REVIEWS OF *ONE DEAD SISTER*

Denley's clean, crisp writing never takes priority over the pace of the plot, which drives along as smoothly as the SUVs favoured by the town's better class. The plot twists and turns like upstate New York's mountain roads, pulling the reader along all the way.
— *Ottawa Citizen*

Bottom line: I enjoyed the book. There are a lot of popular female sleuths out there and Kris Redner deserves to have a place among them. The trick to any good mystery is to create suspense, keep the reader guessing, and Denley does that to a tee. — *Ottawa Sun*

Denley has many fans in the Ottawa area, but *One Dead Si* a wider audience. — *National Post*

READERS' COMMENTS ABOUT *ONE DEAD SI.*

"Randall Denley's third novel *One Dead Sister* (General Stor Publishing House) is a well-paced and suspenseful thriller b. a decades-old murder mystery, political ambition, and a wor backwoods atmosphere into a tightly written page-turner."
— Roger White, Arthur Ellis First Crime Novel Finalist, author of *Tight Corner* (BPS Books)

"More a drama-thriller than a mystery, One Dead Sister is dese. ...g oi a major literary prize. The clean, crisp writing delivers clearly drawn, colourful characters; vibrant descriptions of surroundings and events are a sensoral delight. This compelling read will leave you torn: you can't put the book down until you've reached the last page, but you don't want it to ever end." — Deborah Richmond

"Wish I could forget what I just read to start the book all over again. An amazing thriller that captivated me to the last page."
— Elisabeth Richard

"Very good writing. Anytime I wasn't reading your novel, I was wondering and worrying about the characters. I think a book that engages you even when you aren't reading it really says a lot about the calibre of the writer." — Cathy Curry

"I'm enjoying it, I've got to tell you." — Steve Madely, CFRA

"Just finished the book. Wow! Can't wait for your next one!"
— Tom Woodward

"A very enjoyable read. The characters were well developed, the plot was interesting." — Doug Casey

"A very good read." — Allan Rock

One Dead Sister

RANDALL DENLEY

OPINICON
PRESS

Published by Opinicon Press

www.randalldenley.com

ISBN 978-0-9781924-4-0

Copyright © Randall Denley 2010

Cover art, design, typesetting: Magdalene Carson

Cataloguing in Publication available at Library and Archives Canada

To Linda, for never losing faith.

PROLOGUE

Kris Redner grabbed the edge of her seat to avoid being thrown into the aisle as the Number 97 bus swung out of the Lincoln Fields station and onto the Ottawa River Parkway. The big red and white articulated roared into the night, the lights of the city on the right and the river on the left, flowing like liquid pewter under a full moon.

After seventeen years of living in downtown Toronto, it amazed her that there were still such vast open spaces right in the middle of Ottawa. It didn't even feel like a city. For just a minute, Kris thought, it was like being a teenager again in the Ottawa Valley, camping rough along the river.

She could live without the congestion of Toronto, but she did miss the subway that had taken her straight from work to her condo at Yonge and Sheppard. Now she had to ride the bus. She could have bought a car, but then she'd have had to pay as much again to buy a space in Colin's building. Who wanted a parking space in a building where they didn't even own a condo?

Riding the bus made Kris feel like she'd gone back in time to some other era. The 1970s, maybe, but without all the good music and dope. At least this bus was air conditioned, helping to cut the heavy early-August humidity.

It was 11:30 p.m. It had already taken her fifteen minutes to get from the *Ottawa Citizen* building only a few kilometres away and it would be nearly midnight by the time she got home to the condo she and Colin were sharing in the Byward Market. Another late day, another scramble to get a column that measured up to what they expected from her. In Toronto, it had been easy to turn the daily drama of crime and the courts into a newspaper column three days a week. Between the gangs and the parade of inept losers going through the courts, she had never been short of raw material. Here in Ottawa, it was different. She'd found the crime boring, the biggest things small. People got all excited about a home invasion that wouldn't even make the news in a real city. And she hadn't yet established the web of connections at the courts that would tip her to the good stuff, if there were any.

It wouldn't have been so bad if the paper hadn't run big promotional ads calling her "Canada's queen of crime," picking up a phrase from some puff piece *Macleans* did two years ago, when she was at the height of her career, covering the Jamestown gang killings like the story was a good mystery novel. The promotional stuff had been Colin's idea. When he had been brought in from Toronto as editor after the ownership change, he'd insisted that Kris come with him as his star writer. They had been in the up phase of their relationship then. It had been hard to say no. Six months later, her decision didn't look as good. The paper was too small, the town was too small, and her relationship with Colin was turning into a dead end.

At least today had been somewhat better than average. There had been a drug killing in Vanier, the French quarter just east of the Rideau River. Kris was learning to be grateful for Vanier. It provided more than its share of stories. In this one, the victim was a small-time dealer who lived in a shabby little strip motel on Montreal Road. The police were working on the theory that he had ripped off his supplier. Whoever had killed him certainly had a powerful grievance. They'd crushed the poor bastard's testicles with pliers. There had been some debate with the desk about whether to include that detail in what the night city editor always called "a family newspaper." Kris had managed to get it in, using the implied clout of being the woman sleeping with the boss. It wasn't her favourite method of persuasion, but you played the cards you had.

Kris shifted her purse on the seat and once again felt the bulk of the odd item that she had pulled from her mail slot just before leaving work. She extracted the bubble-wrapped envelope from her black leather handbag, which was big enough to carry an Uzi. She hadn't paid that much attention to the envelope when she had picked it up, but now she was intrigued. Good things came in anonymous brown packages.

Kris tilted the envelope to read the postmark in the artificial light of the bus. The ink was smeared but a single word jumped out at her as if it were written in forty-eight-point type. Osborne. It was her hometown in upstate New York, a place of many memories, most of them bad. It had been twenty years since Kris had left Osborne, vowing never to look back. The murder of her sister, the death of her father, the descent of her mother into alcoholism; all that had been pushed down into the dark mental cavern where she kept memories she didn't want to deal with. Now, she felt those memories climbing to the surface again.

Kris exhaled and set the envelope down on the bus seat beside her. It was time to think rationally. Osborne was old news. She was no longer the scared teenager who had fled in fear for her life. In her mind, Osborne was some kind of gothic place of doom, but she was sure that in reality it was just another pokey little Adirondacks tourist town. Surely there was nothing there that could harm her. Osborne had done about as much damage to her as it was possible to do, but she had survived.

The smart thing would be to throw this envelope into the garbage unopened, she thought. Why allow her past to intrude into the present?

She could tell by the feel of the item in the envelope that it was probably a videotape. How could that possibly hurt her? She eased open the gummed end of the envelope and pulled out the tape. It was dusty and scratched, as though it had been kicking around for years and had been recorded on multiple times. Who still used videotapes, she wondered? The information on it must be old and the person who sent it didn't have the technical capacity to convert it to a DVD.

Kris put the tape back in the envelope and put the envelope in her bag. Colin had a video player for his collection of vintage Second World War movies. Maybe she'd take a look at it when she got home. For a person in the newspaper business, curiosity was like an itch. Sooner or later, she knew she'd scratch it.

She turned her attention back to the bus. One of the few benefits of public transit in Ottawa was that it gave her a chance to eavesdrop on the criminal element, who seemed to constitute the majority of the customers late at night. What kind of criminal was so bad at his chosen line of work that he still had to ride the bus? she wondered. Still, it was a place to pick up possible stories. Last week, two kids had sat in front of her talking calmly about a guy they'd stabbed at their school like it was nothing. The whole thing had been covered up by the school administration. It was small potatoes, but it made a decent column by Ottawa standards.

The prospects were limited tonight. The only other passenger on the bus was a black guy, maybe twenty, dreads, muscle shirt, pants hanging off his ass. The look on his face said he was either stoned, or just lost in thought. In Toronto, she would have been wary of him, alone in a subway car late at night. She relaxed when she saw the University of Ottawa backpack at his feet. Probably an accounting student who watched MTV.

Kris looked out the window at the dark night beyond but could see only her own reflection in the bus's smudged glass. She still thought of herself as young, but what stared back at her was a somewhat hard-looking thirty-nine-year-old with bags under her blue eyes and short black hair that hadn't been combed since yesterday. But what did she expect, after a fifteen-hour day and pounding out 1,100 words on deadline? She didn't have time to fuss about her appearance. It didn't seem to bother Colin.

Colin. Now there was a problem. What had she been thinking? The new *Citizen* editor was the most blatant stickman in the newsroom, and she'd gotten tangled up with him. Colin Legover, as the women at work called him back in Toronto. Colin usually scored with some girl reporter fresh out of Ryerson, not someone who had been around the block, like Kris. She could see why the others would fall for his British accent and his war stories, but what was her excuse? She detected bullshit for a living.

Still, Colin had a kind of seedy charm that she found intriguing. The British did decay well. She once compared him to a heavier Ralph Fiennes. She could see he was flattered that she thought he looked like an actor, but wounded by the word heavier. His own description of himself as "wiry" would be challenged by any good editor.

Kris had taken up with Colin after a long night, too many martinis, and the crash of a short relationship with a terrifically boring stockbroker. The man actually wanted to talk to her about derivatives, whatever those were.

She had been after nothing more than quick sex with a colleague she had mistakenly believed shared her philosophy about romance. Any man was good for a weekend. Some were even good for a week. After that, it was time to start looking. She thought of it as chain smoking, lighting a new lover while the old one was still warm.

She had assumed Colin would see things the same way, but it turned out that all four of his marriages were sincere. The man simply loved to be in love, and now she couldn't get rid of him. Kris was fairly sure that they would have broken up by now if they had stayed in Toronto, but when it was announced that he got the job in Ottawa he had asked her to come with him, not just as a lover, but as a colleague. Then they had moved in together because Colin had bought a condo downtown. Probably not a smart move, Kris could see now, but it had made some kind of practical sense at the time. Now, she'd have to find a graceful way to dump him, and it was complicated by the fact that he was her boss.

The bus was downtown now, passing through the silent Centretown streets where the government office towers emptied out promptly at 4:30 each day. It seemed impossible for something to look cold on such a hot night, but the central business district felt like winter at all times of the year. It was a colourless world of concrete and dirty glass. There wasn't a soul on the street. The buildings were small by Toronto standards, but still big enough to make a person feel insignificant.

The bus pulled to a stop on the Mackenzie King Bridge and Kris got off. It was only two blocks to the condo on Rideau, but she didn't enjoy the walk in the daytime, less so at night. Those two short blocks, she thought, illustrated Ottawa's confusion about what it was. To her right, the Desmarais Building formed the edge of the University of Ottawa campus. It was a modern, bright, slice of curved glass. Ahead of her she could see the twenty-four-storey condo tower that she called home. It was a utilitarian concrete tower without even a touch of imagination. Beside it, a twin was being built, the construction crane looming over the building. In between was a series of nineteenth-century buildings that were as tired and dirty as their inhabitants. Like bad meat in a fresh sandwich, they spoiled everything that was around them.

The Ottawa Mission was the number one home for the homeless. It occupied a four-storey stone building and a shorter red brick building next door. As Kris walked by the Mission, she braced herself for the usual reception. There was always a gauntlet of drunks leaning against the front of the building, bearded men in someone else's old clothes who still thought it made sense to whistle at her and make comments about various parts of her body. What did they think, she was going to be attracted to them?

Kris reached into her handbag and put her hand on her container of pepper spray. She was used to dealing with criminals on a daily basis, people who were far more dangerous than these losers. But the criminals knew she was a reporter. To the guys leaning against the red brick wall of the Mission, she was just meat on the street.

There were only three of them tonight. The rest must be under the bridges partying with their pals. Kris kept her eyes straight ahead. She could have chosen to walk on the other side of the road, but she was damned if they were going to make her do it. She knew how to handle herself, if it came to that.

As she passed them, Kris could smell sweat, cheap wine, and cigarette smoke. Only one looked up. The other two kept studying the sidewalk, lost somewhere in their past. The one who was alert enough to notice her removed a greasy Montreal Canadiens ball cap and said, "Evening," like they were on a small-town street somewhere. God knows, maybe he thought they were.

Two minutes later, Kris was in the lobby of the condo building, waiting for the elevator to take her to the fifteenth floor. The lobby was a cool expanse of gleaming pink granite, scrupulously clean and a world away from the life just around the corner at the Mission. The place wasn't really her style, but Colin loved it. It was right around the corner from all the restaurants in the popular Byward Market, and you could see Parliament Hill from the living room window if you craned your neck just the right way.

The elevator door pinged open, and she stepped in, then was swept up and away from the life on the street. Kris supposed she should be more sympathetic to the guys from the Mission, given her own family's history of abusing drink. Maybe they reminded her too much of her uncle. After things had fallen apart in Osborne, she had sought refuge at his place up near Killaloe, in the Ottawa Valley. Martin Redner had been off the grid in just about every way possible. It had been a long three years.

As Kris entered the condo, she was met with the usual silence. Colin was out glad-handing at social events almost every night. It was a relief, in a way. She had never quite grown used to living with someone, especially not in 1,200 square feet. He'd likely be home within an hour, having had a few beers too many and ready for sex. He was good at it, she had to admit, but sex wasn't at the top of her list after a long, hard day.

As she looked around the condo, Kris got a fresh reminder of what chaos her life had become. The white leather sofa was covered with unread copies of the Sunday *New York Times*. A bag of trash she hadn't had time to get to the chute sat beside the kitchen garbage can, and a pizza box gaped open on top. Yesterday's dirty dishes were still stacked in the sink. Neither she nor Colin believed it was their responsibility to clean up and they were in a bit of a standoff.

The place could really use some fresh air. Kris cranked open the living room window, but the early August air was heavy with humidity and the stink of diesel. Some genius had figured that eighteen-wheelers should go right through the centre of downtown, and they ground their way by the condo all night. She closed the window again, and turned up the air conditioning instead.

She dumped her bag on the black granite kitchen countertop, pulled out a package of Matinee Extra Mild and lit one. She was trying to cut down on smoking, but it was her first cigarette of the day, if you counted the twenty-four-hour period that had just begun at midnight.

She opened the fridge. Seven Sleeman's Cream Ale, a dozen eggs, and a litre of milk. She twisted the cap off one of the

Sleeman's, drained half of it, and put the bottle down on the counter. Turning the kitchen tap on full cold, she stuck her head under and soaked her face and hair in the cool water until she felt both numbed and cleansed. Then she unbuttoned her white short-sleeved blouse, removed it, and used it to quickly dry some of the water from her hair. Tossing it over a kitchen chair, she sat on the living room's red and black Persian rug and turned on the TV. The main item on CNN was another suicide bomb in the Middle East.

Kris knew she probably shouldn't watch whatever was on the videotape from Osborne, but she also knew that she eventually would. Might as well get it over with. She retrieved the tape from her bag and turned on the VCR. The picture was grainy and indistinct, the lighting inadequate. It appeared to have been shot in a basement, probably of an old house. There were stone walls and a room so large that its extremities disappeared into gloom. The bottom of a staircase was visible on the right side of the screen, and now she saw the legs of people coming down it. Two men, then a woman in a dress, then another man.

The camera must have been on a tripod, because it didn't follow them as they moved to the left of the screen. They momentarily went out of the frame, then one of the men said, "Bring her over here. Line her up."

She could still see only the lower halves of their bodies, but someone adjusted the camera, moving it up. Now three men were visible. They had black ski masks over their heads. They looked like they were about to hold up a bank, but the masks didn't exactly go with the rest of their clothing. One wore jeans and a T-shirt, the others khaki chinos and plaid shirts. They looked like two preppies on their way to college. One was tall and almost too thin. The other was stocky and barrel-chested. His shirt strained at the buttons.

The girl had on a white uniform, the sort a waitress or maid would wear. Her hands were tied behind her back and a black gag bit deeply into her mouth. She had long dark hair, but Kris only got a quick side glimpse of her face.

Now only the two preppies were visible as the camera panned to the left. They led the girl to a battered-looking wooden table and pushed her roughly onto it, face down. One of the preppies took a length of heavy rope and wrapped it around the table and her upper body, pinning her firmly in place.

It didn't take much imagination to know what was going to happen next, Kris thought. Some crank had sent her a porn tape. If it had come from Canada, she'd have dismissed it as a prank by some cop who was angry with her, maybe a crude way of telling her what she deserved. But from Osborne? Was it a guy who had lusted after her in high school, Googled her, and wanted a kinky thrill? No, that didn't make sense. People did some weird shit, but she hadn't exactly been the hottest girl in high school. Why would anyone even remember her now? And yet, someone had.

Kris was tempted to pull the tape out and throw it in the garbage, but she decided to let it run. There had to be a point to this.

The taller of the hooded preppies said, "Who's first?" The other reached into his pocket and pulled out a coin.

"Heads or tails?"

"Heads."

The shorter, stocky one flipped the coin in the air and caught it deftly.

"Tail. I win," he said. That line brought a laugh from the other two. She was getting the impression the shorter one was the ringleader.

He turned to the girl and lifted the skirt of her uniform, ever so slowly. He then swiftly ripped her panties off and threw them on the basement floor. The other two clapped. The shorter one then momentarily disappeared from the camera and returned with some kind of stick or switch. With what appeared to be a practised motion, he flicked it and laid a hard blow on the girl's buttocks. Her body jerked up spasmodically and she gave a muffled cry.

This was no porno pretend. This was real.

Kris had had enough. She began to fast forward the tape. If only the girl had been able to do the same. She wrapped her arms around herself and shivered. Suddenly the apartment felt cold and she felt exposed without her shirt.

The fast-forward gave the action a jerky, silent movie look

that would have almost been comical, if it hadn't been so evil. Once the first preppy was finished with the switch, he took the girl from behind, then his friends took a turn. The one with the jeans was last. Low man on the totem pole. Kris guessed that their ages were about what the clothing implied. Late teens or early twenties.

As the last boy finished, she slowed the tape to normal speed. Having acted out their fantasy, the three seemed unsure what to do next.

"Now what?" one of them said, turning toward the camera. She thought it was the one in the jeans, but the sound was indistinct.

"Turn the camera off," said the shorter preppy. This was much clearer and his tone implied that he was used to being obeyed. Then he paused, as if thinking.

"No, first this," he said.

He reached down and untied the gag, saying to the girl "Smile for the camera and tell us how much you enjoyed it."

He twisted her face toward the camera and the girl let out a scream that hit Kris like an electric shock. It was immediately followed by a scream of her own, a howl that seemed to start deep in her guts.

The face on the screen was that of her sister, Kathy Redner. Died August 14, 1981. Osborne, New York. Age fourteen.

1

Nearly two weeks had passed since Kris had arrived in Osborne after driving south in the middle of the night through the twisting roads of the Adirondacks. She was sure Colin must have thought her mad. She had been struggling to get her suitcase out the door when he arrived home at one a.m. She had muttered something about a family emergency and demanded the keys to his company Prius. Thank God he was too drunk to ask a lot of questions, although there had been plenty since.

Driving through the dark mountains, she felt as if a vortex had sucked her into the past, back to a world that was deceptively familiar and yet strangely foreign. She had adjusted to Fahrenheit degrees and driving in miles like it was a default position, but it hadn't been so easy to adapt to the pace of life in Osborne. It was maddeningly slow, like nothing was ever going to happen, and no one was in a hurry to get to tomorrow.

Even though she had spent the first sixteen years of her life in Osborne, it was somehow disconcerting to drive south and end up north, on the edge of America in a world where everyone drove pickup trucks or SUVs, a land dominated by woods and mountains where people had limited impact, existing in little towns that relied on tourism or a single major employer, if they were lucky.

Coming back to Osborne was a decision that Kris had second-guessed a dozen times, but what choice did she really have? Having seen the tape, she had to find out what had happened to her sister. Kathy would have done the same for her. When Kathy's body had been found in the woods outside of town, the story was that she must have been picked up hitchhiking, then killed. Kris had never bought it. Her sister didn't hitchhike, called it stupid. Kris had always felt there was more there. The tape seemed to prove that much, at least.

No one had ever been charged. Kathy's death was a mystery, but not one that much interested the good people of Osborne. Most had treated her inquiries with indifference or even outright hostility. Kathy Redner's death was old, bad news, and no one in Osborne wanted to dig up the past.

The reason wasn't hard to figure out. It was standing right in front of her. There was a stiff breeze coming in off Lake Champlain, but it wasn't strong enough to muss Senator Lowell Osborne's perfect coiffure. At forty-eight, his hair was still dark, with just enough distinguished silver on the sides to indicate his experience. His casual, hands-in-his-pockets posture was offset by a navy suit and blue oxford button-down shirt. The effect was further modulated by a red tie, which was artfully askew. It all reeked of image consultants, Kris thought.

She leaned against a maple tree, out of the sun, watching him work the crowd. It was more than eighty degrees, and she appreciated the shade.

The senator's people were good, she had to admit. It was a small crowd, no more than a hundred, but they were packed in tight, so the television cameras lined up behind them would give the impression of a seething mass of supporters.

The senator was positioned on a low dais, just high enough to raise him up above the masses, but not so high as to obscure the bold, red Osborne Industries sign in the background. It stood in front of a three-storey stone building with deeply inset windows, the trim freshly painted white. To Kris, the nineteenth-century industrial relic looked ominous and gloomy, even in the bright, late-August sun.

She remembered when her father would take her to the shoe factory as a child, how large the machines had seemed, and the overpowering smell of the leather. He had died there, electrocuted while trying to fix a malfunction in the main electrical panel, just one week after her sister's death. She shivered, but told herself the factory was just a building. No ghosts.

Those two deaths had unhinged her mother, whose steady drinking rapidly escalated into alcoholism. She and her mother had endured six painful years together, with Kris forced to become the adult in the relationship. Then it had ended with her mother's suicide. At sixteen, Kris had finally escaped from Osborne and vowed never to look back. Tragic story. Tough luck. Move on. Now the videotape had drawn her to a place she was sure she'd never visit again.

Since her return to Osborne, Kris had found out much more about her sister's life and death, but the crucial interview subjects had remained uncooperative. They didn't have much incentive to help her dig up dirt on the man who virtually owned the town and was an up-and-coming young Republican star and early favourite for the presidential nomination.

She actually felt hostility in the town, as if people were watching when she walked down the street. She was the unwelcome one who had come back to stir up trouble.

She'd told Colin a bogus story about how the sick cousin she'd rushed down to visit had put her onto a hell of a tale about an unsolved murder and a rich American political family. She wasn't sure he'd really bought her pitch, but he had given her two weeks to work on it. Now that was stretching into three, and he'd set that as an absolute limit. Colin said he was getting all kinds of pressure from the publisher because the paper was doing a relaunch in September and they were expecting big things from her.

Kris knew she should have confided in Colin, told him everything, but she was worried that he'd think what she was really doing was either overly dangerous or unlikely to produce a result. Maybe both.

When she had pitched it, she felt it obvious there must be a connection between the Osborne family and her sister's death. Kathy had worked at the senator's family camp on Cooper Lake that summer, and her body had been found in the woods, partway between the camp and town. Although the video finally showed some of what had happened on the day of Kathy's death, the link to Lowell Osborne and the identities of the men on the video remained elusive, and time was running out. Kris had felt that her ability to interview, to get people to open up, would at least give her some idea of what had really happened to her sister, but in a couple of days, she'd have to give up, return to Ottawa, and find a way to explain to Colin that there really wasn't a story. Not one that she could find, anyway.

That would be bad, but the worst part would be never knowing what had really happened to Kathy. It was something she had put from her mind for all of those years, but now that she was back, the wound of her sister's death was reopened.

She'd considered taking the tape to the police, but Kris knew how they worked. There would be absolutely no use giving it to Osborne's Mickey Mouse little force, and even the state police were unlikely to be truly interested. A cold case involving a teenaged victim from a working-class family, all dead except the annoying sister, wasn't going to push itself to the top of any detective's list. The tape was a prime piece of evidence, but only if you could identify the three men on it. And even at that, their assault didn't prove they'd killed Kathy. There were obvious chain of custody and authenticity issues, too. The police would file it, she was sure of that.

Kris brought her attention back to the present, leaned over to the much-shorter woman standing beside her, and asked, "So what do you think?"

Betsy Larson had been dutifully writing down everything the senator said on her steno pad. Kris would be surprised if the senator's speech varied a word from the prepared text his handlers would distribute at the end, but she supposed taking notes made Betsy feel like a real reporter.

"I think he's fabulous," she said.

Kris gave a noncommittal humph. If any other journalist had said that, the sarcasm would have been a given. With Betsy, no. Although she had the title of editor of the *Osborne Republican–Patriot*, Betsy's entire previous journalism experience had consisted of two years on a Boston suburban weekly. Kris considered it a hobby job, the type taken by earnest wannabes who played at journalism.

"Cigarette?" Kris asked, lighting one for herself.

Betsy wrinkled up her nose, as if she'd just stepped in dog poop. It was a pert little nose that seemed the perfect accessory to her too-white teeth and complexion of the sort usually only seen in cosmetics ads.

Kris and Betsy had been in school together from third grade to when Kris dropped out at sixteen to head to Canada. They had never been close, not exactly being from the same social class, and the years at Osborne Public and Teddy Roosevelt High were about all they had in common. She'd wager that Betsy had belonged to a sorority in college. Cheerleading wasn't out of the question. At that age, Kris had been working the night cop desk at Toronto's tabloid newspaper, the *Sun*, and developing a taste for tequila.

Betsy wore a pink cotton jacket and skirt, her blonde hair tied back in a ponytail. Kris didn't think she'd ever worn pink in her life. She found Betsy a bit tight-assed, but at least she was friendly. Betsy had been helpful when Kris had spent a couple of days in the morgue of the newspaper, reviewing the clippings about her sister's murder. The *Republican–Patriot* had been a daily then, and it had done a decent job of covering the story.

The crowd broke into what seemed like genuine laughter, and Kris realized that she had stopped listening to what the senator was saying. He had apparently told a joke, and his listeners had found it awfully funny. No surprise, given that most people in Osborne either worked for the senator or were beholden to him in some way. One person could pretty much own a town of 5,000, and the senator did. He even controlled Betsy's twice-weekly paper.

Kris wasn't surprised to see all the major television networks covering the senator's speech. The media were always interested in the hot new thing and there was a strong chance he would be it. Lowell Osborne had the right blend of youth and experience as well as a smooth, made-for-television style and no connection whatsoever to Sarah Palin and the nutbar right wing of the party.

When she had Googled the senator, Kris found that newspapers across the country were all writing the same story about the fresh and appealing new candidate. The senator was a story because he was a story, a media snowball starting to roll down the hill. Reporters, eager to be the one who said it first, were already hinting that Osborne could be the Republican Obama.

Lowell Osborne turned directly toward the cameras, which were clustered at the left side of the crowd. Kris was sure his likeliest sound bite was coming up. With his best look of sincerity, he said, "Jobs for Americans. Jobs in America." The senator was wisely restricting himself to sentences that the voters could easily digest. Better yet, sentences that would fit on bumper stickers.

"Some might talk about tariffs and protectionism. I say we need to give American industries a chance to compete against foreign firms that pay their workers twenty-five cents an hour. Without jobs, America is going to lose towns like Osborne.

"Here at Osborne Industries, we are leading the way. Americans have been wearing our shoes since 1898. Made right here in Osborne. I suppose I could have shipped those jobs offshore, made more profit, but it's not the responsible thing to do."

The crowd cheered that line. Kris suspected most of them were shoe factory employees on their lunch hour.

The senator had picked a perfect backdrop for today's speech, Kris thought, but it was also one that brought back far too many memories for her. For a moment, she thought the senator's offer of an interview at the factory where her father died was a calculated move, but that was probably her imagination. She was hardly a player in the senator's life. More like an annoying fly, at best.

She had been chasing his staff for an interview for a week. Finally, they had found a five-minute slot for her. She wasn't used to that kind of treatment. Back in Canada, her reputation got calls returned, fast. But here, she was a foreign journalist working on a story about a long-ago crime the town would rather forget.

In a way, Kris was surprised the senator had agreed to an interview at all. The best line of defence against the media was to say nothing, especially when even a denial drew you into a story with no upside. Perhaps his willingness to give her a few minutes indicated how truly unimportant the senator thought she was.

She had no illusions the senator would give her anything useful, but she wanted to see the look on his face when she asked him about Kathy. She couldn't mention the videotape, though. That was her ace in the hole. Holdback evidence, her police contacts would have called it.

The senator looked as if he would be going on for a while, so she turned to enjoy the view. It was the town's best feature. To her left, Lake Champlain stretched to the Vermont shore, the water sparkling in the late August sun. The Green Mountains were purple humps in the haze of the distance. Behind her, the first peaks of the Adirondacks rose. It had been a surprising comfort to return to these natural markers of her youth.

Nature had been kind to Osborne, but man's efforts were less successful. The Ausable River cut through the middle of the town and helped power Osborne's shoe factory. The senator was fond of pointing to this nineteenth-century technology to show how green he was. To the west of the river, on Dumont Hill, was a cluster of magnificent pre-Civil War homes that housed the town's small elite. She had forgotten how beautiful the houses were. The shoreline was mostly taken up by the senator's own estate. The stone Federal-style house, with its wrap-around verandah, had been built by Lowell Osborne's great-great-grandfather, the founder of Osborne. Naming the town after himself had been an early genetic indicator of the size of the Osborne ego, Kris thought.

On the east side, where the working people lived, rundown clapboard and doublewides were the norm. Growing up, Kris had been on the wrong side of the river. It was a barrier she couldn't cross with the "better" people of Osborne, even now. Kris had to smile at their pretensions. Even a backwater had an upper crust.

Osborne did its best to look like some little town in a Norman Rockwell painting, but Kris knew the happy townspeople had a clear sense of their own self-interest. All their hopes centred on Lowell Osborne. His shoe factory kept the town alive, and his presidential dreams gave everyone a reason to believe that there might be a future. With luck, Osborne could become the next Crawford, Texas.

Betsy snapped her notebook shut. The senator had completed his speech and was reaching down into the crowd, shaking hands.

"Isn't he great?" Betsy said.

"Terrific."

Betsy gave her a look, knowing she was being mocked. "Come on. I know you don't like him."

"Why would I dislike him? I've never met the man."

In truth, Kris preferred criminals to politicians. At least they were up front about their intentions.

"I know he's been hard to get an interview with, but I don't think he even knew your sister, and he's got so much on his plate.

You'll like him, once you get to know him."

"I don't think I'm going to get to know him, Betsy. I've got a five-minute interview. I won't be having him to the house for dinner."

Betsy reddened. Her husband, Dr. Tom Larson, was one of the senator's oldest friends, and she had social access to the great man. Betsy was fond of dropping little bits of information about what he'd said and done when he'd been over to visit her and Tom at their place on Dumont Hill.

Kris saw a stocky, broad-shouldered man with a grey suit and a grey crewcut coming her way. Bud Naylor, the senator's chief of security. It must be time for her five minutes with the famous man. She knew Naylor was only in his late forties, but he had the jowly face of a bulldog and fleshy red lips that made him look as if he'd just consumed something raw. Naylor's upper body was that of a man who once lifted weights, but now only lifted beer cans.

Naylor nodded to Betsy and said, "Kris Redner?"

From his tone, she wouldn't have been surprised if the next thing he told her was that she was under arrest. Naylor wasn't a former cop, though; he was an ex-Marine. She'd checked him out.

"Sergeant?" she said.

Naylor took a half step back, caught off guard. Recovering, he said "Not anymore. The senator is ready to see you now."

Naylor turned and headed back toward the factory. Kris quickly caught up with him, so not as to be trailing him like a child.

"I thought Allen Gibson would be handling this," she said.

The senator's chief spokesman was the one who had actually set up the interview. Despite the prestigious title, she doubted if the senator had any additional spokesmen at this stage in his campaign. To her, the guy was just a flak. If he was like any other one she'd ever met, his sole skill would be helping his boss say nothing.

"He will," Naylor said.

"Oh, I suppose he's tied up with the other media and sent you to fetch me."

"The senator sent me. Gibson doesn't send me anywhere."

Kris was pleased that her little shot had found a soft spot. She knew Naylor's type well from all her years covering the police. Heavy, rough, overbearing, couldn't stand women. It was important to show them you weren't intimidated. Most of them were puppy dogs, once they knew that you bit.

Naylor took her around the back of the building and through a door with "Office" stencilled on it in faded gold script. She followed him down a short, wood-panelled corridor and into an office about the size of an average living room. There was a view of the millpond beyond the factory and six mallard ducks gliding along the surface, green heads glinting in the sun. The room was so dominated by a huge, battered oak desk that at first she didn't see Gibson in an armchair to the left.

She was startled when he suddenly rose and said, "Al Gibson. Glad to meet you."

Kris found herself shaking hands with a short, prematurely balding man in his thirties with a disarming grin. Just like his boss, the official spokesman had a red tie, pulled loose.

"Have a seat," Gibson said. "The senator's just going to be a minute. *The New York Times* wanted some additional quotes."

"Well, I hope it doesn't cut into my five minutes too severely," Kris said, emphasizing the words, five minutes.

Gibson laughed and waved his hand. "The senator is tight for time, of course, but frankly, Ms. Redner, I can't imagine that he's got a whole lot to tell you. The connection, again, is that your sister was in his family's employ as summer staff at the camp?"

"That's it. Like I told you on the phone, I'm working on a newspaper story about her murder. A cold-case piece with a personal twist. I like to touch all the bases. The senator's so personable, I thought he might remember some of those summer students."

Gibson smiled, acknowledging the real intent of her remark. The senator, Kris had discovered, had quite an eye for the ladies, and the younger the better. The lovely Terry Osborne, age twenty-five, was his second wife, and Kris's old buddy Chris Walton, the *Star*'s Washington bureau chief, said Osborne's extracurricular activities made Bill Clinton look like a monk.

Bud Naylor had gone out through a door at the rear of the office and now he was back, with the senator.

Lowell Osborne crossed the room in two vigorous strides,

and then clasped Kris's proffered hand in both of his. "Kris Redner. Good to see you," he said, as if she were a favourite cousin he'd just had the good fortune to run into. The senator made and held eye contact, his intense blue eyes projecting an intimacy that Kris was sure must impress a lot of other people. Enough to get him elected to the Senate three times, anyway.

She gracefully extracted her hand from his grip and said, "Senator, a pleasure. Shall we get right down to it?"

She pulled a notepad and tape recorder from her purse and set the recorder on the edge of the desk. As soon as he saw hers, Al Gibson pulled out two recorders and turned them on.

"I hope you don't mind if Al and Bud sit in," the senator said. "No secrets here."

"Of course. As I'm sure your people have explained, I'm doing a piece about the murder of my sister here nearly thirty years ago."

"Yes, and let me say how sorry I am for your loss. Such a young girl. I remember the incident somewhat. I was home from Yale that summer and I spent some time up at the camp."

In Kris's world, the word "camp" meant a tent and a fire. To the rich in the Adirondacks, a camp was usually a series of log buildings on a private estate overlooking a mountain lake. In Osborne's income bracket, they owned the lake, too.

"It was a bit of a shock to us. Not many murders in Osborne. She was a summer employee there. Am I remembering that correctly?"

"Yes. It was her first job. She was working as a maid, waiting on tables, that sort of thing."

"I might even remember her. Long, dark hair?"

"That's it."

The senator seemed pleased with the sharpness of his memory. Al Gibson nodded his approval, too. "Beyond that, I'm afraid it all gets a bit hazy. I think there were several girls working there that summer. I didn't get to know them, of course."

No, of course, Kris thought. Why would a rich frat boy from Yale bother to get to know a bunch of kids from the wrong side of the river?

"Now, I remember your dad," the senator said. "Fine man. My

father held him in high regard. Terrible thing, the factory accident. And then your mother."

He let that thought trail off. "But things seem to have worked out for you, Kris. I understand you're quite successful up in Canada."

The senator's smile was so warm that for just a moment Kris almost thought he really cared. Asking about your family was one the politician's oldest tricks. Al Gibson had done a good job of briefing.

"That's right," Kris said. "Once I sink my teeth into someone, I don't let go until I've got the whole story.

"Tell me, Senator, does the main lodge at your camp have a big stone foundation?"

The senator's eyes hardened for just a moment, she was sure of it. It was a chancy sort of question, but she was tired of sliding down the senator's Teflon wall. She certainly hadn't ruled out the idea that he might have been one of the three men in the video.

"Well, I'm not much of a student of architecture. I've never really thought about it. Why in the world do you ask?"

Al Gibson was tapping his watch. "Senator, time to go. We've got a chopper to catch," Gibson said.

"Right. Sorry I couldn't take longer, Kris, but I've really nothing more to add. Surely you'd do better talking to some of the people from the east side."

The senator rose from behind the desk.

"Good luck with your story," he said, and then he and Gibson made a quick exit through the door the senator had come in.

Bud Naylor was still leaning against the wall at the back of the office. "I've got a couple of things to add," he said. "Turn off the tape recorder."

Kris switched it off. Naylor was part of a group of boys who had hung out with the senator growing up. What did he know?

"I'm not sure how much you know about your sister, Kathy," he said. "You were what, ten when she died?"

"That's right."

"I'm a plain speaker, Ms. Redner. Your sister liked to hang out with older guys. Word was, she was a hot little fuck who'd head off into the bush with anyone who wanted some. Didn't surprise me, what happened to her. She would have ended up as the town whore, instead of your mother."

Kris felt as if she'd been slapped. "Look, you bastard . . ."

Naylor held up a meaty hand. "Listen up. Your sister wasn't worth ten cents. Neither was your whole goddamn family. Your mother was a drunken slut and your uncle was a draft dodger. Now you come poking around trying to somehow tie the senator up in some crime from thirty years ago. It had nothing to do with him except his family was good enough to give summer jobs to some of the no-hope kids in town, see if it would straighten them out."

Kris felt pinned to her chair by his words, and what she feared was the truth of them. Kathy was often out late at night with boys much older. It had been the subject of screaming fights between her sister and her mother.

"The senator's got a real shot at the nomination. Trash like this would end up in the supermarket tabloids, looking like Chappaquiddick. I know how you media people operate. The senator's worked too long and hard to see it all pissed away by someone like you. It's my job to protect him from that."

Naylor reached out and grabbed Kris by the left shoulder, digging his fingers in so hard that her arm went numb. He lifted her bodily to her feet and started to march her to the office door. "Now get out, and I don't want you contacting the senator again. One word about him in your story, and we'll have lawyers sue you so hard your career will be over. But the scariest part is, you'll have to deal with me, and I'm your worst goddamn nightmare."

Kris was trembling, both from fury and the pain in her shoulder. Naylor had taken her by surprise, but she wasn't going to let herself be manhandled by him. As they got to the door of the office, she suddenly dropped down to a crouch, freeing herself from Naylor's grasp. She thrust herself to her feet and turned, driving her right fist hard into the security chief's prominent Adam's apple. As he staggered back in pain, she closed with a well-placed kick to the groin.

"Pass that on to the senator," she said. "And Bud, fuck you."

There were some advantages to growing up rough.

2

Kris winced in pain as she turned the wheel to pull onto the main highway. Naylor had a grip like a crocodile's jaws. Good thing it was only five miles to Jasper's Lakeside Tourist Cabins, the low-end dump she was staying at west of the town.

She wondered if he had broken something in her shoulder. At least the son of a bitch would probably be icing his balls by now. It was a fair trade.

Her surge of adrenaline had been followed by a crash that left her weak and trembling. When Naylor had laid his hand on her, he had pulled away the protective cloak that journalists like to think prevents them from being personally affected by the trouble on which they report. In Toronto, she had routinely interviewed scumbags who'd stick a knife in you if they didn't like the look on your face, but they had always acknowledged her as a non-combatant, someone from outside their world. Naylor's action told her that none of that mattered in Osborne. She was just a woman asking too many questions, a problem to be solved.

She wondered if the senator had instructed Naylor, or if he was just showing initiative. He seemed more like the following orders type, but a bulldog like Naylor relied mostly on instinct. Protecting his master would be basic to the breed.

One thing was certain. Naylor had made a mistake. If the idea of a link between Osborne and her sister's death was so ridiculous, why the overreaction? That, and the look on the senator's face when she referred to the room where she thought the video was shot told her they knew something.

Kris's little Prius shuddered as a mammoth black Ford pickup, canoe in the bed, passed her blind on a curve. The Prius had been perfect in the city, but here it was like a toy car. The only thing missing was a key in back, to wind it up. People in the Adirondacks drove men's vehicles. Even the women. The hybrid Toyota, with its Ontario plates, said wimpy outsider.

The driver cut it tight, forcing Kris so far to the right that the front wheel caught the gravel. Her shoulder screamed as she fought to get the car back on the asphalt. The lakeside road to Westport wasn't the place to go in the ditch. There was nothing but trees and steep lakeshore between Osborne and the tourist cabins.

She could see Jasper's just ahead on the right. It was high on a rocky promontory that jutted into Lake Champlain. Eight cabins, probably built sometime in the 1950s, she'd guess. Still all original, to put it charitably. They were dark brown, in Adirondack style, and didn't look bad from a distance. The rotting wood, sagging screens, and moss-covered shingles were only apparent closer up. A hand-painted wooden sign at the road said Monthly or Yearly Rentals. That was the first clue that the "tourist" cabins didn't attract many tourists. Rick Jasper had hourly rentals, too, Kris had observed, but he didn't advertise those.

Still, the place was cheap, on the water, and not in Osborne. That was what she had been looking for when she'd rented Cabin 3 by the week. She pulled the car up under the pines in front of her cabin and was happy to see L.T. Hill's red Chevy Blazer parked in front of Cabin 5. He was the one person in Osborne who gave her any kind of feeling of security or protection, and she needed that now.

The last thing Kris had been looking for when she came to Osborne was a man. She already had one too many, but she'd learned long ago that you didn't question the good things fate brought you. There were enough bad ones to offset them.

She eased herself awkwardly out of the Toyota and unlocked her cabin. The smell of damp and wood smoke reminded her of her Uncle Martin's place in the Ottawa Valley, where she had spent three rather unpleasant teenaged years. He had been her only available refuge after her mother's death.

The cabin was basically one room, with a corner partitioned off for a toilet, sink, and shower. An ancient, hulking, kitchen woodstove dominated the space, its chrome trim long ago turned to rust. There was a screen porch at the back, though, that overlooked the lake, and that was where Kris spent most of her time. The two banker's boxes that held the clippings and notes she'd accumulated so far sat on the table, a piece of Adirondacks kitsch made of half-sawn logs and painted brown, like everything else inside and outside the cabin.

She'd just set her purse on the table when there was a knock at the screen door. She turned to see L.T. Hill's substantial frame filling the doorway. Even through the screen, she could see the look of concern on his broad, tanned face.

"Hey, you okay?"

Kris shrugged, the movement causing her to wince in pain.

L.T. entered, the screen door slapping shut behind him. "What happened?" His soft, North Carolina accent added a courtliness to his voice. When he had first met Kris, he had actually called her ma'am.

"Bud Naylor was trying to give me a message."

"That security clown? Let me take a look."

L.T. unbuttoned her white cotton blouse and slid it off her shoulder. She was always amazed at how gentle his big hands were. His two most remarkable features were those hands, and his eyes, the bluest she had ever seen on a man.

Kris glanced down and saw four purple welts where Bud Naylor's fingers had dug into her shoulder.

"You'd better tell me what happened," L.T. said. "I think I could lay charges."

L.T. was the youngest officer in Osborne's eight-man police force. At twenty-six, he was also a lot younger than her, but what the hell, Kris thought. Of all the men she could have met down here, it had to be a cop. Back in Canada, she made a point of fending them off, but there was no work conflict in her relationship with L.T.

The Colin conflict, she preferred not to think about. There was going to be some real awkwardness when she got back to Ottawa, but that was a problem for later. She had plenty of others ahead of it in line.

"Don't go getting official on me. It won't help," she said. "You can get me the ice pack out of the fridge, though."

L.T. took the black, flexible ice pack from the freezer compartment of the fridge, a relic from the time when refrigeration was still a novelty. He wrapped it in a tea towel and placed it on her shoulder.

She eased her blouse back up over the ice pack. It was hardly the first time he'd seen her with her shirt undone, but she felt exposed in her white lace bra, and her nipple had hardened in an annoying and inappropriate way.

Turning a kitchen chair backward, L.T. sat and draped himself over it before running a hand through his short blond hair. He wore his usual navy T-shirt and tight jeans, the shirt stretched taut across his upper body. L.T. always changed out of his uniform back at the station, because Jasper was worried that a cop around the tourist cabins might scare off some of his dodgier business.

"You want to tell me about it?"

"Not much to tell. I asked the senator a few questions about my sister's death. She was summer staff at his family's lodge when she died. He sort of remembered her. All very friendly. Then the senator and his flak left and Naylor made it really plain that I wasn't to ask any more questions or even mention the senator in what I'm going to write. If I did, he'd be my worst nightmare. Just to prove it, he clamped down on my shoulder and tried to pretty much drag me out of the senator's office."

"That's bullshit. Those guys act like they own this town."

"They do own it," Kris said quietly. "Once you've been around here a bit longer, you'll see how it works."

L.T. was a free spirit who used police work as a short-term way to support his athletic endeavours. He had told her he'd stay in Osborne until he'd hiked all forty-six of the High Peaks. He was already looking into a police job in Hawaii, for the surfing.

"I've seen plenty already," he said. "Enough to let me know this isn't a place to stick around. Chief Brewster acts like we're the senator's private security force. I caught one of the groundskeepers from the senator's camp going sixty in a thirty this week, and the chief cancelled the ticket."

Kris was sure that was among the least of the favours the chief had offered Lowell Osborne over the years. His outstanding attention to the senator's needs was probably all that prevented Osborne's little force from being replaced by the state police.

"So are you just going to let Naylor get away with this?" L.T. asked. "That's not like you."

"Oh, I wouldn't say he got away with it entirely. I don't think he was expecting a kick in the nuts. His eyes were pretty well crossed when he went down."

L.T. slapped his hand on the table. "Ha! Good girl. I knew you wouldn't take that." He smiled, a bit more relaxed now. "I don't suppose you actually got anything out of the senator?"

"Not much."

"So where does that leave you?"

It was something they'd been avoiding talking about. L.T. knew she was due back in Canada in a few days.

"I was about ready to give up. Kathy's death was a long time ago. People forget things, and there's nothing in it for them to stir up old trouble. But the way Naylor reacted, perhaps there is something there."

"Maybe I could help."

Kris had deliberately avoided dragging L.T. into her investigation. With the attitude of the police down here, it wouldn't do anything but get him into a mess. He had offered her simple, uncomplicated sex, and she'd taken it, his bed the one warm, safe place in an otherwise hostile environment. She had no right to expect anything more from him.

"I know how much this means to you," he said. "I've got no future here anyway. Why not let me see what I can do?"

Kris made a decision then that she'd thought about many times in the two weeks she had known him.

"Do you have a VCR?"

"Yeah, an old one I picked up at a garage sale. Don't tell me you want to watch a movie."

"Not exactly."

Twenty minutes later, the tape finished and the pictures of her sister's rape were replaced by a black and white graininess.

L.T. turned off the television, and sat silently for a moment on the couch beside her. His cabin was identical to Kris's except for the sprung grey couch, which made his a "deluxe" and cost ten dollars more a week.

Finally, he said, "My God, Kris. Why didn't you tell me about this?"

"I didn't tell anyone. Whoever those three boys in that cellar were, odds are they are still around town. What do you think would happen if word got out that I had a tape of them committing the crime?"

L.T. nodded, acknowledging her trust. "Right. And you've

heard nothing from the person who sent you the tape?"

"No. I hoped that by showing up here, being visible, she'd contact me."

"She?"

"I just think it's a woman. Partly from the handwriting that was on the envelope, but mostly because it's the sort of thing a woman would feel outraged over, more than a man. No offence."

"Outraged, maybe, but she sure sat on that tape. If it had been in hand at the time, that could have made a lot of difference. Who investigated the killing?"

"A guy called Barry Fish. Osborne police. He died ten years ago."

"Have you tried to talk to the chief, find out what we knew at the time? That file will still be active. They never close a murder case until it's resolved."

"I talked to Larry Brewster. He won't tell me a thing. Some mumbo jumbo about jeopardizing a case, if and when they get a suspect. Larry will crack this case some time after he figures out who killed Jimmy Hoffa."

From the look on his face, she could see that Jimmy Hoffa had been forgotten by people L.T.'s age. Even though they were only thirteen years apart, it sometimes seemed like more.

"Look, Kris, why don't you stay down for a few more days? I could take a look. See what the department's really got," he said.

She touched his hand. All she had was Labour Day weekend. Tuesday morning, she had to be back in Ottawa to give Colin the bad news, at least the journalistic part of it. Until then, what more harm could a little more digging do?

"Now, on that tape," he said. "You mentioned three guys, but did you notice anything else?"

Kris had looked away during most of the replay of the tape. It had been painful enough to watch when she didn't know who the victim was, but seeing the rape of her sister once was enough. She answered L.T.'s question with a shake of her head.

"Two things," he said. "At one point, you can see all three of them and the camera is moving. Then one of them turns toward the camera and asks what to do next. There was a fourth person involved in this, and I think he was the ringleader."

3

The lake was so smooth it didn't look real as the first hint of sun edged up over the Green Mountains. Kris scrunched up into her fleece housecoat and adjusted her position in the Adirondack chair, which was still damp from the morning dew. The chair sat on a bald rock at the highest point of the stony promontory, as if it had been placed there for contemplation. There was a quiet she was tempted to describe as unnatural, but what could be more natural than the silence that exists in the absence of people? L.T was still in bed, and none of the other cabins were occupied. There wasn't even a boat out on the lake yet. Kris pulled a cigarette package from her pocket, then shoved it back in. There was no need to enhance this day.

The quiet of the lake and the smell of the pines reminded her of the canoe trips she and Kathy used to take with their father and their grandfather Charlie Redner. He had been one of the last of the old-time mountain guides. When she was a girl, it seemed as if there were nothing about nature he didn't know. She had learned the proper way to set a campfire, paddle a canoe, and snare a deer. It was illegal, but her grandfather didn't worry too much about that kind of thing. He was his own law in the bush.

Her father's face was frustratingly hazy in her mind. When she had left home, she took no picture with her, and had none now. She remembered a tall, strong man with dark hair and an easy smile. He always smelled like aftershave. Old Spice, she thought. He liked to carry her on his shoulders when she was young, lifting her as if she had no weight at all. Mike Redner would have been just Kris's age when he died.

She remembered Kathy's brown, muscular body digging in with a paddle, and how she could swim all the way across the lake, as comfortable as an otter. Four years older, she was able to do the things Kris only wished she could. She had kept those images from the past locked away, like a forgotten photo album. They seemed as if they were from some other life where the sun always shone and you had family to care for and protect you.

The difficult years after the death of her father had eroded most of those happy memories. Now, when she wanted to recall them again, she found she had so few. Still, back in the Adirondacks, she felt closer to all of them than she had in years.

Kris ran a hand through her short hair. When she had been a girl, it had been long, down to the middle of her back. Kathy used to brush it for her, one hundred strokes a night. After she died, Kris had cut her hair and kept it that way.

She decided on the cigarette after all. Taking a deep drag, she began to feel a bit more like herself.

Bud Naylor's words still rang in her ears. The town whore. It was a cruel take on her mother, but she was sure Naylor wasn't the only one who thought that way.

At her father's funeral, her mother, Candy, was so disconsolate that she practically had to be carried by two friends walking on either side of her. The double blows of the deaths of her husband and daughter within a week were too much. Who were the friends? Kris couldn't remember now. They didn't stick around long, that was for sure. For a little while, everyone felt sorry for Candy Redner and her daughter Kris. Then Candy started drinking heavily, finally hanging around bars to cadge free drinks. They didn't hear much from people after that. Finally, Candy began bringing her boyfriends home. She had been a beautiful woman with lustrous dark hair, green eyes, and the big breasts men seemed to find endlessly attractive. By the time the drinking became uncontrollable, there wasn't much of that beauty left, but there was still enough for certain kinds of men.

After her mother's suicide, Kris left and ran away to Canada to the grudging hospitality of her uncle. It was that or become a ward of the state. Living with Martin Redner, she often wondered if she had made the right choice.

Whoever had killed Kathy had taken Kris's childhood and family, too. It seemed terrible to say it, but she considered herself as much of a victim as her sister.

A victim. She had fought hard to avoid living her life as one.

She had become tough, strong, cynical. An observer who didn't let anything get to her. Now, back in what she still acknowledged as home, she felt more vulnerable than she ever had in the roughest parts of Toronto. She was a girl from the wrong side of the river again, reminding everyone of a story they wanted to forget. The only one on her side was L.T., and she wasn't even totally sure she could rely on him. He was willing to play white knight, but would he stick it if things got difficult?

She had to decide what to do next. Yesterday's little show was unlikely to be the limit of Bud Naylor's repertoire, and he would want revenge for her well-placed kick. She didn't frighten easily, but Naylor was on his own turf and seemed to make his own rules. And now she had drawn L.T. into the whole mess. He could certainly take care of himself, but his tendency to think the best of people, unusual in a cop, could leave him vulnerable. She was sure L.T. would be a bit naïve about the kind of stakes Osborne and Naylor were playing for.

No more naïve than she herself had been almost three weeks ago when she had driven across the border at Ogdensburg, confident she could locate the person who had sent her the tape, then dig in and find out what really happened to her sister. She hoped to produce enough for the police to take the case seriously, maybe even find Kathy's murderer.

At the least, she had expected to write a story that would hold publicly accountable the people responsible for Kathy's death. She hadn't imagined just how unfriendly and impenetrable her old hometown would be. She had worked her way methodically through interviews with Kathy's old girlfriends and old boyfriends, sure the puzzle would piece itself together the way it usually did. It seemed most had lost touch with her that last summer, Kathy's first venture into the adult world of work. She had spent most of her time at the Osborne camp. That's where the truth was to be found, Kris was sure, but the people directly involved had refused to speak to her. They all seemed to know what she wanted as soon as she said her name, and they all claimed to know nothing.

She didn't believe it for a minute.

The police had been another dead end, the investigating officer long deceased, and the chief completely unhelpful.

Until her encounter with Naylor, she had almost been willing to give up. His ferocity convinced her something was being covered up, something damaging that involved the senator directly. L.T. had been right about the tape. They had watched it again and there was definitely a fourth person in play. Was Lowell Osborne the director of that evil production or a participant? One or the other, she'd bet.

Knowing that increased her compulsion to keep going, but it wouldn't make the story any easier to get. Kris had been awake much of the night, thinking about what to do next. If she was going to stick with this, to drive deeper, she knew she had to admit the truth. She wanted to nail whoever raped and murdered her sister to even the score for what they had done to her. God knows how horrible Kathy's end had been, but Kris had been sentenced to live on: to attend her father's funeral only a week later; to watch her mother decline into an alcoholic stupor and suicide; to spend her teenaged years in a cabin in the bush with her crazy coot of an uncle, Martin.

Kathy was dead and gone. Unless you believed in ghosts, she would never get a bit of satisfaction from whatever justice Kris could bring to her killers. Justice — or revenge? she wondered. Maybe it didn't matter which.

Kris knocked another cigarette out of the pack and lit it. She couldn't work without one. She realized now that she had come at the story from the wrong direction. Sometimes that was what it was like, scoping out a story. No one held up a sign saying "THIS WAY." Often you didn't know you had gone down the wrong road until you'd done it. She'd focused on Kathy's friends and tried to pursue the police investigation, but the people at the camp that summer were the ones who knew the truth. She had to push them harder.

She pulled a slim reporter's notebook from the pocket of her housecoat, fished for a pen, then wrote five names in the notebook. At the top of the list was Dr. Tom Larson, Betsy's husband. He knew more than he was saying. She was sure of that. Then she wrote down Bud Naylor's name. The stockier guy on the video could easily be a young Bud Naylor, and he'd already demonstrated his appetite for violence and his low opinion of her sister. He would tell her nothing, but she needed to find out more about him. He was a player — that was certain. Then two more names. Sharon Sloan and Liz Harper. Both had worked at the camp that summer with Kathy and both had rebuffed her efforts to interview them. Time to try again. Finally, one last name. Pat Osborne. Kris should have tried her sooner. Pat Osborne hadn't been in town that summer, but if you wanted the dirt on a guy, you talked to his ex.

She only had four days to nail the story that had eluded her for nearly three weeks. She had already sent Colin a strongly fictional summary of the story, complete with pictures she'd taken with her little Canon point-and-shoot. Colin expected to see her in the newsroom Tuesday morning, and if she didn't come back with the goods, he would fly into one of his rages. He was unpredictable when angered. Kris knew he could banish her to night rewrite if he felt like it, despite their relationship. If they still had one.

Colin was clearly seething over the way she had vanished in the middle of the night and the meagre information she had given him about what she was really up to. In the two and half weeks she had been gone, they had exchanged only a single phone call, and all they talked about was extending her deadline.

Getting some kind of publishable story would be the best way to mollify Colin, short of a long bout of forgive-me sex, which she really couldn't imagine. Not after L.T.

Kris circled Tom Larson's name. Kathy's friends had told Kris they thought Tom and Kathy had dated that last summer. Kris had been surprised at the idea of her sister with a boy from Dumont Hill. She was an awfully pretty girl, though. At a certain age, that made up for a lot.

The one time she'd gotten together with Betsy and Tom, for a drink at a waterfront restaurant, Kris had raised it with him. He seemed a bit embarrassed, and from the look on Betsy's face, it was news to her. Finally, he had said "I'm sorry, Kris, I'd almost forgotten her. I'm afraid I dated a lot of girls in my younger years, before Betsy stole my heart."

Kris had nearly gagged on that cheeseball line. She'd have bet money that within twenty-four hours Betsy received a dozen red roses.

"So you actually dated her the summer she was killed, but you didn't think that would be helpful to me, for my story?" Kris had replied. It wasn't a gracious thing to say, but how many more people in Osborne were like Tom Larson? People who actually knew something about Kathy's last summer of life, but had conveniently forgotten all about it?

"Well, as I say, I was home from Harvard that summer and I probably dated half a dozen local girls. Nothing serious."

Right, Kris thought. The three Fs. Find 'em, fuck 'em, and forget 'em. She knew the type, but she was disappointed to think that Tom Larson fit it. She had liked him right away, partly because he was a link with the outside world. He had only recently returned to Osborne after spending years in Boston and New York. Tom's easy, urbane conversation had been a relief after weeks of people whose horizons didn't extend beyond the upcoming deer hunting season, or this week's episode of *Survivor*.

"So, Tom, you were home from Harvard. How old would you have been?" Kris had asked.

"Nineteen. Why?"

"Weren't you a little old for my sister?"

"What was she? Seventeen, maybe?"

"Try fourteen."

"Really?"

Tom looked shocked, but not as shocked as Betsy. She quickly rallied, though.

"Tom started dating me when I was fifteen and he was twenty-one. If you want to get the good ones, you have to start early."

It wasn't clear whether she was the one starting early, or Tom, but he liked the concept.

"Right, exactly," he had said, giving Betsy a hug.

Kris felt that she had pushed it as far as she could, without totally alienating Betsy. Kathy had been a mature fourteen. That much was becoming clear. A good-looking girl got to be a woman pretty fast in a town like Osborne. At least now she could see why Tom had "forgotten" dating Kathy. If a guy nineteen was dating a girl fourteen, it wasn't for her conversation.

Although she had let it go at the time, now she felt that she ought to push deeper, perhaps even confide in Tom about the videotape. He might be her best link to what Kathy's life was like that last summer. She had to get someone from the inside to open up. Despite his not volunteering the information about her sister, Kris's take on him was still that he was an intelligent, decent man who would do the right thing.

Perhaps he really had forgotten about Kathy. Kris was painfully aware that the cataclysmic event that had changed her life was nothing but a gossipy story from long ago to most of the people in Osborne

She finished her cigarette and threw the smouldering butt toward the water twenty feet below. The lake was so calm, she could see the brief sizzle before it disappeared.

It was time to get going. She had work to do.

4

Patricia Osborne advanced across the terrace, her high heels clattering on the flagstones. Betsy said she had been a former beauty queen, and Kris could still see it in the high cheekbones and trim figure, so well accentuated by her red silk dress. Her glossy black hair was chin length, and looked as if it had just been cut. Although the temperature had shot up to eighty-five degrees, the woman appeared as fresh as a refrigerated rose.

Unlike the senator, the former Mrs. Osborne had been extremely approachable. As soon as Kris had told her she was doing a true crime book, and Lowell Osborne might feature in it, his ex-wife had told her to come over right away. The bit about the book was an exaggeration, but Kris thought it would sound more intriguing than a newspaper story to be published in a city far away.

Patricia Osborne extended a perfectly tanned hand, with the kind of glossy, red nails that could only be found on a woman who was a complete stranger to physical work. "Hi. Call me Pat," she said.

Her grip was firmer than Kris would have expected. Home gym, probably. There was actually room for both a gym and a basketball court in Pat Osborne's house. It was the most ostentatious building in town, a three-storey steel and glass monstrosity that shone like a lighthouse beacon in the afternoon sun. People said you could actually see it from the Vermont side. Soon after buying the property, Pat had wreckers demolish the mansion that had stood on the site since the middle of the nineteenth century. Closets were too small, Betsy had said. She knew all the gossip.

Pat gestured toward a white summer chair with a soft, cotton cover. The terrace offered a view of the lake and the grounds that swept down to it. Below them, an actual Japanese gardener was trimming the shrubs. A jug of sangria was on the matching white table."Drink?" Pat asked, pouring herself a large one.

"Sure, thanks. Quite a place."

Pat gave a dismissive wave, as if it were the first time she'd thought about it. "A summer spot. My home down in Cocoa Beach is a little grander."

Kris smiled, but she was thinking that Pat Osborne was going to be awfully hard to like.

"So, I'm intrigued. A true crime book, with Lowell in it. What's your angle?"

Kris explained about her sister's murder and the connection to the Osborne family.

"Well, I'm afraid that was before my time. I was Miss New York when I met Lowell. He had just finished at Yale, and was a gofer for Senator Will Lewis. Lewis wanted to get into my pants, but Lowell beat him to it.

"As it turned out, I'd have been better off with Lewis. He's dead now, and left his widow a tidy estate."

"You don't seem to be suffering."

"Not financially, no. My lawyer wrung every possible nickel out of that bastard. It seems he hardly even misses it. Did you know he's going to add a wing to the old house, just to accommodate the children from his current marriage? It's like he's running a breeding farm.

"More Osbornes. Just what the world needs. That's why he left me, you know. I couldn't give him an heir."

Pat took a healthy slug of the sangria. Unlike the wine-based fruit drink Kris was used to, this one seemed to contain a sizeable portion of vodka.

"Have you met little Terry?" Pat asked.

"I'm afraid that I'm not exactly part of the senator's social set."

"No, I suppose not.

"Her tits aren't real, you know," Pat said. "Mine are."

For one dreadful moment, Kris was afraid that she was going to show her. She rushed to change the topic. "Well, I hoped you might be able to tell me about the senator's life as a young man, around the time that my sister was killed. Who his friends were, that kind of thing. I know the two of you weren't together then, but I suppose he must have talked about that. You were married, what, twenty years?"

"Nineteen, and then he traded me in like a used car. As soon as Lowell possesses something, he wants the next, better thing. I'm sure you've heard about his infidelities."

Pat looked out toward the lake. Kris thought the other woman was about to cry, but then she composed herself, leaned toward Kris and said, "Look, I think Lowell Osborne leaves a slime trail everywhere he goes, but what's his connection with your sister, really?"

"She was spending almost all her time at the camp that summer, and the senator was at the camp. I'm just trying to understand the situation."

Pat put her glass on the table with a clumsy thump. "Ah, of course. You're assuming Lowell was screwing her. Why not? He consumes women the way some men consume potato chips."

Pat's expression changed as a further level of understanding set in. "God, you don't think he did it, do you?"

"No, no, of course not. But it might have been someone associated with the camp. I'm just trying to get a full picture."

"Let me tell you, Lowell Osborne doesn't do any of the dirty work. When he decided he wanted a divorce, he sent Bud Naylor over with legal papers. I suppose you've met Bud."

Kris pulled back her blue T-shirt, to show Pat Osborne a bit of the damage Bud Naylor had done to her shoulder. The bruise was now a combination of green and purple. "The five-minute interview the senator gave me concluded with Naylor practically dragging me from the room and threatening to be my worst nightmare."

"The son of a bitch. And I suppose Lowell was long gone by then."

"On his way to the chopper."

"Typical. What are you going to do about that?" she asked, pointing to Kris's shoulder.

"Keep icing it."

"No, I mean, are you taking some kind of legal action? Did you at least complain to Lowell or that press toady he has?"

"No, I settled out of court. A swift kick seemed to square things up."

Pat smiled, a bit lopsidedly. "I always wanted to do that," she said wistfully. "He's had it coming for years."

"Tell me about Bud."

"Hardly our sort of person, but he was Lowell's pal when they were kids. Bud's father was a Marine general, mind, and he's a big backer of Lowell's, but Bud has always been a boor. Lowell went to a public high school here. I suppose he couldn't choose the sort of people he had to brush up against."

"I know. I went to the same one."

"Oh, of course."

"So why is Bud still hanging around after all these years?"

"He thinks Lowell's going all the way. We all do. I think Bud imagines himself as secretary of defence, something like that. With my luck, the bastard will be elected president and I'll get to watch the lovely Terry be First Lady, after I spent nearly twenty years building Lowell up, helping him every inch of the way."

"He sounds like a real snake, but people seem to think he's a charmer."

"Oh, he is. I don't think he's yet met the girl he can't talk the pants off of. Lowell's always selling himself. He's relentless."

"So he and Bud, they would have still been hanging out when Lowell was at Yale?"

"I suppose so. Bud went straight into the service. Refused his father's demand that he train as an officer. He has no education, you know. But he's always kept coming back to Osborne. He follows Lowell around like a stray dog, looking for some kind of free meal."

"Or something to chew on," Kris said, rubbing her shoulder.

Beyond the fact that Pat Osborne hated her former husband, Kris wasn't really getting a lot that was useful.

"How old were you when you first met Lowell?" Kris asked.

"Seventeen. If you are wondering, does he like them young, yes. Little Terry was all of twenty when he married her. I'm surprised he didn't find her a bit old."

"My sister was only fourteen, although I suppose she seemed older. All the guys she dated were quite a bit older than her."

"Ah, yes. I know the type."

Kris was sure she did.

Pat leaned closer, and lowered her voice. "Look, if I weren't half looped, I'd never tell anyone this, but when Lowell and I were first married, he had me dress up in one of those little schoolgirl plaid skirts, then he'd spank me. He really seemed to enjoy that."

And the poison princess was probably long overdue for a spanking now, Kris thought. But Lowell Osborne's semi-kinky little scenario also reminded her rather forcibly that her sister was wearing a maid's uniform at the time of her rape. "Well, they all have their peculiarities, don't they?" Kris said.

Pat Osborne poured herself another glass of her special sangria and topped Kris's up as well.

"Other than Bud, did he have other friends here he was particularly close to?" Kris asked.

"His brother, Billy, would have been around the camp that summer. He's two years younger."

"Billy? I haven't heard anything about him." The official biographies of Lowell Osborne didn't mention any siblings.

"Well, Billy's a bit of a black sheep. He runs a lawn service in some dreadful little town up near the Canadian border. Ploughs snow in the winter. Lowell's money keeps him off welfare. Billy dropped out of being an Osborne long ago. Probably a smart move," she said with a tight little laugh. "And Tom Larson, of course. He was a little more Lowell's style. At one time, Lowell wanted to be a doctor, too, until he discovered how much work it was. Those two go right back to grade school."

"What's your take on Tom?"

"Betsy got a good one. He's smart, he's nice looking, and he doesn't sleep around. You know, sometimes when you reach for too much, you end up with nothing."

Kris thought she could use a bit of the kind of nothing that Pat Osborne was experiencing, but she knew what the former beauty queen meant. If your goal was to be First Lady, the odds of coming up short were pretty good. Everyone made moral compromises on the way to the top, and if you didn't get to the top, all you had left were the compromises.

"My impression of Tom was about the same," Kris said. "Then I found out he actually dated my sister that summer. He didn't tell me, even knowing that I was trying to find out everything about her death."

Pat shrugged. "We can't tell the truth all the time, Kris. I gather you've come down here like you're everyone's conscience. Maybe people here think that what they did so many years ago is none of your business."

She smiled after saying that, but it just added bite to her words. Kris's original hope that Pat would prove to be an ally was fading.

Kris smiled back, with just as much ice. "It is though, because someone here killed my sister and, for all those years, he's gotten away with it. I won't bore you with the details, but after Kathy's murder my whole family collapsed. So I think it matters, and I think Lowell Osborne knows something about it. Something he's not going to tell me, because any kind of association with a scandal will be used against him by his opponents. That's not what I call standing up. I hoped you might do better."

Pat looked away, then glanced at her watch, a petite affair with diamonds encircling the face. "Give me a piece of paper and a pen," she said.

Kris tore a sheet from her notebook.

Pat scrawled a name on the paper, folded it over, and passed it to Kris.

"Talk to her. She was the one Lowell was screwing most often that summer."

Then Pat Osborne stood and was gone in a swish of perfume.

5

L.T. was trying to stay cool, but his heart was pounding with the kind of adrenaline rush he always got before a big game. It had been five years since his days as a running back at Duke, and he had forgotten how much he missed that feeling.

He had tried to think of a legitimate reason to pull the Kathy Redner murder file, but he'd come up dry. Everything before 1999 was locked in the basement records room of the sprawling building that served as Osborne's town hall, police station, and fire hall. He was just going to have to go down and get it, but it needed to be when no one else was in the station.

It looked as if that moment had come. Jackson and Adams were both on the road. The chief had gone to the Rotary Club lunch and hadn't come back. As long as someone else was buying, he probably wouldn't.

L.T. was at his desk, catching up on the paperwork on three kids he'd arrested for break and enter. They'd gotten into six homes on Dumont Hill, cleaned out all the audio equipment and televisions. They'd been pretty good at the breaking in, but it all came apart when one of them tried to sell the stuff out of the back of his dad's minivan in the parking lot of Roosevelt High. Cops might not all be the brightest people in the world, but they were usually saved by the fact that the criminals were dumber.

Not the guy who'd killed Kris's sister, though. L.T. hadn't wanted to discourage her, but the idea of cracking a cold case from nearly thirty years ago was a real long shot, at best. Not that he minded the idea of her sticking around for a bit longer to try.

He was trying not to fall in love with Kris, although he found himself thinking about her first thing every morning, and then most of the day after that. She was leaving so soon, what would be the point in getting entangled? He loved her intensity and passion, though. She was a woman, simple as that, not at all like the football groupies and cheerleaders who just liked to show him off.

He had to admit the idea of having sex with a woman that much older had been what first attracted him. He felt like he'd have to be a damn fool not to go for it. The timing had been good, too. The hiking and climbing in the state park were great, but life in Osborne itself was beyond dull, and the police work was just one step more challenging than being a security guard.

He was the only officer on the force who was not from Osborne, and he didn't fully grasp the politics of the town. Some people you gave a ticket to, others you warned. Some got an escort home, others got a ride to the station. It had more to do with their address than the offence.

L.T. already had applications in to three forces in Hawaii. The answers couldn't come soon enough. The little squad room, with its cheap wood panelling and ten-point buck on the wall, felt like someone's basement rec room, not a police station. It was a place where he would never belong.

The only reason he'd gotten the job, he knew, was because he'd been a college football star. Larry Brewster had actually introduced him to the other guys as "L.T. Hill from Duke, All-American in his junior year." And torn knee ligaments in his senior year. So much for dreams of the NFL.

L.T. looked out the window at the parking lot in back. Three cruisers were parked in the shade of a big maple, but there was no one in sight.

He headed down the back staircase to the records room, wondering if he was being stupid. This little side investigation could cost him his job if the chief found out. Not that he valued the job, but being fired wouldn't do much for his prospects in Hawaii.

Well, to hell with it, he thought. He said he'd help Kris and he would. Where he came from, a man's word still meant something. Besides, that videotape had been sickening. The sons of bitches who did that to her sister deserved to be brought to justice.

The basement under the police station was part of the original 1840s building and he could smell the must of age and feel the damp from the limestone walls. The stairs seemed to be original, wooden treads worn thin in the middle by generations of cops and town bureaucrats. It was a hell of a place to keep records, he thought, but Osborne's police force was unlike any he'd worked for.

He used the key he'd taken from the hook by the door to open the room and turned on the light, a single dull bulb in a wire cage on the low ceiling. All four walls were lined with file cabinets. The oldest were obviously on the left. They were oak. The next bank beside them looked like they were army surplus, khaki and battered. Hard to say what war, but not one that took place recently. The right wall and the one beside L.T. had modern metal cabinets.

This was going to be easier than he thought. Someone had been bright enough to file the cases by year. There were only two drawers devoted to 1981. Crime had never been a big business in Osborne.

L.T. pulled open the lower of the two drawers and started to thumb through it. Parker, Price, Queen, Raymond, Redner. He pulled the file folder out.

Empty.

L.T. went back to the drawer, thinking the contents might have been accidentally replaced in an adjoining file.

Nothing.

He'd expected to find full notes from the investigator, crime scene photos, forensics, an autopsy report. If someone had pulled the file, why wouldn't he have taken the folder, too?

L.T. caught a sniff of Jack Daniels, then felt a meaty hand on his shoulder.

"Can I help you, son?"

It was Larry Brewster, two sheets to the wind.

"I was looking for a file."

"I can see that. Which one?"

"Kathy Redner. That old murder case. People have been talking about it. I thought I'd see what it was all about."

L.T. felt the same way he had when his mom had found the magazines under the bed. He knew his excuse was weak, but it was the best he could think of on such short notice. He wasn't a good liar.

The chief furrowed his face in concentration, his bushy black eyebrows coming together like two caterpillars. In the close confines of the records room, he smelled like a distillery. Brewster couldn't have been more than fifty, but the drinking had made him look much older. His face was as round as a basketball and always flushed, like he'd just run a mile, even though the last time he'd run anywhere was certainly in a different decade. His uniform shirt strained to contain his belly.

"I think you're bullshitting me, son," he said. "You banging the sister? Can't think of any other reason why you'd want to look at that file. The two of you up at Jasper's, it must be pretty handy. Can't say I blame you. This is a hell of town for a young fella to try to get laid in."

"Hey, Chief. That's my business."

"Yep, and what happens in this police station is my business. I thought I'd mentioned it, but one of the things you need to know is when to keep out of stuff that's not your concern.

"I don't know what the Redner girl's angle is, but there's nothing good in it for this town. That puts her on the other team."

The chief looked L.T. straight in the eyes with the expression of fatherly understanding that had probably wrung confessions from decades of young car thieves and vandals.

"I need to know, L.T., whose team are you on?"

"Yours. Our team," he said quickly. "I was just curious. You're right, Chief, I am seeing her and I wanted to know what the facts of the case really are. Now Kris, she's real upset about her sister, but that's the way relatives are. I thought if I looked at the facts, maybe I could straighten her out. Hell, there's not much chance of a cold case like that being solved. She's got to get over it."

"Maybe you can tell me, L.T., why's she down here now, anyway? Her sister's death is ancient history. What's got her all riled up now?"

A damn good reason, L.T. thought, but it wasn't one he was going to share with Larry Brewster. He just didn't trust him.

"Hard to say. I guess it's just something she's always meant to follow up. It's been nagging at her. She's trying to turn it into a story for that paper of hers, with the senator being so much in the news and all."

"How much longer you figure this is going to go on?"

"I think she's due back up in Canada next week."

The chief smiled for the first time.

"That's good news, son. Anything else you can tell me?"

"Well, I don't think she's found out a lot. Folks here just don't seem to remember much about her sister. I'd say she struck out."

The chief's smile grew wider. "Good, L.T. I knew I could count on you. Funny she hasn't come to talk to me. I figured she would. That's why I took the file out myself."

L.T. distinctly remembered Kris saying that she had approached the chief and he'd refused to give her any information.

"I was just a young officer like you when it happened. I wanted to refresh my memory. It's on my desk, for safekeeping. Got to tell you, though, there isn't much there. The best theory at the time, as I recall, was that she was hitchhiking home from the senator's camp. Got picked up by a stranger, and killed. You know how tough it is to solve a crime like that. Guy passing through, probably never been back here. No connection to the victim, other than deciding he wanted a piece."

"So she was raped, then?"

"Well, I don't know that it was rape, but she spent some time in the bush with him. Kathy Redner was kind of a slutty kid, as I recollect.

"Didn't really know her myself," he added quickly.

L.T. let that slide. "Murder case, why didn't we bring in the state police?"

"Well, I do remember them taking a bit of a look, but it was sensitive. Girl worked at the Osborne camp. Osbornes have always swung a lot of weight around here."

The chief gave L.T. his look of stern understanding again. "That hasn't changed. I imagine someone suggested that we could handle it."

L.T. knew what Kris would call that. A coverup. It wasn't necessarily so, but he'd bet that not too much effort was put into solving the case, once it was attributed to a mysterious stranger passing through. Certainly not anything that would connect the murder back to the Osborne camp.

"So I guess you're telling me we don't really have a whole lot to go on. I'll pass that on."

"Good stuff. Hey, why don't you come on over for the game Sunday? We're having most of the boys over for a barbecue. I'm doing a whole pig. Won't be like you're used to back home, but after a few beers, I'll bet it tastes just as good."

In the year he had been in Osborne, it was the first social invitation L.T. had had from the chief. If that was the reward for being on the team, he'd have to figure a way to get back off again. "I'd love to, but I had a day of trout fishing planned."

The chief winked.

"Trout fishing, right. I get it. You enjoy yourself, young fella."

The chief winked again, just to underline the idea that he understood how L.T. would really be spending his day.

L.T. was thinking that Sunday would be a perfect chance to have a little look at the chief's desk, since he and the boys would be at the barbecue. One thing you learned when you were a cop is how to tell when people are lying to you, and he hadn't detected more than a light odour of the truth in anything Larry Brewster had to say.

6

Kris pulled the Prius into an angled parking spot on Main Street. It might be the main street, but parking was never a problem. Things were always slow, even during the tourist season. It was no surprise. Other than half a dozen rundown stores selling second-rate crafts, girlie dust-collectors, and the standard souvenir crap, there wasn't much to attract a tourist to Osborne.

Stepping out of the intense late summer sun into the dimness of Vieth's All-U-Need took Kris back more than twenty years. It was the place she had to walk to for groceries when she wasn't old enough to drive, and her mother wasn't in a condition to get behind the wheel. When she returned to Osborne, she found it almost unchanged. There was still a big cooler of beer at the back and three little aisles of canned goods and cereals, things that wouldn't go bad too fast. The only real difference was the ten-foot-long rack of videos and DVDs on her immediate left as she came in. The wooden floors still dipped and creaked in all the same places, and there was a slight, familiar odour. Mothballs and dust, she thought.

Like most people in Osborne, Kris now had no reason to go into Vieth's. She had been getting her groceries over in Elizabethtown, or up in Plattsburgh. She didn't really understand what kept Vieth's in business. Maybe it was the cigarettes stacked high behind the counter.

The store itself seemed ageless, but Sharon Sloan hadn't been so lucky. The first time Kris had seen her, she was riding in the back of a white convertible, waving to adoring crowds. The Lake Champlain Princess.

Now, she was standing behind the counter at Vieth's, sucking the last bit of evil from the stub of a cigarette. Decades of bleaching had turned her hair a dead yellow, dark at the roots, and she had put on maybe fifty pounds, the bulk only partially hidden by a baggy green sweatshirt. Although she was only in her mid-forties, she looked easily a decade older. Kris could just see the remains of what had made her attractive in the fine line of her nose, and the fullness of her lips. If this was the girl Lowell Osborne had been tied up with back in 1981, he'd done well to check the best before date, she thought.

"Hi," Kris said, as friendly as she could manage. "It's me again, Kris Redner."

It had been only last week that Kris had attempted to interview Sharon Sloan by phone, after some of Kathy's old friends identified her as a girl who worked at the camp that summer. Sharon had rudely blown her off. Now that she knew Sharon had actually been Lowell Osborne's girlfriend, Kris was determined to be more persistent. Surely Sharon must know what had gone on up at the camp.

"Yeah, I know who you are. What do you want now?"

The tone was somewhere between wary and hostile.

"I'll take a pack of those Virginia Slims," Kris said. As Sharon turned to get the cigarettes, Kris said, "I know about you and Lowell Osborne. We really need to talk."

Sharon shoved the cigarettes across the counter and looked around the store. There wasn't another customer present, nor much likelihood of one.

"I suppose I could give you a couple of minutes," she said. "I feel kind of sorry for you."

Kris tried not to show her surprise. If someone this pathetic felt sorry for her, how low was she? And why would Sharon feel sorry for her? "Cigarette?" Kris asked.

"I shouldn't," Sharon said, but she accepted the one Kris knocked from her new pack. Kris lit one for herself.

Sharon took a long drag and said, "So you told me last time you're working on a newspaper article about your sister's death. I can't be in it. I have an understanding with Lowell that I won't talk about our past."

Kris imagined the understanding involved cash. She could readily see why Lowell Osborne wouldn't want Sharon Sloan's face on the grocery store tabloids with a headline of "Senator's Former Lover."

"Of course, but we could speak on background."

Background, deep background, off the record, all were synonyms for I won't quote you. They were meant to reassure a source and had real meaning, if it was a source you wanted to quote again.

"I only ask because I'm trying to understand the situation my sister was in that summer," Kris said. "Tell me about you and Lowell."

"It was a long time ago. We were all different people then."

Kris could easily imagine the outline of Sharon's life. Lake Champlain Princess. The most beautiful girl of the summer. Thinking she had found her rich prince. Then fall came, and the prince went back to Yale. The princess got stuck in the dungeon of Osborne.

"You were Lake Champlain Princess that summer, right?"

Sharon laughed.

"Yeah, fuck of a lot of good that did me."

"You must have known Kathy from up at the camp."

"A bit. She was four years younger, but we worked together."

"And the work was what, maid? Waitress?"

Kris thought she already knew the answer to that question, but it was usually good to start with some easy ones, to establish the rhythm of the interview.

"Whatever they needed done. It was Liz Harper, myself, and your sister. Lowell's father used to bring his big-shot friends up from New York to fish and drink. We were something for them to look at, then clean up their mess afterwards."

"For you, it was a little different than that, wasn't it?"

"Lowell was screwing me, if that's what you mean. I was in love, but he was just filling in time until he went back to school. I haven't seen the prick in years. Not to talk to, you know. You can't miss him driving around town in his limo. Now, they are saying he could be president. It makes me shudder. That guy lies so often I think he's forgotten what the truth is.

"He told me that he'd remain faithful when he went back to school, just to keep any of the local boys from getting their hands on me. He had me reserved for a little quick sex over Christmas. He dumped me on New Year's Eve, but not until after he'd celebrated."

Kris nodded sympathetically. "Yeah, he's a real bastard. And what about Kathy? Was she involved with anyone at the camp that summer? I take it there must have been guys working there, too. Students?"

"No, old Mr. Osborne kept two regular staff on year round. George Henderson. He died a couple of years ago. Bobby Edwards. He still works at the camp. Have you talked to him?"

"No, I didn't know about him. Is he . . . ?"

"A no-brain boozer who lifts and carries for the Osbornes. I'm sure your sister wouldn't have been interested in him. She was a fourteen-year-old kid."

"People keep telling me she was an old fourteen."

"That happens around here."

"Now, the camp itself. I've never been there. Do any of the buildings have a big stone foundation?"

If Kris had to bet who sent her the videotape, Sharon Sloan's name would be at the top of the list. She had a motive, and she had been at the camp that summer.

Sharon looked away, suddenly interested in something happening in the street. "What's that got to do with anything?"

"I have a reason for asking. I thought you might know what it is."

"You know, Kris, I've probably said too much already. You don't know what it's like. You're not from here anymore. Lowell Osborne owns this town. Most everyone works for him, or they depend on someone who does. Osborne knows everything that goes on. The police work for him, you know."

"That's a little paranoid, isn't it?"

"Sure," Sharon said, blowing out a cloud of cigarette smoke. "What would I know? I'm just a clerk in a sad-assed grocery store."

"Sorry," Kris said. "That's not what I meant. But how could Osborne control the whole town, really?"

"I'm surprised you don't know. Power. He's got it. Some fear it. Others want a share of it. Either way, they're lined up to kiss his ass. If the guy does become president, they all think there's going to be some kind of tourism boom, and they'll cash in. Just like that shit-ass little town down in Texas, where George Bush is from."

"Well, I'm not afraid of him," Kris said. "If he had anything to do with my sister's death or is covering up for someone who did, I'll be kicking his ass, not kissing it."

Sharon looked nervously around the store, as if concerned that someone might have heard Kris's comment. "Well, good luck to you, but I can't help you. I went up against Osborne once. Bud Naylor ran me off."

"Me too," Kris said. She undid a button of her white blouse and slid it off her shoulder to show the bruise. It still looked grotesque, but at least the pain had begun to subside.

"Fuck, some things never change, do they?"

"Not unless someone makes them change," Kris said.

"There's way more to this than the death of your sister, honey. Trust me, you don't want to get into it."

"Yeah, I do. Way more like what?"

Kris knew she was on the verge of losing Sharon and this would probably be her only shot.

"It involves your mother. Surely you must know that."

Her mother? What did she have to do with all of this? "My mother was a drunk who killed herself, but that was years after Kathy's death. I don't understand."

"Check out what your mother was doing that summer. That's all I'm going to tell you."

Sharon began to rearrange the cigarettes on the shelf. Kris knew the interview was over, but she was more confused than when she walked through the door. Her mother and Kathy hadn't gotten along. Too much alike, perhaps. But how did that connect to Kathy's death?

7

L.T. Hill unzipped his golf jacket and tossed it in the basket on the back of the power cart. The morning had started cool, with a fresh wind off Lake Champlain, but now it was beginning to heat up. The green of the tenth hole was located on top of a hill that rose at nearly a forty-five-degree angle from the tee box. They were at the highest point of the course. Below him, the fairways spread out like one of those aerial views they showed on TV, the lake to his left, the mountains to his right.

The hole was 430 yards straightaway, but the angle of the hill was so steep that it was going to eat any drive as soon as it landed. This hole was going to be all about the second shot. L.T. selected a five wood, thinking the five's extra loft might gain him a few yards. His shot sounded solid off the tee, but it turned into a long, lazy slice that hit the edge of the fairway and bounded into heavy grass on the right. The sun had finally come out from behind the clouds, glaring in his eyes, but he thought he could find the ball. Mountain View Golf and Country was a good course, but the rough wasn't too rough. The groundskeepers didn't want to make it overly difficult for the members who were paying the freight.

The mayor was next up. He took a short, choppy backswing, his arms having difficulty getting beyond his belly. The ball went sky-high and landed on the fairway, about 120 yards out.

"Not bad, Fred. Right down the middle. It'll play," the general said. His own swing was lean and compact, like the man. L.T. figured the general was only about five eight, but he still looked fit enough to be in the corps. Even his khaki pants and tan golf shirt looked vaguely military. Only his thin, white brush cut gave away his age.

His drive was low and straight, bounding up to end beside L.T.'s, but in the short grass. The heavy morning dew was almost gone, but the general's ball rolled into a shady spot, kicking up a little spray of water.

A few strange things had happened to L.T. Hill since he'd been in Osborne, but this was the weirdest. He'd had a call about nine o'clock last night from General Jack Naylor, USMC (ret) inviting him for golf the next morning. The general's usual partner couldn't make it, he'd heard that L.T. was quite a golfer, and he wondered if he wanted to have a go.

From the general's tone, it was clear it was more of an order than an invitation. He had been told to be ready to move out at 0800 hours. Mountain View Golf and Country. The course boasted that it was the Adirondacks' best, but at $150 a round plus cart, it was well beyond L.T.'s means. The general had picked up the tab this morning, apparently all for the pleasure of L.T.'s company. He'd played a lot of rounds like this during summers back in Wilmington, out with town big shots who wanted to mention that they'd played golf with L.T. Hill, the Duke star.

Just like at home, they'd talked about his days at Duke, and what team he liked in the Atlantic Coast Conference that fall.

L.T.'s first inclination had been to say no to the invitation. He loved golf, it was his second sport in college, but he could do without spending four hours with a couple of old duffers who wanted nothing but football jock talk. That part of his life was behind him.

Kris had been with him when he got the call, and when he scribbled down what it was, she nodded for him to go. A golf invitation from Bud Naylor's father had to have something to do with what he had come to think of as their investigation. He had no choice but to go.

L.T. and Jack Naylor waited in their cart on the right side of the course, pausing while the mayor lined up his second shot. So far, the conversation had been as dull as he'd imagined it would be. The mayor had been on about some sewer issue, and Jack Naylor just wanted to talk football. To L.T.'s surprise, he hadn't gotten started on war stories. That was a relief. Naylor would be Vietnam era, and L.T. had heard enough about that from his own father.

L.T. was sure the general had something he wanted to say, but all he could do was play the game and wait to see what happened. At least the course was interesting, full of odd holes and surprises. The company wasn't much, but it took a lot to spoil golf.

The mayor hacked his second shot, sending the divot farther than the ball.

"I'm afraid Fred isn't a natural," Jack Naylor said. "Too bad the senator couldn't make it. You'd have found him a good match."

Here we go, L.T. thought. The general had mentioned earlier that Senator Lowell Osborne was his usual partner, the guy L.T. was filling in for. It sounded like he was about to hear more about the senator, but L.T. decided not to bite on the mention of Osborne's name and said, "I'm having trouble keeping ahead of you, sir."

L.T. had shot thirty-nine on the front nine. Not bad for not having played in more than a year, and using rented clubs. His own were back home in North Carolina. The general had shot forty. He seemed to know every inch of every gully and hill of the rugged course, and he played the smart, controlled game of the older man.

"Hell, I wish I could still swing like you do," the general said. "You're doing fine, especially without a chance to reconnoitre. There's a lot of blind holes on this course."

Never knowing what was around the next turn was a feeling that L.T. was starting to get used to. He found his ball buried in the thick grass. It was going to be tough to get out, and the green was still 180 yards away, on top of a hill. Seven iron, he thought. Give it hell and hope for the best.

The ball exploded from the grass and arced upwards, disappearing from sight somewhere over the brow of the hill.

"Hell of a shot," the general said. "I think you're on. Maybe even through the green."

He took a six iron and lofted the ball gracefully, landing on the front of the green and rolling toward the pin.

L.T. whistled.

"Well done, sir."

"You can stop calling me 'sir.' My military days are long done. Jack will do."

They got back in the cart and the general gunned it up the

path and parked behind the green. The mayor was well off to the right, looking for his ball. The general said, "There's a little bit of business I want to discuss, L.T."

L.T. showed a look of surprise, as if the thought had never occurred to him.

The general stopped the cart, pushed his sunglasses up on his head and turned to L.T. The older man's face was deeply lined, but not in that kind of friendly-old-guy way. It was more like terrain that had seen a lot of battles. His hard dark eyes grabbed L.T.'s own, and held them.

"I've been talking to Larry Brewster and to my son Bud. You know Bud?"

"We haven't met, but I know who he is."

And if I got half a chance, I'd knock him on his ass for what he did to Kris, L.T. thought.

"Good. They were telling me about an interesting situation. Now Bud, he gets concerned about every potential problem that might affect the senator. That's his job, but it's his way, too. Bud's one hundred per cent loyal to the senator. We all are here. Myself, I'm co-chairman of his campaign.

"We all back Lowell because of who he is, but there's a big picture, too. With the terrorist threat the world faces, we can't afford a weak president. I know. I've been on the front lines. I've seen boys sacrifice their lives for this country. America needs to be strong. Lowell understands that."

L.T. was beginning to wonder what defence contractor the general lobbied for.

"Now some of his opponents, and the Democrats, they just want to talk about higher taxes and more social programs. That's what makes America weak. This country needs Lowell Osborne in the White House, L.T., and there's a number of us determined to get him there."

L.T. didn't consider himself political. His take on politicians wasn't as black as Kris's, but from what he knew, they were all there for themselves first. Guaranteed the general had some angle besides love of country and love of Lowell Osborne.

There was no point in arguing, though. His job was to find out what the general wanted. "Yes, sir. Folks from my part of the country know the importance of the military."

"Good, good. Now I don't suppose you follow the game of politics, L.T., but it's high stakes and dirty. There's some out there that will try to find any way they can to smear their opponent, even if it's not true. The damage is still done. Lowell doesn't play that way, but the people around him have to realize that others do.

"Now, here's where you come in."

Even though he realized he was nothing more than a pawn in whatever game the general was playing, L.T. was still eager to find out what his move was supposed to be. He fought the urge to drop his guard, though. The general was going to try to talk him into doing something, just the way he'd no doubt talked a lot of other young guys into charging some no-name hill in the middle of the jungle.

"Bud tells me this Kris Redner is a bit of a problem. Her sister dies, what, nearly thirty years ago? And now she shows up here, rooting around in the past, just when the senator's campaign is beginning to build. It's a fact that her sister worked at the senator's family camp that summer. It's a fact that someone killed the poor girl. It's a big stretch to say that has anything to do with the senator, but you know how the media work. Something like 'Senator denies knowledge of teenaged employee's mysterious murder' is a sure sell for those grocery-store rags and scandal blogs. Then the legitimate papers will report that it has been reported. The thing could take on a life of its own.

"It's all a crock of shit, but there's no saying how much damage this media maggot could do."

It took all L.T. had to remain impassive, not give away his feelings. Media maggot? He assumed the general was testing him, to see if he'd rise to Kris's defence.

"I also hear she's been talking to the senator's ex. Now there's a bitter bitch, heavy into the booze. God knows what line of bull she's been serving up.

"L.T., between you and me, I'm suspicious of who this Redner woman is really working for. Every campaign has people digging deep into their opponents' pasts. A murder with a peripheral tie to the senator would be like gold for them."

The general paused, the worried look on his face suggesting that he was contemplating some unspeakable horror. "Anyway, the point is we need to neutralize her," he said.

Neutralize? L.T. knew military men never used a clear word if they could use a euphemism. Was neutralize like terminate with extreme prejudice? "How do you mean, sir?"

The general laughed. "Hell, I don't mean kill her, son. That would be an overreaction. We just need to discourage her. Convince her there's bugger-all to find here. Get her back up to Canada, quick as we can.

"Now, I won't mince words. I know you've been screwing her. No harm in that, but it isn't serious is it?"

L.T. gave an easy laugh. "No sir. Not at all. But she's a good-looking woman, living about twenty feet from where I do. I'm a young guy."

He let a shrug tell the rest of the story. It wasn't really true, but he'd been asked the same kind of question so often about some airhead cheerleader that he had the answer down pat.

"Good, glad to hear it. You're way too young to take women seriously. Hell, we probably all are."

The general had a warm, manly laugh. It was the kind of thing that could make you like him. L.T. reminded himself the guy was a shark, and he was a minnow.

"The thing is, we need to keep a real close eye on this Kris Redner. We need to know what she knows. And we need to find a way to send her packing. I mean ASAP. Within days."

"The chief told me much the same thing."

"Damn straight, but I want you to report right to me. I'm point man on this. It's a political matter, not a local police matter.

"Now you are probably wondering, what's in it for you? I know you're not from here, you don't owe the senator a damned thing. So I just thought you ought to know, and I've discussed this with the mayor, that the chief is planning on retirement within a year.

"Now someone like you, outside policing experience, some profile, already on the force, would have the inside track. It can be a damn good job. Pays on a par with chiefs in much larger towns. Company car, if you don't mind an unmarked."

The general laughed and L.T. forced a smile. Jack Naylor acted as if he were making a hell of an offer, but L.T. would rather be buried alive than spend the rest of his life in Osborne, caddying for the likes of the senator and the Naylors.

"As the chief, your job would be to protect Osborne. That starts with protecting the Osbornes. The town wouldn't be much without them," the general said.

"No, sir."

"Right now, you're in a position to do the senator a favour, L.T. Now, that's a fine position to be in, because the senator's a man who can easily return a favour. Did I mention that a membership here comes with the job?"

L.T. knew that he could only give one answer. Saying no would tell them he was on Kris's side. That would end any ability he had to find out what the senator and his team were up to, and it would put him on the enemies list. Apparently a bad place to be.

He didn't want to act like a fool, though, bought off for the promise of something down the line that was never going to be delivered. If he was going to sell out, it needed to be convincing. What would he do if he were really the kind of guy they thought he was?

The general stopped the cart behind the green. Their balls were on the far edge, within ten feet of each other. They saw the mayor's cart heading off to the right. In the woods again.

"You've been straightforward, General," L.T. said. "I appreciate that, and I'll return the courtesy. I have to tell you that I don't see myself being chief in Osborne."

The general glared at L.T., his salesman's mask dropped.

"Make up your mind, son. Offer's good today only."

"Now, I have no problem helping the senator out, but I think work like that would be worth $50,000. Cash. I have plans after Osborne, and once the Kris Redner problem is solved, I'd be on the road."

The general's laugh was more of a snort.

"Damn, Boy, I like that. You know what you want, and you go get it. We'll call it a consulting fee. Half up front. Welcome aboard."

8

They were late for Betsy's party, and L.T. was taking the Blazer too fast in the hairpin turns between Jasper's and town. The sun filtered through the row of trees on the lakeside as if it were coming through a vertical blind, giving the illusion of even greater speed. Cops all drove like race-car drivers, Kris thought.

"I still don't believe it," she said. "They offered you chief, and then $50,000 instead?"

"I wouldn't say they offered. They told me the job was coming up, I'd be a strong candidate, all that. The general seemed to like it when I asked for cash on the barrelhead. Shows that I'm greedy, but not stupid. Just the kind of guy they're looking for."

Kris thought it had been dangerous for L.T. to agree to take that money. Now he was inextricably drawn into her situation. If it had been anyone else, she'd have worried about whose side he was really on. The senator and his handlers obviously considered her to be a serious problem, but was it because they were actually covering up something about Kathy's death, or just because they feared the fallout from whatever she would write?

"Slow down. I'm not in that big a rush to get to Betsy's."

L.T. touched the brakes. "Hell, what am I thinking? I'm not in any rush at all. Only you told me we were late."

Betsy had said to arrive at seven. It was a quarter after. No big deal to Kris, but Betsy was so anal she'd probably had two events organized for the period between seven and 7:15.

It was a bit awkward, though, because Kris had blundered right into the middle of Betsy's dinner party. She had phoned that afternoon, to ask if Betsy and Tom would like to get together and meet L.T. Kris knew it was the kind of girlie thing Betsy wouldn't be able to resist and it was also her best way to try to corner Tom. She was sure now that he knew a lot more about what happened at the Osborne camp that summer than he'd let on. Sharon Sloan's comment about Kris's mother had been bothering her all day. What could her mother possibly have had to do with Kathy's death? Maybe Tom could explain.

It turned out Betsy had a dinner party planned for the evening, but two guests had dropped out and she'd be more than happy to add Kris and L.T. Betsy actually sounded eager to have them come. Kris suspected it was partly because their presence would correct a disturbing imbalance in Betsy's table plan, but she'd been asking pesky questions about L.T. for a week. There weren't many secrets in a small town.

Then Kris corrected herself. It was true that small-town nosiness made your business everyone else's, but there were obviously a lot of things about Osborne that she didn't know.

Kris and Betsy had been to coffee a few times and out for drinks with Tom once, but she'd never been invited to the big house. Kris had to admit she was looking forward to it, not the least because of her own inherent nosiness.

She adjusted her black dress, which had crept halfway up her thighs.

"Don't do that," L.T. said. "I was just enjoying the view."

"Keep your eyes on the road, Buster."

It had taken some convincing to get L.T. to come along, and even more to get him into some respectable chinos and a button-down shirt. She'd actually been a bit surprised to find that he owned anything but T-shirts and jeans.

As the truck climbed up Dumont Hill, Kris was impressed again by the stateliness of it. These houses had been built in a time when money and craftsmanship had a happy partnership. Long before the kind of monstrosities favoured by people like Pat Osborne.

The houses were built of stone, brick, or clapboard, almost a primer on how housing styles had changed over the slow course of development of the town. As a child, Kris had often looked up at these houses, wondering what that world would be like.

The lawns were a startling green, despite the recent dry weather. On some, underground sprinklers hissed their jets of water into the air. Only a few brown leaves marred the perfection. She'd read in the *Republican–Patriot* that some kind of blight was causing the maples to drop early.

As they pulled into the circular drive in front of Betsy's house, they saw her on the front verandah. She waved, then Kris was sure she stole a quick glance at her watch.

Betsy and Tom Larson's house was at the very top of Dumont Hill, a white clapboard with three gables, a verandah on three sides, and crisp green trim. A literal-minded owner had named the house Three Gables sometime in the nineteenth century, and it had stuck. A discreet sign on the gatepost at the foot of Betsy's driveway reminded visitors of the name.

Dumont Hill itself wasn't that high, but stepping out of the car, Kris could see well out onto Lake Champlain. It certainly beat the view of downtown Ottawa offered by Colin's condo.

Betsy gave Kris a quick embrace. She wore quite a lot of a perfume that smelled like jasmine and a short, low-cut blue dress. Kris found it discouraging someone her own age could look so much younger. Betsy could pass for twenty-five, at a distance. Money must be good for the skin.

"So glad you could come, Kris."

"No problem. Betsy, this is my friend, L.T. Hill."

She extended her small white hand, and L.T. took it in his large, tanned one.

"Ma'am."

Kris hoped he wasn't going to do his Southern boy, super-polite, don't say a word, thing.

Betsy cocked her head to one side, and smiled. "So, L.T., I don't think I know too much about you."

"Just a friend of Kris's," he said. "I'm a police officer. Maybe you've seen me around town."

"Ah," Betsy said, as if trying to decide whether L.T.'s job status was a plus or a minus. "Well, come in."

Kris was sure she had told Betsy that L.T. was a cop, but that news was always a conversation stopper. It was as if people were afraid they might blurt out their secret crimes, although Kris doubted Betsy had ever done so much as roll through a stop sign.

The foyer was big enough for a square dance. A heavy oak staircase led up to halls both left and right. Kris could see the dining room, to her right, set for eight. A chandelier hung low over a walnut table. The wine-coloured walls emphasized the feeling of richness and age.

"Everyone's in the kitchen," Betsy said. "Come on back."

She led them down the centre hall and into a kitchen that felt as old as the house, but had been updated with the granite countertops and stainless steel appliances that everyone now found essential. French doors opened onto a perennial garden surrounded by a white picket fence. Kris had seen houses like this before, but only in magazines.

There were no signs of dinner preparation, but Kris could hear the clatter of pans behind a door to her right. Caterer in the summer kitchen, she guessed. Betsy didn't seem like the sort of woman who would actually cook.

Tom Larson and the four other guests stood in front of a big fieldstone fireplace, drinks in hand. Kris recognized the mayor and his wife, an attractive redhead who looked ten years younger than her husband, but a full-sized beer gut and a bald head could put years on a man. Liz Harper, as she had been back when Kris still lived in Osborne. Kris remembered her as a confident teenager. She had been a brunette then, but those things happened. Liz had worked at the camp the summer of Kathy's death, but had flatly refused to answer any of Kris's questions, practically slamming her front door on Kris's toes. Would her presence be awkward, or a bonus?

The other fellow was a stiff, white-haired man who actually wore a bow tie and had on his arm a wife of his own vintage. Kris had the feeling that it could turn out to be a terrifically long evening.

Tom Larson provided the only hope of relief. He would stand out in any room, but especially in this company. Tom had a physical presence that seemed to fade the rest of the people in the room into sepia. The first time she had met him, he reminded her of a younger Tom Selleck, and now the impression was reinforced by his Hawaiian shirt with palm trees on it. Tom had the same thick, dark hair and brushy moustache as Selleck, whom she'd had a crush on when he played the charming older man on *Friends*. When he stepped forward to clasp Kris's hand, it was as if they were the only two people there. He had those soulful brown eyes she always fell for.

It was stupid, she knew, allowing his looks to affect her judgment. It wasn't as if she was actually attracted to him, but she had always found herself flustered around really good-looking people. L.T. was the exception. She'd been relaxed with him from the first moment.

"Kris, so glad to see you again," he said. "Betsy keeps telling me all about you."

Kris immediately wondered what "all about her" would consist of, coming from Betsy. Her other question was, how had Betsy managed to land this guy?

She recovered her wits enough to say, "Tom, this is my friend, L.T. Hill."

"L.T. What does that stand for?" Tom asked, shaking L.T.'s hand.

L.T. wasn't going to like that, Kris thought. It had taken a week to convince him to tell her that his full name was Lester Tubman Hill. His parents hadn't left him many options.

"You wouldn't believe it if I told you. How you doing, Tom?"

Now that he was standing beside L.T., Kris could see that Tom was only of average height. Just a moment ago, he'd seemed much larger. She also had to remind herself that he had dated Kathy, but hadn't told her. And that he'd artfully deflected her requests for an interview on the topic of the summer her sister died. Was Tom just another deceptive charmer like Lowell Osborne?

"You probably don't know our other guests," Betsy said. "This is Fred Tremblay, our mayor, and his wife, Liz, and Dr. Will Hooper and Helen Hall–Hooper."

Now Kris remembered Dr. Hooper. She had been to see him a few times as a kid. He seemed startlingly older, but it was more than thirty years ago. Helen Hall–Hooper was an aging grande dame, in a pink twin set complete with pearls. Her hair was a brassy shade of blonde and her makeup looked as if it had been applied by an undertaker.

L.T. surprised her by saying, "Hi, Fred. I didn't know we were going to meet again so soon."

"That was a fine round of golf you played, L.T. What'd you shoot in the end?"

"Eighty-one. It's a bit high, but I haven't played in a while."

"Damn, I'm never going to shoot eighty-one in my life. Maybe you could give me some pointers out at the driving range."

"Sure," L.T. said

Kris quickly changed the topic to avoid L.T. getting committed to hours of tedium teaching this fat old fart to golf. "Dr. Hooper. So nice to see you again. I was once a patient of yours."

"Forty-five years as a doc, pretty much everyone has been," he said. He and his wife smiled in unison, she regally, he displaying teeth that were a reminder that doctors didn't have dental plans. From the blank look, it was clear that he didn't remember her at all.

"I think we should sit down," Betsy said "We're a little behind, but no problem, Kris."

Betsy ushered them into the dining room. Naturally, there were place cards telling them where to sit. Their names were written in an elegant, looping script, and clasped in tiny pewter hands. Kris was relieved to find that Tom was on her right hand, at the head of the table. Will Hooper was to her left. He smelled vaguely of age and antiseptic.

They seated themselves and Betsy said, "I'm so glad you could join us, Kris and L.T. I thought you should meet some of our best friends."

Kris wondered how these two couples, so much older, could possibly be Betsy's best friends. Betsy was a climber, though, and Fred Tremblay was the mayor and Will Hooper was a socially connected doctor from one of Osborne's oldest families. What about Tom Larson's old friend, Lowell Osborne, she wondered. Were the Osbornes the guests she and L.T. were replacing?

Two servers had appeared with bowls of a yellowish-orange soup. They were town teenagers in white smocks, trying to look professional. It was the sort of job Kris might have found herself doing at that age, if she'd stayed around Osborne.

She saw L.T. eye the soup uncertainly. She imagined his experience with dinner parties was rather limited. She'd have to be sure to reward him later.

"What a fascinating soup," Helen Hall–Hooper said. "What is it, dear?"

"Summer squash," Betsy said.

Kris tried hers and nodded encouragingly at L.T. It actually wasn't bad.

Betsy raised her wine glass. "Before we start, I'd like to make a toast. To Kris, an old friendship renewed. We've enjoyed your stay here, and hope you return soon."

Everyone raised their glasses, smiling. Then Kris said, "Betsy, I'm not leaving yet."

Betsy's look of surprise was mirrored by the other guests around the table. "Oh, I'm sorry," she said. "I understood that you were due back in Canada on Tuesday."

"I am, but I don't have quite everything I need for my story yet."

"Kris is writing about the tragic murder of her sister so many years ago. I'm sure you all remember that," Betsy said.

"How's it going?" she asked, nodding encouragingly. "I thought maybe you weren't going to get enough to tell the story."

"There's always a story," Kris said. "Part of the story here is how a small town seals over a wound like that, but it doesn't heal, it infects. I have to say, I'm surprised at how unwilling people have been to help me. Kathy was one of us. For all we know, the person who killed her is still in town."

Kris knew she had stepped beyond the bounds of good manners, but she was fed up with the smug little people in this town and their stonewalling. Screw tact. It was time these people heard the truth.

"Oh dear," Mrs. Hall–Hooper said. "I understood he was some kind of transient."

"That was a theory at the time, but nothing was proven. The investigation was abandoned pretty quickly," Kris said.

"Kris," Tom said gently, touching her forearm. "You have to understand that the people here, at this table, are all willing to help, but it was a long time ago. If the police couldn't solve it . . ."

Willing to help. That was rich coming from the guy who hadn't even told her what he knew, she thought. It wasn't the time to raise that, though. Even she had limits.

"I understand that," Kris said, "but there's a Lowell Osborne factor. Kathy worked at his family's camp that summer. Not to say that her death had anything to do with that, but as soon as the senator's name comes up, people clam up. Even people with direct knowledge of Kathy's life that summer."

The remark was meant for Tom, but Kris could practically feel the heat of Liz Tremblay's angry glare.

"Lowell's a popular guy here," the mayor said. "He's pretty much the key to our economy and people think he can become president. They see a situation where something might come out in the media that could hurt him — well, they protect their own. That's only natural."

L.T. cut in, before Kris could dig herself any deeper. "Absolutely, Fred. As a police officer, I see that kind of reaction all the time. Now tell me, how'd you get into politics?"

"Me? Hell, I'm just the guy who runs the hardware store. Someone had to be mayor, and they stuck me with it. Lowell Osborne's the only real politician in this town."

"Do we need two?" Betsy asked.

Everyone laughed at her little joke, relieved to find an easier topic. Kris decided that she'd made her point. "Tom, tell me about your new clinic," she said.

She smiled and nodded as Tom Larson told her about the generous endowment from Lowell Osborne that had led to the new clinic downtown. They could even do day surgeries there, and save people the drive up to Plattsburgh.

"Lowell and I go way back. When he offered to build a surgical clinic, and have me run it, I felt it was something I wanted to try. Sometimes you have to give back, and I have great memories of Osborne. Betsy was keen to come home, of course."

Tom went on about his plans to attract three more doctors. Will Hooper was helping out for now, but he'd be taking retirement soon.

Tom seemed excited about it all, but he had left Boston to come here. It didn't make sense, unless Lowell Osborne had offered him an obscene amount of money. Everything seemed to lead back to Lowell Osborne, Kris thought. Maybe Sharon Sloan had it right. There didn't seem to be a person in this town who didn't either work for him or owe him a favour.

She caught L.T.'s eye. Helen Hall–Hooper was bending his ear about something. At least they had served the roast beef by now.

L.T. held her gaze and said, "Kris, Mrs. Hall–Hooper was just telling me about something you might find interesting."

Kris couldn't imagine how that could be true. Perhaps L.T. just needed rescuing.

"Yes, dear. The ladies auxiliary at St. Matthews is having a fundraising tour tomorrow. Three of the great camps have agreed to open up to visitors, including Cooper Lodge, of course. Tickets are still available."

"Oh yes. The great camps are very interesting. My grandfather used to be a guide, you know," Kris said.

Cooper Lodge was the Osbornes' camp. Kris hadn't been able to find any legitimate reason to get past the security and onto the grounds. The tour was an ideal chance to look around. At the least, she could get pictures for her story. She was thinking a two-page spread, but it would be a problem without art.

The mention of camps and guides set Will Hooper off on an interminable ramble about fly fishing on the local lakes. At least L.T. seemed to enjoy it.

By the time they had finished dessert, Kris was dying for a smoke. Liz Tremblay too, apparently. She reached into her purse and pulled out a pack of Virginia Slims and a lighter.

"You will all have to excuse me for a moment," she said. "Habit calls."

"I'll join you," Kris said. Liz didn't look overly pleased, but there was no polite way to refuse.

Together on the front verandah, they looked out on the lake as twilight began to turn everything in the distance to shades of mauve. The hardware store must be doing well, Kris thought. Liz Tremblay had heavy gold bracelets on each arm and an expensive-looking red suit that was perhaps inadvisable with her current hair colour. There had to be some payback for marrying Fred Tremblay. Kris couldn't imagine getting in bed with a man like that.

"I didn't think I'd see you again," Kris said.

"It certainly wasn't my idea."

"I was talking to someone the other day who mentioned you."

"And who would that be?"

Liz took a strong draw on her cigarette, as if to speed up the burning time and escape Kris's little inquisition.

"Sharon Sloan."

"Ah yes, the Lake Champlain Princess. I came second. I'm afraid that Sharon peaked rather too soon."

"It seems so. You've done an awful lot better."

"Well," she shrugged, as if the outcome would always have been obvious.

"Sharon was telling me about life up at the Osborne camp the summer you two worked there."

It was a bit of an exaggeration, but in an interview, it always paid to imply you knew more than you really did.

"Was she now?"

"I know we got off on the wrong foot, but I could really use your help," Kris said.

"Yes, you asked for it so graciously." The acid in the answer could have burned the paint off Betsy's porch.

A polite person would have taken that as a hint to shut up, but a pushy newspaper columnist just kept asking questions until the subject walked way.

"You can probably understand how I feel. My family's been through a lot. Actually, Sharon said my sister's death had something to do with my mother. Does that make sense to you?"

Liz flipped the remains of her cigarette into Betsy's carefully manicured flower bed. "A word of advice, Kris. You're not going to find out anything about your sister, and you're just pissing people off. We're not all as nice as Betsy."

Liz stepped closer to Kris. Even in the fading light, she could see the intensity in her eyes. "Some things are best just left as a mystery, Kris. That way no more harm is done. Understand?"

Liz turned and went back into the house, but her rebuke was still ringing in Kris's ears when Tom stepped out onto the verandah.

"I thought maybe I needed to rescue you. Liz isn't exactly an admirer."

"So she was saying."

"Your comments at the dinner table were pretty pointed."

"Actually, they were mostly directed at you."

He didn't seem surprised by her statement.

"I realize that. You have to appreciate I'm in a difficult position."

"Yes, what with Lowell Osborne owning your ass and all."

Tom's response was quick and sounded at the edge of anger. "He doesn't. I made my own decision to return here, but Lowell is a friend. Loyalty means something to me."

"Me, too. That's why I'm here. What would you do in my place?"

Tom shrugged. "It's difficult to imagine being in your position, but I'd like to think I'd do the same thing. Why now, though?"

Kris could see Tom was on an information-gathering mission himself. She matched his shrug with her own. "It was time. Way past time." She paused, then said, "Tell me about the connection between my mother and my sister's death."

"Your mother?"

His surprise seemed genuine, but was it because she knew of the link or because the link was news to him? "She's involved in this," Kris said. "What's your understanding of how?"

"Well, you'd know far more about that than me. I was simply a friend hanging out up at the camp that summer. There were rumours, of course."

"Yes," Kris said, as if she knew all about them. She had been ten years old, and all she had known was that her sister and her father were gone. She didn't understand why then, and she didn't really now, either.

"What did you make of the rumours?" she asked.

"I suppose they were believable, but I don't see how they connect to your sister's death."

"No," Kris said, still fishing, "but why did you find the rumours believable?"

"Well, I didn't really know your mother except to see her occasionally, but she was certainly a beautiful woman. And Lowell's father, let's just say he and his son were much alike."

Her mother. Lowell's father. Kris suddenly felt weak at the knees. Now she could see why Kathy got the job at the camp so young and she had a pretty good idea who the person with the video camera was, the one three boys deferred to.

"Kris, are you all right?" Tom asked.

No, she thought. I'm all wrong, and I've been all wrong since the day I returned to Osborne.

9

Low clouds hung like a kind of high mist, obscuring the view of Cooper Lake. The rain was holding off, but what had fallen overnight had brought out the damp smell of forest. Heavy stands of spruce trees hemmed in the camp, giving it a claustrophobic feel in the weak light. Kris shivered inside L.T.'s too-big camouflage rain jacket.

Lowell Osborne's main lodge loomed a couple of hundred feet to her right. It was a two-storey log structure that looked like the small sleeping cabins to her left, but on a much grander scale. There were upper and lower verandahs and a cobblestone chimney that rose into the mist and disappeared. Even from that distance, Kris could see that the building rested on a massive foundation of quarried stone.

This was the place where her sister had died. She was sure of it.

The brochure said the lodge was on the tour, but Kris would just have to wait for her moment to investigate. In the meantime, she continued to play tourist, hanging at the back of about twenty-five gawkers who had laid down twenty dollars to see the great camps. They had to be especially nosy to come out in this weather, at ten o'clock on a Sunday morning, with the camp a twisty forty-minute drive up into the High Peaks.

She liked the size of the group. It was big enough that she wouldn't be immediately noticed as missing when she found the opportunity to get a little bit lost and look around on her own. With a baseball cap pulled low over her eyes and the hood of the raincoat up, Kris hoped no one would recognize her. Her face had become all too well known to the Osborne retinue.

Kris hated perky women, especially perky young women, and their guide, Tessa, couldn't have been much perkier. Blonde hair, 200-tooth smile, body of a bikini model. She had proudly informed everyone that she had worked at Senator Lowell Osborne's camp this summer and in a few days she'd be heading back to Brown.

Bully for her, Kris thought. She was sure that the senator would have handpicked this one. She pronounced his name with a kind of breathy excitement, as if he were a movie star.

"To your left, you will see the boardwalk leading to the five sleeping cabins. As this is still a private camp, only the cabin used by the fishing guides will be open today."

Things were certainly more genteel at the Osborne camp than they had been back when her sister had been raped. Now the sex was provided by college girl groupies who probably thought they were on some kind of internship.

Kris had hoped that visiting the camp would give her some sense of Kathy. This was where she had spent most of her last summer, maybe even the last day of her life. Kris understood why Kathy was so reluctant to come home that summer, beyond her youthful wildness. Her mother was already showing the signs of the alcoholic irrationality that would overcome her after Kathy's death. Her father was the one who kept things on track, but his status as a supervisor at the factory meant he worked lots of extra, unpaid hours. The Redner house in 1981 was not a good place to be.

And what about the affair with Osborne? Surely Kathy must have known about it, working at the camp. Knowing what her mother was doing, how she was betraying their father, must have fuelled the fights between Kathy and Candy Redner. Kris tried to imagine the camp as it had been for Kathy back then, but she couldn't see it. All she had was a cold, empty feeling.

The real emotion she felt was toward her mother, and it was a burning anger. Where had old man Osborne fucked her? In one of the cabins ahead? On his boat? In the big lodge?

Kris remembered afternoons when her mother came home flushed and unnaturally excited, eager to arrive before her husband got back from work. As a child, she had just put it down to drinking, but now it made a kind of twisted sense, her mother and Lowell Osborne's father. Candy Redner always had grand dreams of what her life could become. Certainly something much more than being the wife of a factory foreman and mother of two girls. In a way, Kris supposed her mother was something like Sharon

Sloan, a small-town girl who saw an Osborne as the way out. All they had to do was spread their legs and make a wish.

But what was the connection between her mother's affair with Osborne senior and Kathy's death?

"We're going to head up to the guide's cabin," Tessa said. "Everyone watch your step. You might want to use the handrail.

"For generations, the Adirondack guides made a living from rich city sportsmen who came to the wilderness to hunt and fish," Tessa said. The girl's voice was as grating as a dentist's drill. Kris was dying for a cigarette, but she imagined sweet little Tessa would slap it out of her hand. Even with the damp weather, the great camps were tinderboxes, and a few of them had gone up over the years.

Only about half the group would fit in the little cabin at once. Kris clustered outside with the rest. She had seen cabins like this many times over the years, and they were always about the same. Bare wooden walls, green shingle roof, everything stained brown, a woodstove. Most had that bloody twig furniture, too. Living rustic seemed to endlessly fascinate the rich, as if being poor were an interesting lifestyle change, but only for the weekend. Kris had grown up with it, and didn't find it quite so amusing.

The first group filed out of the cabin and Kris jostled in with the rest. She found herself squeezed up against a large woman with too much hairspray.

"You will see that some of the old-time guides carved their initials into the door," Tessa said, pointing, as if they couldn't identify the door on their own.

There were half a dozen initials there, but the ones that caught Kris's eye were C.R. Charlie Redner, her grandfather. It had to be. She knew he'd guided at most of the great camps, including this one. The initials were grey and weathered, much the same way she remembered Grandpa Charlie. He had a big, droopy moustache and a face that was lined and seamed like an old catcher's mitt. As a girl, fairy tales had told her that being deep in the dark forest was the scariest place to be. He'd shown her how to master it, so that she felt safer in the woods than she ever did on the roughest streets of Toronto. The forest was generally free of people, still the most frightening animal out there.

Tessa was nattering on about the important role the old-time guides played. Sure, Kris thought, until fish finders and power-boats and ATVs. By the time she knew her grandfather, guiding was almost extinct. He survived on odd jobs and the occasional generous client from the old days.

"All right, watch your step again," Tessa said. "We're heading back down toward the lake. The senator has generously offered to let us take a look in the boathouse, where we can see his collection of antique speedboats.

"The great camps were started by a man called W.W. Durant, over at Raquette Lake," Tessa said. "Most of the folks that owned them came up from New York City. What was different about this camp was that it was built by a local man, the first Lowell Osborne, in 1905. He was the senator's great-grandfather. Now the senator, he's the fourth Lowell Osborne."

That was at least two too many, Kris thought. It seemed as if there had always been a man called Lowell Osborne running the town. Like English kings, or popes, they couldn't even come up with a different name.

The boathouse was as wide as a four-car garage. Its brown clapboard walls slumped a bit to the left, supported by cedar pilings that had shifted over the years. Around it, the water was still, without a breath of breeze.

"In the old days of the camps, there were very few roads, so the only way to visit your neighbours was by boat," Tessa said. "These old mahogany or cedar boats didn't go very fast, but they sure had style. The senator has four of them, and he takes them out on special occasions, like the Fourth of July."

She gave the tourists her big smile. Kris would bet the senator had given little Tessa a ride in one of his wonderful antique speedboats. She noticed that the seats were wide and quite comfortably upholstered.

Kris wondered if Tessa was this year's version of Kathy. How many had there been over the years? Rich men liked amusing toys, whether they were pretty girls or fine boats. At least they kept the boats. The girls got traded in every year.

Kris knew something of what that summer of 1981 had been like, from Sharon Sloan's perspective. What about Liz Harper — or

Tremblay — now? Had Liz also had her turn in that cellar, spread on the table and videotaped? Kris knew all too well the stupid things women would agree to do when they were young and in lust.

Kris's fellow tourists crowded into the boathouse to stare at the boats. There was plenty of room for them. The place was like a small barn. A heavy yellow rope ran across the front of their moorings, to prevent the spectators from actually touching the senator's prized possessions.

Liz's warning had kept rolling over in Kris's mind. Some things are best left as a mystery, so no more harm is done, she had said. Kris supposed Liz must mean harm to Lowell Osborne. Like so many others in the town, Liz seemed to feel a kind of protectiveness toward Osborne. It went beyond his money, his power, and his undoubted charismatic appeal. He was the one person from Osborne who was going to make it in the big world, to give their little town meaning. There was something in that for everyone. Even old girlfriends would eventually get their fifteen minutes of fame in *People* magazine, or at least in the grocery store tabs.

"All right," Tessa said. "Now we are going to have a look at a very special place. It's a gazebo on a little rock island about one hundred feet offshore.

"Don't worry, you don't have to swim."

There were a few twitters of amusement at her joke.

"There is a boardwalk that connects the gazebo to the shore. It's where the senator goes to think. He's drafted some of his most important bills there," Tessa said.

Kris hung back as the others traipsed out the boardwalk to the gazebo. She could do without seeing where the senator drafted his bills. It must be nice, though, to have your own little retreat out in the middle of a lake. She did most of her thinking in a newsroom while more than a hundred other people talked on the phone, chatted, and hammered on their keyboards.

Her fellow tourists were almost invisible, one hundred feet out in the lake. Tessa's voice carried clearly as she touched on the highlights of the senator's legislative career and the great thoughts he had thought while sitting in the gazebo. Kris was pretty sure she knew who would have told Tessa *that* exciting story.

There might just be time for a cigarette. She pulled the pack from under her coat and quickly lit one. Two quick drags and she could already start to feel her brain return to normal.

Kris pulled her little Canon point-and-shoot from the pocket of the camouflage jacket and got a few quick shots of the lodge. The quality wasn't great but the pictures had a dark, ominous feel to them. She knew Colin would be crying for art before she even wrote word one of her story, already laying out the pages in his mind. She hadn't decided yet how she would handle the bit about her mother, if it proved to be true. It was embarrassing and deeply personal. Maybe the readers didn't have to know every detail.

She'd even had a difficult time telling L.T. what she'd learned. When they'd talked about it last night, in bed, she was afraid he'd think her whole family was trash, that they'd brought their tragedies on themselves. She half-believed that herself, but she knew it was victim-think. What Kris really feared was that she and her mother weren't so different. Candy Redner had just made the mistake of marrying and having children before her real personality took over.

L.T. had been understanding, but she knew he had been shocked. He immediately asked whether her mother's affair with old man Osborne had anything to do with Kathy's death. It was a question she couldn't answer.

The curiosity seekers were already coming back. Kris flipped her cigarette into the lake and found that littering the senator's property was curiously satisfying.

Seeing Kris by herself, Tessa affected a look of concern.

"You missed the gazebo," she said, the disappointment evident in her voice. "Are you all right?"

"Bit of a headache. Thanks for asking."

"Well, the Great Lodge is our final stop," Tessa said. "This way, everyone."

The Great Lodge, Kris thought. The Osbornes couldn't just settle for calling it the lodge.

The wooden steps up to the lodge were steep and slippery, fitted into the rock where niches and ledges offered an opportunity. As Tessa ushered the visitors in, Kris was impressed in spite of herself. The lodge was open the full two storeys, straight to the ceiling, where cedar rafters and wooden roof planks were visible. Half of the building was one large room, dominated by a cobblestone fireplace big enough to walk into. The red and blue plaid furniture looked as if it were actually used. It was too big to call cozy. She supposed "grand" might be an appropriate adjective.

"This is the Great Hall," Tessa said. "All the guests from the cabins gather here before moving to the dining room, which is to your left."

The Great Lodge. The Great Hall. Cooper Lake. Cooper Lodge. Osborne the town. Osborne the family. What a linear, literal-minded bunch, Kris thought.

"In the far corner, you will see a black bear, killed by the senator himself right here on this property," Tessa said.

Kris nearly laughed out loud. At least the senator didn't tell her he killed it with his bare hands. She'd bet money the snarling stuffed bear carcass had come from one of the Adirondack curiosity shops that dotted the state park like blemishes on a teenager.

"We are going to move to the dining room now, where the senator has provided cookies and coffee for his guests."

Probably baked the cookies himself, Kris thought, and they would be the biggest and best anyone had ever seen. She was dying for a coffee, but she saw her moment to check out the cellar. But where was the way down? If it was in the kitchen, she'd never get to it.

She quickly scanned the wood-panelled walls and saw a door subtly inset in the far corner of the Great Hall. Did it lead down?

L.T. pulled his Blazer into the far end of the town hall parking lot, under a big oak. There was no way to make a red SUV inconspicuous, but there was no use advertising his presence, either.

He knew that what he was about to do could get him fired, but he had told Kris he'd help. There wasn't much he wouldn't do for Kris, including going to that boring party last night. What a bunch of stiffs. At least she'd made it up to him afterwards.

Taylor and Hancock's private vehicles were both parked, and two patrol cars were gone. Good. There was only two-man coverage on Sundays, and there wasn't much chance of seeing the chief, who'd be busy with his pork barbecue. The police office was a white prefab addition that stuck out the back of the historic clapboard municipal offices like an afterthought. It looked closed up, mini-blinds drawn.

L.T. crossed the parking lot with a deliberately slow walk, as if he were in no particular hurry. It was always hard to say who could be watching. At least the murky, wet weather would keep people indoors.

The chief had been so helpful in pointing out that the Redner murder file was on his desk, that it seemed a shame not to follow up and take a look. Maybe there was nothing in it, but the $50,000 offer from Jack Naylor had convinced him that someone had something to hide. That file was a good place to start looking.

He'd stashed the money inside the oven of the woodstove back at Jasper's. It was evidence, if it came to that. He'd just have to remember not to light a fire.

He unlocked the office and stepped inside. There were eight metal desks in four groups of two. Each had a computer, but they were mostly used to generate the paper forms that filled stacks of banker's boxes piled high around the edge of the room. There were a few small, human touches. Most of the desks had pictures of family. Taylor's had a plant, a big spindly thing that stretched vainly toward the dirty windows. L.T.'s own desktop was clean. Across the back were the chief's office and another slightly smaller one beside it, for the deputy. There was no deputy, though, so it was used as a lunchroom.

L.T. walked quietly across the office and tried the chief's door. Locked. He took a credit card and fiddled with the lock until it snicked back. He'd seen the chief do the same thing himself when he forgot his keys. There didn't seem to be much need for good locks inside a police station.

Larry Brewster's office was more like a den than a workplace. The walls were covered with pictures of the chief with the mayor and various state politicians. There was a big one of him and the senator. There were also shots of him and his hunting buddies with a deer, and him and his fishing buddies with a string of trout. A largemouth bass was mounted on the wall. A good one, L.T. thought, more than five pounds. He was supposed to be fishing himself, today, but it was a miserable morning for it. That was his cover, though: Just stopped to get some paperwork on his way out to the trout stream.

L.T. tried the chief's desk drawers, but they were locked. Getting them open was going to be a tougher challenge than getting into the office itself. He'd have to hope that the chief still had the file on top of his desk. There was a litter there of newspapers, old McDonald's boxes, and file folders. He sifted through it. Much of the material was related to a jewellery store robbery that was coming to trial soon. Two cokeheads from Plattsburgh had walked into Jefferson's on Main with guns and walked out right into the arms of the chief, who had been having a burger next door. L.T. still remembered the *Republican-Patriot* going on about the "heroic apprehension of armed robbers." Over a couple of drinks later, the chief had shared the fact that he'd nearly shit himself when he saw the guns. The cokeheads, new to crime, dropped their guns and surrendered as soon as they saw him, assuming that they were surrounded by cops.

At the bottom of all that was a wad of documents more than half an inch thick, held together with an elastic band. The word Redner was scrawled in capital letters across the top. L.T. smiled. This was going to be easier than he'd thought. He couldn't take away the material, but he would give it a quick read.

He'd just removed the elastic when he heard footsteps coming up the stairs to the station. A voice he recognized as Taylor's said, "Is that Krispy Kremes I see?"

"Uh-huh. Don't worry, Chuck. I got extra for you."

L.T.'s mind raced, but his body was frozen. How would he explain being in the chief's office? There was no way. Quickly, quietly, he stepped to the office door and clicked it shut.

"You got your keys?" Hancock asked. "My hands are full."

The main door opened with a screech. It needed oil, but it wasn't clear whose job that would be, so it never got done.

L.T. crouched behind the chief's desk. It was a reflex that he knew was pointless. Taylor and Hancock weren't going to come into the chief's office. The question was, how was he going to get out?

"Save anything with chocolate for me," Taylor said. "I'm going to take a crap."

"All right, but wash your hands, for Christ's sake."

L.T. heard the sound of Hancock's computer booting up, then the clicking of keys. He tried to stay calm and silent, to breathe evenly. He was starting to cramp up already, but he didn't want to move for fear of knocking something over and alerting the two on the other side of the door.

The toilet flushed, then the washroom door slammed.

"Why'd you get a dozen?" Taylor asked. "We can't eat that many."

"Some of them are for my kids. Here, have one. They're fresh."

Hancock's words were garbled, his mouth already full.

"Fucking paperwork. I hate it," Taylor said. "Sometimes that's all this job is. Good day for it, though. We could drive around out there looking at bugger all the whole day."

"I know what you mean," Hancock said, "but the chief said he wanted a visible presence. It's Labour Day weekend, after all. Tourists."

"Fuck me. Tourists. What would a tourist be doing in Osborne?"

"Lost, maybe."

They both laughed.

"Our presence is visible," Taylor said. "You just have to look in the parking lot. I see L.T.'s truck is out there, by the way. What's up with that?"

"Who knows. I don't see him here. It'd be just like that guy to come in on his day off, though. A real eager beaver. Man, that's the last thing we need."

And screw you, too, L.T. thought. Lazy hacks like Taylor and Hancock were what gave small-town police forces a bad name. If he knew those guys, they would settle in for the rest of the day, barring the unlikely eventuality of an actual call for service. They'd probably put the Yankees game on later. He supposed he could try to wait them out, but it was a dodgy play. The night duty officer would be in at the end of their shift.

He turned to the Redner file. At least he could accomplish something while he waited for an escape plan to come to him. The first thing he saw was the pictures.

They showed a slight, dark haired girl, obviously young. She was face down on the forest floor, her neck twisted at an unusual angle. Welts were still visible across her buttocks. There were several more shots from different angles. Then a morgue shot. L.T. thought he was looking at a younger, thinner Kris. He shivered at the idea.

Murder was just another crime until you saw the body. Then it wasn't so academic. He'd been involved in only one homicide case in his five years. It was on his first job, back home in Wilmington. Seventeen-year-old kid had shot his mom while she was sleeping. The bedroom had been a nightmare of blood and stink. It had taken weeks to get that smell off his skin.

He flipped through the coroner's report. Death by strangulation. There was no mention of the welts, nothing about the rapes L.T. knew she had endured. What was with that? The report was signed by Will Hooper, the doctor he had met at the Larsons' house.

Officer Barry Fish had questioned four men in connection with Kathy Redner's death. Bud Naylor, Tom Larson, Lowell Osborne, and Bobby Edwards. There was no mention of whether Osborne senior had been at the camp that day. Edwards, the handyman, had been immediately ruled out. He had been drinking with friends at a bar downtown at the time Fish suspected that Kathy Redner had been killed. Solid alibi. Half a dozen witnesses.

The three boys, who had all been in their late teens, had been at the camp that day, for a barbecue. According to their witness statements, they'd taken two girls and a two-four of beer up to one of the guest cabins for a little party. The girls, Sharon Sloan and Liz Harper, backed up their story. They'd been there all afternoon and well into the evening of August 14, the day of Kathy's death.

Odd party, L.T. thought. Two girls and three guys. Maybe they liked to share. He remembered the videotape.

Fish had questioned the few homeowners in that part of Westport Road, to ask if they'd seen her hitchhiking, or any cars pulled off the road. Nothing.

There was one final detail. The body had been discovered by Officer Larry Brewster, responding to an anonymous tip. An anonymous tip about a body in the woods? That didn't wash with L.T.

There was a loud scraping as either Hancock or Taylor pushed back his chair.

"You got that jewellery store shit?" Hancock asked. "I'm going to be called to testify about questioning those two losers. Need to refresh my memory."

"No, I don't have it. Chief's got it, I think."

L.T. held his breath as he heard the door handle of the chief's office grind.

"Locked," Hancock said.

"I think Larry still keeps a spare key under the coffee maker. He can never remember to bring his own."

Spare key? L.T. hadn't known about that. He heard the door of the lunchroom open.

"Yep, it's under here. What a dumb-ass place to put a key."

L.T. knew he had maybe ten seconds. He put the elastic back around the paperwork and stuck it under the mess on the desk. The chief would never remember the exact order of the disorder.

The window. It was the only option. He unlocked it, but it screeched and jammed part way up. It would be a tight fit, but he had no choice but to try to squeeze through it. He went feet first, the sill scraping him as he pushed through, then landed awkwardly on the wet grass. No time to close the window.

He crouched tight against the building as he heard Hancock say, "Dumb fuck didn't close his window. At least the rain didn't get in."

The window closed with a slam.

L.T. felt totally focused. It was the same feeling he'd had when he burst free of coverage, and only the end zone lay in front of him. He still needed one more move. If he got in his truck and drove off now, it would look pretty strange.

Twenty feet to his left and down three steps was the dispatch office for police, fire, and the town's one ambulance. He didn't know which girl would be working today, but they were all about the same. Brushing himself off, he headed toward the office. A little flirting time would certainly explain his presence at the station. He could stop back in the police office later, tell the boys about it. Well past the flirting stage themselves, they still loved to talk about what they'd like to do to those young dispatch honeys.

Kris closed the door quietly behind her and took a penlight from the pocket of her coat. It was supposed to have some kind of krypton beam, but its light was quickly swallowed by the gloom below. There was a strong smell of mildew, dust, and rodents.

There was no railing on the open staircase, and she took the steps slowly. Every one she stepped on responded with a creak that sounded impossibly loud to her. Rationally, she knew the sound couldn't be heard over the clamour of voices upstairs, but she still stepped as lightly as she could.

At the bottom, she shone her light around the windowless room. Immediately to the right of the stairs, there was a concrete block wall that divided the space in two, much newer than anything else down there. Beams as big around as her body were laid on it, and she supposed the wall must have been added to keep the old structure from sagging. Her flashlight beam just barely reached the far wall, but the cut limestone definitely looked like what she had seen in that horrible video.

The room seemed to be a place to collect things that had become irrelevant long ago. There were snowshoes, a rack of bamboo fishing rods of the type her grandfather used, antique dressers crusted in dust, and even an old green cedar-strip canoe, its canvas bottom torn open.

Kris willed herself to explore the room. She hated basements. They were the locale for all of her childhood nightmares. Small wonder. When her mother was drinking, it didn't take much to push her into a fury. She would scream at Kris, telling her how bad she was, then lock her downstairs and spend the afternoon with her bottle. School was Kris's only escape.

Their own basement had been a creepy place, full of spiderwebs and dirt; it was dark and damp. This one wasn't any better. She'd forced herself to forget how many afternoons she'd spent alone, crying in the dark. Now it all came rushing back. She was filled with dread, and the thought that this might have been the room where Kathy was raped and murdered intensified the feeling.

She took a deep breath. That was a long time ago. She was an adult now. She needed to stay focused.

She had to determine if this room was the one where Kathy died. Kris took the little digital camera from her coat pocket and took a series of quick pictures of all that she could see. The images looked even more eerie in the camera's viewfinder.

The flash momentarily blinded her. She couldn't see her watch. How long had she been downstairs? The real difficulty would come in getting back upstairs without being noticed. If questioned, she had already decided to say she had been looking for the washroom.

She worked her way down the wall that divided the big room. What was on the other side? Probably more of the same kind of junk, she imagined. Perhaps this wasn't really where Kathy had been killed at all. That room had seemed neat, almost tidy. There had been nothing in it but the scarred table that the three men had tied her to. The clutter she saw around her had probably been here for many decades.

She worked her flashlight beam down the stone wall. She would only be here once. She should definitely check to see what was on the other side.

She saw a door, deeply inset into the stone, and worked her way toward it, careful not to trip on a pile of old ski poles. It was locked with a stout steel hasp and a padlock that was much newer than anything else she had seen in the basement. Whatever was on the other side of that door, someone had gone to some trouble to keep it private.

The floorboards creaked above Kris's head as the tourist group re-entered the main hall. She had taken too long.

She could hear Tessa say, "We have a special surprise for you. Your host, Senator Lowell Osborne, would like to greet you and answer any questions you might have about the camp."

Shit, Kris thought. She was trapped.

10

When L.T. pulled the Blazer into the driveway at Jasper's, he was surprised not to see Kris's car in front of her cabin. It was after one. How long could a house tour take? He'd never been on one, and never intended to. Paying good money to wander through some rich guy's place, make you feel bad that you didn't have what he did, what was the point?

Kris had been determined to go, though. He'd tried to talk her out of it, sorry that he'd even brought it to her attention in the first place. Snooping around the camp couldn't be a good idea. She had already set off alarm bells with Osborne. The house tour gave her a good chance to get on the property, but what she really needed to do was see if she could find that cellar where the video had been shot. If it wasn't at the camp, maybe their whole theory was off base.

L.T.'s cabin was cold and damp, an early taste of fall. With any luck, he'd be out of Osborne before the first snow. One winter in the Adirondacks had been enough. It had been a novelty at first, but then it was nothing but cold and bad driving.

He wanted to light the woodstove, but first he had to remove the money from the oven. What were you supposed to do with $25,000 you couldn't really explain? It wasn't that bulky, but it didn't seem like something you could just leave lying around. Jasper had a key to all the cabins himself, and some of his clientele were definitely the wrong sort of people. He could hardly put it in the bank, though. That would create a trail and leave questions he couldn't answer.

L.T. decided maybe he should bury it, once the rain stopped. For now, he put it on the kitchen table, then got a small fire going with some cedar kindling and a copy of the *Republican–Patriot*. At first, a bit of smoke leaked out of the top of the stove and into the cabin; then the fire caught, sucking air in with such vigour that it rattled the cast-iron door.

His quick manoeuvre out the window had been successful. Taylor and Hancock hadn't even questioned it when he walked in the door, spent a few minutes on paperwork, and told them about the little honey he'd been talking up down in dispatch. Annette. "Nice rack," Taylor had said, as if she were a deer.

There were a number of things he had found disturbing in his quick examination of the Redner murder file. Fish had done the basics, but it didn't look like anyone had really busted his ass. It was a homicide. How many of those did they ever get in Osborne?

The crime scene photos had clearly shown the results of the whipping he had seen on the video, but the post-mortem made no mention of it. That couldn't be right. If Kathy really had been picked up by a stranger on the highway, what were the chances that he'd have engaged in a little S and M before raping and killing her? Pretty unlikely. A crime like that involved a high risk of getting caught in the act. The killer would have been in a hurry. All that should have been obvious to Fish.

There was nothing about the beating in the rest of the report either, like no one was even looking at that. And Larry Brewster finding the body after a tip. The chief said he had the file out to refresh his memory. You didn't forget finding the body of a dead girl. Maybe that explained how he got the top job.

Lowell Osborne, Tom Larson, and Bud Naylor had all admitted being at the camp that day. L.T. had the advantage of knowing about the video, Fish did not, but having them all alibi each other was a little too easy. Three guys, two girls. That left an odd man out, where L.T. came from. And what did the girls really know?

There was no saying for sure that Osborne, Larson, and Naylor were the three men in the videotape, but it was a reasonable conjecture. The date information on the tape told them it had been made on the day Kathy died and they had all been at the camp that day.

That still left open the question of who the fourth man was — the guy behind the camera.

If the police had had the videotape at the time of the original investigation, it would have come out a lot differently. Now, it was of little, if any, legal value. Any half-decent defence lawyer would attack it as a fake, and no one knew where it had come from or where it had been the past thirty years. Without an eye-witness to go along with the tape, it wouldn't lead to charges.

It was still a time bomb, though, L.T. thought. If that tape showed up on the Internet, Osborne would be finished. In politics, truth didn't matter as much as perception. Maybe that's why they were reacting so strongly to Kris's digging. Did they suspect she had the tape? He hoped not, because they would want it back, and that would be dangerous. The only good thing was that he'd probably be the first person they'd ask to retrieve it.

He pushed aside the faded green curtain on the front window and looked out at the rain pouring off the porch roof. Visibility was lousy, the roads slick. He hoped Kris hadn't had a problem with that little toy car of hers. He was tempted to set off toward the Osborne camp, see if she needed help.

He picked up his car keys, then put them back down on the table. Kris wasn't the kind of woman who liked to have a man come running to her rescue. Not that she'd likely need rescuing. She wasn't at all like the honey-sweet southern blondes he'd made a specialty of in college.

He heard a crunching on the gravel in front of the cabins and looked out. It was the little Toyota.

Kris quickly opened the car door and made a dash for L.T.'s cabin, hat pulled down over her eyes. He held the door open as she practically came sliding in, spraying water over the worn pine floor. She removed the hat, ran her fingers through her short hair, and then gave him a long and wordless hug, snuggling against his red and black plaid shirt. It was the first time she had felt secure all day. Driving back from Osborne's camp, she had kept checking the rear-view, to see if someone was following her.

"You okay?" he asked.

"Yes, and I found the cellar. Or I think I did, anyway. One side was locked, but it has to be the same room. The big cut stones in the foundation look just like the videotape."

"Yeah, but they can be found in a lot of places around here."

"No, it was the spot. I know it."

It would sound stupid to say that she could feel Kathy's presence in that cellar. It was the sort of thing that made her eyes roll when some other reporter had it in his copy. But she'd felt something, all the same, when she was waiting for her chance to get back to the main floor.

"How'd you get into the cellar, anyway?" L.T. asked. "Surely that wasn't on the tour."

"Not exactly, but I'm resourceful," she smiled. "I just waited until the crowd of busybodies was headed in a different direction, then I slipped downstairs."

"So it was easy?"

"Getting down was easy. Then they all came back to this big room in the main lodge, and I was trapped downstairs."

"So how did you finally get out?"

"I caught a break. Someone asked about the second-floor gallery. The senator told them it was a sleeping verandah and invited them all up to take a look. By that time, I was on the other side of the door and I just slipped out."

"Did he recognize you?"

"I don't think so. I was wearing a ball cap and I put on sunglasses."

"Sunglasses? It's a rainy day."

"What was I supposed to do, wear a ski mask?"

L.T. laughed.

"I felt like a burglar myself today."

"You got the police file?"

"I got a look at it. I couldn't take it away. I was just about to take a peek when Hancock and Taylor showed up. I locked myself in the chief's office long enough to scan it, but I had to make a quick exit out the window."

"Oh God, L.T."

He was putting himself in danger for her, and she was so afraid of something happening to him. Her sister's death had already set off a chain reaction that had destroyed her whole family. Now she was starting it all up again.

She held him again, feeling his warmth and strength.

"Don't you think you should get out of those wet things?" he asked.

It was the best idea she had heard all day.

11

Kris pushed through the undergrowth, trying not to let branches slap back at L.T. The leaves were damp from morning dew, her shirt wet to the elbows. It was still cool, but the day had come in clean and fresh, yesterday's storm gone down to plague the people on the eastern seaboard.

The pool was a good hour's hike off the main trail, the path just a suggestion of an opening through the pines. She was navigating it from memory, but it was a memory long distant. The last time she'd walked this path, she had been following behind her grandfather, who knew this part of the state forest as well as a city man would know the rooms of his house.

He'd taught her to identify landmarks, and she still remembered some of them: a sharp outcropping of rock shaped like an anvil; a stand of birch like a white island in the sea of evergreens. Now she could see the last of them just ahead, a deep fissure in the rock that ran parallel to Goodkind's Creek.

She had just begun to hear the waterfall. That meant they were within a few hundred yards of the stream. It was only a ten-foot drop, but the rushing sound carried, competing only against the sigh of the wind and a few bird calls.

"There had better be some fish in here. I know a lot of places closer," L.T. said.

"There's no rush," she said. It was Labour Day, nine a.m., and L.T. was working nights. They had the day to themselves.

"This was my grandfather's special spot."

"The one where he used to take the New York City outdoorsmen?"

"No, the one where he used to take me. No one else comes back here. They didn't then, anyway."

L.T. nodded in understanding. Their long hike off the main trail wasn't just about fishing.

When they finally reached the pool, it seemed much as she

had remembered it, but smaller. The water dropped from a projecting rock, fanning out in a feathery spray. There was room to sit behind the waterfall, and not be seen. As a child, it had been Kris's favourite place. The pool itself was perhaps thirty feet long and ten feet wide. Its surface churned where the water dropped into it, then smoothed into a silvery, fluid, calm before funnelling into a ripple of rapids. A lone birch tree had rotted and collapsed into the pool about two-thirds of the way down, its butt still on the bank and its top beneath the pool, branches like ghostly white fingers under the water.

"Look at that tree," L.T. said. "There's going to be some trout hanging in that."

"Your line will be hanging in it, too," Kris said.

"Watch the fly fisherman at work," he said. "I'll drift it along the surface and they'll rise to the bait."

He had already selected a fly and was flicking the line in the air above the pool. He landed the fly just past the turbulence of the little falls, and let it drift slowly toward the partially submerged tree. There was a swirl at the surface, and the fly disappeared. L.T. set the hook. "Good one," he said.

"Keep it out of the branches."

He worked along the side of the pool, using the current to keep the trout clear of the obstruction. The fish let itself be carried downstream, then made a rush toward the tree. L.T. steered it back toward the shore, the long fly rod bending. He had the fish past the tree now, into the deepest part of the pool. It dogged down, but soon tired, and L.T. worked it in to the shore. "Not bad," he said. "About fourteen inches."

Kris whistled. "Most girls would be happy with eight."

L.T. reddened. "Aren't you going to fish?"

"Not yet."

She had brought L.T.'s spinning rod, worms, and a few small Mepps spinners, although she hadn't fished since she and her Uncle Martin used to canoe into Algonquin Park for trout. For now, she was content just to watch L.T. in her special place. He wore hiking boots, lightweight khaki shorts, and a white T-shirt that stretched across the muscles of his chest and back. His broad face was shadowed beneath a navy Duke ball cap. Kris had not yet forced herself to decide if she was in love with him, but she knew she was in lust. She had a fleeting thought about Colin, but that world seemed so far away.

L.T. worked the fly rod with a kind of natural grace, but in an hour of fishing, he was only able to get one more, a ten-incher that he threw back.

"One fish," he said. "That's not enough for dinner. Are you going to help me out?"

"Show you how, you mean."

"So you think that after I've worked this pool with a fine array of flies, you can dunk in a worm and get one I missed?"

"Yep."

Her grandfather had only fly-fished when he wanted to impress the sports. They liked the old-timey craft of it. When he wanted to catch a fish, he knotted a worm on a hook, added a sinker just large enough to take it down, and let it drift. The key was to get it to the bottom, he said, then lift it just off the stream bed. Fish were like people. Sometimes they liked to sit on their asses and have their food brought to them.

Kris baited the hook and tested the drag on the ultralight spinning rod. With a flick of the wrist, she dropped the bait into the pool and stopped it what she hoped would be just short of the sunken tree. She lifted the rod tip to raise the worm up, and imagined it in the clear brown water, swaying tantalizingly in front of a fat trout.

She felt a tap, tap, then a hard hit as a trout took the worm in. If he had driven farther into the branches, the fish would have been safe, but he headed towards the deep water at the centre of the pool, following the same pattern as the one L.T. had caught.

"Jesus, first cast," he said.

The fish bent the lightweight rod and stripped line, but Kris didn't try to play him for too long. He was dinner, after all.

The brookie was a couple of inches bigger than L.T.'s, and deep, his speckled sides flashing in the sun.

"You see? You just need the right technique. Same thing as I was telling you last night."

"You've really got your mind on one thing, haven't you?" L.T. said.

"There's something about you that turns my thoughts that way," she said. "Come on, I'll show you my favourite place."

"I thought this was your favourite place."

"It is, but there's a little shallow cave behind the falls. You can still see out, but no one can see in. Come on," she said, already heading toward the water.

"We'll get soaked."

"Good point," she said. "I can solve that problem."

Turning her back to him, she stripped off her denim shirt, white tank top, bra, jeans and panties. If she had been planning to do this, Kris thought, she would have worn something sexier than white cotton.

Without looking back at L.T., she dove into the pool. The water was numbing. A half-dozen smooth strokes took her to the falls. She pulled herself up on a rock, slippery with moss, turned to L.T. and gestured for him to follow. He said something, but she couldn't hear him with the sound of the water cascading behind her.

She walked through the falls and into the little space behind, which had a smooth, damp, stone floor and a couple of round boulders that made good seats. She could see L.T.'s outline through the sheet of water, like looking through a hazy glass. He was still standing on the shore.

God, if he doesn't come along, this is going to be embarrassing, Kris thought.

Looking around, L.T. shucked off his T-shirt, shorts, and underwear and slipped into the pool. A minute later, he joined her behind the falls. "I never know what to expect from you," he said.

"Good. I'd hate to think that I'd become predictable already."

He quickly explored the little space. It was about six feet deep and the width of the water curtain in front, the result of erosion in some far distant time. "This is pretty cool," he said. "Kind of a Huck Finn thing."

"I don't remember Huck Finn hanging around with naked girls. You must have read some heated-up Southern edition."

"I just saw the movie, but you're right. They left this part out. So, now what?"

"Don't you have any ideas?" she said.

"One."

"That ought to be enough."

Half an hour later, they lay together on the stone, finally

beginning to cool off. Kris was sure that she must be covered with bruises and scrapes. She snuggled into L.T. Now that the passion was over, the discomfort was kicking in, but she didn't want this to end.

"I love this place," she said. "You can be back here and no one in the world knows it. It's safe. I didn't have many safe places when I was a kid. Did you?"

"My childhood looks like a TV show compared to yours. My daddy's a Baptist preacher, my mom teaches school. We were brought up to love God and books."

"So how did you end up as a football player and cop?" she asked, directing the conversation away from any more comparisons between L.T.'s family and hers.

"The football was a way to go to college for free. My folks didn't have much money. Good way to meet girls, too," he laughed. "As far as being a cop, that's more from the God side. I was brought up to believe that people who do wrong should be punished. You've got to catch them first, though."

"That's the thing isn't it? Take our friend the senator. We know he was at the camp the day Kathy died. It's hard to imagine that he isn't one of the three men on that videotape. The way he's reacted to my presence tells us he has something to hide. But to actually nail him, that's going to be tough."

"Legally, yeah. It's likely there were at least two eyewitnesses to your sister's death. One of them would have to turn. Or maybe the girls. We don't know what role they played."

"Be honest, L.T. Do you think I'm going to get anywhere with this?"

She could feel his shrug. "Well, we know quite a bit more than we did. We've got the other side jumping. Depends on what you want to get out of it. It's not just a story, is it."

"Probably not. When I came down here, I was looking for justice. Showing the world what Osborne did is one way to get it."

Kris had to admit the story was now not just about Osborne, but about her mother, too. Had she really been involved with old man Osborne — and if so, what role had that played in Kathy's death?

"You say you were looking for justice. Has that changed?"

They were getting to a topic that Kris had been putting off, but she supposed this was as good a time as any.

"Maybe. I've been thinking that there could be something more important." She paused, and ran her fingers slowly down his chest. "So what are we doing, L.T., you and I?"

"Trout fishing?"

"You know what I mean. You've been laying it on the line for me. That makes me think I might be something more to you than an older broad you're screwing because there isn't any young stuff available."

He laughed. "Hell, yes. You're the most amazing woman I've ever been with. It's about a lot more than sex."

He hesitated, then said, "I suppose you're asking if I'm in love with you?"

Now it was her turn to shrug.

"If I was, I'd be in a bad spot," he said. "You're going back to Canada any day, and I'm heading to Hawaii soon. I just haven't allowed myself the luxury of feeling that way. Our lives have intersected here, but we're heading in different directions."

"It doesn't have to be that way," she said.

"No, but it probably will be. I thought you were the hard-nosed realist?"

It's not quite that, Kris thought. She had lived her life in a protective shell, unwilling to treasure anything that could be taken away. Too much hurt, too soon. There was an empty place in her life, and she was trying to fit L.T. into it. When Kris had begun to investigate Kathy's death, she hoped maybe something good would come from it. She hadn't anticipated this.

"Sorry," she said. "You bring out the tiny emotional side of me."

"Don't apologize for that," he said.

12

It was a call Kris had dreaded making, but it was seven-thirty p.m. the day before she was to return to Ottawa. She could hardly put it off any longer. Colin had a right to know that she wasn't coming home yet.

She had fortified herself for the task with a cigarette and a Scotch on the rocks. It was a blend, but not bad. She had taken up her favourite position in the Adirondack chair on the point, an ashtray on one chair arm, her glass on the other. A north wind swept whitecaps down the length of the lake and brought a chill to the early evening. She wore a red fleece pullover, but it was almost time to start thinking about coats. She looked at the cell phone and shivered a bit.

It had to be the wind.

She wasn't sure how to play it with Colin. Technically, this was a business call, but their unresolved personal relationship coloured everything. Now, with L.T., things had become much more complicated. She could only explain L.T. to Colin as part of telling him it was over. That didn't seem like something to do over the phone.

The two were so different. Unlike Colin, L.T. took time with her pleasure, like it meant something to him. As a lover, Colin certainly got the job done, but he showed the ill effects of a life-time of deadlines. His style was go like hell, one eye always on the clock. Her time with him always felt as if it were stolen from something else, something more important. She had cursed herself for getting involved with him, but a sort of inertia had quickly set in. He was eager and close at hand.

It was a bit more than that, too, if she was being completely honest with herself. Colin had a kind of boyish vulnerability behind the tough-talking foreign correspondent act. She liked that, although God knew she wasn't the first person to feel that way. Colin's conquests were legendary, and she knew the boyish thing could just be another layer of his act. You were never really sure with Colin.

She also had to admit that she had been reluctant to dispose of a lover without another in sight. Even living together, their relationship had consisted mostly of hurried sex and shop talk, but it had filled a need, and she had been touched by the idea that the man was actually in love with her.

She punched in their home number, telling herself not to worry too much about Colin. His dick would lead him to the next woman as reliably as a compass pointed north. On the other hand, he had a reputation as a serial monogamist. She only hoped he wouldn't get into personal stuff, not today.

He picked up on the fourth ring.

"Wendover."

"Hey, it's Kris."

"Yes, my dear. I still recognize your voice."

He sounded somewhat breathless, but it didn't prevent him from getting in the dig. She had called him only once in more than two weeks, and that to wangle more time for her story.

"Did I get you at a bad time?"

"Not at all. Just on the balcony having a pint. Bit of a rush to get to the phone. Will I see you tomorrow?"

"Afraid not. That's why I'm calling."

"Really? What's up?"

The disappointment was obvious in his voice.

Kris described the manhandling she had received from Naylor, leaning on it as proof of the senator's connection to her sister's death and hoping it would boost Colin's determination to get the story.

"Bloody hell," he said. "Who does this bloke think he is? Have you gone to the police?"

"No, I think the town police are in Osborne's hip pocket."

"Are you all right, then?"

"I think so. They're trying to run me off, but what are they going to do really?"

"I'd be careful, if I were you. This Naylor sounds bloody unstable. You say he's ex-military?"

"Marine."

"No telling what a chap like that is capable of. Look, Kris, I want you out of there today."

She ignored that and said, "The story has taken a kind of twist. It seems my mother was somehow involved with Senator Osborne's father. I'm not sure yet how that relates to my sister's death but I'm not leaving until I find out."

"So you're saying your mother was . . ."

"Apparently fucking the senator's father. That casts doubt on how my father died, too."

It was the first time Kris had said that thought aloud. Her father's electrocution at the Osborne factory, so soon after her sister's death, had long struck her as too coincidental. If he had found out what was really going on with his wife and daughter, Mike Redner would have sought revenge. The Osbornes certainly had the power to make his death appear accidental.

"Well," Colin said. "I suppose that must be rather difficult. The whole thing is starting to sound like a bloody soap opera. What's the actual status of the story?"

Kris had already started working up an outline for a story about how she didn't get the story, how the death of her sister still remained a mystery. She knew she wouldn't really be satisfied with that, though, and neither would Colin.

"It's coming, shaping up. I'm thinking a two-page spread with art. I've got pictures. Personal column, a mystery, all I've been through here. That sort of thing. I'm putting it together as I go, but I need a few more days to explore this angle with my parents."

"Bloody hell, Kris. Have you been following what's going on up here?"

News of Canada seldom slipped through the impervious membrane of the border and she hadn't used her laptop to log on to the *Citizen* Web site in two days. Events in what she would have thought of as her real world now seemed far away and quite unimportant.

"I'm afraid I haven't."

"A teenage girl was killed in a drive-by shooting on Elgin Street yesterday. It's gang related. The city's in a bloody uproar.

I gave it three clear pages today but the *Sun* still kicked our ass with a good piece on the shooter. Without you here, they're killing us on the police angles."

"What about that police reporter, Suzy Morin? Isn't she on top of it?"

"To a degree, but this is a story that needs your touch. Someone who can put words to the outrage the community feels. I need you back here. Tomorrow."

It was politely put, but Kris recognized that Colin had just given her an order. At least she took some small satisfaction in knowing that Suzy Morin wasn't getting the job done. The bitch had had her nails out ever since Kris appeared and started to show her how the job was done.

"Look," Colin said, lowering his voice. "It's not just the paper. I need you back, too. You've only called me once in two weeks. We need to talk. Why not give the New York State thing a rest? When the action subsides up here, maybe the two of us can go down together, really dig into it."

Kris almost had to laugh at the thought of Colin trying to deal with people in Osborne. It had been difficult enough for her, and she was sort of a local.

"I don't think that would work, Colin, but it's a kind offer. You've got dozens of reporters, surely you can cover for a few more days without me."

"I've already been covering," he said, his voice more strained. "Today, I had the publisher in my office, slapping the *Sun* on my desk and asking me when we were going to start doing our job. He asked where you were and I had to tell them you were covering some story of high political intrigue in the States. Let me tell you, he wasn't impressed. Acted as if I'd lost my bloody mind. I assured them you'd be back on the job Tuesday morning. There's a meeting in the publisher's office at nine a.m., where I'm to lay out my plan for getting ahead of the *Sun*. Not having you there simply isn't an option, I'm afraid."

"Sorry, Colin. I'm not leaving now. This guy Osborne's connected to my sister's death. I've no doubt of that. And he's got a real shot at the Republican nomination. It would be irresponsible not to tell this story and if it works out the way I hope, every major news organization in the U.S. is going to be scrambling to match us."

"Yes, well, I'd enjoy that, but I repeat, I expect to see you here tomorrow."

Kris had a sense she was on the verge of throwing away her job, but she simply couldn't leave without knowing what had really happened to her family. It was difficult to imagine Colin actually firing her, but the publisher could demand it. Colin was on thin ice himself. This was his first crack at being editor of a major paper, and with the new owners, there was no room for error. Kris knew she was asking a lot of him.

"I'm quite certain I can make it back by the end of the week," she said. "Just tell them I'm working on this shooting from outside the office."

"Kris, I can't help but feel that you're trading on our personal relationship when you make that kind of request." The anger in his voice was barely contained now.

Kris felt like telling him to stick the personal relationship in the orifice of his choice, but it wouldn't be smart. Colin could be vindictive when crossed.

"I've already given you more time than I would anyone else to chase something that just doesn't seem to be coming together. Your job, Kris, is to cover crime here, in Ottawa. I'll remind you that when I was hired, I insisted on having you at quite a substantial salary."

"I'm aware of that," she said. When Colin had dragged her along from Toronto it was certainly for more than professional reasons but it wasn't the right time to remind him of that. "What are you going to do, suspend me?" she asked.

"In fact, I am. I'm going ask Morin to undertake the crime column. I need someone I can rely on."

Kris hung up, her heart racing. There was nothing more to be said.

13

General Jack Naylor's black Lexus was parked just where he said it would be, on a long, deserted stretch of Northport Road, so heavily forested that it seemed gloomy even on a sunny Tuesday morning. L.T. pulled his cruiser in behind the car. If anyone asked, it was a traffic stop.

There had been a message for him from the general when he got in to work, summoning him. It was something he could have done without, after working until midnight the night before, then pulling an early shift today. He felt groggy, not as alert as he should be for this.

L.T. walked over to the Lexus and tapped on the window. It powered down and he said, "What's up?"

"That's what I hope you'll be telling me, son. I expected a report back by now. Have a seat," the general said, gesturing toward the passenger side.

"It would look better if I didn't, sir. Why don't you step out of the vehicle?"

The general shrugged and opened the car door. He was easily six inches shorter than L.T., who figured that at least helped even out the power imbalance. Naylor wore his usual military casual, khaki pants and windbreaker over a white shirt with a button-down collar.

"Let's get to it," the general said. "What about the Redner woman? I hear she was at a dinner party on the weekend telling people she wasn't going back up to Canada as scheduled. Doesn't have everything she needs for her story yet."

Betsy Larson, L.T. thought. She worked for the senator, but then it sometimes seemed like the whole town did, one way or another.

"Just a few more interviews, she tells me. Between you and me, I don't think she's got enough to go on, but she's not the kind of person who gives up easily."

"You're damn right she doesn't," the general said, "but I thought we had an understanding. You were going to figure a way to get her the hell out of town. We made a down payment on that. What have you got to show?"

"I've been urging her to give it up, giving her my professional perspective. One woman isn't going to come in alone and solve a cold case that's nearly thirty years old. I've also made it clear that I'm heading out of town soon, just in case she had any personal reasons to stick around."

"I suppose that's a start, but if you want the other twenty-five grand, you're going to have to do better than that. I only pay for results. Now, what's she telling you? Is she finding anything out?"

L.T. rubbed the side of his face and allowed himself a bit of an embarrassed grin. "Well, to tell you the truth, sir, we spent most of the weekend in the sack. My feeling? She's given up, but she's just sticking around out of pride. Those people at Betsy's party thought she was leaving on the weekend, and some made it pretty clear that was a good thing."

The general nodded, seemingly not paying much attention to what L.T. had just said. "All right, son, that's good to know.

"Look, I've got something else for you, and it would double your money, but before I even tell you about it, I need to know that I can trust you absolutely."

The general stared at L.T., his cold, dark eyes squinting as if he could see right inside his head. L.T. nodded and looked serious, while trying to keep his own eyes opaque, to keep the general out. The man had presence, he had to admit that.

"There's something I need you to get for me," the general said. "If you can produce it, there's another fifty in it for you."

"Fifty? Must be very important. What is it?"

He was pretty certain he could make an accurate guess.

"A videotape. I think Redner has it. It was something made years ago, bunch of kids horsing around. If it showed up now, got on the Internet, it could be embarrassing. It's possible to misinterpret what was going on."

"Sir?"

"You don't need to know what's on the videotape, L.T. In fact, I don't even want you to look at it. It's an old tape, and I doubt that she's carrying around two. She hasn't said anything about a tape, has she?"

"No sir. Not a word."

"Could be back in Ottawa, I suppose, but I doubt she'd let it out of her possession. Here's what I suggest you do. Push her on why she got into stirring up this whole damn mess now, so many years later. Act like you don't think there could be any good reason for it. She trusts you. She'll show you the tape to prove her point.

"Now if you do see it, remember it was just some kids who had a few too many beers. Nothing to do with the senator whatsoever, but someone who's out to get him is making it out to be something else. I'd bet on that. You see, L.T., when you rise to the top of the ladder, there's always some little person trying to knock you down."

"Yes, sir. I know that. What should I do with the tape if I find it?"

"Secure it and report to me immediately."

"But she's going to figure out that I took it. Seems like no one else knows about it."

"Mess up her place. Make it look like a break-in. Christ, man, do I have to tell you how to carry out every order?"

The general's face was beginning to redden, and L.T. could see that the man's hands had clenched into fists. He was clearly dissatisfied with any answer other than "Sir, yes sir."

"Sorry, I don't have that much experience in breaking the law."

"The law is there to control the masses, L.T., to let us maintain some order. The people who make the laws weren't meant to be constrained by them. Someone has to be in charge."

L.T. didn't remember that point from any of those poli-sci courses he took at Duke, and certainly not from the sermons he'd heard growing up in his daddy's church. Most of the crooks he'd caught just wanted to have stuff without working, but the general had elevated breaking the law to the level of philosophy.

"When I get it, then what?"

"We'll arrange a meet."

The general withdrew a small leather card case from the inside pocket of his khaki windbreaker. "This is my cell phone number. Call any time. I expect to hear from you within forty-eight hours. If this doesn't work, then you're not our man, L.T. and we'll have to go another route."

He hated to think what that would be. Nothing as benign as having him snatch the videotape, that was for sure.

"I'm counting on you, son. You make this work for you the way you can, you're going to be doing a lot of surfing in Hawaii soon."

"Yes, sir," L.T. said, with a big grin that he hoped made it look he was the kind of person who would enjoy a little betrayal for money. The sheer size of the sum made it easier. No matter how you looked at it, a total of $100,000, tax free, was a big pile of cash.

14

Kris pulled her car up beside a black Lincoln Navigator. If she'd opened the tailgate of the thing, she probably could have parked right inside. It was in front of a four-car garage that formed the west wing of what the senator had quaintly referred to as his "town house." Was the SUV too big to fit into the garage, she wondered, or was it already full of cars?

The invitation to lunch had come in an embossed manila envelope, hand-delivered by one of the senator's household staff. She had declined the offered limo ride, but she couldn't turn down the lunch. Except for their brief conversation at the factory, the senator had succeeded in eluding her for weeks. Now he was inviting her to his place, like they were old friends. Something had changed.

She took a minute to collect herself before getting out of the car. This meeting was likely to be a confrontation, and she was still stinging from the one with Colin last night. He'd been more brutal than she expected. When this was all over, she'd have to decide between begging to get her job back and telling him to fuck himself. But then what? Her guts had been churning all night over the likely self-destruction of her career, and the whole thing was complicated by the fact that they were living together. She wouldn't even have a place to stay. But Kris kept telling herself she had to put those worries to one side and push ahead. She'd already chosen her course.

Kris stared at the senator's mansion. It looked even more imposing up close than it did from the road. Windward, as she knew his place was called, was a house in town, but it certainly wasn't a townhouse of the sort people would think of back in Ottawa, an aluminum-sided row house huddled up against a bunch of others the same. Eight white columns supported a verandah the full width of the house. Seven second-storey windows were deeply set into the heavy cut stone blocks, and flanked by white shutters. The house gave the impression of having been there forever, just like its owners.

The senator came out a side door, where the garage addition joined the main house. He wore jeans, loafers, a button-down-collared blue shirt, and a red pullover sweater, cashmere, she thought. He would have fit nicely in a Ralph Lauren ad. Even though he was almost certainly a figure of evil, the senator wore his blandness like camouflage.

He waved and smiled, as if he were actually happy to see her. By the time Kris had slung her big purse over her shoulder, he was at the car, extending his hand.

"Senator," she said. "This is a surprise. I thought you had nothing more to tell me."

"There are a few things I'd like to clear up," he said. "Why don't you come in?"

He turned and she followed him toward the house. No flak, she noticed. No Bud Naylor. No human Dobermans of any kind. It made her suspicious.

He held open the door he had come from, so she could enter first. It led directly to a dark hall with natural cedar wainscoting turned dark with age. The walls were plaster, painted white, but the ceiling was also cedar, the narrow strips formed in an intricate pattern of squares. The walls were covered with portraits of stern-looking men, the pictures illuminated with little brass lights like in a gallery. Previous Osbornes, she assumed.

"Sorry, it's a bit gloomy in here," he said. "Let's go into the conservatory."

The hall led to a round room made almost entirely of glass. She could see blue and white dishes set for two on a white wicker table.

"This is a little more comfortable," the senator said.

It was a clear day, and she could see for miles up the lake. In the near distance, two sailboats worked close to each other, racing.

"The conservatory was a late Victorian addition. The house itself was built in 1845," the senator said. "We're about to add an east wing. Terry finds it a bit cramped.

"Would you like a tour?"

She'd had about enough of touring the senator's properties for one week.

"No thanks. I get the picture. What did you want to tell me?"

"Please, have a seat."

He gave her that charming smile that had carried him so far in life. His flawless teeth had almost certainly been capped, Kris thought.

Grudgingly, she perched on the edge of one of the white wicker chairs that filled the conservatory. An ornate metal birdcage stood in one corner, providing an elegant prison for about a dozen blue and green budgies. They flitted about nervously and seemed to be studying her.

"First, I'd like to offer you an apology. I understand Bud Naylor conducted himself extremely inappropriately after Al and I had left the office. I've spoken to him about it, believe me. You have to understand, Bud spent his career in the Marines. Subtlety isn't their style. He's also fiercely protective of me. Anything that he thinks poses a threat puts him on red alert."

"And he thinks I'm a threat to you?"

"Yes, because you are. Bud put his point poorly, but any story that contained a phrase like 'senator denies involvement in teen's death,' could be politically lethal. I'm sure a woman of your experience knows that."

"So let me just ask you flat out, Senator. Were you in some way involved in my sister's death?"

He smiled and shook his head. "There you go, asking me to give you the denial quote. The thing I don't understand, Kris, is why in the world you think I have anything to do with those tragic events? And why are you pursuing them now? I know newspapers love to dig up old stories simply because twenty-five or fifty years have gone by. Surely there must be more to your coming down here than some instinct toward anniversary journalism?"

"Yes, there is," she said. "But Senator, you know reporters never reveal sources. You're just going to have to trust me."

Kris returned his look of sincerity. Two could play the smiling game.

A dark-haired young man in a white shirt and black bow tie discreetly appeared in the door of the conservatory. "Would you care for a beverage before lunch, ma'am? Sir?" he asked.

The senator gestured inquiringly toward Kris.

"Nothing for me, thanks," she said. She could use a drink, but she didn't trust the bastard not to put rat poison in it.

"Nothing, then, Buxton," the senator said, dismissing him.

She wondered what it must be like to lead the senator's kind of life, with Buxton and God knew how many other flunkies lined up to wait on you. It was easy to see why he was so afraid of losing it.

"Kris, you're a respected journalist. I'm going to assume you have some reason for doing what you're doing. But I want you to understand my thinking, to consider the bigger context. Let me share a few things with you."

The senator looked down, almost shy, before saying, "This is stuff I wouldn't tell anyone."

It was all Kris could do to keep from rolling her eyes up. She was familiar with the technique. The rich and powerful seemed to know the fastest way to co-opt a journalist was to make her feel like one of them. Take her to lunch, give her a little inside knowledge. Kris had to admit the illusion that they were equal to the power elite often made reporters roll over and beg for more.

The senator leaned toward her and lowered his voice. "Truth is, the shoe factory has been losing money for years, but I choose to keep it going because closing it would be such a blow to this town. I believe all that stuff you heard me say about jobs in America, for Americans. We've got to stop the outsourcing, Kris, so towns like ours can compete on an even footing.

"Folks here need me representing them, too, to make sure they get a fair shake from government. I'm sure you know I hope to move that representation to an even higher level. What you're getting into could jeopardize all of that. I don't just mean for me, but for the town. Hundreds of jobs, families that depend on my success and credibility to make sure they can feed their kids."

Kris was curious to see how far he would go down this path. Pretty soon, he'd be talking about his little dog, Checkers.

The budgies shrieked and noisily flapped their wings as they competed to get at the seed holder. Even the bloody birds depended on this saintly figure, Kris thought.

"Oh, spare me," she said. "Senator, you're just worried that I'm going to fuck up your chance to get into the White House."

He shook his head, with the look of a parent who is saddened by the behaviour of a wilful child. "Well, of course," he said. "For all the reasons I've just raised.

"Let's not get distracted from the main reason I asked you here. I want to offer you any help my office can give in solving the mystery of what happened to your sister. Now, I have no reason to believe that her death was anything but what it seems. She was almost certainly picked up by a passing motorist and assaulted."

Right, she thought. And Larry Brewster found the body based on an anonymous tip. She'd love to mention that detail, but it would make it obvious how she'd gotten it. It was a fact that hadn't been in the news stories.

"I can understand how frustrating the uncertainty must be. I'm not without influence. I could definitely persuade the police to review the case again. Perhaps we could even hire a private investigator.

"I'm here to help, Kris. There's no reason why we need to be on opposite sides of this."

His smile was disconcertingly personal, almost intimate, as if he'd just caressed her with his splendid offer. Seduction took many forms.

"Very generous," she said. "Let me think it over."

With enough encouragement, she was sure Larry Brewster and the senator's private detective could probably even find some drunk from the wrong side of town to charge with the crime.

She picked up her purse and was rising from her seat when the senator reached out and touched her forearm. His touch was surprisingly warm and gentle.

"There's another thing," he said. "It's a long-standing matter between your family and mine that has to be cleared up. When your dad died in that terrible electrical accident at the plant, my father naturally wanted to offer your mother a pension, to help out. It wouldn't replace your dad's earnings, of course, but father wanted to do something. He regarded his employees like a family."

Kris distinctly remembered her father describing old man Osborne as a "cheap prick" who wouldn't give him a raise. It was the first she'd heard of the so-called pension. Guilt money, she thought. The stories about her mother and old man Osborne must be true. The feeling that her father had been killed because he'd found out too much was growing much stronger.

"Your mother refused to take the money. I suppose she wasn't well, with her condition, but she somehow blamed Father for the accident. It was a terrible shame, because I know your family could have used that money.

"In any case, Father continued to put it to one side, in an account, hoping that one day she would be well and agree to take it. That never happened, of course, but we still pay the pension into the account. By rights, it's yours. Even though the annual sum is modest, it has added up over the years. Actually, I believe that it's somewhere near a quarter of a million dollars now."

Kris did the math. A payout of a little better than $80,000 each for the three members of her family the Osbornes had eliminated one way or another. A bargain from the senator's perspective.

"Isn't that interesting," she said. "Mother never spoke of it. I suppose I should just take that quarter mil and head back to Canada, buy myself some new shoes."

He shrugged.

"You can mock me, but the money's there. I'm quite sincere."

"I'm sure you are. What if I asked for a million, cash, to settle everything? Maybe I could retire and devote myself to poetry."

For just a moment, he looked as if he were considering it.

"Of course, that would be absurd," he said. "The money I mentioned is strictly a pension, owing to you as the last remaining member of your family."

The last of the troublesome Redners, she thought, and felt the cold realization that there was little to prevent them from eliminating her, too.

"Tell me, Senator, since you've raised it. What was the relationship between my mother and your father?"

"Relationship?" The senator appeared confused, as if the idea just didn't compute.

"I'm sure you must have heard. People say your father was fucking my mother around the time of my sister's death. Casts my dad's 'electrocution' in an interesting light, too, doesn't it?"

The senator shook his head, as if clearing the offensive suggestions away.

"This is just so out of line, I don't know how to comment," he said. "My mother and father were very happily married. Please don't drag your family's problems across my doorstep."

"Happily married in much the same way you and your ex-wife were, I expect," Kris said. "And what about little Terry? Does she know you like to step out?"

The senator got to his feet, some colour finally showing under his tan. "That's enough. We're done here."

"We certainly are," Kris said. "And you can stick your money. This isn't about money. And it isn't about power, either, and those are the only two things you can understand."

With that, she turned to leave, pausing ever so briefly to open the rather large door on the budgie cage. The first of the little blue and green feather bombs made its burst for freedom as she left the conservatory, with a flight path that led it directly toward the senator's hair.

"Oh shit," were the last words she heard as she stepped back into the morning sun.

15

Kris parked her car directly in front of Vieth's. She was going to get some real answers from Sharon Sloan this time. No more hints and mysteries.

First, she had to get a grip. Kris was still steaming from her meeting with the senator and the thought that he was probably washing bird shit out of his hair was small consolation. The more she thought about his offer, the angrier she became. Lowell Osborne figured, after all that had happened, that she could either be sweet-talked or bought. She supposed those were the two cards he had to play, but why now? He'd blown her off for weeks.

The senator had seemed genuinely surprised when she brought up the connection between his father and her mother, but was that because it was news to him, or because he was shocked that she knew?

As Kris walked up the front steps of the store, she noticed that it was one of those crisp, clear, fall days, the kind she would enjoy if it were another time and another place. The store's wooden screen door slapped shut behind her. It looked just as it had the last time she was in, the stock perhaps just a bit dustier. The only real difference was in Sharon Sloan. Her left eye was bruised and puffy, its appearance made more lurid by the bare neon lights overhead.

When she saw Kris enter, Sharon immediately headed through a door covered by vertical strips of heavy plastic, and disappeared. Kris figured it must be the stockroom.

What was she trying to hide? Fight with a boyfriend?

Kris went up to the door and called Sharon's name, but there was no response. "Come on Sharon, I know you're back there. Look, I just need to buy some stuff. If you got in a fight with your boyfriend, or whatever, it's none of my business."

Sharon Sloan came back through the plastic strips, tentatively looking around the store and keeping her left side turned away from Kris. "I shouldn't be talking to you," she said.

"Hey, I need food like everyone else. What am I supposed to do, drive to Elizabethtown for a loaf of bread?"

"All right. Make it fast, please. I don't want people to see me with you."

The tough, wiseass stuff was gone. Something had happened to Sharon since Kris had spoken to her last. "Look, I can see someone punched you out, but what's it got to do with me?"

Sharon stared at Kris, her good eye burning with anger. "Nothing. It was my fault."

"I doubt that. Look, why don't we go out back, have a smoke? No one will see us there."

Sharon looked down, bit her lip, then said, "All right."

She went back through the door, and Kris followed, brushing aside the heavy plastic. The storeroom was stacked high with boxes containing cartons of cigarettes. It smelled of cardboard and damp. A single bare bulb, hanging from the ceiling, provided a dull light. Sharon sat on one of the cartons and Kris followed suit, pulling out a pack and offering a cigarette to the other woman.

Sharon lit it with a Bic, took a couple of drags and said, "What do you want?"

"I want to know who did that to you, and what it has to do with me."

"Who said it had anything to do with you?"

"You took off as soon as you saw me, and then you told me you weren't supposed to talk to me. Who's telling you that?"

"Who do you think?"

"Osborne?"

"Not Osborne, no. He doesn't do anything directly. Bud Naylor came by my house on the weekend, with a couple of men. They seemed to think I was helping you. I told them I wasn't, but they said they wanted to make sure I didn't forget."

"So he gave you the shiner?"

"That was just the finishing touch."

"Come on, Sharon. What did he do to you?"

There were tears running down her face now, smearing the pancake makeup she'd used to try to disguise the damage.

"He put me over his knee, like I was a child. Then he pulled my pants down and smacked me so many times that I couldn't sit down for a day. Part way through, he ripped my panties away and showed the others everything I had. He got off on it too, the bastard, I could feel that. He's a fucking sadist. When he was done, he gave me the shot in the face, just as a reminder, he said. He told me that if I so much as said hello to you, he'd be back, and next time, he wouldn't be so gentle. That's what he actually said. Gentle. The prick."

Kris was stunned. She'd known Naylor could be violent, but now it seemed like he was out of control. If he'd do this to Sharon Sloan, just because of a suspicion that she was helping Kris, what did he have planned for her? Now she began to wonder if the senator's offer was some kind of last chance.

"That was assault," she said. "You need to go to the police."

Sharon gave a harsh laugh, and took another drag on her cigarette. "Yeah, right. Osborne owns the police. You know that."

"Take this straight to L.T Hill. He'll lay charges. I guarantee it."

"Which will then get thrown out. And what will happen to me after that?"

"Just being charged with a crime like this will ruin Bud Naylor. Once it hits the media, the senator will have to dump him."

"Yeah, well, that would be sweet, but it's not worth it. Osborne will be there to come back at me long after you and your boyfriend have moved on."

Kris let the boyfriend comment pass. She supposed that everyone must know her business. It was a small town, after all. "Maybe there's a way to get Osborne himself. I think you do know something that you haven't told me. Bud Naylor must think so too."

"Haven't got a clue what you're talking about. Look, I have to get back out front. Let me go first, make sure there is no one in the store. Then get your stuff and get out."

"These people have beaten and humiliated you. Not to mention the way Lowell Osborne treated you years ago. Why are you protecting them?"

"I'm not protecting them. I'm protecting me. And don't you tell me how to do it."

"All right," Kris said, backing off. "Look, Sharon, there's one more thing. You told me to find out what my mother was doing that summer. I know she was hooked up with old man Osborne, but no one will give me any details. Tell me what really happened and how it connects to my sister's death."

Sharon shrugged. "She never told you?"

"Not a word. I was only ten when all this happened, remember?"

Kris offered Sharon a second cigarette and was encouraged when she took it.

"I don't know how it started," she said. "By the time I came up to the camp that summer, your mother was there three, four days a week, in the afternoon. Bud Naylor used to fetch her from town. I guess Osborne didn't want to be seen with her back here. People would talk. They kept it really quiet. I think only the people who were actually at the camp knew what was going on, and we all understood to say nothing.

"She spent most of her time up at the lodge, with Osborne. We didn't see that much of her, really."

Kris remained silent as Sharon looked away and took a long drag on her cigarette. Sharon's story was a reluctant précis that told her little more than she already knew. As a child, she had attributed her mother's afternoon absences to her drinking. Like so much of what she thought she knew, it was only a small part of the truth.

What had motivated her mother? Was it sex, the attraction of power, or something more?

"Do you think they were in love?" Kris asked, regretting the question as soon as it left her mouth.

Sharon snorted, blowing smoke from her nostrils.

"Love? There was a lot of fucking that summer, not much love. The women there all wanted something from the Osbornes and they wanted something from us. Turns out, they got what they wanted; we didn't."

"But what about Kathy? How does my mother's affair connect

to my sister's death?" Kris asked.

Sharon shrugged. "Your mother got Kathy the job at the camp, even though she was really too young. Maybe the rest was just fate."

Kris really didn't want to ask her next question. "Do you think old man Osborne might have been involved with Kathy too, that my mother . . ."

"Pimped her out?" Sharon said. "I doubt it. Your mother wanted the old man for herself."

Kris nodded. Sharon's supposition actually constituted good news in the sad narrative of the Redners and the Osbornes. Maybe there was some kind of limit.

"You know my father was killed a week after Kathy," Kris said. "We were told it was an electrical accident at the factory. I wonder if he found out what was going on with my mother, confronted Osborne?"

Sharon appeared to consider the idea, then said, "Beats me. The old man and your parents are all dead now. Does it really matter?"

Yes, Kris thought. Yes, it matters how much Redner blood is on the Osborne hands. In courts, she had never agreed with the approach that said you paid in full for the first crime and the rest were free. Every life taken was of value.

They both heard the slap of the screen door in the front of the store.

"That's a customer," Sharon said. "I've got to go. You head out the back way. The alley leads around to the main street."

When Kris got back to Jasper's she was surprised to see L.T.'s cruiser parked in front of his cabin. That was a first. Jasper would be pissed, she thought. There would be no hourly rentals today.

She went into L.T.'s cabin without knocking, and found him sprawled on the ragged couch, in his uniform.

"They know we have the video," he said. "Jack Naylor just offered me fifty grand for it."

"Shit. I think I know how they found out. I was just talking to Sharon Sloan. Bud Naylor was over at her place on the weekend and laid a beating on her. I've suspected for a while that she was the one who sent me the video. She was at the camp that day, and she has it in for Osborne."

"A beating? What's she doing about it?"

"Nothing. She's too afraid."

L.T. got up off the couch and held her silently for a moment. In his arms, she felt safe again. Then she broke off the embrace and pulled one of the wooden chairs away from the kitchen table, turned it around and sat down, leaning forward against the back of the chair.

"How'd it go with Osborne?" L.T. asked.

She forced a laugh. "My bribe makes yours look like pocket change. He had some mumbo jumbo about a pension that should have gone to my mother, after my father was killed at the factory. It's not large, but after nearly thirty years, it has built up to a quarter of a million bucks."

L.T. whistled. "Serious cash. The two of us could spend a lot of time in Hawaii with that."

For just a second, Kris wondered if he was serious.

"Did he say anything about the videotape?" L.T. asked.

"No. I'm sure they will never officially acknowledge it exists. Too many questions would flow from that. He did offer me all the help I needed to solve Kathy's murder, though. He's even willing to pay for a PI."

"Do we get to pick him?" L.T. asked. "Maybe we could get the guy who helped O.J. track down Nicole's killer."

"I told him what he could do with it," Kris said. "He even gave me a political speech about how much the people here needed him to give them their factory jobs and fight for them in Washington. It would be a pity to let a little thing like murder get in the way of all that good work."

"Right, it's all about the big picture," L.T. said. "The general gave me forty-eight hours to come up with the video, or I'm out. How do you want to play it?"

"Did you actually tell him I have it? Maybe he was just fishing."

L.T. shook his head.

"Give me some credit. I was shocked. First I'd heard of any video."

"How does he think you're going to get it?"

"Push you on why you are chasing down Kathy's murder, after all this time. He figures you will show me the video to convince me."

"He had that part right."

"Once I find out you've got it, I'm supposed to mess the place up, like it was burglarized. Then I call him and arrange a meet."

"You really think he's going to pay that kind of money?"

"Judging by what the senator offered, it would be a bargain."

"I wouldn't trust anyone from the Naylor family. I'm betting he intends to rip you off for the video. He knows you couldn't exactly go to the police."

L.T. shook his head. "He'll pay. Anything else's too risky. What if I took the whole thing to the state police, told them I was playing it undercover. They can't take the chance. Besides, fifty grand is small change in a political campaign.

"You know, I've been wondering where the general is getting all the cash. The way he talks about a strong America, it makes me wonder if he's a front for defence contractors. Someone's awful keen to push Lowell Osborne to the top."

"I'll e-mail our guy in Washington," Kris said. "If the general has got those kinds of connections, he can find out."

She didn't want to give up on a possible chance of trapping the general into telling the truth. "What if you turn it over to them, but wear a wire?" Kris asked. "We could get the general to talk about what's on the tape."

"Won't work. His official line is that it's just a bunch of kids horsing around after having a few beers. Some people would misinterpret what it all means. I'm sure he'd tell me that he was just doing his job, reducing risk to the senator. I'm the one who would end up in trouble."

"Yeah, well, fuck him then. Let him stew for forty-eight hours, then tell him you couldn't find any sign of a tape. I'm not just going to give it to him. If we put that tape with a witness, then we've got something. I think maybe I can get Sharon Sloan onside, with a little more persuasion."

L.T. came around behind her chair and began to massage the tense muscles of her shoulders and neck. "If they don't get that tape back, they are definitely going to Plan B, and I'm worried about what that might be. We don't have a fix on just how ruthless these people are. They've got a lot at stake."

"What do you suggest?"

"Find another old tape and a second VCR. Copy the one we've got and give them the copy. They won't know the difference. Sounds like they haven't seen this tape since it was made. That will at least buy us some time."

"Let me think about it," Kris said.

16

Number 38, Washington Street, was not really as Kris had remembered it. Her father had kept the white clapboard of the narrow, two-storey house immaculate, spending countless hours up a ladder scraping, then painting. The new owners weren't so inclined. The paint flaked, hanging in dry strips, and the walls themselves bulged in places, betraying rot.

The little verandah where her father liked to sit and smoke had been crudely enclosed with sheets of plastic. The front lawn was an array of uncut weeds, and an old black Ford without licence plates filled the tiny driveway.

Kris's memories of the sixteen years she had spent on Washington Street were mostly of people and events, so much so that she found the physical place surprisingly unfamiliar. The trees, a row of maples up each side of the street, had suffered badly from age, but still provided a canopy over the worn, broken pavement. It was almost similar to a street from the west side, until you took in the details. The white houses were like a line of decayed teeth, faded with age, some missing. A late afternoon mist of rain made the whole street seem even more grey and depressing.

Kris had avoided the east side of town since she had come back. Too many bad memories. She knew she'd eventually return to Washington Street, though. What she had found out about her parents' troubled life made her want to assess her childhood street again, to see it through adult eyes. It was still hard to believe the soap opera that had played out in the old clapboard house. Kris hadn't told L.T. about the extra details she had learned from Sharon. He knew enough about the embarrassing situation as it was, and Kris felt she still hadn't gotten the whole truth.

Sitting in her car, parked across the street from her old house, she wished she hadn't come. The state of the house her father had poured so much love and energy into was an unpleasant reminder of how temporary everything was. The things we care for and tend are so rapidly destroyed by those that follow. She herself had consciously left no mark. No husband. No children. No house for anyone to drive by in the future and look back on the things that had been. With nothing to lose, Kris had thought she couldn't be hurt. She could see now that was wrong. We all have something to lose.

Coming back to Washington Street had been a mistake, Kris thought, but she had felt the need to reconnect with her family in some way. A trip to the Lakeview Cemetery was just too morbid. Three headstones together, a space reserved for hers. She wasn't one to hang around cemeteries, trying to communicate with the dead. They were long past listening.

Kris had been antsy sitting around the cabin waiting for L.T.'s return. They had found a bunch of old tapes in one of the junk stores on Main and used one to make a copy of the original, the horrible scene of Kathy's rape erasing a birthday party for an anonymous and forgotten child.

L.T. had called Jack Naylor, explaining that he had done as the general suggested, and it all played out just as he had hoped. Kris had shown him the tape, and now he had it. They arranged a meet for five p.m. at a lookout twenty miles outside of town.

Kris had been suspicious of the location, scribbling on a notepad that L.T. should meet the general downtown, someplace public, but it was too late. The order had been issued and the general was gone. At her urging, L.T. had taken his service Glock. Fifty thousand dollars was a lot of money to hand over. Most people would prefer to keep it if they could. She had seen nothing yet to indicate that the Naylors were worthy of trust, although the general appeared to be a little bit smoother than his son.

She lit a cigarette and continued to look at the old house, memories of all that had taken place there coming back unwilled.

Before Kathy died, there had been happy times. She remembered her mother and father putting out a Sunday picnic supper on the old wooden table in the backyard. Ham, devilled eggs, and jellied salads. Her mother would drink beer during those picnics, quite a bit of it, but it made her flirtatious, and her father liked it. Even through child's eyes, she could see that. There had been all the Christmas mornings in the front room, gathered around a sparse tree her father had borrowed from the bush. There had never been too much in the way of presents, but Santa had always come.

She supposed they had been a normal, working-class family until that summer of 1981. Then the Osbornes came into their life. She wondered how Osborne had first connected with her mother. Had he merely seen her walking down the street and decided to pluck her like a ripe piece of fruit?

Whatever it was, that moment had led directly to Kathy's death, and a week later, her father's electrocution at the shoe factory. She still remembered the night of his death vividly. There was a storm, heavy rain battering at the windows of their house. Her parents were in the living room, both drinking and arguing, as they had done most of the few days since her sister's death. She could understand better now what they were arguing about. The call had come around nine. The storm had knocked out power at the plant, and they needed her father to fix it or the morning shift would be cancelled. Her mother didn't want him to head out in the storm, but Kris remembered his saying that a lot of people would go without pay if he couldn't get the power up by morning. He put on a dirty, yellow oilskin and a battered black felt hat and went out the door. Kris had watched from the front window as the car's tail lights disappeared up the dark, wet street. It had been the last she had ever seen of her father. Her mother had said she was too young to see him in his coffin.

Unlike Kathy's death, her father's had seemed straightforward. An industrial accident, the timing horrendous. Now she was almost sure it was more than that.

She still didn't know what to make of Lowell Osborne's talk of a refused pension. Her mother had never worked, and after her father died, she had to clean houses to support Kris and her drinking. Surely either labour law or decency would have dictated some kind of help for the widow. She ought to have been due something because her husband had died on the job. Of course, just because Lowell Osborne said there was a pension, and it had been refused, didn't mean it was so. Probably he was just looking for some kind of plausible way to give her a large sum of money without its appearing to be the bribe that it actually was.

There was another way to sort out the facts, though. Any father, faced with his daughter's murder, would have demanded to know how it happened and who was responsible. Did the official explanation of events appear as thin in 1981 as it did today? If her father had seen the results of Kathy's whipping, he would have been suspicious. There was no love lost between her family and the Osbornes, either. She distinctly remembered her father describing the young Lowell Osborne as "a lazy snot who has never worked a day in his life and had everything handed to him."

Her father had opposed Kathy's working at the camp. It was far from home and required her to sleep over some nights, but his major objection had been because it meant working for the Osbornes.

Kris remembered, during one of her parents' many fights, her father saying, "Does every goddamn penny this family has have to come out of the Osbornes' pocket?"

Her mother had expressed no objection to Osborne money at the time, being as willing to drink up their dollar as anyone else's. Strange, then, that she wouldn't take the pension. Had her mother not taken the money because of guilt over how her husband and daughter had died?

Had her father found out something about what had gone on up at the camp? In the five long years that followed her husband's death, her mother had never given any indication that he had. Candy Redner had simply refused to speak of the past. Candy. Just the mention of the name was enough to put Kris off sweets. Candace, really, but Candy suited her best. Candy the bar girl, hanging around with men who were dirt, just for a free drink. At least she didn't sell herself, but she might as well have, the way she was giving it away. By the time the various "uncles" started coming to visit, Kris was old enough to understand what was going on. So did the kids at school, who taunted her about being the daughter of the town slut. She left home at sixteen, and a year later, her mother was dead. Kris hadn't come home for the funeral; hadn't come home at all until now.

She looked at her watch, a cheap Timex she had picked up in town. Osborne wasn't exactly the kind of place to wear her Rolex, and the gift always reminded her of Colin. It was five-thirty. L.T. should be back soon. His transactions with the general so far had been brief, and the kind of deal they were doing today wasn't one anyone would want to linger over. She had been unconvinced about giving them the copy. It confirmed what she knew, and that knowledge was dangerous. L.T. had argued that they already assumed she had the tape, and were prepared to use any means necessary to retrieve it. Handing the tape over was the safest thing. Without the tape in hand, her description of those long-ago events wouldn't be credible, and she couldn't do them any more harm. Or so they'd think. It would buy her and L.T. a bit more time to dig.

In the end, she'd agreed, but reluctantly.

Lost in her thoughts, Kris had stopped paying attention to the house. She jumped when someone knocked on the driver's side window, and turned to see a girl about the age she would have been when everything started going to hell. The girl's pink jacket was shabby, but she had an iPod clipped to the waist of her jeans and headphones hanging around her neck.

"I live across the street," she said, pointing to Kris's old house and offering a gap-toothed smile. "Are you lost?"

It was a good question, Kris thought, but she said, "No, just thinking for a minute. What's your name?"

"Brie," the girl said.

At least something had changed on the street, Kris thought. Now the parents were naming their children after cheese, even if you still couldn't actually buy the cheese in town.

Kris and Brie both turned, startled by the sound of a siren that called the volunteer fire department into action. Even so far distant from the municipal building, the end-of-the-world, air-raid howl still shattered the silence of Washington Street. Kris wondered what could be burning on such a wet day, and hoped that no one was hurt.

17

The Prius turned into the lane leading to the cabins, wet gravel crunching under the wheels. As the wipers cleared the misty rain from the windshield, Kris expected to see L.T.'s truck parked in front of his cabin. When it wasn't there, she felt a vague, tingling unease, then realized he had probably been called in to deal with the fire. Even though he was off duty, the small size of Osborne's police department sometimes meant everyone worked.

Whatever the problem was, it was somewhere on the main road west out of town. She'd seen two police cruisers go screaming by, lights and sirens going, as well as an ambulance. The doors of the firehall had stood open when she drove past, all three pieces of equipment gone.

In her real life, she would just phone police dispatch, find out what was going on, but she had no standing here. Still, it might not be difficult to get the dispatcher to share. She imagined it had been quite a while since Osborne's emergency services had seen this much excitement.

Kris ran quickly from the car to her cabin, the smell of the pines almost overwhelming in the rain. Inside, the place was cold and dank. She fired up the electric heater and looked the police number up in the tattered phone book that was kept in the kitchen drawer. Not that the cabin actually had a phone, but she had her cell.

Her call was answered on the second ring.

"Osborne Police," a young woman said, the breathless excitement in her voice not quite concealed.

"Hey, I'm calling from the newspaper. I see ambulance, fire and police are out. What's up?"

"MVA on the West Lake Road, fifteen miles out. Gas tank is ruptured and a person is trapped inside."

Kris felt the first cold finger of panic.

"What kind of vehicle?"

"Some guy rolled his Blazer. Who is this again?"

Kris punched off the phone, shoved it in her pocket and ran for her car. The little Toyota sprayed gravel as she floored it out of Jasper's driveway and onto West Lake Road.

Please, God, she thought. Let him be alive.

She whipped the car down the road, gas pedal flat to the floor. Her heart raced and tears ran down her face. Pictures of L.T. flashed through her mind like a collection of snapshots. Standing in her doorway with his easy grin; massaging her neck; hiking back to her grandfather's favourite spot; making love behind the waterfall.

She had never been utterly sure about her feelings for L.T., but now, in the moment where she feared losing him, her need for him was absolute.

There was little traffic on the lake road, but Kris recklessly bypassed what there was, pulling out blind on a hill to pass a wheezing pickup truck. She didn't care about herself right now, she just had to get there in time.

The flashing lights of the fire trucks were visible a mile off, bouncing off the wet forest that came right to the edge of the road, the damp pavement a narrow channel cut through its primitive immensity.

One fire truck was parked across the road, stopping traffic a few hundred yards from the actual accident scene. Three cars and a big black pickup had pulled off to the side of the road, half a dozen people out of their vehicles, looking ahead to see what had happened. Kris pulled in behind the pickup, grabbed a notepad and her digital camera off the front seat and began to sprint up the centre of the highway. As she neared the fire truck, a cop stepped out and raised his hand, signalling her to halt. He was heavy and middle-aged, his wet uniform clinging to his belly. Hancock, his name tag said.

"Media," Kris said, waving the tools of the trade. "Down from Plattsburgh."

Hancock squinted at her, as if she looked familiar, then said, "All right, but don't get underfoot."

She ran past the fire truck. Now the view of what lay ahead

was clearer. She saw a red Blazer, on its side. The pavement was scarred where the truck had slid before ramming into a stand of spruce trees. The impact had compacted the vehicle, as if it had been stomped on. The raw smell of gasoline filled the air, and it made a rainbow stain on the highway.

Firefighters were prying the passenger door open with a large metal bar, while three more cops and two ambulance attendants stood back, watching. The firefighters worked steadily, but to Kris it looked as if they were going in slow motion. Why didn't they hurry?

When she reached the little clot of uniformed men, she was out of breath, but managed to gasp, "Media, Plattsburgh," to justify her presence.

Drawing in a desperate lungful of air, she said "The driver. Is he going to be all right?"

One of the ambulance guys, young, crewcut, said, "We couldn't get a response and we can't get in. He's trapped behind the wheel on the bottom. They'll have him out in a minute."

They all turned to see a red GMC Suburban pick its way around the other emergency vehicles. The driver parked it and jammed a fire helmet on his head as he got out. He was a big, broad-shouldered man still wearing a mechanic's greasy overalls. She recognized Vic Desmarais, the volunteer fire chief, according to what was painted on the side of his truck. He was one of the few people she still remembered from school. He took no notice of her.

"Jesus Christ!" Desmarais shouted. "Let's get some hoses ready. We've got bloody gasoline all over the place. Wash this highway down!"

Desmarais waved urgently for the three firefighters whose truck was blocking the road to move up and get into action.

"Why don't they use the jaws of life?" Kris asked.

"Mechanical extrication?" one of the cops said. "They don't have it. Too expensive."

Desmarais was at the Blazer now, adding to the leverage being exerted on the heavy metal bar. His effort was enough to finally spring the crushed passenger side door open.

Now he waved up the ambulance guys. One of them scrambled up the vehicle, and into the cab.

Come on, come on, Kris thought. Say he's okay.

When the crewcut ambulance attendant wriggled back out of the cab and dropped to the ground, she knew from his body language.

She sunk to her knees, wordless, gasping for breath.

"He's gone," the ambulance guy said, loud enough for them all to hear.

"All right. Let's get him out of there, get this cleaned up," Desmarais said, his tone resigned now, no longer urgent.

"Hey."

They all turned to see Hancock running toward them, belly bouncing.

"Just ran the plates," he shouted. "That's L.T. Hill in there."

The cop standing beside Kris threw his cap on the ground and said "Ah shit. L.T. Hill?"

Desmarais looked confused. "Hill?" he said.

"One of ours," Hancock said. "The new guy."

"Fuck," Desmarais said. Then he ran back to the Blazer, signalling his men to follow.

"Come on, let's get him out. Now. This goddamn thing could catch fire."

Kris was still on her knees on the cold, wet pavement, shivering as the icy rain trickled down her back. Now, in death, L.T. was getting the comradeship and consideration that had been denied him by his fellow officers. She supposed he would have found it funny, but they would never share another laugh again.

They were making progress now in getting whatever was left of L.T. from the truck. Kris watched the scene in front of her with horror and guilt in the certain knowledge that she had sent L.T. to his death.

18

Police Chief Larry Brewster slid his heavy white mug of instant coffee nervously from hand to hand, the bottom grinding against the rough surface of Kris's wooden kitchen table. His face was haggard and grey, his khaki uniform rumpled.

"I thought I should come by," he said. "L.T. has no people around here, and I understood that the two of you were . . ." Brewster searched for the right word, and settled for "close."

Closer than even Kris had realized, until L.T. was gone. He'd crept up on her, getting inside her guard, then getting nearer to the core of her than anyone else ever had. She'd told L.T. things about her past that she didn't think she'd ever share.

After the ambulance drove away with his body, Kris had come back to the cabins. She had felt numb, drained, but then the sight of his empty place set her off again. She felt as responsible for his death as if she'd steered the truck into those trees. He'd died on her errand, sacrificed himself in her vain quest.

She'd finally fallen asleep just before dawn. Larry Brewster had awakened her at nine, getting his obligations out of the way early. She was sure she must look like hell, with her mussed, unwashed hair, an old red fleece bathrobe wound tightly around her. Right now, she didn't care.

"So, the accident. What do you think caused it?" she asked.

"We haven't completed our investigation yet, but it looks like speed. There's a tight turn there, the road was slick. L.T. liked to drive too fast. Those damn SUVs roll over easy. Once they flip, you're screwed."

She remembered how quickly L.T. drove, but always with great confidence. His vehicle was hardly a sports car, but he seemed to be able to handle it like one.

"You're right," she said. "He did drive fast. But he was a good driver."

"Of course he was, but cops all like to push it. It's a fine line."

The chief reached out and patted her hand, as if he were a kindly uncle. Even though she knew that L.T. hadn't trusted him, she almost let down her guard. There was no one with whom she could share the real story of L.T.'s death. If his suspicions had been right, though, the chief was here on a fishing expedition for the senator.

"Where was he going, did he say?" the chief asked.

"No, I have no idea. What direction was he heading?"

"West."

From the timing of the accident, she would have thought east. The way the truck had spun around, it was difficult to say at the site. The fire trucks hadn't been called out until five-thirty. He was supposed to have met the general at five, but it sounded as if he'd never reached the rendezvous. What had happened all that time?

"I think he left here just before four-thirty," she said. "What time did the accident take place?"

"We're not sure yet. We got a cell phone call from a passing motorist just before five-thirty."

"A motorist? Did he stop to help?"

The chief shook his head, not hiding his look of disgust.

"I don't know what the hell is the matter with people. Who-ever the guy was, he just drove on. Probably couldn't have done anything useful anyway, but you'd think most people would stay."

"So you say that was five-thirty, but he'd left an hour before, and was only fifteen miles outside of town. Anything about that strike you funny, Chief?"

"Well, that's a lonely stretch of road. Sometimes you can go a long while without a vehicle passing up there."

Kris wasn't so convinced that he was going west. Once she'd pulled herself together, she would drive back to the accident scene, check the skid marks. If he hadn't met with the general yet, then it was unlikely that Osborne and his gang were responsible for L.T.'s death. They wanted him to arrive at the rendezvous, so they could get that videotape. But if he'd already met with them, he was expendable. Could they have arranged something, driven him off the road?

"L.T. kept quite a lot of stuff in his truck. What will happen to it?" she asked.

"Yeah, there was a load of outdoor stuff. It's all back at the station. I guess we'll send it on to his folks, if they want it. If not, we'll put it in the annual stolen bike sale we have."

"Nothing unusual in the truck, was there?"

Like $50,000 in cash, she was thinking. If the money was in the truck, did it quietly disappear into someone's pocket?

The chief shook his head, interested by her question. "Unusual like what?"

Now she had trapped herself. It was a bad question to have asked.

Kris looked down, willing her face to redden.

"Some, how can I describe them, personal items. We were . . ."

The chief held up both hands in protest.

"Enough said. I didn't pick through every little thing. Has nothing to do with the investigation of the accident. Why don't you stop by the station, sort out anything that's yours. Just sign for personal items, no need to describe them."

"Thanks, Chief. You're very understanding."

She wondered what kind of things the chief thought she and L.T. kept in that truck — kinky sex toys?

"Will there be a funeral here?"

"No. We've sent the body back to his folks in Wilmington. They are looking after everything down there."

"You sent it back already?"

"Yep. Coroner had a look. Doc Hooper."

"Cause of death?"

"Blow to the head, I'd say. We haven't seen the official report yet."

She hadn't been able to see L.T.'s body after the accident. Now it was gone. It made the whole thing seem surreal, as if he had just disappeared.

"Well, I guess that's about it, then," the chief said. "I just wanted to fill you in. L.T. Hill was a fine officer, by the way, well respected. Hell of a football player, too. Did you ever see him play?"

"No, that was before I knew him."

"I suppose you don't follow college ball, being up in Canada. He was a big name. This story is going to be in all the papers. I've already had calls from half a dozen reporters."

For all that L.T. was, he would be remembered for his ability to run with a football. What a stupid world, Kris thought

"Chief, I do appreciate you coming by. Very thoughtful. I'll be around to the station to pick up those few things. When do you think you'll complete your investigation of the accident? I'd just be interested to see what you conclude."

The chief's look was warier now. "It's going to play out about like I told you. Just a matter of the paperwork.

"I suppose you'll be heading back to Canada now. Not much to keep you here."

That confirmed the primary reason for the chief's visit. Without L.T., the Osborne gang was lacking its inside info on Kris's plans.

"Oh, within days," she said. "Just a few little things to tidy up."

No use giving them a further reason to come after her. L.T.'s death was probably just a horrible accident, but she wasn't leaving Osborne until she found out what really happened. She owed him that much.

Kris showed the chief to the door, and then saw that a second police cruiser was parked in front of L.T.'s cabin, two officers loading his clothes and personal things into the back of the vehicle.

"We're going to box it all up, FedEx it back down to the parents," the chief said. "Nothing in there that you want, is there?"

"No," she said quickly, thinking of the $25,000 down payment from the general. L.T. had said that he was going to bury it. Had he? She didn't want Osborne's filthy money herself, but if he'd left it somewhere where it could be found, it would raise more awkward questions.

"Well," the chief said, putting on his hat. "I guess that's about it. Have a safe journey back."

19

As much as Kris distrusted the chief, she had been sorry to see him go. With his car and the other cruiser parked out front, she had felt a momentary sense of safety. She doubted very much that the Osborne police were the good guys, but there was surely a limit to what Lowell Osborne and the Naylors would pull right in front of them.

Now, an hour later, she was all too alone. She and L.T. had been the only two long-term rentals at Jasper's. Over the past three weeks, the occasional budget-minded tourist had rented a cabin, but after Labour Day, Osborne's anemic tourist industry pretty much shut down.

She had locked the cabin, but its flimsy wooden door wouldn't withstand a single well-placed kick. The thin white curtains that she had pulled closed didn't even shield her from anyone who wanted to look in. She peered out the window, as she had done several times already, but saw nothing more than pine trees bending in the wind that whipped across the point. The only sign of life was a single black squirrel sitting on the picnic table in front of her cabin, sunning itself and chattering as the wind ruffled its fur.

Rationally, Kris told herself that she wasn't in any danger right now. But what would it be like after dark?

She realized that it was stupid to stay there like a sitting duck, in the first place they'd look for her. If L.T. hadn't given them the copy of the tape, they'd be coming to get it, and her cabin was the logical place to find it.

She wanted to phone Colin, just to hear a familiar voice, but after the way things had gone during their last call, she felt that door was closed. And what would she tell him? That her boyfriend had been killed in a car crash and she thought some guys were coming to get her next?

No, the thing was to take action. To get moving. First, Kris thought, she had to check L.T.'s cabin, see if she could find that $25,000. She only hoped that the police hadn't already done so. She didn't want to leave a trail that would allow anyone to suggest later that L.T. had been a dirty cop.

Kris had had a hell of a time trying to find a hiding place for the video in her Spartan cabin. No bigger than a single-car garage, it wasn't exactly a likely spot for concealment. She had finally settled on duct-taping the video to the underside of the kitchen sink. It wasn't a bad hiding place, but it wouldn't stand up to any kind of a thorough search.

She got on her hands and knees, reaching awkwardly under the sink. She could feel the video, but the duct tape had done a better than expected job of holding it in place. She pulled open the utensil drawer, looking for something with which to cut it away. Among the usual collection of garage sale odds and ends was a six-inch paring knife of reasonably decent quality. It had a solid black handle and some weight to it. She used the knife to cut away the tape, stripping the sticky remnants off and stuffing them in the garbage. She put the tape in her big black purse, thought a moment, then dropped the knife in, too. It wasn't much of a weapon, but it was better than nothing.

She locked the door of her own cabin and crunched across the gravel driveway twenty feet to L.T.'s. As she had hoped, the police hadn't bothered to lock it. The empty brown interior seemed lifeless now, as stripped and anonymous as if he'd never been there. One white sports sock dropped by the bed was the only sign of L.T.'s presence. She willed herself not to visualize the times they had spent together in this little room.

He hadn't told her where he was going to put the money, and she hadn't thought it important to ask. After checking under the bed, inside the couch, inside the toilet tank, and her own idea of a hiding place, up behind the sink, she finally thought to check the woodstove. A risky place to store paper, but perhaps a good one because of that. She found the money, neatly bundled, in a copper side container that was used to boil water. She remembered her Uncle Martin having one like that in his Ontario cabin. Many times she had had to start the thing early in the morning, on days when he wasn't inclined to get up. The money made a compact brick, 250 $100 bills. She put it in her purse, for now. Maybe she'd give it to the poor.

Kris had been to the police station only once, the day she first asked about the investigation of Kathy's death, and Larry Brewster had brushed her off. The station, really just an extension of the municipal building, looked cheap and improvised, like so much in Osborne, Kris thought. It was a white, aluminum-sided extrusion that jutted out from the original, clapboard building and filled most of the parking lot. She was happy to see the chief's car there. Going through the stuff from L.T.'s truck was the logical first step in searching for the copy of the video, but she didn't want to have to explain the whole thing again.

She sat in her car for a moment, steeling herself for what she had to do that day. Her natural inclination was to release herself into grief, lock herself away and cry L.T. out of her system. She didn't have the luxury of doing that. If she was going to find out what really happened to him, she needed to act and she didn't have much time. She had to suppress her feelings for now. Fortunately, her life's many sorrows had given her lots of experience.

When she walked in to the little office, Larry Brewster was standing by the desk of the officer she recognized from the accident, Hancock, and they were laughing, apparently sharing a joke. The period of mourning for L.T. hadn't even lasted until lunch. Maybe they had all chipped in to send a Hallmark card to his family.

The place lacked any of the sense of hustle or urgency she always associated with real police stations. It looked more like a small insurance office, and maybe, in a way, it was.

"Chief?" she said. "I'm here to get my things."

"Oh, right," he said, offering a half wave. She was aware that Hancock and two others she didn't know were sizing her up. Their thoughts were easy to read. Something like, "So this is the woman L.T. Hill is banging." Was, she corrected herself.

"It's all in the property room," the chief said. "Quite a mess of stuff."

The chief gestured for her to follow him, then headed through a door and down a set of stairs that led back toward the municipal building. The stone walls reminded her of the cellar of Osborne's lodge. From her position above the chief, she could see that he had a bald spot on top, about the size of the palm of her hand. The bulky cop moved awkwardly down the stairs, as if he were carrying a sack of cement strapped to his middle.

"Bad place to keep stuff," he said, "but we're short of space. The town has been talking about a new police station since I started working here. I don't suppose I'll live to see it happen."

"I'm sure it doesn't reduce your effectiveness," she said, letting him take that any way he wanted.

At the bottom of the stairs, they passed a locked door, and she said, "What's in there?"

"Records," he said hurriedly. "Old stuff. We rarely go in there."

Where L.T. had gone to look for Kathy's file, before finding it on the chief's desk, she thought.

The property room was next to the record room and had an identical metal door, heavy and encrusted with layers of once-white paint. The chief unlocked it with a key he took from his pocket.

"Now, we've got evidence from a number of cases in here, valuables," he said.

She could see a number of DVD players and televisions stored on the shelves, and a box labelled "Jewellery Theft." Before he could go any further, she cut in.

"Look, Chief, I'm not going to steal any of the stuff. Just give me a minute, will you?"

Apparently remembering their earlier conversation, he got a bit red-faced and scratched the back of his neck, uncertain about this breach of procedure.

"Why don't you just wait in the hall. If I'm lugging out anything big, you'll spot it."

"No problem, no problem," he said. "We just have procedures, that's all. I'll have to make you sign for anything you remove. Just for the records."

"Right — it's not like you need L.T.'s stuff for a charge, or a trial. There was no crime committed, right?"

"Of course not. We are going to FedEx this stuff to his parents, like I told you. I just want to make sure it's all intact."

"Did you go through it all, itemize the things?" she asked. If they had, her trip would be in vain, but she was betting they were too sloppy or lazy to do it right.

"We should have," the chief said, rubbing a whiskery jowl, "but I don't think there has been time yet. Look, just take what's yours, we'll organize the rest and get it going. I'll be right out here in the hall if you need me."

"Thanks," she said, forcing a smile.

He returned it, like they were on the same side now.

The goods from L.T.'s truck were contained in a large cardboard box and a black duffle bag big enough to hide a body in. She quickly scanned the box. Two softballs, a bat, hiking boots, a football, a fly rod in a blue case, the spinning rod she had used, and a green canvas creel. She opened the creel, but it contained nothing but an assortment of trout flies. She removed one and slid the hook through the material of her T-shirt, like a brooch. It would be the only physical reminder of L.T. she had.

The duffel bag seemed more promising, but held nothing but a catcher's scuffed, red shin pads and mask, cleats, two ball gloves, and a uniform jersey. The bright yellow shirt had his name across the top, then "McGRUER'S ESSO" in bigger letters. It was where L.T. always bought his gas, a man of habit in small things. No videotape, no $50,000. Kris closed the bag, sealing in the stink of athletics.

She took the fishing rod and stepped back into the hall. "Just a fishing rod, I guess, Chief. It's always hard to remember what you keep in someone else's car."

"Yeah, I suppose," the chief said, apparently unfamiliar with this particular dilemma. "So you're done, then?"

"All set," she said, following him back up the stairs. He made even slower progress than on the way down, gravity being no longer in his favour.

Halfway up, she said, "Tell me, what do you do with wrecks like L.T.'s truck? Doesn't look like you have a pound."

The chief's back stiffened and he hesitated just a bit between steps. "Vic Desmarais tows them, keeps them locked in his compound until we give the go ahead to release them. Why do you ask?"

"Oh, just a reporter's instinct. We're always asking questions," she said.

Vic Desmarais's garage would be her next stop.

"That Blazer is a write-off, but we have to hang onto it until the insurance company sends a guy down from Plattsburgh for a look-see. They'll cut some kind of a cheque for L.T.'s estate. I'm sure his parents could use the cash."

"Do you know them?" Kris asked.

"Daddy's a preacher. That's all I know. Those fellows are always short of dough, unless they have their own TV show."

They were back in the office now, Kris being stared at again by the other three cops. There wasn't a friendly word or look among them. Did they blame her for L.T.'s death, or did they just know she had been branded as trouble?

She felt stupid, standing there with a fishing rod, and quickly reached out to shake the chief's hand. It was soft and disconcertingly wet.

"Thanks for your help," she said.

He didn't reply, and after she closed the door, she heard laughter again from inside.

Vic Desmarais's garage was on the far-east side of town, the first business that trucks saw as they entered Osborne. He had twelve pumps and a parking lot that was big enough to handle eighteen-wheelers, two of which were idling in the pull-in area. The garage itself was a squat, grey, stucco building, the original finish chipping off in hand-sized flakes. It had four bays, each with a vehicle up on the hoist. Behind, an eight-foot fence with three strands of barbed wire curving out on the top prevented access to row after row of battered and crushed trucks and cars.

An oval sign on a thirty-foot-high white pole had "DES-MARAIS'S GARAGE" in big letters that followed the curve of the sign. The words "Gas, Wrecker, Repairs" in the middle succinctly summarized the services offered.

Kris had been surprised to see Vic Desmarais at the accident scene. They had known each other in the early years of high school, but his was one of the many faces that she had forgotten, until yesterday. When she had moved on, she hadn't taken much baggage. Or so she had thought.

Kris parked away from the gas pumps and walked toward the garage, avoiding the oily stains that marked the asphalt. Despite herself, she got a bit of a lift from the warmth of the sun. It was another perfect September day. Nature was cruelly indifferent to human tragedy, she thought.

A mechanic with the name "Josh" embroidered on his coveralls sat at a deeply soiled brown metal desk, filling in a yellow form on a clipboard. He was young, maybe even good-looking if someone cleaned him up.

"Hey, Vic in?"

Josh looked up, apparently surprised to see a woman at the garage. "We got your car in here?"

"No, I just need to talk to Vic."

Josh smiled now, white teeth, his thoughts as obvious as a newspaper headline. Vic Has Girlfriend.

Kris was suddenly aware that she probably looked like hell. She'd hardly slept, no makeup, she'd just let her short hair dry whichever way it wanted to. She was wearing stained jeans and a white T-shirt that was maybe too tight, now with a fishing fly stuck in the top of it. Maybe that's why the cops were laughing.

"He's in the yard," Josh said. "I'll go get him. Who should I say is here?"

"Kris Redner," more businesslike, now. "It's about the accident yesterday, with the Blazer."

Josh nodded, disappointed.

Kris remained in the doorway of the little office. She didn't fancy sitting on the one chair, its yellow foam padding hanging out. It was even filthier than the rest of the room. The floor tiles were curled and chipped, and the window probably hadn't been cleaned since it was installed. The place was a hole, but it looked as if Vic was making money; probably a success story by Osborne standards.

He surprised her by coming up behind her.

"Kris?" he said, then smiled when she turned to face him. He was about L.T.'s size, maybe even broader, wavy black hair with just a touch of grey. He wore the same greasy blue coverall as yesterday, or its twin, and heavy workboots, one steel toe shining through the scuffed leather.

"Jesus Christ, Kris Redner. I haven't seen you since high school."

He held out a hand to shake, saw that it was slippery with oil, then pulled it back again.

"Actually, you saw me at the Blazer accident yesterday, but you were pretty busy."

"Yeah, that was a bad one. Josh says you're here about it. What's the connection?"

"The driver, L.T. Hill, was a friend."

"Shit, I'm sorry. How can I help?"

She wondered if Vic was someone she could trust. He had a connection to the Osborne police, but her gut instinct said that he was all right. It seemed unlikely that he was someone whom Lowell Osborne or the Naylors would have any real influence over, or even know. Vic was way on the wrong side of town.

"I'm looking for something that was in the car," she said. "A videotape. It's background for a story I'm working on."

"Hey, are you on television?" Vic asked.

"No, I work for a newspaper up in Ottawa. I'm here on assignment."

"Oh right, Ottawa."

She was glad the name of the country's capital city was familiar to him. Kris had been in Canada long enough to adopt the irritation Canadians felt when Americans showed a lack of curiosity about the nation that was rumoured to lie to the north.

"Let's take a look," he said, leading her through the garage toward the wrecker's yard in the back. All four mechanics downed tools as she passed, staring with open curiosity at the woman with whom Vic was so friendly. Kris sometimes wondered if Osborne men had ever seen a woman who hadn't spent her whole life in the town.

"You say you're looking for something," he said. "You might not be the only one. The whole interior of that vehicle was torn up."

"Not because of the accident?'

"No, after."

"Cops say anything about that?"

"Not a thing. I mentioned it to them, they told me it was just a traffic accident, don't worry about it."

"That's not right," she said, her mind filled with a horrifying image of L.T., trapped and dying in the truck as Naylor or one of his underlings looked for the tape. Once L.T. had failed to show, the general must have sent them after it. Why had she ever agreed to go along with his idea of giving them that copy? She should have pulled the plug on the whole thing as soon as the general had made his first pitch to L.T. But he had seemed so confident, so sure he could handle it.

"No, it's not, but they just pay me to haul away the wrecks, not figure things out," Vic said.

"They don't seem to pay anyone to figure things out around here," Kris said. "That's one thing I've noticed since I came back."

"Yeah, it's not exactly CSI," Vic said. "Those fucking guys, someone broke into the garage last year, took over ten grand in tools, it took them three days to come around, write up a report. Never caught them, either. I'm telling you, we should have the state police in here, like everyone else."

"The senator wouldn't like that," Kris said.

Vic laughed. "Didn't take you long to pick up the thread, did it? If the senator doesn't like something, it's not happening."

They walked through a long row of battered Chevs, Chryslers, and Ford pickups, most with doors hanging off or hoods sprung and engines removed. The ground was rutted with the tracks of a heavy truck and still held puddles where they were deepest. There was a stink of oil and rusting machinery.

"So how did you get the police contract?" Kris asked.

"Only wrecker in town," Vic said. "It's not because they love me, that's for sure. That and being fire chief. It gives me a certain status as a good guy."

"And are you a good guy?" Kris asked. "I haven't met many since I came to Osborne."

"That's a strange question, Kris. I'm not part of the group that lines up to kiss Lowell Osborne's ass, if that's what you mean."

"Something like that. Jeez, the lineups must be brutal, huh?"

Desmarais smiled. "The Blazer's at the back here."

She saw L.T.'s familiar truck, its top crushed in on the driver's side, windows broken out, and the body battered like someone had gone after it with a baseball bat. There was a stained, star-shaped crack in the windshield that she decided she wouldn't dwell on.

Kris opened the passenger door with a scraping of metal on metal. She saw what Desmarais had meant. The glove compartment was hanging open, its contents spread on the passenger seat. The carpets were torn up, plastic side panels ripped from the doors. Even the fabric of the roof had been cut away.

"Whoever did this, I hope to hell the driver was already dead. Makes you sick thinking about it. You say this was all over a videotape?"

Kris thought she might be willing to trust Vic, but it was too early to decide that.

"I don't know what they were looking for," she said. "I'm looking for the tape, but only because I need it for my story. I don't know why anyone else would want it."

"What's the story about?" he asked.

"Tourism."

She went around to the driver's side of the truck. The plastic that covered the gauges had bent and shattered, but she could see the trip odometer. L.T. faithfully reset it every time he got gas. It read 14.7 miles. So he had never made the rendezvous, but Kris still had no idea whether the general had recovered the tape.

"When you get a car in like this, traffic accident, is there any kind of investigation of mechanical failure, whether that might have caused the crash?"

"Sometimes, if there is no apparent reason for the crash. This time, the police were sure it was speed and wet roads. Makes sense to me. The roads are nasty in those turns on a wet day. You've really got to watch yourself."

"Do me a favour?" Kris asked.

"Name it."

"Would you mind checking this truck out, see if there was

any problem with the brakes or steering, whatever? Something that might have contributed to the crash. I'll pay whatever it costs."

"Hey, don't worry about that. I'll take a look at it myself. Should be able to get at it later today. Tomorrow morning at the latest. How's that sound?"

"Great, Vic, thanks."

He smiled, then looked down and put his hands in his overall pockets.

"Look, Kris, it's good to see you again after so many years. This is going to sound funny, but I sometimes think of you. As the one who got away, you know what I mean? Pretty much everyone else from high school is still here in town. That's sure not the way we thought it was going to go, back then."

"You've done all right, though."

"Yeah, it's okay. You know what I wanted to be?"

"I don't remember," she said. "All I wanted to be was out of here."

"Yeah, well, I wanted to be an actor. Crazy huh?"

She looked him over appraisingly. She could see it. He was big, good looking, nice smile. How much more was required?

"I don't think so. You should have gone for it."

"Yeah, well, I got married at twenty-one. Three kids . . ."

"Well, I should be going," she said. She wasn't in a mood to hear his life story.

"Okay, well, great to see you again. Is there somewhere I can reach you, let you know if I find anything?"

"I'm not going to be home much. Let me get back to you," she said.

"Fine. I've got some stuff to do back here. Looking for a tranny for a Chrysler minivan. Those things eat them. Can you find your way back?"

"No problem, and thanks again."

As she picked her way back through the mud and ruts of the wrecker's yard, she hoped that Vic hadn't been acting when he said he wasn't on the Osborne team. She'd rather that word of her continued inquiries didn't find its way back to Osborne or the Naylors right away.

20

The green door of her cabin hung crookedly on its hinges, the handle smashed from the splintered wood and lying on the verandah floor. The screen door gaped open.

Bastards.

Kris's anger was followed by a quick shiver of fear, which she immediately suppressed. She stuck her purse and the videotape under the seat, took out the six-inch paring knife and got cautiously out of the car. There wasn't another vehicle in sight. Whoever had broken in was surely long gone, but she didn't want to let down her guard.

A big oak tree to the left of the cabin placed it in the shadow of the late afternoon sun. Kris couldn't see clearly inside, but there was no visible movement. The only sound was the shrieking of a blue jay.

She stepped onto the creaking verandah, and stopped.

"Whoever's in there, get out. Now," she said, in her best imitation of a cop's tone of command.

Nothing moved.

She cautiously eased the door farther open, the damage causing its bottom to drag on the floor. After what she had seen done to the Blazer, she expected the place to be ripped up, but this was a more thorough, leisurely job. Everything had been emptied from the kitchen cupboards and piled in a heap on the floor. Pots, dishes, flour, sugar, rice, every bag or box slit open. Milk, beer, and eggs from the fridge had been tossed on top. Flies buzzed and crawled around the whole mess, and it was already beginning to stink. The fridge door was open, the light on, but it had been cleared out. A stream of water ran to the floor from the freezer compartment. The kitchen table had been turned over, to see if anything was attached to the bottom. It was a hiding spot she had considered at one time.

Kris moved cautiously to the little partitioned corner that served as a bedroom. The mattress had been pulled from the bed and slashed in several places, the pillows cut up. Her entrance caused feathers to float in the air. The four doors of the cheap wooden dresser had been wrenched open, and her clothing tossed around the room. In the midst of the chaos, there was one point of order.

On the top of the little dresser were three sets of her underwear, neatly arranged in pairs. The cups of each of the three bras, black, red, and blue, were slit from top to bottom and gaping open. The matching black and red panties had the crotches ripped out, and then had been carefully placed below the bras. The blue panties were intact, except for a large stain of semen, not yet dry. Its funky odour filled the little room.

Kris suddenly felt dizzy and dropped to her knees.

Bud Naylor. She remembered what he had done to Sharon Sloan, and probably to her sister as well. This was almost certainly his calling card.

The search of the cabin wasn't that big a surprise. It was the next logical step. She wasn't prepared for the other part. Seeing her things displayed this way, knowing that Bud Naylor had pawed through them, used them, made her feel violated. The tearing and cutting suggested a tremendous anger. What would he do when he got the chance to unleash it on her?

She briefly considered calling the town police, but that would just bring another group of men through her bedroom. A second violation. She was sure they'd attribute the break-in to teenage vandals, too. They certainly wouldn't be asking Bud Naylor what he'd been doing that afternoon.

Kris numbly picked up her overnight bag, which had been tossed in the corner. Ignoring the underwear, she gathered up her T-shirts and jeans, stuffing them into the small black suitcase. She couldn't stay here anymore, that was obvious.

With a broom, dustpan, and plastic garbage bag, she began to clean up the mess. No use leaving it so Rick Jasper could see her humiliation, too. She was certain the tourist camp owner would be billing her for the damage to the door. He didn't seem like the type to have insurance.

After fifteen minutes of sweeping and shovelling, she finally got to the mess in front of the fridge. Half a dozen beers were imbedded in the flour, rice, and sugar. She pulled one out. Not cold, but after rinsing it under the kitchen tap, she cracked it open. It went down so quickly, she tried another.

Kris had just snapped open her third beer when she heard the knock at her screen door. She jumped, reaching toward the counter for the paring knife.

When she turned, there was Betsy Larson, peering into the dim light of the cabin, Tom silhouetted behind her. Kris groaned. Betsy was a bit tough to take at the best of times, and after all she had just been through, the only company Kris wanted came in a brown bottle.

"Kris?" Betsy called, her voice singsong. "We came to see if you were okay."

Kris banged the bottle of beer on the counter and walked to the screen door, in no hurry. She looked through it without opening it.

"I brought you flowers," Betsy said, holding up large multi-coloured bouquet that she had probably just cut in her own garden. Daisies were the only type Kris recognized. Flowers weren't really her thing.

Kris held the screen door open. As unwelcome as Betsy and Tom's visit was, she supposed it might be well-intended, and she still had a modicum of the insincere pleasantry that kept society's wheels greased. Good thing they hadn't come one beer later.

"Hey, what happened to your door?" Betsy asked, once she was inside. Tom inspected the damage, running his fingers along the broken wood.

Betsy reared back as she almost stepped in the remains of the mess on the floor.

"Kris, what's going on?" Tom asked.

"Break-in," she said tersely. "Probably some kids."

"Jesus, they really tore the place up," Tom said.

"You should have been here an hour ago," Kris said.

Betsy hugged Kris, enveloping her in perfume and soft, bare arms. She wore a white sundress with spaghetti straps. Kris stiffly accepted the embrace, not reciprocating. There hadn't been a whole lot of hugging in her family and she had never developed the habit some women have, of embracing and kissing every time they saw each other.

Tom hung back near the door, unsure of what to do. He was more sombrely dressed today, black golf shirt and black Dockers. Casual mourning clothes, she guessed. His look of sympathy seemed genuine, although he'd certainly had lots of opportunity to develop it in his line of work.

"This is awful," Betsy said. "What must you think about people here?

"We just came by to express our condolences about L.T. It's just so terrible. He seemed like a really nice young guy."

"Yes, he was."

Kris wasn't offering much, trying to read Betsy. She worked for the senator, and Kris was certain that a combination of loyalty and hero worship would compel her to report back on everything about Kris, on the off chance the senator hadn't already been fully apprised of the latest effort to drive her off. That was one of the things she didn't know; did the senator approve Bud Naylor's adventures in advance, or was Bud showing initiative? One thing was certain. Her knee hadn't caused any permanent damage to his testicles. It must be time for a tune-up.

Since she had walked in the cabin door, her emotions had been swinging between rage and fear. Rage was beginning to gain the upper hand. Who did this bastard think he was, anyway?

"What are you going to do about this?" Tom asked, gesturing around the cabin.

"Clean it up," Kris said. "But if I ever find out who did it, he's going to be sorry he was born."

There was a message to take back to Bud and the senator.

"Did they take anything?" Betsy asked.

"No. There was nothing valuable here. That's probably why they went nuts, tore the place up."

"You should call the police," Tom said.

Kris shook her head.

"I don't think so, Tom. Larry Brewster and his boys aren't going to bust their asses over a break-in at a rental cabin, especially one rented by me. Let's be honest, I'm not very popular in this town."

"No, you're not," Tom said. "But not everyone in Osborne thinks the same way. Like you, some of us have actually spent a little time in the real world. We're not all just a cheering section for the senator."

Tell that to Betsy, Kris thought, immediately wondering if the senator had ever made a run at her. Was the generous funding for Tom's clinic a guilt payment?

"Really?" she said. "I thought you and the senator were old friends from way back."

"We are, but that doesn't mean I approve of everything Lowell does, or has ever done."

Tom was looking right at her now, as if Betsy weren't even there. Was he referring to her sister's death, telling her something, without telling her? She fought against her tendency to give Tom more credit than he was due. She had been attracted to his handsome, strong face and gentle manner the first night she had met him. Lowell Osborne was supposed to be the charmer, but she found him utterly slick and phoney. Tom was more her type.

Kris shook her head. What was she thinking? L.T. just dead, and she was letting her judgment be affected by the good looks of a guy who could be one of the three who raped her sister.

"Kris? Are you okay?" Betsy asked.

"Yes, sure. Just a bit shaken up by all of this."

"Look," Betsy said. "You can't stay here tonight in all this mess, no proper door. Why don't you stay at our place? We've got plenty of room."

Betsy looked so concerned, almost motherly, that Kris feared another hug couldn't be far off. The idea of staying over was attractive. The alternative was one of the cheap motels on the east side of town, but even that wouldn't offer much protection. She needed to be someplace where Naylor couldn't easily find her. He was obviously out to get the tape, and he wasn't going to stop until he found it.

Betsy and Tom smiled expectantly, sure she would take up their generous offer. She wondered if they had already made up the guest bedroom, knowing what they would find when they got to her cabin.

Kris decided to go with her instinct. She just didn't trust them. In their house, asleep, she might as well be right in the hands of Bud Naylor.

"Look, that's really kind," she said. "I was thinking I might actually hit the road. My suitcase is packed. Things here haven't turned out the way I hoped."

"No, and I'm sorry about that," Tom said. "You were trying to do the right thing."

"Well, if you think you should go, I certainly understand it," Betsy said. "After all you've been through."

Betsy and Tom were trying not to appear too eager, but she was sure that if she had a hat, they'd be handing it to her. Kris would bet that their next stop would be to tell either Naylor or Osborne that the problem was solved; the nosey journalist was going home.

"Well, it would be best," Kris said.

It would be useful for the other side to think she was running home, even if it was the last thing she'd do. She had a few other plans, and Tom and Betsy's report just might give her a bit of breathing space.

21

Kris edged the car carefully onto the soft, narrow gravel shoulder. Were it not for the half-dozen sheared-off spruce trees, she could have driven right by the spot. Where yesterday there had been fire trucks and police cars with their lights flashing, now there was silence, except for a light wind sifting through the trees. The hill that the road was cut through banked up steeply, and the trees had already darkened the pavement with their shadows. Perhaps she should have waited until morning, but she wanted to check the crash scene before someone else had the same idea, if it wasn't already too late.

She walked up the centre of the road, not a car in sight in either direction. There was perhaps half a mile of straightaway ahead, but visibility behind was limited by the tight turn that had proven too much for L.T.'s Blazer.

Kris willed herself not to think about L.T. It would take away her ability to look at the situation logically. Looking back down the road, she tried to visualize what had happened. He had come out of the turn, obviously too fast. Fifty feet ahead, she could see the road surface was scraped, flakes of red paint adhering to its surface. By that point, his truck had flipped. What she didn't see were any skid marks. Surely, losing control, he'd have put on the brakes. It was instinctive.

Kris walked back down the road to where the turn began. No tire marks of any kind. She was no accident scene specialist, but there was something wrong with that.

Turning back, she headed to where the truck had come to rest among the trees. The smell of the sap from the broken spruces filled the air, their trunks white and jagged. There was still a suggestion of the smell of gasoline.

The tops of the trees had been pushed back into the forest. She supposed a works crew would eventually come and cut them up. Around the base of the ruined trees, she saw the usual detritus of an accident. Shattered glass sparkled on the ground, along with fragments of headlights and turn signals. One hubcap rested on its side, leaning against a tree trunk.

Kris edged toward the mess, her shoes slipping in the loose gravel. At the bottom of the ditch, turned upside down, she saw a baseball cap. Picking it up, she recognized it as L.T.'s navy Blue Devils cap, with its capital D, and a stylized picture of the devil inset. The hat was still damp from yesterday's rain, and dirty from the ditch. She brushed it off, then clutched it to her.

When the tears started, she made no effort to hold them back. Since his death, she had tried to suppress her emotions, to be controlled, focused, as if this were just another murder story. Who was she trying to kid?

Poor L.T. He'd tried to be her white knight, and he'd gotten knocked right off his horse.

Then she saw something else, farther up in the ditch. Wiping the tears from her blurry eyes, she recognized a familiar black, oblong shape. A videotape. It must have been thrown clear on impact, just like the hat.

She scrambled along the bottom of the ditch and picked it up. The case was old, broken now, and the tape itself unfurled in a twisted loop. In his efforts to rip apart the truck, Naylor had read L.T. wrong, assuming everyone would think like him. If you had something valuable, you'd hide it. It would be like L.T. just to set the tape on the truck seat. And why not? He was on his way to give it up.

Kris considered putting the tape back where it had lain, see if Naylor would think to look for it, but he hadn't been smart enough to do it yet. From what had happened back at her cabin, it was clear he assumed she still had the tape, and that the rendezvous with L.T. had been some kind of trick.

Well, that was the way it was going to play then. Straight up. No more tricks. Her against Naylor and Osborne.

She took the tape and hurled it as hard as she could, into the forest. It disappeared without a sound.

Kris got Colin on his cell phone, caught in Queensway traffic, the usual six-lane rush hour snarl of people heading downtown. She was parked at the lookout where L.T. and the general were to have had their rendezvous, the undulating green forest spread out before her.

"Kris? I'm surprised to hear from you," he said, his tone as cold as Wellington Street in January.

"It's been a bit busy down here."

"Glad to hear it. Late for a meeting myself."

Colin obviously hadn't mellowed since their last conversation, but she needed to talk to someone and he was the only possible ally she had.

"Look Colin. I'm sorry about the way things went the last time we talked. You just don't understand how important all of this is to me. Now, don't be an ass. I need to talk to someone I can trust. I really need you to help me work this through."

"Oh, well, all right then," he said, his tone still gruff, but softer.

Kris almost smiled. She had figured the request for help would appeal to his chivalrous side.

"Things aren't going too well down here," she said, then told him how much Osborne's handlers had offered to get the tape, the strategy with the copy, and about how L.T. had died trying to make the delivery.

"Who was this chap L.T.? I don't remember your mentioning him."

"A neighbour," she said quickly. "He offered to help. I never should have let him."

"Well, his choice. Are you all right?"

"Not really."

"I'm sure the accident must have been a shock."

"It's worse than that. The senator's head goon came to the cabin where I'm staying, when I was out, ripped the place up and . . ."

She lowered her voice, even though there was likely no one within miles.

"God, Colin, he tore up my underwear with a knife, then jerked off on them."

"Wanked on your knickers? Fellow's a bloody deviant. I've heard enough. I want you out of there, now. Just get in the car and drive."

Kris put the cell phone down, fighting to control her emotions. She was swinging from anger to tears. Just like a hysterical bloody woman, to choose a phrase popular with Colin.

"Kris? Can you hear me?"

"Yes. Look, there are some things I need to tie up. This accident, for example. I'm not convinced it was an accident. The guy comes around a tight corner and his truck just flips, no sign of skid marks or any attempt to brake. That makes me suspicious. I've got a mechanic going over the vehicle."

"I'm not sure what your obligation is to this chap, Kris, but it's not up to you to investigate accidents. If you actually think Osborne's people might have tampered with the truck, doesn't that make it obvious that you're in danger? You're in the middle of a great, bloody forest. If these blokes decide to snuff you out and toss your body in the bush, it would never be found."

She had thought the same thing, and it made her shiver.

"I'm sorry, Colin. I just can't walk away from this. There's no way those people would be reacting the way they have if they weren't responsible for my sister's death. Now another person has been killed. I set that in motion. I've never backed off a story in my life, and I'm not going to start now."

"You know how much I admire that, Kris, but this isn't just a story. It's become an obsession. It's too personal. If this were happening here, I'd pull you off."

"Well, you can't pull me off this, Colin. I'm suspended, remember? I'm staying on these bastards until I get the truth."

"Still, it's my responsibility to see to your safety. You initiated that story on company time. And, of course . . ."

"No need to say it, and I'm staying," she said. She didn't want to hear any more about Colin's affection for her, but it was still a relief to think they were no longer at war.

"All right then, if you must, but I'm coming down and this time I insist. You can't do this by yourself. Two heads, and all of that. Look, Kris, I've been in war zones around the world. These backwoods bullies don't intimidate me."

She imagined him sucking in his gut and puffing out his chest as he said it. Colin, lubricated by a few pints, was fond of regaling his colleagues with tales of his narrow escapes from death in Lebanon, the Falklands, and Afghanistan.

"Oh shit," he said, and she heard the cell phone fall to the floor of the car.

After a moment, he said, "Sorry, nearly sideswiped a bus. Where were we?"

"You were staying in Ottawa, and I was taking a couple more days to get to the bottom of this. I really appreciate your offer, I do, but I know you're terribly busy. I'm going to be all right. It all sounds worse than it is. Remember, they can't really afford to harm me unless they've got the videotape. It wouldn't do to have it floating around out there. And if I do need help, you will be the first one I'll call."

"Well, I don't like it," he said. "I want you to check in daily."

"All right, don't worry. I can handle it. And Colin, get a hands-free phone, for God's sake."

Kris ended the call. She felt that her tone had been confident, maybe even convincing. She hadn't persuaded herself, though. Perhaps she was just being stubborn, even stupid, in refusing his offer of help. Looking out at the vast, indifferent forest spread in front of her, she had never felt more alone.

22

Patricia Osborne's house looked even more garish at night than it did in the daytime. The centre of the building was a triangle of bronze glass, rising a full three storeys. You couldn't see through the glass, but it glowed from within with a warm light. Two-storey glass wings projected from either side of the central area. These were lit externally by spotlights strategically placed in the deep band of shrubbery surrounding the bizarre structure.

The heating bills must be horrendous, Kris thought, but she didn't suppose Pat Osborne worried much about that.

Kris knew her plan was off the wall and she was prepared for it to go south in a hurry, but her instincts said it wouldn't. If there was any truth to the observation that the enemy of your enemy is your friend, then Pat Osborne ought to be a very good friend indeed. In the time Kris had spent in town, the senator's ex-wife was the only person she had found who didn't fear him. What was better, she loathed him. Kris also needed a place to stay where Bud Naylor wouldn't come looking, and the former Mrs. Osborne's house seemed like just the spot.

She walked up the paving-stone front path and rang the doorbell, amused to see a security company sticker on the glass sidelight of the door. How did you keep someone from breaking into a house made of glass?

Kris expected some kind of servant to answer the door, and was surprised to see Pat herself, in navy silk pyjamas and gold sandals, a cigarette smouldering in her right hand. Even without makeup, she was still a beautiful woman.

"Well, this is a surprise," she said. "Just in the neighbourhood?"

"Something like that. I thought you might be curious about how my story is developing."

Pat took a discreet look at her little diamond-encircled watch.

Even though it was only nine o'clock, she looked as if she were ready for bed. Then it struck Kris that she might have company. "Look, if it's a bad time . . ."

"Not at all. I was just thinking about a nightcap. Join me?"

"Sure. One thing. Do you have a garage? I'd like to park my car inside."

Pat looked at her quizzically but said, "There's a carriage house around back. I'll open one of the doors with the remote. Come in the back way."

Then she closed the door and was gone.

Kris intended to vanish for the evening, if all went well, and leaving her funny-looking little Toyota with its Ontario plates parked in front of the house wasn't exactly going to aid the cause.

In the dull light, the garage appeared to be made primarily of steel. One pewter-coloured door slid silently up, and Kris pulled her Toyota into an open bay, beside a Boxster, a green Ford Taurus, and some kind of monster black SUV that looked just like the one Lowell Osborne had. His and hers, she wondered? She locked her own car, and slung her purse over shoulder, the videotape still safe inside.

Pat was standing behind a pair of French doors that opened onto the terrace where they had had drinks just a few days ago. As Kris headed toward the big house, she opened one of the doors and beckoned her to come in.

The kitchen had a granite counter about the size of a bowling lane, and cupboards of glass and steel. It let you see everything inside, but the dishes were meticulously organized. A cosy table big enough for twelve was on the other side of the counter.

"Cigarette?" Pat asked, knocking two out of her pack.

Unfortunately, it was an offer Kris could never refuse. She intended to quit, soon, maybe once she got back to Canada. "Sure," she said.

Pat handed her one, then lit them both with a gold lighter with the initials PO on the cap in a fancy italic script. Nothing in Pat Osborne's life was ordinary, Kris thought, although she had been surprised by the Taurus. It was the old model, an anonymous-looking thing. Must be for the houseboy to fetch groceries.

"At this hour, I prefer a little bourbon. You?"

"Sounds fine."

"Water?"

"Ice if you've got it."

If you've got it, Kris repeated to herself. What was she saying? The woman probably had ice cubes with her initials on them.

Pat took a bottle from under the counter and poured two generous portions into short glasses. "Why don't we go into the great room," she said. "It's more comfortable."

It was the first time Kris had heard the term "great room" used, outside of real estate ads and decorating magazines.

The room lived up to its name. Three storeys high, it featured a solid wall of glass looking out on Lake Champlain. Kris could see the ferry heading to the Vermont side, and the lights of Burlington in the distance. She sank into a leather armchair, and Pat took one the same on the other side of a coffee table that had a glass top on a base of what looked like industrial steel bars, bolted together.

"You like metal," Kris said.

"It lasts; one of the few things that does."

Perhaps her unusual house had been designed by a psychologist, not an architect, Kris thought.

"So, I assume you visited the woman whose name I gave you. Was it productive?" Pat asked.

"Sharon Sloan? Up to a point. I think she knows quite a bit more than she's willing to tell me. I nearly had her persuaded, but Bud Naylor got to her first."

Kris decided to omit the stuff about her mother and old man Osborne. That was none of Pat's business. She did describe Sharon's humiliation at the hands of Naylor and his two goons, remembering Pat's own story of how her former husband liked to spank her, then thinking again of the whipping that Kathy had received. Lowell Osborne and Bud Naylor shared an interest in the corporal punishment of women, that much was certain.

"That's disgusting," Pat said, wrinkling her nose just the way Betsy did. Maybe it was something they taught you in finishing school.

Then Kris related most of what had happened since they had

spoken last, leaving out the part about L.T, but finishing with the ransacking of her cabin that afternoon, and the defiling of her underwear.

"Are you sure that was Bud?" Pat asked. "I mean, I rank the man somewhere between a dog and gorilla, but still, that sounds like the work of a pervert."

"I didn't take a DNA sample. I understand he has a couple of guys working with him, but the anger tells it me it was Bud. He had to be alone. I don't think a guy would whip it out and do something like that, another guy there."

Pat shook her head. "Despite all that," she said, "I don't think you're really any closer to proving who killed your sister."

It was a bleak appraisal, but Kris couldn't really argue with it. There were three people in the rape videotape. Bud Naylor, Lowell Osborne, and Tom Larson had all been at the camp that day. And there was almost certainly a fourth man operating the camera. Old man Osborne, she wondered? Proving any of it was the problem. Everything Naylor and the senator had done could still be motivated by nothing more than fear of being smeared with the tape.

"You're right," Kris said, "but I haven't given up and I won't walk away. Sharon Sloan, Liz Tremblay, the senator, Bud Naylor, and probably Tom Larson all know what went on that day. I've got to get one of them to crack."

"Tom? You really think he had something to do with this? I read him as one of the good guys," Pat said.

"Maybe, but he was there. And he'd dated my sister earlier, but didn't tell me about it."

"None of that makes him a killer."

Kris wondered what Pat's interest in Tom Larson really was. She had spoken favourably of him the last time they had met, too. Something about being good looking, but doesn't fool around. How had she found out?

"From that list, who's your choice?" Kris asked.

"Bud," she said, without a flicker of hesitation. "Lowell wouldn't have the courage."

"I'll have to take your word for that," Kris said, wondering if Pat was still covering for her former husband, even though she obviously disliked him.

"And don't forget the other man," Pat said.

"Other man?"

"Billy. Lowell's brother. He was at the camp that summer, but I couldn't tell you if he was there that day. I've got a picture of them all together. Just a minute, I'll get it," she said, rising and disappearing towards the middle of the vast house.

Billy, the lawn-cutting guy. Pat had mentioned him briefly during their first visit, but Kris had forgotten all about him.

The photograph showed a smiling Lowell, wearing swim trunks, with his arms around a hairy-chested Tom and a thinner, younger replica of himself. Billy. Bud stood to the right, behind the other three, his arms crossed over his chest. In the group, but not. He had the same crewcut, but about fifty pounds less weight.

Pat turned the photo over. "The camp, summer, 1981," was written on the back in dark ink that had smeared a bit on the glossy paper.

"Why have you got this?" Kris asked. "I thought you had washed Lowell Osborne out of your life?"

"A box of his junk got mixed in with my things when I moved," she said. "I keep forgetting to send it back."

Kris noticed that Pat had refreshed her drink when she went to get the picture. She was still sipping hers, the American whisky raw after the scotch she was used to.

Pat settled back into the leather chair. "You're in danger, aren't you?"

"Yes, probably."

"Is that why you're here, to seek my protection?"

As if she were a queen, able to offer sanctuary. Kris felt like ditching the idea right there, but she didn't have a better one.

"I'd like to stay the night, if it isn't too ridiculously inconvenient. I'm sorry, I know we've only met once, but I can't go back to where I was staying, and I don't know where else I'd be safe."

"Makes sense. They won't think to look for you here. If they do, I've got an alarm system. "

Kris hoped she didn't put too much faith in that. It would connect either to her ex-husband's tame police force, or some security company guy who'd drive by later carrying nothing more threatening than a flashlight.

"Anyone else in the house?" she asked.

"No, none of the help sleep over. People think it must be wonderful, having servants, but one does value one's privacy, as well."

"Of course," Kris said, as if she had much the same concern. Every time she thought Pat was getting a bit more down to earth, she put her tiara back on.

"Tell me," Pat said, "do you actually think they mean to kill you?"

"Probably not, but I wouldn't want to bet on it."

"Here's what I don't understand, then. Why are they still after you? If their goal today was to frighten you, I'm sure they succeeded."

Kris shrugged, not willing to concede the fright. For just a moment, she considered telling Pat about the tape, but dismissed the idea. Although she had turned to her for help, that didn't mean that she trusted her. Besides, the last person in town she had shared that information with was now dead.

"I wish I understood it," she said. "I can only imagine they want to keep up relentless pressure until they see me drive across the border."

Pat nodded. "Well, they have an enormous amount at stake. The media are really beginning to pick up on Lowell. I understand *Newsweek* is working on a cover story. Any scent of a scandal and they will be on him like jackals."

"You almost sound sympathetic."

"Not at all. I'm cheering for the jackals."

Pat drained her glass and said, "I'm turning in. Beauty sleep. Let me show you to the guest room."

The so-called guest room turned out to be only slightly larger than the condo Kris had owned back in Toronto. Everything was white and glossy, from the ceramic tile, to the wall colour, to the bedspread. The ensuite bathroom was large enough for a cocktail party. A row of windows offered the same view out across the lake as the great room on the far side of the house.

"The windows have power blinds," Pat said. "The controller

is on the nightstand. Anything else you need?"

Kris tried to think of something, just to see if Princess Pat would go and get it, but the room appeared to be as well-equipped as one in a luxury hotel.

"No," she said, "but thanks for this."

"No problem."

Kris knew she ought to feel perfectly safe, but she still locked the bedroom door and wedged a chair under the handle. Pat had been Lowell Osborne's wife for a long time — too long to totally trust her.

23

Kris woke with the first light, not having mastered the intricacies of the power blinds. There was no haze across the lake, and from the bank of windows, she could see the sun coming up on the Vermont side.

She had slept soundly, except for one interruption around midnight, when she had awakened suddenly, sure that she could hear the doorknob turning. There had been nothing further, though, and after half an hour, she had drifted back to sleep.

Kris stripped and stepped into the glass-sided shower. Like everything in Pat Osborne's house, it was oversized. A vertical row of spray heads attacked her body from every angle. It felt good, in contrast to the grungy metal stall at the cabin, but the disconcerting thing was the number of large mirrors on the walls. Showering, she had no choice but to look at some view of herself.

Even through the steam-fogged glass of the shower, she could see she was starting to go to hell. Her breasts weren't bad, just a little lower slung than they used to be. Her stomach certainly wasn't as flat as it had been. Turning, she examined the other side. Who knew what her own ass looked like, really, but she had always been assured it was a good one. To her, it looked saggy.

At thirty-nine, she knew she was at a turning point. The choices were constant exercise and maybe a little discreet cosmetic surgery, or turning into one of those nondescript, pear-shaped, middle-aged women that no man would look at twice.

Maybe it would be a relief.

She felt her legs, stubbly from a week without shaving. There was a pink Bic razor and a can of shaving cream in an alcove that also held a variety of soaps and shampoos. Turning off the water, she lathered her legs and slid the razor up them.

L.T. had always remarked on how smooth her legs were and

how he liked them that way. She had drawn the line when he suggested she shave her pubic hair. It would have been the look he was used to with the twenty-year-old cheerleaders who had preceded her. Lust did make her stupid, almost like a man, but this was where she said no. It was trouble enough shaving her legs without adding to the list, and a wax job was totally out of the question. He claimed that oral sex was far better when bare, and she could see it from his perspective, but there was a limit to what she'd do for a man.

Thinking of L.T., she touched herself, then turned the shower back on. Massaging one breast, the other hand between her legs, she lost herself.

A few minutes later, both relieved and ashamed, Kris wrapped herself in a soft white bath towel. L.T. had been dead only two days, and already she felt like she needed a man. It was as ridiculous as her dependency on cigarettes.

When she came downstairs, Pat was already at the table, eating a grapefruit. She wore designer jeans with a crease, a black silk shirt and the gold sandals from last night. Her chin-length black hair didn't have a strand out of place.

"Good morning," she said. "Sleep well?"

"Yes, thanks." There was no need to mention the doorknob; it had probably been her imagination.

"What's the plan for the day?" Pat asked, with the enthusiasm of a camp counsellor.

"My plan? I thought I might drop in on Sharon Sloan again. Of all the people on my list, I still think she's the most likely to co-operate."

"Perfect. When do we leave?"

"We?"

"It's obviously not safe to be running around town by yourself. I thought you might appreciate some company."

It was something Kris hadn't thought of, but it might be a useful complication. If Naylor planned to make any sort of move against her, he couldn't very well do it with the boss's former wife hanging around.

"Sure, why not?" Kris said, although she felt quite capable of constructing a list of reasons.

"Great! This will be fun," Pat said, as if they'd just agreed to go shopping for sweaters. Kris wondered if she might be on something. It was early in the day for booze, but Pat seemed unnaturally enthusiastic.

"Do you think what I have on will be all right? I put on my grubbies. That should make the poor woman feel less uncomfortable," Pat said.

Grubbies, Kris thought. She'd gone more poorly dressed to parties.

"No, it will be fine. Good choice."

She poured herself a coffee from the carafe on the countertop and said, "When we get to Sharon's, let me do the talking, okay? Interviewing is what I do, and I think I've developed a bit of a rapport with her."

"No problem. Now, you can't go driving around in that car," Pat said. "It will make it too easy for them to spot you."

For a thrilling moment, Kris thought she was going to offer use of the Boxster, but she said, "Let's take the Taurus. No one will notice us in that."

"All right," Kris said. "I don't suppose you happen to have a handgun?"

"Oh my, yes. One that will fit in a purse, or something more intimidating? I have a nice little Walther, but I've also got a Colt .45 semi-automatic. My dad's army gun. It makes a tremendous amount of noise, and it can blow a very large hole in people."

"I don't intend to be blowing any large holes in anyone," Kris said, "but the Walther might be handy. Just in case."

A couple of years ago, Kris had spent quite a bit of time at the shooting range with some cop buddies. They were firing Glocks, but the Walther should be okay. Show them you've got the gun, and look like you'll use it, the cops had told her, and you'll probably never have to pull the trigger. Even Bud Naylor would be smart enough not to gamble against a loaded gun.

Kris finished her coffee and said, "Let's go, then. I want to get to Sharon Sloan before she goes out for the day."

"I'll get the guns. Mind if I bring the .45?"

"I'd rather you didn't. It's not like we're going to a shootout. It's just a little bit of insurance."

"All right," said Pat, disappointed. "I'll just put it in the trunk then, in case."

"Whatever."

Kris imagined this was going to be the most excitement Pat Osborne had had in quite some time. She just hoped Pat could keep her mouth shut. If not, she'd be in the trunk, too.

Sharon Sloan's place was on the far east side, 470 Independence Road. Kris wondered whether the town council had been showing a subtle sense of humour when the street was named. Welfare Alley would have been more appropriate. It was a street of one-storey houses with small windows, peeling paint over decayed clapboard, and defeated shingles. Every other driveway held a car of 1980s vintage, some of them on concrete blocks.

Sharon's house was the same kind of low-rent rectangle as the rest, but someone had tried to improve it by painting it a shade of green that was too close to lime. A thin flower bed ran across the front of the house, the flowers wilted from lack of water. There was no car in the driveway.

"Do you think she's home?" Pat asked.

"I hope so. I don't know if she even has a car."

They parked a couple of houses down the street and walked back, the nondescript Taurus as out of place on this street as if it had been a limo.

"I didn't even know this neighbourhood was here," Pat said.

"It's about four blocks from where I grew up. Our street wasn't quite as bad, though. The houses there were actually respectable once. Even when I was a kid, this was a street with a reputation."

Pat looked warily from side to side.

"Don't worry," Kris said. "They're not dangerous. They're just poor." It was actually the rich you needed to watch out for, she thought.

Kris knocked on Sharon Sloan's front door, which had been painted a shade of purple that someone thought went with the lime green. The curtains on the small front window were drawn, but she could hear the cry of a cat inside.

"Sharon? It's Kris."

She waited a minute, then knocked again. There was no response, and no sound from inside except the cat. She tried the handle, but it was locked.

"Not home, I guess," Pat said. "Maybe we should get going."

"Not yet."

Kris walked down the narrow gap between Sharon's house and the one next door, a converted trailer with a porch and roof added on. The back wall of Sharon's house hadn't been painted and was a dingy white almost the colour of ash. The interior door was open, and there was a wooden screen door that didn't quite fit the sagging frame. Kris could smell cigarette smoke coming from inside.

Since she obviously wasn't going to be invited, Kris walked in. Sharon Sloan sat at the kitchen table, an overflowing ashtray in front of her, a cigarette in her hand. Her bleach-damaged yellow hair hung limp, and Kris could tell that it had been days since it had been washed. An old purple bathrobe was cinched tightly around her waist. The room was small and confined, the floral wallpaper yellowed from years of smoke. Several days' dirty dishes filled the sink and overflowed onto the counter.

"Get out," Sharon said.

Ignoring that, Kris said, "Sharon, this is Pat Osborne."

"Jesus Christ, what are you bringing her around here for? Are you crazy?" Aiming her cigarette straight at Pat, she said, "Haven't you people done enough to me?"

"Hey," Pat shot back, "I'm not with Lowell anymore, and believe me, I've suffered from him as much as anyone."

"Yeah? I've gone by your house. Now you've seen mine. I guess you earned it, though. You fucked him for longer than I did."

Pat gasped and instinctively jerked her head back, as if she'd been slapped.

"Sharon, can it," Kris said. "Pat's helping me out. She's on our side."

"Our side? I didn't know you and I shared a side."

"I think you do. You're the one who started all of this. If it wasn't for you, I wouldn't be here, and L.T. Hill wouldn't be dead."

"Don't put that off on me," she said, pointing her smoking cigarette at Kris now. "What's that got to do with me?"

On the drive to Sharon's house, Kris had been thinking about how to play the next part. She didn't want to tell Pat about the videotape because she didn't really trust her. She was the closest thing Kris had to an ally, though, and maybe hearing the story would bring her fully on side.

"L.T. was helping me. When he died, he was en route to a meeting with Jack Naylor to turn over the videotape. They say the crash was an accident. I'd be surprised if that's true."

Pat looked at her curiously, obviously wondering what videotape Kris was talking about.

"Shit," Sharon said, snubbing out the cigarette. "Why would you give that tape back to them?"

"It was a copy, to get them off my back. I've still got the original, but it's no good without someone who can identify the three men in it, and tell us what happened afterwards."

"What is this tape?" Pat asked.

"It's a video of three men raping my sister on the day she was killed. I believe it was shot at the Osborne camp. Sharon sent it to me, and that's why I'm here," Kris said matter-of-factly.

"Good God, was Lowell . . . ?"

"I don't know," Kris said, "but Sharon does. That's what we've come to find out."

"Wait a minute," Sharon said. "I've never said I sent you that tape."

"No, but we both know you did. Bud Naylor suspects it, too. Has he been back?"

"No, but if he hears about you being here, he will. What do you want from me?"

"The truth. When you sent me that tape, you must have wanted to bring Lowell Osborne to justice. I can't do that without your help."

"Justice? What are the chances of that? I just wanted to fuck him up, for all that he did to me. He showed me what I could have, then took it away. I wanted him to know how it felt. I saw on the Internet that you had become some kind of big newspaper writer and I figured you'd know how to do it. And plenty of reasons, too."

So much for the idea that Sharon Sloan had some kind of altruistic motive, Kris thought. She obviously couldn't care less about Kathy. Just like everyone else in town.

"Well," Pat said, pulling a mickey of Jack Daniels from her purse, "I think we'd better have a drink."

"It's a long ways from noon," Kris said.

"It's noon somewhere. Sharon, where do I find the glasses?"

"Cupboard," she said, gesturing toward the working part of the little kitchen.

Pat opened the cupboard door, careful not to touch the mess on the countertop. She selected three glasses and gave them a quick rub on her shirt tail.

Back at the table, she poured a good shot and shoved it across to Sharon before offering the second one to Kris.

"No thanks, you go ahead," she said.

Pat topped it up a bit more, then clinked glasses with Sharon. "To Lowell Osborne, may his hide be nailed to the wall," she said.

The two women each took a healthy gulp and nodded to each other, at last finding common ground.

Kris gave them a minute, then said, "Sharon, all that you've done so far will be for nothing unless I know who those three men are. Tell us what you saw."

"I didn't see anything. I wasn't there."

Kris felt herself deflate, but tried not to show it. Come on, Sharon, she thought. You can do better than that.

"Let me ask it another way. Do you know anything about the three men in the videotape? I think they were Lowell Osborne, Bud Naylor, and Tom Larson. Am I wrong?"

"Tom? He had nothing to do with it. I know that for sure."

"How can you be so certain?"

"He was in the same room as me, screwing Liz Harper. Afterward, he fell asleep. I was with him the whole day."

"The same room?" Pat asked.

"Yes, Lowell liked to watch other people have sex. You must know that."

Pat ignored her comment, but blushed.

"So Lowell, was he there, too?" she asked.

"He was with me," Sharon said, giving Pat a faint echo of the look of triumph that she would have had thirty years ago.

"The whole time?" Kris asked.

"No, but for several hours. Then he went out for more beer. He was gone maybe an hour. I can tell you, there was no chance of him participating in that thing on the tape. After what he and I did, he didn't have anything left."

Sharon smiled again, her haggard face almost grotesque. It was difficult to square the teenaged temptress with the woman they saw before them.

"All right, if Lowell Osborne and Tom Larson weren't on the tape, who were those men?" Kris asked.

Sharon picked up her cigarette pack off the table. Empty.

Pat pulled hers from her purse and passed it over, gesturing for Sharon to keep it. She lit one, slowly drawing on it, then was silent for a minute, as if trying to take herself back to that day.

"I can't say for sure. The only people I saw at the camp the day your sister was killed were Tom and Lowell. But if Lowell was around, Bud was never far away. He didn't have a girl, so he was the fifth wheel that summer, kind of hanging out in the background. The guy who was in charge in that video? I'd say that was Bud. Beating women was always his thing. Still is," she said, shifting uncomfortably on the wooden kitchen chair.

"And the others?" Kris asked.

"I'm guessing Billy, Lowell's brother, was the other well-dressed one. He was two years younger, a follower. He trailed Bud around the way Bud did Lowell."

"Billy?" Pat said. "Do you really think so? I don't know him that well, what with the situation in the family, but he seemed to be laid-back, almost docile."

"That age, they've all got the hormones," Sharon said. "Billy would do anything Bud told him to do. Anything."

"What about the third man?" Kris asked.

"Probably Bobby Edwards. He was a handyman at the camp. Older guy. I suppose he was only in his thirties then. He was usually the third one."

"Usually the third one? I don't follow," Pat said.

Sharon held her hands in front of her, and turned away from Pat.

"Look, it's just . . . It's not related. You don't have to know everything. Talk to Edwards. He still works out there. See what he says."

"We will talk to him," Kris said, "but Sharon, we do have to know everything. What are you not telling us?"

"It's really embarrassing," she said.

Kris wondered what could be more embarrassing than to be sitting there looking like a derelict, chain smoking, telling other people how you'd screwed up your life. A kinder person would see Sharon as a victim, but Kris had always hated the passivity of that word, and had spent her whole life trying not to be one. To her, saying that you were a victim was just an excuse for not fighting back.

Pat poured Sharon another shot, and one for herself. Sharon shrugged, deciding to tell her story.

"It was like an initiation," Sharon said. "I was really drunk on the night of mine. I would never have done it otherwise."

Kris said nothing, knowing that Sharon had decided to confide in them and that silence was the best way to draw her out. One of the things she had learned as a crime columnist was that people were surprisingly willing to tell you about the bad things they had done, either to brag or to seek forgiveness. Silence from the interviewer seemed to create a vacuum that drew it right out of them.

"It was like what you saw in the videotape," Sharon said finally.

Pat looked at Kris questioningly.

"They tied my sister to a table face down, stripped her, whipped her, then took turns screwing her," Kris said. She felt no need to elaborate on that terse description. Just those few words held enough horror.

"When they had a new girl at the camp, they'd break her in," Sharon said. "That was the term they used. Break her in. Like a horse."

"Who were they?" Pat asked, gently.

"Always Bud. He was the first in, and he was brutal. He'd pound you until you were numb. Then Billy. Then Bobby, the hired guy, would come in third. That was the final humiliation."

"Jesus," Pat said. "Where was Lowell while all this was going on?"

"He was the cameraman. Like the director of the film. It was the first summer they'd had a video camera, and it was a new toy for them. Lowell, Tom, and the rest would watch the videos on their poker nights."

"Who else was initiated?" Kris asked.

"As far as I know, every girl who worked at that camp. If they didn't go along, they were out of a job. If they did, it was a nice summer of hanging out with the rich boys."

"And that summer, was there anyone besides my sister?"

"Liz Harper. She was after me. I was Lowell's girlfriend by that time. So I thought. Lowell made me strip and watch what they did to Liz. After, they made us do things together."

Something else Tom had forgotten to tell her, Kris thought. Wouldn't Betsy find that story fascinating.

"God, why did you go along with it?" Pat asked.

"I was young. I was drunk. I was horny. I thought Lowell loved me, and this was what it would take to keep him. All of that," Sharon said. "Was it any better for you?"

Pat waved the question away. "My relationship with Lowell has nothing to do with this."

Kris remembered the anecdote about how Lowell liked to make her dress up like a schoolgirl, then spank her. Was he just reliving his wild days, or did he share his wife with Bud, the way he had shared his girlfriend?

"I'm sure he was a perfect gentleman by the time he got to you, princess," Sharon said with a leer that indicated the opposite.

Pat rose from her chair, and said, "That's enough for me. Kris, let's go."

"We aren't done yet. Sharon, did you see those three men rape my sister?"

"I already told you, no. I don't even know if Lowell knew about it. As I said, he liked to watch. He was plenty busy observing Tom and Liz going at it, but I don't think he would have missed something like the initiation of your sister. They'd already tried to set it up a week earlier, but she wouldn't go for it. Kathy was young, but she knew more about boys than I did, when you got right down to it. The evil of them, I mean. I understood from Lowell that they were going to fire her over it. You see, it wasn't rape exactly. Not for me or Liz. We'd agreed to go along with it. Not knowing how bad it would be, of course. But they were smart, thinking ahead about what would happen if it came back on them."

Kris could see it now. To please his master, Bud had decided to initiate her sister by force, then brought Lowell in at the last minute as cameraman. But Kathy hadn't gone along, and then she'd run off. It wasn't difficult to see why Lowell Osborne couldn't just let her run to town with a story about being raped.

"What do you think happened after my sister was attacked?" Kris asked.

"I don't know. The story everyone has always believed could be true. She ran away from the camp. That made sense, after what they'd done. Then she was picked up hitchhiking and attacked. That was a lonely road. A really bad place to hitchhike."

"Just a coincidence, then?" Kris said.

Sharon shrugged.

"Maybe, I just don't know. Any way you look at it, though, she wouldn't have been on that road if it weren't for Bud."

"If Bud is to blame, why are you going after Lowell?" Pat asked.

"Bud didn't do anything unless he was told to do it by Lowell, or he was trying to please him," Sharon said.

Despite her bitterness toward her ex-husband, Kris could see that Pat was still trying to find a way to limit Lowell Osborne's culpability. It must be difficult to have spent so many years living with a man, and only now find out what he was really like.

"How did you get the tape, Sharon?" Kris asked.

"After your sister was killed, I was worried, afraid that they'd do something to me. I thought the tapes would be insurance against them. Besides, I was sick of the idea of them watching us whenever they wanted to.

"Lowell kept the tapes in a cabinet in the main lodge, in the same room where they made them. I took all of them."

"You've still got the rest?" Kris asked. "Can you see the people involved in any of them?"

"No, they always wore those stupid masks. And in Liz's tape, and mine, they had us ask for what we were about to get at the beginning, then thank them for it when they were done. That was Lowell's idea, being able to show that it was just sex games, not rape. That's why Bud did the same thing at the end, when he asked your sister to say how much she liked it.

"I eventually destroyed the other tapes. Your sister's was the only one I thought I could really use against them."

"Do they know you had the tapes?"

"Not for sure, but they've always suspected it. After your sister was killed, I told Bud that I could get him in a lot of trouble if he ever tried to do anything to me."

"But you still kept dating Lowell?"

Sharon hung her head. All the things she had already said didn't seem to bring on shame, but this did. "At the time, I thought he loved me, that he had nothing to do with the rest of it."

Pat Osborne had listened to all of this with a look of increasing alarm. Finally, she drained her glass and banged it on the table. "Manipulative bastard. I'm sorry I ever let him touch me. And when I think of the other women he had, and what he must have been doing with them. The money I took from him is nothing. I want his balls."

"Now you get it," Sharon said. "Pour me another."

Her words were already beginning to slur. Kris wondered how long it had been since Sharon had eaten.

Based on what Sharon had just said, Lowell Osborne was undoubtedly a bigger piece of slime than she had imagined, but there was nothing in Sharon's story that said he knew about, or was involved in, her sister's death. He wasn't in any of the videotapes, either. Osborne might actually be innocent of any direct involvement in her sister's death, but it was easy to see why he was so concerned. Any honest description of the events of that summer thirty years ago would destroy his political career. Kris knew she didn't have enough, though, not yet. It reminded her of Bill Clinton and that big-haired country singer he had taken up with. Just that one story wasn't enough to do him in. People needed to see the whole picture.

The problem was how to back the story up. She didn't like to imagine a future libel case in which Sharon was her key witness. A lawyer would pick her apart. If they could get Liz Harper to tell the same story, it might be different, but Liz had made it clear that she had no interest in digging up a past that must be intensely embarrassing to her.

Tom Larson would make a credible witness to the events of that summer, but if he was really the stand-up guy people took him for, he would surely have gone to the police the day her sister was killed. Kris had to assume he was part of the cover-up.

At least Sharon's story had given her a couple of good new leads, and the clearest idea yet of what had really happened on her sister's last day of life. She'd have to track down Billy, to see if he might be the weak link. And the handyman. His story about being in a bar at the time of the killing might be true, but what had he been doing beforehand?

She had a lot to do and not much time to do it in. Bud Naylor and Lowell Osborne wouldn't be content to see her hanging around town much longer, and she was becoming increasingly worried about what they might do to solve that problem.

24

"I have to talk to this guy," Kris said. "Do you want to come in or wait here?"

Pat looked at the filthy, oil-stained pavement of Vic Desmarais's parking lot, then down at her gold sandals. "Do you need me?"

"Not for this."

Or for anything else, Kris thought. Now she was thinking twice about having let Lowell Osborne's ex-wife tag along and find out about the videotape. Kris had been tempted to take her back home after Sharon Sloan's place, but decided it was safer to keep Pat with her, so she would know what she was up to.

On the phone, Vic had said he had something for her, and she should come by as soon as possible. He wanted to discuss it in person. It couldn't be good news — that much she knew.

Vic was at the desk in the little office, filling out bills by hand. He wore the same blue coveralls he had had on before, "Vic" on the pocket. Kris paused in the doorway and said, "Hey Vic, what have you got?"

He looked up and smiled, almost too eager to see her. Kris wondered if he might have had a crush on her in high school. Or maybe he had just been married too long. Either way, she was glad she had worn her baggy blue sweatshirt, L.T.'s cap pulled down over her uncombed hair.

"I went over that truck from top to bottom," Vic said, getting up from behind the desk. "Let's go out back and I'll show you what I found."

Kris smiled, nodded, and followed him through the shop, once again drawing stares from the mechanics. Vic was obviously proud of whatever he had discovered, and he was going to tell her when he was ready.

When they were halfway back down a lane of crushed and

scavenged pickup trucks, he said, "I didn't want to talk about this back in the shop. The boys are always on the lookout for a bit of gossip, and this isn't something I want going around."

When they got to L.T.'s red Blazer, Kris felt a chill. It was impossible to look at the truck without thinking about his last moments, trapped inside. The two sprung doors stood open. The crushing of the cab made it impossible to close them.

Vic wiped his oily hands on a red rag that he took from the back pocket of his coveralls, then leaned in to the driver's side.

"Look at this," he said, holding up the seat belt strap. It was no longer anchored to the floor.

"Defective?" Kris asked.

"No, cut nearly through. Clean cut, new. With the force of the collision, it was bound to give way.

"There's more," he said, and pointed to the engine compartment. The hood was already up.

Kris peered in, but the mass of hoses and metal didn't mean much to her.

Vic leaned into the opening, the upper half of his body almost out of sight. He pulled up a thin metal tube with a long thin gash in the side.

"Brake line," he said. "Someone sliced it. Every time he put on the brakes, he'd lose a bit of fluid. Then they'd go right down. Touch them, and there would be nothing there. That explains the lack of skid marks."

So it was murder, Kris thought. The Naylors had set out to kill L.T. as surely as if they had put a bullet in his head. Finding a way to make it look like an accident would be the general's doing, based on everything L.T. had told her about the way the old man operated. Make it look like an accident, then count on the town's tame police force to do their usual shoddy job. Assuming Larry Brewster wasn't in on the whole thing from the start.

"What do you want me to do with this?" Vic asked. "Normally, I'd say go to the police."

"Not much point," Kris said.

"I didn't think so, either. Do you mind telling me what this is all about?"

The look on his face was one of concern, not just curiosity.

Kris figured she owed him an explanation, for his effort.

"L.T. Hill and I have been investigating my sister's murder. There are still people here who were involved, and they are apparently prepared to do anything to keep me from proving it."

"Your sister? That must have been, what, nearly thirty years ago? I thought about her when I saw you yesterday, but I didn't want to say anything. You know, bring up old bad news."

"There seems to be a lot of people in this town who don't want to hear about old bad news," Kris said.

"You know what I mean," he said. "I just didn't want you to think I had you pegged as the girl whose sister was killed. I remember who you really are."

"Most people just think I'm trouble, trying to drag up something that will make the town look bad."

"The town, or Lowell Osborne?"

"Is there a difference?"

Vic smiled, then his expression was instantly serious again.

"Yeah, to most of us. The Osbornes have acted like they own the town, as far back as anyone can remember. They've never understood the difference between owning things and owning people."

"Seems like they own a fair number of people, too. Most of the ones I've met," she said.

"Don't put me on that list. Look, Kris, I'm going to sit on this until you tell me different. I take it the people involved are Osborne or Bud Naylor. I remember your sister worked for the Osbornes the summer she was killed."

"You're on the right track," she said. "Don't say anything to anyone about this. You saw what happened to the last guy who tried to help me."

Vic looked at the truck, and shook his head.

"Yeah, well, fuck them. They don't scare me. Look, if you need any kind of help, any kind, you call me."

He pulled a grubby business card from his wallet, then wrote another number on the back in pen.

"That's my home number. If you can't get me at work, I'll be there."

Kris took the card and slipped it into her purse. She didn't imagine she'd ever use it. The last thing she wanted was to encourage another guy to get in the way of Bud Naylor and Low-ell Osborne. This was her fight.

Back at the car, Pat Osborne was applying a candy apple red polish to her fingernails. Kris had smelled the strong odour twenty feet away.

"That took forever," Pat said, as Kris got back in the driver's side.

"They sabotaged L.T.'s truck," she said, her tone flat. "The brake line was cut." With all that Pat already knew, Kris figured this extra piece of information couldn't hurt.

"Oh, no. They killed him?"

Even after all she had heard that morning, Pat's face still expressed disbelief.

"That's the picture."

Pat capped the polish and blew on her nails. "Are you going to be able to prove that?"

"I could prove that the car was sabotaged. Not who did it."

"I just don't believe that Lowell could be involved in that," Pat said. "I mean, he's a lying, deceitful womanizer, but he's never been violent."

"No, he delegates that to Bud. In this case, maybe to Bud's father. The plan was a little too subtle for Bud himself."

"The general? You think he's involved in this? I always thought he was a straight arrow."

Kris was rapidly concluding that Pat's ability to judge other people was not her strength.

"The general offered L.T. quite a lot of money to convince me to drop the investigation," she said. "Then he said he'd pay him even more if he got the videotape and turned it over. That's where he was going when he was killed. He never made the rendezvous. I guess their estimate of how many times he would brake before he got there was off a bit. They didn't know how L.T. drove."

Pat shook her head. "I just can't believe this. Lowell is like a son to the general. He's always encouraged Lowell, helped him along. After Lowell's own father died, he kind of took up that space. We used to have him to our house at Christmas and birthdays. I just don't see Jack Naylor doing this."

"Why don't we go ask him?" Kris said.

25

Kris knew she was breaking one of the first rules of journalism. You talked to all your secondary sources and gathered every fact before confronting the main subject of your story. You didn't want to ask questions until you knew as many answers as possible, and could infer that you knew even more.

She'd had an e-mail from Chris Walton, the *Star*'s man in Washington, with a lot of background on Jack Naylor's defence contractor connections. He was on the board of three different corporations. Kris had only had time to scan the information from Walton, but the picture was pretty clear. Old soldiers never died. They became defence lobbyists.

Ideally, she would have interviewed Billy Osborne and the handyman before confronting Naylor, but L.T.'s death had changed the game completely. Kris had proceeded as if she and Osborne were playing chess, but the Naylors had just turned over the board and knocked all the pieces onto the floor. It was time to show them she could play the same way.

The general's house was surprisingly modest for Dumont Hill, a bungalow with a fake stone facade, fresh white woodwork, and a lawn and shrubs that looked as if they had been trimmed by a barber. A black Lexus was parked in the driveway, and Kris pulled the Taurus in tight behind it.

The general answered the door, a newspaper rolled up in his left hand. He removed a pair of black-rimmed reading glasses and gave Kris a quick once over, apparently not recognizing her. Then he saw Pat, and Kris could tell he was trying to figure out what it all meant. Kris was surprised by how small he was. She had expected someone more like Bud, big and beefy. The general was trim in his khaki pants and a green golf shirt, but his white hair revealed his real age.

"Hello, Pat," he said, over Kris's shoulder. "Who is this?"

Kris didn't wait for Pat to answer and said, "Kris Redner. We haven't met."

She didn't offer her hand.

The general showed just a flicker of surprise. "Ah yes, the woman investigating the death of her sister. I've heard about you."

"I'm sure you have. Can we come in? I'd like to tell you more."

The general hesitated, then stepped back, gesturing for them to enter. "We can use my study," he said, pointing to a room on the right.

The walls were panelled in dark wood and covered with military memorabilia, pictures of the general in uniform in various deserts and jungles, framed medals and citations. A thick navy rug bearing the Marine Corps insignia covered most of the oak floor. The general sat in the worn black leather chair behind his desk and indicated that Pat and Kris should sit in two similar ones side by side in front. She felt as if she were there for a job interview.

"Pat, how have you been?" the general asked, ignoring Kris.

"Surviving. You?"

"Busy with Lowell's campaign. We're getting ready to go national. Quite a challenge."

"I'm sure you're up to it," Pat said. "You were always the master organizer, Jack."

He shrugged away the compliment, if that's what it was.

"I assumed we would be able to count on your support, Pat," the general said, moving his eyes quickly to Kris, then back to Pat. "Now you seem to be playing on a different team."

"My support? Good God, Jack. After Lowell dumped me and took up with that girl, you think you can count on my support?"

"I'm sorry that things didn't work out for you two, Pat, and I know Lowell has his faults. We all do. But the country needs him."

Kris had grown impatient with being ignored. "Tell me, is there anything you wouldn't do to get him elected, General?" she asked.

"I'm sorry, I don't follow."

"I'm sure that you do. L.T. Hill told me all about your schemes. You didn't really think he was working for you, did you?"

Kris reached into her purse and pulled out the $25,000, held tightly together with an elastic band. She flipped the money on the general's desk and said, "Here, I think this is yours."

He looked as shocked as if she'd thrown a dead fish in front of him. "I know nothing about this," he said.

"Sure you don't. I'll bet you'll tell me you didn't pay L.T. that money to encourage me to give up, then offer him another fifty grand to get you the videotape."

"Videotape?"

The general was feigning mystification, but his face was getting redder.

"You know, the one that showed three men raping my sister on the day she was killed. I believe your lad Bud was one of them."

"That's an extremely serious allegation."

"And I don't hear you denying it."

"I wouldn't lower myself. It's absurd."

"Is it? You must not have thought so when you so urgently needed L.T. to get that tape back."

The general had picked up a fountain pen with the USMC insignia on it, and was tapping it on the surface of his desk. He considered for a moment, then said, "Let's say, hypothetically, there was such a videotape. It would almost certainly be fake, the work of one of the senator's opponents. We're playing a high-stakes game, Ms. Redner, and some play it dirty. Nevertheless, it would be in our interests to obtain and suppress such a tape. Any kind of scandal would be disastrous for Lowell's prospects, even if it were subsequently proven to be groundless. Momentum is key. We can't afford anything that takes it away."

"So a tape like that would be worth just about anything to you, wouldn't it?"

"I wouldn't go that far. I think we would be prepared to pay full value. Assuming there was such a tape."

The general picked up his reading glasses from the top of his desk and put them on. They magnified his eyes, making them dominate his face. Kris was surprised that his eyes were so colourless and dark. It was almost like staring down into a pit.

"I take it you've brought me something to look at, and want to talk price," the general said.

Kris was momentarily sorry she had the tape with her. A man

like the general would certainly keep a gun in his desk drawer. But she also had the Walther in her purse, and Pat Osborne as further insurance.

"I'm not trying to sell you anything, General. If I wanted money, I'd have taken Osborne's offer of the $250,000 pension."

"That would have been wise. It was owing to you, from your father's unfortunate accident."

The general almost managed a look of sympathy. Kris wondered how stupid he thought she was.

"There's another question," she said. "What a strange coincidence. My sister is murdered, then just a week later my father is killed in an industrial accident. After being called back to the Osbornes' factory late at night. I wonder what he had found out?"

The general laughed, but it was dry and mirthless.

"You seem to see evil around every corner, Ms. Redner," he said. "This is just a small town."

"But with its share of drama, all the same," she said.

Kris took the cigarette pack from her purse, lit one, then offered it to Pat, lighting hers off the end of the first one. She didn't bother to look for an ashtray, knowing there would be none in the general's pristine, orderly study.

He looked with alarm at the cigarettes and said, "I'd rather you didn't smoke."

"Me too, but what can you do? What I really wanted to talk to you about, General, is L.T. Hill's death."

"Traffic accident, I understand. Driving too fast."

"Let's cut the bullshit, General. The brake line had been tampered with, and the seat belt nearly cut through. You simply misjudged how many times he would brake between town and the rendezvous point, and the crash happened on the way there, instead of on the way back. You certainly went to quite a bit of trouble to find the tape, ripping up the inside of the truck. Tell me, did it bother you, him lying there dying?"

The image of what she had just described nearly brought Kris to tears, but she fought them down. This would be the worst time to act like a woman.

The general whipped his glasses off and dropped them on the table. "Where did you get this nonsense?"

"Does it matter? We both know it's true."

"If so, I'm sure you'd have gone to the police with it, and I rather doubt that you have."

"Larry Brewster? Give me a break. The first thing he'd do is come running to Osborne or you, asking what to do next."

"I should hardly need to warn you about slander, Ms. Redner. I'm surprised that a journalist of your experience would be throwing around these kinds of allegations with nothing to back them up."

"Did I say I had nothing to back them up? Here's the thing, General: I honestly don't know what role Lowell Osborne played in my sister's death, but the way you and your son have been acting, it makes him look guilty. Why don't you try telling the truth?"

"Truth is really a matter of one's perspective, don't you think?"

"Maybe in your world. But to get back to my sister's death, I know you didn't kill her, but you are covering up for whoever did. Don't you think it's gone on long enough?"

The general shrugged. "Look at it another way. What would be gained by bringing this matter up again? Surely, so many years after the fact, there is no evidence sufficient to convict anyone in your sister's death. All that would happen is that a number of people's lives would be ruined, and your sister would be just as dead in the end."

Kris saw it about the same way, but had no compunction about ruining the lives of anyone involved with her sister's death. They'd had it coming for a long time.

"A number of people? Who did you have in mind?" she asked.

"It's not who I have in mind, Ms. Redner, but which ones you are prepared to smear in your misguided search for justice. I suspect your list includes Lowell and every friend he had as a young man."

"Would you care to narrow it for me?"

"Hardly. I'll remind you that I know nothing about the events that actually took place the day your sister died. My goal, my only goal, is to protect Lowell from harm.'

The general paused, as if making a decision, then said, "Since we are putting our cards on the table, what if I were able to get you what you want in exchange for the tape? I assume you still have it?"

"Of course. It's in Pat's safe deposit box."

Kris hoped that Pat would be smart enough not to reveal her surprise.

"Pat's safe deposit box," he repeated, smiling as if he didn't believe her story for a minute. He turned to Pat, shaking his head slightly.

"Pat, what in the world has gotten you tangled up with this woman?"

"Jack, if Lowell was involved in that girl's death, he should be held to account for it. I'm surprised you can't see that," Pat said.

"Ah, Pat, you were always rather easily led, weren't you?"

Kris figured Pat and the general could fight it out another day. "You say you can give me what I want. Be more specific," she said.

"The person who killed your sister. What if I were able to determine who it was, and hand him over to the police?"

"Who are you going to give me? The drunken handyman?"

The general's surprise was too obvious. "Handyman?"

"I don't think we are getting anywhere here, General. In fairness, I wanted to bring you up to speed on where my story is now, and give you a chance to comment. I'm afraid that you are going to be in it."

Kris took a steno pad and pen from her purse and flipped it open. She then reached in and showed him her microcassette recorder. Excellent little Sony. It could pick up conversation even while inside her purse.

"You can't rat trap me with that old trick," he said. "Our conversation was off the record."

"It's too late to say that now. You've acknowledged that I'm a journalist. Surely you didn't think this was a social call. Any final comments?"

The general rose from his chair and pointed a finger at her. "Yes. Get the hell out."

Kris put the notebook back in her purse, then ground her cigarette butt into the navy carpet.

"My God. Do you know what that carpet's worth?"

"No, but I'm sure you do. You seem to have a dollar value for everything."

26

"**M**y God, Kris, I thought I was a mouthy bitch. I can't believe the way you went after Jack Naylor. Do you think that was wise?"

They were back in the Taurus, driving away from Dumont Hill toward downtown.

"Maybe not, but he had it coming. He's to blame for L.T.'s death. I've no doubt of that. He's been sitting back pulling the strings, enjoying the idea that no one knew what he was up to."

"Great, but if he's as dangerous as you think, aren't you just daring him to act? If he was smart enough to kill your boyfriend, why do you think he can't get at you?"

"I don't," Kris said, her voice low. "As long as that tape is out there, they will keep coming for it, but they were going to anyway. I was fed up with Jack Naylor thinking he was the only one who knew what was going on.

"I doubt that he bought the idea of the tape being in your safe deposit box, but thanks for not blowing it when I said that it was."

"I was too surprised to speak. Where is it really?"

"In my purse, but it didn't seem like a good idea to tell Naylor that."

"I suppose not. We need to find a better place for it."

"Agreed."

Kris parked the Taurus about half a block from the Crowsnest, the bar that Vic Desmarais had suggested would be the most likely place to find Bobby Edwards. In another town, the Crowsnest would have been a trendy tourist bar, hanging out over the edge of the lake on pilings, its weathered clapboard walls giving it that look of an authentic fishing shanty. In Osborne, it was a cheap place to serve serious drinkers. Kris could smell the beer before they even got through the door. A neon Budweiser sign glowed dully in the dirty window.

"So you think Bobby Edwards is going to be in here?" Pat asked. She sounded dubious.

"I understand he next to lives here. It's the bar he was supposed to be in on the day my sister was killed. We need to get to him before someone else does."

If they haven't already, she thought.

Kris pushed the door open, the light causing a dozen drinkers to look her way, eyes blinking like moles. It didn't look like much had changed inside the bar in the years since Kathy had been killed. The drinkers were slumped around a small collection of Formica-topped tables, sitting on mismatched wooden chairs. They wore T-shirts and jeans, or uniforms with their names stitched on the shirts. Working men having an early lunch. None of the shirts said "Bobby."

"Ladies," the bartender said, obviously surprised to see any in his establishment. He was a smiling, freckled, redhead, thinning hair swept back, black golf shirt tight over his paunch.

"What can I do you for?" he said, smiling at his time-worn witticism.

"We're looking for Bobby Edwards," Kris said.

"Really? I knew if Bobby hung around this bar long enough, he'd get lucky. Did he win the lottery, too?"

"Not exactly. Which one is he?"

She slid a twenty across the bar, to improve his memory.

He pocketed it, and said, "Bobby's not here right now, but he will be. He's a lunchtime regular. I'll be sure to point him out."

"You serve food?" Pat asked.

"Liquid lunch," the bartender said. "There's a vending machine in the back, though, has chips if you're hungry."

"Thank you, no."

"We'll wait for him," Kris said. "I see you have a deck over the water, any chance of sitting there?"

"The patio? I could open it, I suppose."

"I think we'd enjoy the fresh air," Kris said.

She put another twenty on the bar. "Bring us a pitcher of whatever you have on draft, and keep the change."

The bartender smiled, as if Bobby Edwards weren't the only

one who was having a lucky day.

"Sure thing, ladies. Go right on out. There's some patio furniture out there."

Kris and Pat walked past the drinkers, who paused to openly evaluate them. Most of their attention was directed at Pat, Kris noted with irritation. She had that hip-rolling girl walk that men always liked. Kris slid open a balky, smoke-stained patio door and stepped out on the deck. There were two formerly white plastic tables and a half-dozen chairs. Kris knocked the major debris off two of them and set them up so that they could look at the lake, but still see if anyone came into the bar. She set her purse under the chair, feeling the weight of the gun and the bulk of the videotape.

Pat looked down at her neatly pressed jeans, then at the filthy chair.

"Don't worry, you can wash them," Kris said, wondering whether she sent her jeans to the drycleaner, or had a laundress come in.

Pat took a white, monogrammed handkerchief from her purse and cleaned the chair a bit more before tentatively perching on the edge of it.

Kris shivered and wished she hadn't left her sweatshirt in the car. The day was clear and bright, but the lake breeze had a bite to it. Still, it was better than sitting inside.

"So Edwards, he's supposed to be the third man, right?"

"If you believe Sharon Sloan," Kris said.

"Do you?"

"Probably. It's a lurid tale to make up. We know what they did to my sister. We just don't know who did what. This guy Edwards seems like he could be the weak link."

"I've seen him around the camp," Pat said. "Heavy-set man, doesn't say much. He's worked for the family for years. I believe his father did, too. We're probably going to find that he's loyal."

"Maybe," Kris said. "We'll see what he says when I tell him the general is willing to give him up as the killer of my sister."

"He didn't say that."

"Not in as many words, but I could tell that's what he was thinking. Besides, Edwards won't know anything more than what we tell him. It's up to us to be persuasive."

The bartender brought their pitcher and two glasses of dubious cleanliness. Kris smiled at him, but suspended her conversation until he had gone back into the bar.

"Fortunately, that's one of my specialties," Pat said.

Kris imagined that with Pat's looks, and later, money, persuading men had never been difficult. The problem with Bobby Edwards was going to be that the other side had money as inducement, too, and they also had fear.

Pat drained half a glass of beer, then said, "What was she like, your sister?"

"I wish I really knew. She was a kid when she died, fourteen years old. To me, back then, she was the older, stronger, bolder person who could do everything I wanted to do. I'm sure she was wild, to some degree. Dating at fourteen, working up at that camp, she had lots of chances to get into trouble.

"You need to understand what our house was like," Kris continued, wondering why she was telling Pat this, but feeling good at being able to tell someone. "My mother drank too much. She just wasn't there for us. Dad worked long hours at the Osborne factory. He was a foreman, responsible for keeping all the machinery running."

"Your father worked for Lowell's? I hadn't realized that before today. The general said something about a pension?"

"He was killed in an industrial accident, just a week after my sister's death. We were left with nothing. A couple of days ago, the senator told me that my mother had refused a pension. It has built up to $250,000 over the years. He wanted me to have it."

Pat's expression said that was a lot of money, even by her standards.

"If there was a pension due, why didn't your mother take it?"

"Good question. It certainly wasn't like her to refuse money. She had to do maid work to get by, but she drank up everything she had. My father's death put her into a real downward spiral. She committed suicide a few years later."

Kris had already mentioned her suspicions about her father's death back at the general's house, but she decided not to go into more detail for Pat. The affair between her mother and old man

Osborne, and all that flowed from it, was before Pat's time in town.

"My God. You must have still been quite young. Who brought you up?" Pat asked.

As soon as she was sixteen, Kris got on a bus for Canada and left her suffocating family home behind. Six months later, her mother was dead. Kris had turned to her uncle Martin, the only other relative she had left in the world. He had welcomed her with less enthusiasm than he would a stray dog. His house in the Ottawa Valley was little more than a shack, but once he saw that she could cook and clean, he grudgingly accepted her. By the end, she suspected he actually liked her, but two years of that was enough. She headed to Toronto and fought her way through Ryerson. She had made her way by serving beer in a pub, spending every spare minute at the school newspaper.

She gave Pat the *Reader's Digest* version.

"An uncle. Up in Canada. Grouchy old bastard who lived out in the bush. As soon as I was old enough, I headed for the city.

"That's me. What about you?"

Kris expected to hear a story about growing up the daughter of a dentist and a housewife somewhere in the suburbs of New York.

"My father was army. A sergeant. We moved around a lot, but we ended up at Fort Drum, up near the border. My mom took secretarial work, when she could get it. We lived on bases in married quarters, never really had a home. The beauty contest was my way out. It got me the job in Washington. What politician wouldn't hire a state beauty queen? I planned to stay in Washington, get involved in government. Then I met Lowell."

"Really," Kris said, surprised. "I would have taken you as coming from the upper crust."

Pat gave an unladylike snort and downed the rest of her beer.

"Hardly, but you pick it up when you become an Osborne. For a family that made its money in shoes and shipping, they certainly have a regal manner. You should have met Lowell's father."

"What was he really like?"

"Lowell Osborne the third? A small-town Republican penny pincher who thought he was an English duke. Used to write the editorials in that little paper of his, as if the world needed to know everything he thought. Lived like a king while paying his workers peanuts. But you know about that."

What had her mother seen in a man like that? Kris wondered. Money, or maybe just a break from the mundane life on Washington Street, she supposed.

"How did he take to you?" she asked Pat.

"Poorly. He berated Lowell for marrying beneath his class. To the old man, marriage was like a strategic business merger. He himself had married a Cleghorn. Banking money."

"And what happened to her?"

"Killed in a car crash, when Lowell was still in his teens."

Kris vaguely remembered her father saying something at the dinner table about the boss's wife being killed in an accident. The workers had been given a half-day off, without pay, to attend the funeral.

"About the only good thing the old man saw in me was my looks," Pat said. "I remember him saying to Lowell, when he didn't think I could hear, 'she has good lines; she'll breed up well.' Like I was a goddamn horse. Unfortunately, it was an inaccurate prediction. Tragically, I left Lowell without an heir, so he had to turn to little Terry to ensure the line of succession. Bastard.

"When the old man died of colon cancer ten years ago, I wasn't exactly overcome with grief.

"Have you got a cigarette?" Pat asked, nervously tapping her fingers on the table.

Kris passed one to Pat and took one for herself. "What was it like, being with Lowell?" she asked.

"In what way?"

"I don't mean sexually," Kris said. "I mean everyday. Is there anything normal about the guy, or is he always working an angle?"

Pat shrugged. "He's a politician. He wasn't always that way, though. When we were young, Lowell was idealistic. He thought he could use his money and his family name to really do something, to change the way things work. He still talks that way but all he wants is power."

"I guess I've presented him with a bit of a complication," Kris said.

"I should think so, judging by the response. We don't know how involved Lowell actually is in all of this, though. The Naylors will protect their man at all costs. It's power for them, too, after all."

An older man wearing a green work shirt and pants and scuffed construction boots had come into the bar and was talking to the bartender, who pointed towards the two women on the patio. Edwards turned in their direction. From the look on his broad, flat face, he was surprised by the bartender's news. He was big-shouldered and solid-looking, maybe six foot two, but with a beer belly that caused his belt to curl forward in a vain attempt at containment. His wallet was joined to his belt with the kind of chain truckers favoured, and a large ring of keys protruded above his right pocket.

Kris tensed and half rose from her chair. Even money Bobby Edwards would run for it, and she had no intentions of letting him get away.

She sat back down when she saw Bobby rub a heavy stubble of beard and smile in their direction. They had said nothing to the bartender about why they wanted to talk to him, and she didn't suppose it was every day that the handyman stepped into his favourite bar and found two women waiting for him. Bottle of beer in hand, he headed toward them, stopping briefly to joke with some of the other drinkers. Ribbing him about his unexpected company, no doubt.

Bobby walked up to their table, his free hand scratching the greying hair on his head, which wasn't much longer than that on his face. He had a what's-this-all-about look. He was a few decades past the point where a name like Bobby would have made sense, Kris thought. Some men never grew up.

Kris rose and shook his heavy, calloused hand. "Kris Redner," she said, "and I think you know Pat Osborne."

"Mrs. Osborne? I haven't seen you in some time. How have you been?"

"All right, Bobby. You still up at the camp?"

"Yes, ma'am."

"My friend Kris is working on a story, Bobby," Pat said. "She thinks you might have some information that could be useful to her."

From the look on his face, this wasn't a situation Bobby had faced too often, Kris thought. He turned toward her warily. "What's it about?"

"My sister was murdered back in 1981, Bobby. I'm writing the story of what was really behind it. I thought you might remember her. She worked up at the senator's camp that summer."

Only a slightly-raised eyebrow spoiled the blandly-neutral look on Bobby's face. It was as if she had asked him about the weather.

"Kathy Redner. Yeah, I remember her."

Bobby sat back in his chair and took a pull on his beer.

Kris realized she hadn't quite worked out how to approach him. She couldn't very well just say, "Hey Bobby, did you happen to rape or murder my sister?"

Pat Osborne jumped in. "It would be helpful, Bobby, if you could just tell us what you remember about the girl that summer, the events leading up to her death. Kris's heard a lot of this from other people, but she just wants to touch all the bases."

"Journalistic thoroughness," Kris said.

"Exactly."

"It was a long time ago," Bobby offered. He took another jolt from his beer and looked out across the lake. Kris thought perhaps this was going to be the sum total of his recollection, but she waited.

"I didn't really know her," he finally said. "She worked inside, I worked outside."

"I understand Sharon Sloan and Liz Harper worked at the camp that summer as well," Kris said, trying an oblique tack. "Do you remember them?"

"Sure, but they're still around town. They were older. It was a little different."

"Different how?" Pat asked.

Bobby looked at them with bloodshot eyes, weighing what to do. "That's not for me to say."

"Suppose I said that Lowell Osborne and Tom Larson were screwing them, what would you say to that?" Kris asked.

Bobby looked quickly at Pat Osborne, then said, "I wouldn't argue with it, but they were single guys, not much older than the girls. That was well before the senator met Mrs. Osborne."

"Don't worry about my feelings, Bobby," Pat said, brushing a hand quickly over his. "I know all about Lowell's habits with women."

"And my sister, where did she fit in?" Kris asked.

"Like I say, she was much younger. So far as I know, she wasn't involved with the boys at the camp."

"We heard about something, and maybe it's just a story," Kris said, "but the idea was that the girls who worked at the camp were put through some kind of initiation. Ever hear about that?"

"Initiation?" he said, shaking his head. "News to me. I was just the handyman. It's not like I was a pal of those fellas."

Bobby had maintained his passive, blank look but Kris noticed a small tic had started near his left eye.

"No, but say Lowell or maybe Bud Naylor wanted you to do something, you'd do it, right?" Pat asked.

"Well, it wasn't up to Bud to tell me what to do. I work for the Osbornes."

"All right, what if Lowell Osborne ordered you to do something, a thing you didn't want to do. Would you go along?" Kris asked.

"When he was a kid, the senator was always telling me what to do, like he ran the place already." Bobby shrugged. "What could I do?"

"You seem like a straight shooter, Bobby," Kris said, wishing it were true. "Let me just ask you flat out. I've got a videotape showing three guys raping my sister the day she died. Two of them are Bud Naylor and Lowell Osborne, I'm quite sure, but the third guy is you. Am I right?"

She wondered which he would deny first, that Lowell and Bud were the other two, or that he was the third man.

Bobby looked back into the bar, to the comfort of his regular companions. His smell of stale sweat was now mingled with the scent of fear. "Where would you get something like that?"

"We were talking to the general this morning, Bobby. Jack Naylor."

Bobby banged his empty bottle onto the plastic table. "Fuck, Jack Naylor told you that?"

Kris didn't reply, just fixed him with her best guilt-inducing stare. Sometimes it was useful to identify two points, and let the source draw his own line between them.

Finally, Bobby looked away and said, "It's bullshit."

"If they forced you to do it, Bobby, it wouldn't be your fault," Pat said.

"I was right here, in this bar, the day your sister was killed," he said, looking directly at Kris. "It was my day off. I spent the whole day drinking. There were witnesses. The police cleared me. You can check that out."

He tapped his heavy forefinger twice on the table, then pointed it at Kris. "And don't believe everything you hear from the Naylors."

"You're saying they're liars?" Kris said.

Bobby shrugged again, and looked out at the lake. A sudden gust of wind brought new-fallen yellow leaves floating onto their table, and Bobby flicked at them irritably. "I've got a job to worry about. I'm not saying anything about anyone."

They'd lost him now, Kris thought, but at least she had created some doubt in his mind about the Naylors. Bobby Edwards wasn't the sharpest guy in town, but he was smart enough to know that it wouldn't be wise to incriminate himself, and they weren't in a position to offer him any kind of deal that would make him turn on the others.

"If you're worried about money, Bobby," Pat began, but Kris touched her arm, stopping her. They wouldn't get the truth by entering a bidding war with Lowell Osborne.

"Is there anything else?" Bobby asked, looking at Pat Osborne.

"No, Bobby, but thanks."

Thanks for nothing, Kris thought. She watched Bobby lumber back to the bar, where he quickly got himself another bottle of beer. She wondered what role he had really played. If he wasn't the third man, then who was?

27

It was 4:35 p.m. Kris tried to picture where Colin would be. After nearly three weeks away, her life in the newsroom seemed remote, almost from another age. She tried his office phone, but it was picked up by Lily Wong, the secretary who worked for him and the managing editor.

"Mr. Wendover's office. How can I help you?"

"Hey Lily, it's Kris. Is Colin around?"

"Kris?"

"Redner, the crime writer, remember me?"

"Of course, sorry, Kris. I didn't recognize your voice. How's your holiday going?"

Some holiday, she thought, but she said, "Great, thanks."

"He's out in the newsroom. I'll get him for you."

So it wasn't just her who thought it had been forever since she'd been in the newsroom. Away a few weeks and they were already starting to forget who she was.

While she waited for Colin to pick up, Kris sipped the margarita Pat had made. She was on the terrace overlooking the garden, where she had first met Pat. She could hear the clattering of pans through the open French doors of the house. Pat's cook had come in early, to make some kind of chicken pasta. They hadn't eaten since breakfast.

Finally, Colin came on the line.

"Good to know you're still alive, Kris. How's the story coming?"

His tone was brusque and she was about to remind him that it was him who wanted her to call in, but she didn't need another fight. "Got you right in the middle of something, didn't I?" she said.

"Still dealing with that drive-by shooting. It turns out that the victim was an innocent person walking down the street. There has been a second shootout, all over some kind of drug deal gone wrong. Two chaps dead, and an eleven-year-old boy took a bullet right through the eye. He's still alive. I've just cleared four open pages, so yes, it's going to be rather hectic. Everyone's been deployed, so there will be a bit of a lull, actually."

It was impossible to hear Colin's story without the adrenalin starting to flow. Breaking news was what everyone got into the business for, and here she was, in the Adirondacks, chasing the cold trail of a long-ago murder.

"Pretty busy day down here," she said, immediately thinking it would seem small compared to what Colin had to deal with back in Ottawa. She decided to lead with the most dramatic fact.

"The crash that killed L.T. Hill? No accident. The brake lines had been tampered with and his seatbelt was cut partway through."

"Surely you've gone to the authorities with that?"

"You still don't see it do you? There are no authorities down here that aren't part of Lowell Osborne's team. Even the state police aren't going to attribute this to the people that did it without a lot more than my say-so."

"What else?" Colin asked.

"I've interviewed Sharon Sloan again. She's the one who sent me the tape in the first place. She claims a handyman called Bobby Edwards was involved. Pat and I interviewed him, too."

"Pat? Who's Pat?"

Kris had forgotten that all her involvement with Pat had taken place in the time since she had last talked to Colin.

"Lowell Osborne's ex-wife. It's complicated."

"I dare say."

"We also talked to Jack Naylor. He's the senior political adviser that I suspect is masterminding the whole attempt to retrieve the tape. He's connected to three major defence contractors, doesn't want anything to spoil the business Lowell Osborne would bring them."

"I like that, a kind of Dick Cheney angle. Get anything out of him?"

"He was obliquely offering to make a deal. If I back off, he'll deliver the person who killed my sister."

"Can he do that?"

"He can come up with someone, but I doubt it would be the

real killer. I think he's hoping to use this handyman as a fall guy."

"Quite a complex story. Is any of this getting you closer to resolution?"

That was the question, Kris thought, and she wasn't sure she liked the answer.

"I've laid it out for them. They know what I suspect, and I'm sure they know I have the videotape. The next move is up to them."

"Good God, Kris. You're telling me that they've already killed this L.T. chap. Now you say the next move is up to them. What kind of a move do you think it will be?"

"I don't know, but the ex-wife is pretty effective as a shield. I'm staying at her place, going around with her. Doing anything to hurt her would be too risky. That would be exactly the kind of publicity they are tying themselves in knots to avoid. Can you imagine the headlines? 'Senator's ex-wife missing, suspected killed.' The husband is always the first one they look at, and these two are famous for their bad feelings. As long as I'm with her, I'm safe."

"Maybe," he said, sounding far from convinced. "What have you got left to do?"

"I need to talk to the senator's younger brother, Billy. Apparently he was at the camp that summer, too, and they don't get along. He might be willing to help. He's about an hour's drive from here, so I'm going to start fresh in the morning."

"Then what?"

"I don't know. We'll see what Billy says."

"All right. Check in after you've interviewed this Billy. I think you should get back up here, write what you've got, and we'll see if we can get it in the paper. It's going to be a rough bloody go with the lawyers, though, I can tell you that."

Kris suspected that Colin's prime concern was getting her safely back to Ottawa. Too much of what she knew wasn't provable, and she could never get into things like L.T. accepting the money from Jack Naylor. The other side would easily twist that to make him look like a crooked cop.

"All right. I'll call you tomorrow. It should be no later than noon."

28

Kris quietly parked the Prius on Oak Avenue and watched the man across the street. He sat on a sawhorse in front of a tumbledown garage, a can of red paint and a brush in his hands, working on a big snowplough blade, the kind you'd mount on the front of a pickup. It would be a while until there was snow, but you could feel fall in the morning air, the crispness and lack of humidity, with just a tinge of woodsmoke.

It had to be Billy Osborne, but it was impossible to see any family resemblance. The man's hair was pulled back in a ponytail that came out the back of his green ball cap, and when he turned, Kris could see he had a full brown beard, the kind that crept right up to his cheekbones and left the impression of eyes peering out of a mat of hair. Despite his background, Billy Osborne looked just like any rough-and-tumble guy from a little town in upstate New York. What was the phrase Colin liked to use? Gone native, that was it.

She was obviously in the right place, because a hand-painted sign on the front lawn announced that it was the premises of Billy's Lawn and Snow. Like most of the others on the street, Billy's house was a big, white clapboard, but it was fancier than the rest, with a turret in one corner. Oak appeared to be about the only good street in Midbury, a town so small that it made Osborne seem like a metropolis. Kris would bet that the few doctors, lawyers, or teachers the town had would all live on Oak. They must not have appreciated Billy's lawn sign and his beat-up Ford pickup in the lane.

She got out of the car and locked it, a big city reflex. Pat had decided not to come, saying she and Billy had never gotten along, and her presence would lower the chances of his co-operating. Without Pat, Kris figured she might as well drive her own car. The Naylors knew she had been using the Taurus anyway, so that little subterfuge had run its course. Kris had to admit she felt safer with

Pat, but the Naylors wouldn't be looking for her up here.

Her feet crunched on the gravel as she walked up the driveway. Billy was intent on his painting, but when she was about ten feet away, he spoke without looking up.

"Whatever you're selling, I don't need it."

"I'm not selling anything, but I have a few questions to ask you."

"I don't do surveys."

"Kris Redner," she said, extending her hand. "I'm a writer with the *Citizen*, in Ottawa. Maybe the name Redner is familiar to you?"

"Sorry, I don't get up to Ottawa."

Billy placed the can and brush on the ground, then stood up. He was a lanky man, well over six feet, but thin inside his blue coveralls. The full beard masked his face, but Kris could tell by his eyes that she had caught his interest. He made no move to shake her hand, though, and Kris dropped it to her side. Warming this guy up wasn't going to work, so she decided to get right to it.

"Kathy Redner was my sister. She was murdered in Osborne, nearly thirty years ago. I'm trying to find out who did it."

His eyes narrowed slightly, but he didn't speak.

"I've been down in Osborne the past few weeks, talking to your brother, the Naylors, Bobby Edwards, Sharon Sloan, Liz Harper. People like that."

"Well, if you've talked to all of them, I doubt there's anything I can add."

He bent to pick up the brush and can, and began applying paint on the blade again. "I've got to get this finished before the paint dries," he said. "Snow season's not that far off."

Kris knew she needed to jolt him. The Osbornes were good at ignoring the truth.

"I know what you did, Billy. You want to talk about it?"

He looked back at her sharply, his eyes searching her more carefully now. Kris felt the reassuring weight of the gun in her purse, then wondered how long it would take to get it out if he became violent.

Then he put the paint down. "With Lowell's campaign, I figured someone like you would eventually show up. We'd better go in the house," he said, his tone flat, almost resigned.

"The verandah would be fine."

"Don't trust me?" he asked.

"Not yet."

He led her to the verandah, and they sat in two battered white wicker chairs with lumpy floral cushions. "You want a coffee?" he asked.

She did, but she didn't want to give him any more time to think his way out of talking to her, if he'd actually decided to open up. Pat had said that Lowell and Billy didn't get along. How would he play it?

"No, thanks," she said.

"All right. Let's get to it. What is it you think I did?"

"Raped my sister. I've seen the videotape."

Billy exhaled sharply, as if she'd hit him in the stomach. Then he looked away, back at the driveway. He didn't say anything.

Finally, he said, "So you think someone raped your sister. What makes you imagine it was me?"

His tone was calm, not the angry outrage of the innocent. Or for that matter, she told herself, the feigned outrage of the guilty.

"There were three men in the videotape. One, I'm sure, was Bud Naylor. I believe another was Bobby Edwards, the handyman. The third man could be your brother, or Tom Larson, but I think it was you. The other two were with their girlfriends that day. Where were you?"

"All that was a long time ago."

"So I keep hearing, but it's my family. I can't let it go."

Then she told him about her father's death a week later, her suspicion that his death was tied in some way to Kathy's, and the effect it all had on her mother.

"I'm sure you know about your father and my mother," Kris said. What a mess those two had started, she thought.

"Yeah, I knew. Dad and Lowell were a lot alike." He looked at his watch and said, "Look, you want a beer or something?"

"Sounds good," she said, although the prospect wasn't particularly attractive. It was ten o'clock in the morning. If it loosened him up, though, it would be worthwhile.

He went into the house and returned a minute later with two Rolling Rocks. She took a sip of hers, and he downed half of his. She couldn't believe she was sitting having a beer with one of the men who had raped her sister. But then, she had done the same thing with Bobby Edwards yesterday. They were all human, in the end, and Billy had only been a kid when it happened. Maybe, like her sister, he had simply gotten in over his head.

"You know, I came up here to get away from Osborne family stuff, but it seems there's no escaping it."

"Families are like that," she said. "I didn't imagine I'd ever come back to Osborne, but after someone mailed me that video-tape, I couldn't just ignore it."

"It's amazing what you can ignore, if you try."

"You must want to get away from it all pretty badly, living up here, cutting grass and ploughing snow."

"It's clean."

"If your brother wins the nomination, you will end up being a news story yourself, you know. People will dig up everything about you and Lowell."

"There's not much to tell."

"I doubt that."

"We don't get along. It happens with brothers. Lowell revels in the money and power. It doesn't turn me on. I've got everything I need right here."

"How long have you been up here?" she asked.

"Ever since college. It started out as a summer thing, while I was at Yale. The original Billy, Billy Cobb, was selling out, so I bought in. Two Billys, seemed like it was meant to work out that way. I figured I'd do it for a few years, see what I wanted to do. Turns out, this was it."

"You went from Yale to lawn cutting?"

"There's a lot of big places outside of town, overlook the river. Owners are rich guys who only come up on weekends. I keep it all looking good for them. It's an honest living."

"And the family businesses aren't?"

"Lowell was going to run those. I wasn't going to fetch and carry for him."

"When was the last time you lived at home?"

"1981."

"The summer my sister was killed."

"That's right."

"Coincidence?"

"Life's full of them."

Billy wasn't looking at her, flicking a bit of drying red paint from his work boot with his thumbnail.

"You're my last chance to find out what really happened to my sister, Billy. I haven't come across one honest person yet."

He worked the piece of paint off and turned to face her.

"I've got obligations."

"Meaning what?"

"A lot of people's lives could be ruined by all of this."

"Let's make a list," she said. "For starters, there was my sister, my father, my mother. And me, of course. Do those lives count for anything?"

He stroked his beard, then looked away. Finally, he said, "It wasn't a rape."

"Really? It certainly looked like it on the video, three guys tying her up, tearing her clothes off, taking turns going at her. Then she screams for the camera. What would you call it?"

"Initiation was the term they used. The other two girls, Sharon and Liz, they'd already done it. They were laughing five minutes afterwards. It was like a show, a pretend rape. Kathy had agreed to do the same thing. She'd seen the other tapes."

"Come on. You're telling me they didn't mind doing it with three guys while they made a movie out of it?"

"They were wild," he said. "They knew it was what it would take to keep their rich boyfriends, too. Your sister had gone out with Tom Larson a few times. I think she wanted him back. Maybe it was a way of showing she was as good as Liz."

Kris had to admit Billy's story was plausible. Oh Kathy, she thought, what were you thinking?

"But my sister was only fourteen," she said.

"Yes, I had no idea at the time. I thought she was eighteen, like the other two. After we did it, she freaked out, ran off."

"You say 'we' did it. Who do you mean?"

"You had it right. We were all drunk. Normally, nothing like this would happen without Lowell's say-so, but Bud wanted to surprise him. I was stupid. A follower.

"After she was killed, I left Osborne, and I haven't been back."

"So Lowell wasn't involved?" Kris said. She hadn't mentioned the fourth person in the room, the cameraman.

"No, like I said, it was just the three of us."

That was a lie, she was sure, but after a month of digging, she had finally found someone who was ready to tell most of the truth. She wished she had been recording this interview, but she had been sure that a tape recorder, even a notebook, would spook him. Would he repeat it later? That would finally allow her to prove what had happened.

"How was she killed, Billy?" she asked softly.

"I don't know. I wish I did. After she ran off, Lowell was pissed, screaming at Bud. If she went to the police, we were all going to jail, he said. Bud said he'd take care of it. You can draw your own conclusions, I guess."

Kris suppressed a smile of triumph. That was the quote she'd been waiting for. She'd told Billy she was a writer for a newspaper and he'd offered the information. She'd put those words in her notebook later, but for the moment, she was content to burn them in her memory. Lowell Osborne was in up to his ears now.

"And where was Tom when all this was going on?"

"I didn't see Tom. I imagine he was with Liz."

"After she was killed, who orchestrated the cover-up?"

"I don't know. I got in my car and headed out. I wanted nothing to do with it."

"Didn't you feel responsible?"

"Of course I did," he snapped. "I've felt responsible for thirty years. I didn't kill her, but I didn't do anything about it, either. I just couldn't send my brother to prison."

Or yourself, either, Kris thought.

"It would have killed my father. Ruined the whole family."

"I know what that's like," she said.

He looked at her straight on, his dark eyes intense.

"I'm sorry. I was seventeen. I had no idea all the grief that thing with your sister was going to unleash."

"Now you're forty-seven," she said. "What are you going to do about it?"

"What do you want from me?"

"I want you to finally stand up, Billy, and tell the truth. The people who did this should be in jail, not running the country."

He stared at the weathered grey floor of the verandah, his thoughts seemingly far away. His silence dragged on to the point where Kris began to wonder if he just expected her to get up and leave. Finally, he said, "If I do this, Lowell will be destroyed."

"Don't you think he should be?"

"Do you think everything he's done since that day in 1981 should be cancelled out by what happened to your sister?"

"The courts can decide that," she said.

"He'll be lynched in the media long before it ever gets to court. You know that."

Kris said nothing. It was true, of course. And she'd be knotting the noose.

Finally, Billy stood up and shoved his hands in his pockets. "I'll do it," he said. "I've been carrying this thing with me for thirty years. That's long enough."

She nodded solemnly, resisting the urge to pump her arm in triumph.

"Here's the way it's going to work," Billy said. "First, I have to talk to Lowell. He deserves that much. I want to convince him to withdraw. If he won't, we'll do it your way."

Kris tried not to show her disappointment. If he talked to Lowell before committing himself on her story, there was an excellent chance that his brother would persuade him not to act. Whatever kind of persuading it took. And withdrawing wasn't all she had in mind.

"All right," she said, smiling to make it seem as if she fully agreed with Billy's plan. "Before you do that, do you think we could do this a little more formally? I'd like to lead you through the events that led up to and followed my sister's death. To get all the details. I'll take notes, and tape it. I'll need that for my story."

She intended to go with what he'd told her, one way or another, but getting the brother on tape would make it rock solid for the lawyers.

"I've said I'll do it, and I will," he said. "First, I talk to Lowell."

"All right, deal."

Even if Billy didn't follow through, she had her story. Lowell Osborne's life was about to get very interesting.

29

The weather began to turn when Kris left Highway 11 and headed south on I-87. Heavy, dark clouds came in from the west, carried by a gusting wind that buffeted the little Toyota. By the time she took the turnoff for Osborne, half an hour later, the rain was so heavy she had to run the wipers on high speed, and it was still difficult to see the road.

When she got back to town, she would call Colin and tell him about the interview with Billy Osborne. At last, she had made some real progress. When she had left his house, she had parked a few blocks away and reconstructed their conversation in her notebook. There would still be an element of doubt until she had Billy on tape, though. With the brother as an eyewitness, the story would fly. She didn't have to nail down exactly what role Lowell Osborne had played on the day of her sister's death. The readers could connect the dots.

She had Sharon Sloan for corroboration, too. Colin didn't have to know what a lousy witness Sharon would be, if it came to a lawsuit.

If she could get the guts of her story in the paper, she knew it would be picked up by the major U.S. news organizations and they would start looking at every dark corner of Lowell Osborne's life. The state police would be compelled to investigate. She hoped Osborne would eventually be charged, along with Bud Naylor and whoever else was involved. Even if he wasn't, her goal would be accomplished. Lowell Osborne had taken away her most precious things, now she would take away his, the dream of becoming president. That would be revenge enough for her to feel she had done all she could for Kathy, at last.

She had been surprised Billy Osborne hadn't raised the problem of his own jeopardy in going public with the story of what happened that day in 1981. Being an Osborne, he probably knew he could cut a deal with the state attorney's office if he was the key witness that enabled them to go after the bigger names.

In good weather, she would be in town in fifteen minutes, in time to see what Pat's chef had in mind for lunch. With the rain, she didn't feel safe going any faster than thirty-five miles an hour. The drivers behind her obviously thought that was way too slow. A red pickup was right on her tail, its heavy grill looming over the Prius. Behind the pickup, she could see a big, black SUV. It looked like the two trucks were glued together.

Idiots. If she touched the brakes, there would be a three-vehicle pileup. Why didn't they pass? She couldn't pull over. The shoulder would be too soft from the rain.

Kris tried to avoid the distraction of the two trucks. It took all her concentration just to follow the curves of the road. It was cutting through the pine and fir woods of the state park, but it would open up in a few miles, once she got closer to Osborne. Maybe they would pass then.

Billy hadn't exactly said when he would talk to his brother, but she was sure he wouldn't let it wait. With the weather, it was unlikely he'd drive down today, but he had given her his cell phone number. Kris would check with him in the morning, make sure he wasn't wavering. Maybe she could re-interview him in town, save another drive up to Midbury. Once she got his story on tape, she'd head back to Ottawa and start writing. She had found out all she was going to in Osborne. It had been a long three weeks, and the welcome she had received had proven one thing: this was no longer home.

The red pickup pulled out to pass, its big tires showering the Toyota with water. For a few seconds, Kris couldn't see at all as the road spray washed across the windshield. She glanced sideways and saw the pickup was still in the left hand lane, slightly ahead of her. What was the matter with this jerk? Why didn't he just pass?

The black SUV had now pulled in tight behind the Toyota, taking the place of the pickup, and boxing her in. Kris speeded up and the pickup matched her, staying beside her about half a truck length in front. She could see the shapes of two men in the pickup and two more in the SUV, but she didn't recognize any faces through the rain-smeared windows.

Now she could see what this was, and her heart started to

pound, her mouth suddenly dry.

The pickup pushed into her lane, trying to cut her off. Kris gripped the wheel harder and fought to keep her little car on the road. If she hit the shoulder, she'd lose control. Her mind immediately flashed to L.T., trapped in his smashed Blazer at the side of the road, the smell of gasoline hanging raw in the air.

This was going to be the end, and it was so easy for them.

The pickup driver jerked his wheel right, smashing into the side of the Toyota with a loud thump and causing the car to skid sideways. Kris regained control, but now the pickup was tight against her driver's door, its sheer size forcing her car to the right. Behind, the SUV hit her bumper, the two of them driving the Toyota off the road like a grader clearing snow.

She braked, feeling another bump from the SUV. The car wobbled as it hit the shoulder. They wanted to make it look like an accident, and just drive away, she thought, but she wasn't going to help them. She slowed the car, pumping the brakes to avoid a skid in the soft gravel. The SUV hit the Toyota again, but she brought it to a halt.

What had just happened had taken only seconds, she knew, but it seemed like far longer. She felt cold trickles of sweat running down her sides.

The pickup also pulled to a stop, half in the lane and half on the shoulder, so close to the Toyota that she couldn't open the driver's door. The SUV halted behind her, its high headlights blinding her from the reflection in the rear-view mirror.

Two men got out of the SUV and ran toward the Toyota. Both were big, and dressed in camouflage pants and black, military-style jackets. She didn't recognize either.

The gun, she thought. Pat Osborne's Walther was still in her purse.

Kris reached for the black leather bag, which sat on the passenger's seat. It seemed as if her arms moved in slow motion. She fumbled with the zipper, and then felt the cold metal in her hand.

One of the men pulled on the locked door, then Kris was covered with wet broken glass. The man stuck his head through the shattered window, tire iron still in hand.

Bud Naylor.

She pulled the gun from her purse.

"Gun," the second man shouted, and she felt a searing pain as the tire iron descended on her right forearm. The gun fell from her numb fingers.

30

It was the same thing again. A cheery female voice telling him, "The subscriber you are trying to reach is not currently available."

Colin Wendover banged his own phone down in frustration. Four o'clock. He must have tried Kris's cell twenty times in the past two hours. Granted, the woman had no more sense of time than a bloody Inuit, but she had promised to check in by noon. All this stuff with L.D., or T.R. or whatever the fellow's name was, that was a pressing concern. If these chaps she was chasing down were playing at that level, she was in danger.

He cursed himself for not following his instinct and heading down there himself yesterday. Her request for more time was really a cry for help and he'd reacted by suspending her. What the hell had he been thinking? Kris liked to put out that she was as tough as nails, and God knew, she had dealt with wrong sorts every day in Toronto and enough of them here, too. But that was different. At least there was some kind of law and order, and the watchful eye of colleagues not far away. Kris was on someone else's turf now, and from the way she described it, the stakes were enormous.

He leaned toward his office door and bellowed, "Lily!"

Lily Wong entered his office, clearly annoyed. "Do you have to shout like that? I'm not your dog."

"No, quite. Sorry. It's an emergency."

"It's always an emergency around here."

"This is what I need you to do."

He thrust a scrap of paper toward her.

"This is Kris Redner's cell number. Ring it every five minutes until you get an answer. And phone down to HR. I think she has an uncle out in the bush somewhere. I want a number for him."

Lily looked sceptical.

"Is this personal?"

"Personal? Of course not. Kris's working on a big story down in New York State. It's critical that I get hold of her today."

She shrugged and turned to go back to her own desk outside his office.

"Oh, and one other thing, Lily. Get me a number for a Pat Osborne, lives in a town of the same name in upstate New York. Pat's a woman, so Patricia, I suppose."

"Right," she said. "But I leave at five."

Colin was tired of Lily Wong's attitude. If she weren't so gorgeous, he'd have fired her long ago.

By 4:45, Colin had determined that Pat Osborne was expecting Kris hours ago, but had heard nothing. She had left early to interview Pat's brother-in-law Billy as planned. A call to Billy had been no more useful. She had left his place late morning, didn't say where she was going. A big storm had come up, Billy said, and he speculated that maybe she was sitting it out. The driving was miserable.

That didn't sound like Kris to Colin, and he hadn't a clue if either one of these people could be trusted. After all, they were the ex-wife and brother of the man she was trying to bring down.

It was time to send in the cavalry, but first he wanted to talk to the uncle, on the off-chance Kris might have gotten in touch with him to discuss her attempt to discover what had really happened to the sister. Kris had mentioned the chap from time to time, but Colin had formed the impression he was a bit of a nutter, living in the bush up north of Ottawa in some place called Killaloe. Still, he might be able to give some insight into the situation down there.

It took half a dozen rings, but the fellow finally picked up.

"Redner," he said, the voice deep and gravelly.

"Mr. Redner, Colin Wendover here. I'm phoning from the *Ottawa Citizen*, about your niece Kris."

"Something happen to her?"

"That's what I'm trying to find out. She's been on an assignment in New York State the last few weeks, but I can't contact her. Based on some of what she's told me, I'm rather concerned. I wonder if she might have called you?"

"Haven't talked to Kris since her birthday back in May."

"Well then, I guess you won't know what's going on. Sorry to have disturbed you."

"Wait a minute. You said New York State. What's she doing down there?"

Colin gave Martin Redner the short version of Kris's attempt to find out who murdered her sister, and her suspicions about Lowell Osborne. As soon as he mentioned that name, Redner said, "Lowell Osborne? Jesus Christ, if she was going to mess with him, why didn't she call me?"

"I understood that you weren't close," Colin said, trying to be tactful. He actually remembered Kris describing the chap as a disgusting old goat who lived in a smelly cabin in the middle of nowhere, or words to that effect.

"I'm the only family she has left," he said. "So you say she hasn't called in and now you can't find her."

"That's it. It's possible she has simply forgotten, but she did tell me that she would phone by noon."

"And your gut says she's in trouble."

"Yes."

"That's all I need to hear. I'm heading down."

"I was thinking the same thing. Why don't we go together?"

"This is Redner family business. Something I should have dealt with a long time ago. There's no need for you to get involved."

"Well, I feel that I ought to. Kris and I are . . ." Colin sought the right word. What was his status with Kris? He settled for "partners."

"Yeah, she mentioned something in May about some English guy she was screwing. Is that you?'

Colin preferred his own characterization of their relationship, but it was apparent that subtlety of word usage wasn't a gift shared by the entire Redner family.

"Our relationship is of that nature, yes," he said.

There was a long pause, and Colin thought the connection might have been broken.

"All right," Redner said. "You can tag along, but don't get in my way."

"Look here," Colin said. "I'm a former foreign correspondent. I've been under fire in Afghanistan, Lebanon, and the Falklands. I can certainly handle myself."

No need to mention how long ago all that was, or that his main physical activity now was golf, Colin thought.

"We'll see. I'll be at the border in Ogdensburg in five hours. Meet me on the Canadian side. I'll be driving an old black Chev pickup, had the shit kicked out of it. One door's red. You can't miss it."

"Five hours? That could be a bit tight. I've some things here that — "

Martin Redner cut him off. "A man like you should be able to manage that. Ten o'clock, that's it. I just hope we're not too late."

31

Kris heard it again. A scurrying noise. It was impossible to tell how far away it was. Sound distorted in the emptiness of the cellar. But it was getting closer.

She willed herself to think of something else but found her mind filled with a memory from childhood; her mother, the smell of gin on her breath, locking Kris in the cellar of their house on Washington Street. It always followed a loud, slurred speech about how bad Kris was, then she was shut in the windowless cellar, so her mother could finish the bottle without interference. She spent hours down there in the dark, imagining that every shape was a monster.

Now, the monsters were real.

They had dragged her from the Toyota, quickly gagging her with a rag and pinioning her arms and legs with duct tape. Then they had tossed her in the back of the SUV as if she were a duffle bag, and covered her with an itchy wool blanket that smelled like a dog.

She must have passed out from the pain in her arm, because when Kris came to, she was in a cellar. Alone, except for the scurrying sound. There was a faint light from the far end of the room. It must be nearly dark. All she could see was one blank, empty stone wall. They had placed her face down on a rough, wooden table. Her head was twisted to one side and held in place by a strap of the grey, sticky tape. Two more straps across her back and thighs kept her pinned to the table like an insect preserved for scientific examination. Her arms were still taped behind her back, and they had lost all feeling. That was probably a blessing. She didn't think her right arm was broken, but the memory of the pain was fresh in her mind. It had come shooting up her arm and seemed to go right through the top of her head.

They had removed the gag, a rag that smelled of sweat. That

couldn't be a good sign, Kris thought. It meant she could scream her lungs out, but no one would hear her.

They would be back soon enough, she knew. Bud Naylor, Bobby Edwards, and two other men she didn't recognize. They were probably upstairs now, having a couple of beers and a nice dinner, looking forward to their evening's work.

She was sure the cellar was the one under the main lodge at Osborne's camp. Even with her head taped in place, she could tell the room was exceptionally long and rectangular. Surely it was the other side of the space she had explored on the tour of the camp. She assumed, too, that the table she was strapped to was the same one her sister had been raped on. They had even put her in the same face-down position.

Bud Naylor was playing the psychological game, trying to reduce her to jelly before he asked his first question.

Well, fuck him.

She drew a deep breath, straining against the tape. Rats or mice? The noise sounded exceptionally loud, but she knew it would be magnified in her ears. Kris just hoped they didn't crawl over her. She wasn't sure if she could handle that.

She tried to imagine that the sound came from a chipmunk, trapped in the basement like her. Something cute and cuddly.

Pat or Billy? That was the question she had been asking herself. One of them had betrayed her. How else could Bud Naylor have known when she'd be coming down the lake road to town?

Her money was on Billy. After nearly thirty years of hiding a secret, he'd agreed to co-operate just a little too easily. The only things that could have motivated him were honour and decency, two qualities that didn't seem to be included in the Osborne DNA. She'd kept herself from questioning it at the time, so eager to think that she finally had Lowell Osborne where she wanted him.

It turned out it was just the other way around.

Now that they had taken her, it seemed so obvious that they could have done it at any time. Somehow, she had convinced herself that her reporter's invulnerability would protect her. In the civilized world, reporters did their jobs without fear of losing their lives, but this was different, it had always been different.

She had never been a mere observer. Not since that videotape arrived in the mail.

She hadn't told Pat when to expect her back, but surely she'd be wondering by now what had become of her. Would she do anything about it, or would she just mix herself a strong drink and wait to see how it all turned out? And what about Colin? She had promised to call by noon. Would he act, or just fret? But what could he really do, back in Ottawa?

Kris had little doubt what Bud had in mind for her. The videotape was all too fresh in her mind. She also remembered the beating he had given Sharon Sloan. For her, that would be just the warm-up, she imagined.

The thing to focus on, the one thing to hold tight to, was survival. They needed to find the videotape. As long as they didn't have it, they couldn't afford to kill her. Once they knew where it was, they'd use her as they liked, then finish her.

How she wished she had FedExed the bloody thing back to Colin in Ottawa, along with all her notebooks. Those, they would already have taken from the trunk of her car, along with her laptop. Maybe they were upstairs reading them now.

Kris was just thankful she wasn't still carrying the tape around with her. Had she been, she had no doubt that she would have been dead already. Early that morning, before Pat got up, she had wrapped the videotape in heavy plastic and tucked it inside one of six stone pagodas that ringed the terrace. She wasn't entirely sure she could trust Pat, but if someone did search for the tape, they would look in the room Kris had been using, not inside the garden decorations. So she hoped.

The door at the top of the stairs opened with a screech of rusty hinges, and she heard the footsteps of two men coming heavily down the stairs. The fear passed up her body like a wave of cold.

They were to the left, behind her. She couldn't see them, but she could smell the beer. One of the men had to be Bud Naylor. The other wore a strong cologne that didn't entirely mask the smell of sweat.

"Hey Bud, what's new?" she asked, determined not to let them see how afraid she really was.

"Still got lots of attitude, have you, Kris? We'll see how long that lasts."

Lights flicked on overhead, causing her to blink after the near-darkness.

Bud circled around so she could see him. A khaki USMC T-shirt stretched across his belly and hung loose over multi-pocketed camouflage pants.

"Going to war?" she asked.

"Something like that."

He continued walking around the table, stopping to her left so he was out of her line of sight. "You're looking pretty vulnerable," he said. "Kind of reminds me of your sister. It's the same table. I suppose a smart girl like you already figured that out.

"You know what? You got the wrong impression from that videotape. She enjoyed every minute of it, little Kathy."

"She was fourteen years old," Kris said, speaking to the empty stone wall.

"Old enough to beg for it," he said.

"Bullshit," Kris said. "Weren't you the loser, Bud? The guy without a girl? I doubt that too many women have ever begged you for it."

He gave a cold laugh. "We'll see who's going to do the begging.

"My job is to get that videotape. We tried to make it easy for you, even profitable, but you just wouldn't play ball. Now it's come to this. Where's the tape, Kris? Last chance."

Last chance to make Bud Naylor's job easy, she thought. She knew her only real chance was to hold out as long as possible, and hope Pat would send someone to her rescue.

"Sorry, can't help you," she said.

"Okay, I'm all right with that. Personally, I was hoping you might say that. I'm going to enjoy convincing you."

Kris felt the tape that held her thighs strapped down give way. She thought of twisting her body, trying to kick, but her legs were dead, lifeless from lack of circulation.

"Nick, cut her skirt off," Naylor said.

Kris cursed the fact that it was the one day she hadn't worn jeans, then realized that it wouldn't have made any difference.

She felt the cold steel of a large knife on the backs of her upper thighs, then heard the sound of her denim skirt being ripped bottom to top. Then it was wrenched off her and thrown to the floor.

"Tie her ankles," Naylor said.

The second man, the one she hadn't seen, roughly took her left leg, tingling now from the returning circulation, and pulled it outward, looping tape around her ankle and down to the table leg. He did the same with her right leg. She was left spread-eagled, totally exposed.

"Having any second thoughts?" Bud asked.

She said nothing, then heard the sound of his belt sliding through its loops.

"God, I love black panties," he said. "It's a shame to take them off."

The second man, Nick, said nothing, but she could hear him breathing loudly. If she lived, she wanted to see them both die, slowly.

He grabbed the black cotton material and pulled up hard, yanking it deep into the cleft between her buttocks, leaving them bare. "There, a compromise," Bud said, his tone almost cheery. "Oh, I wanted you to know, by the way, that I'm fully recovered from that kick you gave me. Not very ladylike.

"You know, I was going to use my belt, but I think I'll use my hand. It's more personal."

His rough, calloused palm smacked Kris's buttock harder than she would have thought possible. She gritted her teeth, determined not to cry out.

The blows fell in a stinging flurry. After six on each cheek, her ass was tender and burning with pain, but she still had made no sound. The worst part was knowing this was just the beginning.

"Looks like I'll have to use my belt after all," Bud said. "Sure you can't remember what you did with that tape?"

"Yes, I remember," she said, trying to keep her voice from showing the pain. "I'm just not going to tell you."

Six blows from the belt came in quick succession, the last one finally forcing her to give a muffled whimper. She could imagine the six big welts that scarred her, and found herself wondering inanely why corporal punishment always came in units of six.

The pain was searing now, and she thought she might black out. Would they stop if she did, or keep going?

"Maybe we need to do this a different way," Bud said. "I don't want to spoil that sweet ass. I'll bet it stings, though.

"Nick, cut off her panties."

She felt two quick contacts of the cold knife, then the two thin pieces of material that held her underwear together at the sides were gone and the panties ripped away, leaving her fully exposed.

"Jesus," Nick said, speaking for the first time. "Sweet little piece."

Kris burned with shame as they examined her, even though she had known from the first minute that this was the way it would be. She frantically tried to think of some strategy to make them kill her, to make it stop now.

Bud ran a rough finger slowly between her legs, pausing to press lightly against her anus.

He leaned in close to her ear and said, "I own you now, little girl, every inch of you."

Then she heard another person coming down the stairs, and the voice of a third man said, "Bud, phone's for you."

"Goddamn it," Bud said angrily. "Can't you see I'm busy?"

"It's the senator, Bud."

"All right, then, bring me that phone."

She heard the third man descend the stairs, then Bud took the phone and went off to the far side of the room. The senator seemed to be doing most of the talking, Bud limited mostly to "uh huhs." Then he said, "Jesus, Lowell, I'm right at the point of finding out what she did with that damn tape. Once we determine that, we can wrap all of this up."

There was another long pause as Bud listened to the senator.

"I know that, I know that," he said, "but who's going to come looking here?"

After a briefer pause, he said, "So what do you suggest, then?

"Yeah, yeah, I suppose. Not so easy in the dark, but I'll get it done. Right now. I understand."

Bud clicked off the phone and said to the other two, "Untie her. We've got to move her. Get that gag back on, and keep her hands behind her back. And Lou, get something from upstairs to cover her up. We can't be dragging her out like that."

Bud's tone was angry, but it sounded almost as if someone else had created the situation in front of them, and now he had to clean it up. She wondered if he was even sane, then understood that it probably didn't matter.

Bud leaned close to her, his breath hot in her ear.

"We're taking you deep into the cold, dark mountains. And you're not coming back."

32

Colin saw what he took to be Martin Redner's pickup, pulled over at the side of the road where the pavement widened leading to the border point. The vehicle appeared to sag to the right, and the tailgate was wired shut. He pulled his BMW in behind it, then walked up on the passenger side and tapped on the glass. The man inside reached over to roll down the window.

"Watch that door. Paint could still be a bit tacky. If you've got any stuff, throw it in back."

Obviously Redner, then.

"Splendid. Let me just park my car."

Colin pulled the BMW into the parking area, hoping it might still be there when he got back. Returning quickly to the truck, he looked in the back and saw a greasy-looking gas can, a chain saw, a battered red tool chest, a military-style knapsack and a hockey duffle bag on the rusted truck bed. He had just had time to stop at the condo and throw a few things in a bag and he was glad he had only grabbed the old Eddie Bauer. He placed it in back, trying to keep it as far from the gas can and chainsaw as possible.

The door of the truck was balky, screeching on its hinges, and he could see the black paint was fresh. Colin settled gingerly on the bench seat, feeling individual springs beneath him. The smell of woodsmoke, tobacco, and ancient sweat had already filled the truck. Colin tried again to remember how long it would take to drive to Osborne.

Redner had still given no greeting, beyond the warning about the paint. "I'm Colin Wendover," Colin said, to get things rolling.

"Figured as much. When we get to the border, let me do the talking."

Eighteen-wheelers were backed up to their right, but there

were only two vehicles ahead of them in the cars-only lane. The border guard was young and serious-looking, black hair clipped short, uniform immaculate. No doubt a kid from a small town nearby who thought he was defending America against terrorism, Colin thought.

"Nationality?" the guard asked.

"American," Redner said, displaying a birth certificate.

"And you sir?"

"British."

Colin passed over his passport as the guard looked at it curiously, puzzled by the idea of someone British crossing at Ogdensburg.

"Purpose of your visit?"

"Visiting a relative in Osborne," Martin Redner said. "This fella here's a family friend."

Colin nodded and smiled.

"Okay," the guard said, handing them back their paperwork. "Have a good visit."

Colin was relieved that the fellow had chosen not to take an interest in the chain saw, and God knew what Redner had in those bags.

As they skirted Ogdensburg, the lights of the town to their right, Colin said, "So you painted the door?"

"Truck like this is good camouflage in the mountains. Plenty of them. Red door would make it stand out."

That conversational sally parried, they drove on in silence for half an hour. They passed through a few hamlets, then there was nothing but trees and emptiness, dimly lit by a moon that kept peeking through the clouds. Puddles shimmered at the side of the road, the last remnants of the afternoon's storm.

Colin pulled his phone from the pocket of his jacket and tried Kris's cell again. Still nothing but the same damned recorded message. Not in service at this time.

He cautiously examined Redner, looking out the corner of his eye. The man's appearance was much like that of the derelicts Colin had to pass on the way to his condo; bearded, with greasy grey hair that hadn't received the attentions of a barber in some time. He wore a red and black plaid jacket, green work trousers with black stains on the legs, and a blue and red ball cap with some sort of service station logo on it. Colin's own khaki cotton pants and navy golf jacket seemed better suited to a weekend at a posh country inn.

The silence of the drive had given him a rare opportunity for reflection. What were his plans regarding Kris, exactly? Their moving in together was precipitous. He could see that now, although it had made perfect sense at the time. After four wives, he knew he'd have to be mad to even consider matrimony again. The financial burden of his past misjudgments was so crushing that he'd be working until the day he died to support them all. Still, he rather fancied that he was in love with Kris. Hadn't quite found the moment to say so, though, and she'd seemed quite distant in the few weeks before she took off so suddenly for New York. He hoped he wasn't on a fool's errand.

It was difficult to believe that this fellow beside him was related to Kris. In the event he was to marry her, this chap would be an in-law. Colin shuddered at the thought.

He rolled down the window an inch. The night air was cool but a welcome relief from Redner's woodsy pong.

The advantage of Redner's rough appearance, he supposed, was that it would enable him to blend in with the locals. And, of course, he was one. A quality local guide was key to the success of any operation. He'd heard that repeated many times by military chaps who knew far more about this sort of thing than he did.

But what was the plan? Redner had told him nothing. They had driven for an hour, and still he had found no need to speak, or to get to know anything about Colin. He felt on about a par with the stuff in the back of the truck. Something that might be useful, but wasn't really part of the main scheme.

After another fifteen minutes, Colin finally gave in to the silence. "Look, Redner, I understand you aren't keen on my accompanying you, but here I am. I'd at least like to be apprised of the plan. What do you intend to do?"

"Apprised, eh? All right. We're going to the cabin where I used to live, to get a few things I need. Then we're going to Osborne's camp to find Kris and get her the hell out of there."

It all sounded delightfully simple, but Colin said, "How can you be so sure where she is?"

"If Osborne has got her, he'll stash her out there. Too risky to keep her in town. The guy's got about 1,000 acres of bush. Plenty of places to hide her there."

"A thousand acres? How in the world will we ever find her, then?"

"It's my home ground. I know where to look."

Colin settled back and looked out the window again. More trees, but the road was steadily rising now. Redner's description had been skimpy, but it was at least comforting to know he had some sort of plan.

"You mentioned that all this was family business, something you should have taken care of long ago. Did you mean about Kris's sister?"

Had Redner known the killer's identity, but let it go for decades, finally forcing Kris to do his work for him? Colin wondered.

"There's been problems between the Redners and the Osbornes, goes back generations. They treated us like dirt, only good enough to fix things for them or show them where to kill a deer. My dad guided at their camp for decades, then they dumped him like yesterday's shit, when he was in his sixties. Left him with nothing. My brother practically ran their damn shoe factory, then he died on the job. Again, we got nothing. This was right after Kathy, my niece, was killed up at their camp. My brother Mike was on to something about that. I thought his death was pretty damn suspicious, but I didn't wait around to be next. Headed for the border, never looked back."

All this poured out, like he had been waiting a long time to say it.

"Ah yes, well, I can see where you'd have a grievance there."

"Damn right. I should have taken the Osbornes on head-on back then, instead of turning tail. I convinced myself it was best to let it go. Now Kris is into it. Damn woman. If she'd just come to me, I'd have warned her off, or helped her. She hasn't been down here since she was a kid. I'm sure she didn't know what she was getting involved in. My fault. I never told her about all of this.

Well, now it's up to me to get her out."

Colin wondered what he had gotten himself into. A few hours ago, it had seemed a fine idea to come charging down here to rescue Kris. He enjoyed stepping in to use his position and power to help young women in distress. Usually, though, it involved something rather less life threatening than this, and his position would mean bugger all in the American north woods. Now, he was tangled up with some hillbilly obsessed with a family feud. Perhaps he should have come on his own, although he had to admit that he wouldn't have had the faintest idea where to start.

"I understand you helped raise Kris," Colin said. "After all that went on."

"Yep."

The man's description of his family's relations with the Osbornes seemed to have exhausted his conversational energy.

Another half hour of driving, the silence broken only by the uneven chug of the old Chev's engine, and they were deep in the heart of the dark state forest. Colin shivered. The night was cool for September, and the truck's heater apparently didn't function. He rolled the window back up, reluctantly choosing the smell over the cold.

Redner startled him by asking a question. "Where was Kris today? What was she doing?"

"She'd gone up to some small town called Middle-something-or-other."

"Midbury?"

"Yes, that's it. She was interviewing Osborne's brother Billy."

"Billy? He left town about the same time I did. What's he got to do with all of this?"

"Apparently she thinks he might have been implicated in her sister's death."

"Billy? I doubt it. Never been much to that boy. Just followed his brother around, did what he was told. What's he doing now?"

"Cuts lawns for a living, apparently."

"Jesus, an Osborne cutting lawns. Hard to imagine."

"She's been staying with Pat Osborne, so naturally I called

her as well, to see if Kris had turned up."

Redner turned to face him, ignoring the road. "Pat Osborne? You mean Lowell's wife?"

"Ex-wife. She hates him, Kris tells me."

"You talked to her?"

"Yes, this afternoon, actually."

"Fuck, why didn't you just take out an ad in his newspaper? You think we can trust this guy's ex-wife? I learned a long time ago not to trust anyone with the name Osborne, no matter how they came by it.

"Tell me you weren't stupid enough to say we were coming down?"

"No, of course not," Colin said, trying to remember whether he might have implied it.

"I spoke to Billy Osborne as well, but only to say that I was her boss, that I couldn't reach her by phone, and I was trying to track her down."

"They'll know she's been missed, then. I won't count on surprise. If I know Bud Naylor, he'll take extra precautions."

"Naylor, that's the thug?"

Redner gave a gravelly laugh. "Talks tough. I kicked his ass once, in high school."

Colin realized he might have put his life in the hands of this strange chap beside him, and he fervently hoped the rematch would be as successful.

33

Kris lay on a thin mattress on the bottom half of a bunk bed, eyes closed and pretending to be asleep. Despite the exhaustion she felt, sleep wasn't a priority. Not when she could count the remaining hours in her life in single digits. She was still bound with duct tape, arms painfully stretched behind her back. Her right arm throbbed where they had hit her with the tire iron, and her shoulders felt like they were pulled out of the sockets. At least they had removed the filthy gag. The dog-smelling blanket from the black SUV gave her a bit of warmth, but she still shivered.

She guessed they were at an old hunting cabin, no more than a mile from the waterfall where she had taken L.T., what seemed like so long ago now. They had come in on a rough bush road, bumping and bouncing through the dark, the driver cursing as he swerved around obstacles not visible until the last moment. She thought the drive had taken about twenty minutes, after a similar time on good roads, but there was no way to know for sure. She felt better, thinking she had an idea of where she was, but she had to admit they could have been anywhere in the vast forest that surrounded Osborne's main camp. There were several of these hunting cabins scattered around the property.

On the far side of the cabin, her two captors sat by a cobblestone fireplace, warming themselves in front of its open fire.

"I don't see why we have to stay up all fuckin' night," the younger one said. "She's not going anywhere, and no one is going to find us back here."

"When you work for Bud Naylor, you follow orders, you don't ask questions," the other one said, poking the fire with a long stick. A shower of sparks danced up the chimney.

The older man was called Lewis. Kris made him as in his early forties, muscular, with a black T-shirt and the same kind of camouflage pants Bud wore. His nose twisted to one side, like he'd taken a couple of good shots over the years, and he hadn't shaved in a few days. The younger one, Nick, was a muscle boy, too, but with spiked black hair and a couple of gold chains around his neck. He was the one who had cut her clothes off. Nick was dressed the same as Lewis, like it was a kind of uniform.

"Bud and I got into some hairy shit together in the Marines, but he knows what he's doing. Follow the sarge's lead and you'll be all right. I learned that fast enough," Lewis said. "If you want to stick with this job, you don't question the man. Besides, he gets his orders from the senator."

Nick grunted in response, then she heard the pop of another beer can opening. The two had been drinking steadily since they got to the cabin. Kris hoped they might eventually fall asleep, or pass out, but even if they did, she hadn't worked out any way to get free of the damned tape. In addition to the strip that bound her hands behind her back, another held her legs together below the knees. Even if she could get off the bunk, she'd have to hop to freedom. Fat chance.

The tape cut tightly into the loose pair of jeans they had put on her, taking their time for a good look as they did so. She imagined the jeans belonged to Lowell Osborne. When they arrived at the cabin, at least they had had the decency to give her a couple of minutes in the outhouse before binding her again. To her surprise, they didn't even insist on watching her. She had frantically scanned the outhouse for something sharp, but the best she could come up with was a loose nail. She had tucked it in her pocket, without a plan, but now it was so inaccessible, it might as well have been back in the outhouse.

"What's this tape they've got such a hard on about?" Nick asked.

"Something from a long time ago," Lewis said. "Doesn't matter to you, does it?"

"I guess not."

"Good. Don't dig too deep into Osborne business. You don't want to piss these people off."

Good advice, Kris thought. Maybe she should have taken it a long time ago.

"When's Bud coming back?" Nick asked.

"Early morning. Then we'll finish up with her."

Finish up. Kris knew the rape would just be another step. If she didn't break, the actual torture would follow. Bud and Lewis would have some experience there, she was sure. God knows what the two of them had done, in the service of their country.

When it was over, they'd bury her back in the woods somewhere. That's where Bud went wrong with Kathy. He left the body for people to find. If he'd taken the time to bury her, it would have saved a lot of grief later. Kathy was probably the first person he had killed, but he'd no doubt had plenty of experience since then.

Kris found it almost comforting to think she would be buried back in the mountains. Home.

Then she fought that thought back. It was too soon to give up. Every hour she held on increased the chances she'd be rescued. Her gut would tell her when it was time to quit.

"Am I going to get a piece of that?" Nick asked. "She looks pretty fuckin' tasty."

"That's up to Bud. We'll see how it plays out."

"I could use some of that right now. How about you?"

"Forget it. Bud would be pissed."

"Do you always do what Bud tells you to do?"

"Yeah, and you do what I tell you to do. Some part of that you don't understand?"

"Jesus, I might as well have joined the fuckin' army."

"You couldn't have hacked it," Lewis said. "We washed out guys like you in basic training."

"Yeah? What can you do that I can't?"

"Think," Lewis said. "I'm going outside, take a leak and a bit of a look around. Keep an eye on the girl."

"You bet."

Kris heard another beer can pop open. If Nick decided to try something, he'd probably untie her, confident he could overpower her with ease. If she could get at the nail, maybe she'd have a shot. It would look awfully good in his eye. See how tasty he'd find that.

34

The headlights showed Colin nothing more than a faint track through the forest, but Martin Redner guided the pickup with all the confidence of a man pulling into his own driveway, oblivious to the branches that slapped and banged against the truck.

"My God, Redner, where are we?"

"My place."

"Place? All I see is trees."

Then they bucked up a hill, and Colin saw a small A-frame cabin, little more than a shed, really. It stood in a clearing of perhaps a couple hundred feet in each direction, but saplings had sprung up in the open space, some as high as twenty feet. In the moonlight, it was impossible to make out the details of the cabin, but it would be a happier home for vermin than people. Surely Redner didn't intend to spend the night?

He pulled the pickup to a stop six feet from the front door and got out.

"Let's go," he said. "We're here."

"And here is where?"

Redner shook his head at the question.

"This is where I lived, before I headed north. Built it myself."

Indeed, Colin thought. Now that he was closer, he could see that the one window in the front had been smashed in, and the roof was covered in some kind of thick moss.

"Why are we here?" Colin asked, still in the truck. "Shouldn't we be going after Kris directly?"

"Like I said, I need to get a few things. It's nearly one o'clock in the morning. We can't find her now. If she isn't dead yet, she'll still be alive at dawn."

Colin got out of the truck and lifted his bag from the back. Dew had left everything in the back of the truck wet. He hoped his heavy sweater was still dry. The air had gotten steadily cooler as they moved up into the mountains.

"Go inside and start a fire," Redner said. "There should still be some wood by the stove. It will work, as long as nothing has nested in the chimney."

"Where are you going?"

"I've got some stuff I need to dig up."

Colin was puzzled by that, but Redner took a spade from the back of the truck and headed off into the bush, disappearing from sight.

Thankful for the moonlight, Colin stepped onto the moss-slick porch of the little A-frame. The solid wood door was intact and opened easily enough. Inside, there was just one room and a sleeping loft across the back. The main piece of furniture was a heavy old wooden table, its top covered in shards of glass from the window, and dust so old it had turned to dirt. A single wooden chair was upturned on the floor behind it. The place smelled of mice and must, reminding him of a cottage he'd rented in the Muskokas years ago.

Colin saw the wood stove at the back of the cabin, near the little galley that had served as a kitchen. The stove was basically a steel box with a black chimney pipe coming straight up and out the roof of the cabin. Beside the stove was a wooden crate full of cedar kindling. Well, it would certainly be dry, Colin thought.

There were a few ancient newspapers tucked in with the kindling. Something called *The Republican-Patriot*, from June 1981. The line story was a car crash. He crumpled the brittle, yellow paper, lit it with his lighter, swung open the door of the wood stove and tossed it in. No use getting anything really going until he found out if the chimney worked.

The old paper disappeared with a whoosh, and there was no sign of anything blocking the chimney, so Colin rolled up some more, arranged the kindling on top and set the lot afire. It took off with a crackling and snapping, and he closed the door of the stove. It wouldn't do to burn the place down.

Almost immediately, he could feel heat begin to radiate. He slipped his little silver flask from inside his jacket pocket and downed a quick nip, the Aberlour burning pleasantly as it went down.

Unzipping his bag, he took out his heavy blue wool sweater. It was Royal Navy issue, picked up at a surplus shop back in London. Had the thing for years. He wondered if he looked like a commando in it. At the bottom of the bag was his SAS commando knife, the real thing, gift from a chap he'd met while covering the Falklands war. He put on the sweater and slipped the sheathed knife through his belt and put his jacket on, feeling considerably more braced. Ready for action, even.

Colin had no idea what they'd have to overcome to get Kris back, but surely it couldn't be more than a handful of yokels. He'd faced far worse. Not as a combatant, of course, but the people shooting from the other side hadn't stopped to make that fine distinction. In Lebanon, he'd experienced bullets whizzing over his head and smacking into a wall not a foot from him. It was the sort of thing that got your wind up a bit at the time, but on balance it was worthwhile. He'd been recounting the story to young colleagues for years. Surefire way to get their knickers off.

None of that braggadocio had ever impressed Kris, though. After what she'd been through in her life — for that matter, what she faced on the streets every day — it took a lot to wow the woman. Tough as nails, he told himself. Surely she'd find a way to get out of this scrape, too.

Redner came into the cabin lugging a metal footlocker shaped like a small coffin. He dumped it on the table without a word and went back out to the truck.

Colin was used to the taciturn rural type. He'd known enough of them growing up in Suffolk. Sheep farmers who spent more time with animals than people, and preferred the four-legged company. Still, Redner was at the extreme. The good news was that they ought to have Kris back within hours, and then they would be on their way home. Assuming Redner knew what he was doing, of course. Colin had to admit to a certain lack of confidence in that regard, but it was too late to question his own decision now. He was in all the way.

When Redner reappeared, he was carrying the red metal tool chest from the back of the truck. Judging by the way his right arm hung, it was a rather complete kit.

Redner opened the tool chest, selected a small crowbar and applied it to the rusty lock that held the metal locker closed. After one quick jerk, it popped off and went skittering across the wooden floor. Redner reached inside and pulled out three long shapes wrapped in heavy dark cloth. The smell of oil filled the air.

"Guns?" Colin asked. He hoped he hadn't shown too much surprise. He hadn't thought about the need for guns, but the people they were up against were clearly dangerous.

"We're not going in there empty-handed. Stored these when I left."

Redner carefully unwrapped a pump-action shotgun, a lever-action rifle, and another rifle that looked a bit more modern.

"What have we got here?" Colin asked. He knew enough about guns to see that all three were sporting weapons, not the brutal-looking semi-automatic stuff he was used to seeing troops carry.

"Remington pump, Winchester 30.30, and a Ruger .308," Redner said. "Duck and deer guns. They'll have to do."

Colin picked up the Winchester, running its fingers along the lever action. "Who was the last chap that fired this?" he asked. "John Wayne?"

"Gun that won the West. Still a damn good deer gun if your range isn't too long."

Redner was wiping the guns with a white rag he had taken from his jacket pocket. "Twenty years underground, these guns have stood up real nice. I oiled them heavy."

"What about ammunition?" Colin asked.

"Plenty of new stuff in the truck," Redner said. He took a hacksaw from the tool chest and made a preliminary scratch on the blade just past the pump.

"What are you doing?"

"Customizing. Sure could use a vice, though. Grab the stock and hold it steady on the table."

Colin did as he was asked, the stock of the gun slippery in his hands.

"Shame to spoil a gun," Redner said, "but a piece like this is only good close up. I'll take off most of the barrel, stock past the grip. Makes it easier to manoeuvre in tight."

The raspy whine of the hack saw filled the little cabin as Redner worked his way through the barrel.

"This gun's for you," he said. "I don't figure you'll have to use it, but if you do, just remember that it holds five shells and you have to pump after every shot. Just aim for the centre of your man and squeeze one off. Pump and give him another. Buckshot; rips 'em up pretty good."

Colin nodded, trying to look as if this were something he did all the time. He was forced to admit that there was a significant difference between firing and being fired on. One was obviously preferable in some respects, but he'd never killed a man, or even tried to. He wondered if he could do it. If it meant his life, or Kris's, he hoped basic survival instincts would kick in.

"When do we head out?" Colin asked, trying to project an enthusiasm he didn't actually feel.

"We'll be moving by five. I want to be in place before dawn."

The barrel fell to the floor with a clang.

"There's two sleeping bags in the truck," Redner said. "Bring them in. Might as well get a bit of sleep. This will be an interesting day."

Colin appreciated the understatement. Quite un-American, and no doubt very apt.

35

Despite her best efforts to stay awake and watch for an opportune moment, Kris had drifted in and out of sleep. Her dreams had been horrible, the scene of being stripped below the waist repeating itself like a tape loop. She could feel the cold blade of the knife gliding across her buttock, in some twisted parody of foreplay.

Now she was awake, and her reality was worse than the dreams.

Lewis was nowhere in sight. Nick, the young one, sat in a chair watching her, his body silhouetted in the faint dawn light coming through the window behind him.

"Beauty sleep over?" he asked.

She didn't respond to his idiotic remark.

He got up and swaggered over to her, adjusting his crotch with his left hand. Then he examined her like a hungry man stepping up to a buffet.

Without warning, he slipped his hand quickly under her T-shirt, forced his fingers up under her bra and tweaked her right nipple so hard it hurt. Removing the hand, he unzipped his fly and said, "How be you get my day off to a good start?"

"Fuck you, you little shit," she spat.

She immediately regretted the words, but maybe this would be the chance she was waiting for, if she could get him to remove the tape. Let him think he was getting his way, then bite down hard. That would take big Nick out of the game.

The cabin door opened with a gust of cool air. Lewis was back.

"Nick, what the hell are you doing?"

"Checking the prisoner," he said.

"Hey," Kris said, talking past Nick. "How about a pee break, here?"

"All right," Lewis said. "Nick. Take the tape off her and take her to the outhouse."

"Should I keep an eye on her?"

"Where do you think she's going to go? Give her a minute of privacy."

Nick slid his fly back up, keeping his back to Lewis, then took a Buck knife from one of the many pockets in his pants, folded it open, and cut away the tape that held her legs together and her hands behind her back. He took her by the upper arm and pulled her upright. Kris's legs tingled as the feeling returned, and she eased her shoulders forward, releasing the tension on them. The pain in her right arm had declined to a dull throb, and she could move all her fingers.

There was no end to the good news, she thought blackly.

She insisted on walking unassisted, her unsteady steps taking her haltingly forward. At least the sneakers they had come up with were something like a fit, unlike the pants, which drooped like a Britney Spears fashion statement.

Outside now, in the first morning light, she recognized the cabin. Her grandfather had used it occasionally for Osborne guests, when they wanted to get the feeling they were deep in the wilderness. It was no more than a mile from the waterfall. Not that it really mattered, knowing where she was, but it gave her a small sense of control.

The outhouse was about fifty feet from the cabin, down a little hill. She tottered toward it, Nick following close behind. He had no gun, she noticed, but she would still be no match for him. She could barely move her arms and legs. Running was out of the question.

"All right," he said. "Take your moment, but leave the door open. And don't worry. I won't look. Plenty of time for that later."

All Nick could think about was his cock. That made him act even more stupid than he really was. She hoped there would be a way to use that to her advantage.

A light, misty rain had begun to fall, and she turned her face up, wetting her parched lips. They had given her almost nothing to drink since they had grabbed her, and no food at all.

Apparently they hadn't intended her to be alive that long.

Crouching over the rough wooden seat, the stink of aged human waste coming up from below, she thought about how powerless she really was. Her idea that she could oppose Osborne had been an illusion from the start. She wondered what it was like for her sister and her father, at the end. Did they have similar thoughts?

On the way back, she could hear the sound of a large engine in low gear, still some distance away.

"Hurry up," Nick said. "Sounds like we've got company."

36

Colin watched spirals of mist curl up off the lake in dawn's slim purple light. It was so still, he could hear himself breathe. In other circumstances, he might actually have enjoyed the unnatural quiet, but he was fifteen feet up a maple tree, his legs cramped from over an hour in the position. Water from the light rain that had fallen earlier dripped from leaves and ran down his neck like cold fingers.

Redner had explained that hiding himself in the tree was a deer hunter's ruse, but he had noted that the man himself was nestled in an outcropping of rocks, fifty feet to Colin's right. He was nearly invisible in his camouflage coat and ball cap.

They'd taken up their positions after a half-hour stumble in the dark, their truck tucked down a dead-end road about a mile from the camp.

He suspected that Redner wanted him safely out of the way if there was any difficulty. He hadn't come this far just to watch, but he didn't fancy the odds of a speedy escape from the tree, either. He'd damn near broken his neck getting up the bloody thing in the first place. Hadn't been up a tree since he was ten, and he didn't intend to climb another, if he was fortunate enough to escape from this one intact.

From his vantage point, Colin could see the lodge beginning to wake to the day. There were lights on downstairs, and a wisp of smoke had started to rise from the huge cobblestone chimney. What had appeared as an indistinct mass in the dark was now visible as some kind of frontier cabin on a grand scale. Four smaller cabins were visible on a ridge behind the main lodge, but there was no sign of life there.

Kris could be in any one of them, Redner had said, but his bet was on the main lodge. It was easiest for her captors, and he didn't think they anticipated a rescue. A single red pickup truck was parked in the gravel drive beside the lodge. Probably no more than two men, Redner had said.

Colin had argued for going in under the cover of darkness, catch them in their beds, but Redner had vetoed the plan. The house was too large, he said. No way to tell where Kris or the guards would be. He wanted to wait until morning, see what they were up against.

Colin had grudgingly concurred. What choice did he have? But he was worried about the delay. What were they doing to Kris while he and Redner dithered? There was no saying these chaps worked banker's hours. Was she injured? Bleeding?

Colin heard a low whistle and looked toward the rocks, where Redner was gesturing for him to come over. He began to gingerly dismount from the tree, stiff legs wobbly on the springy branches. Holding the shotgun in one hand, he manoeuvred down a series of branches that acted like steps.

The soft, leafy earth felt good under his feet. Now that he was back on the ground, he could admit to a touch of vertigo. No need for Redner to know, though. Running in a low crouch, Colin made his way to the rocks.

Redner was examining the house with a large pair of binoculars. "I see one guy in the front area, drinking a cup of coffee," he said.

"There must be more. They wouldn't leave her with one man," Colin said.

"That's what worries me. This is the easiest spot for them to bring her, but there's no saying she's here. If they got a heads-up from Billy or the ex-wife, they'd have moved her."

"So what do we do?"

Redner held up his hand to silence Colin. The man had come out of the house to gather an armload of firewood from a pile by the door. He was heavy set, with an iron-grey crewcut, green work pants and a baggy red sweater.

"Bobby Edwards, it looks like to me," Redner said. "He's been a handyman around the camp for ages. Probably lives in the lodge full time. Looks pretty relaxed, too. Not a good sign."

"Edwards? Kris mentioned that name. If I recall correctly, he's one of the fellows she thinks raped her sister."

Redner spat in the dirt. "Yeah? Let's ask him."

"So what do we do? We can hardly just walk up to him, can we? Two fellows with guns?"

Redner looked at Colin as if he had just observed that the sun rose in the east. "Right. That's why you're going to leave your gun here and go to the door and knock. When he asks, tell him you're a hiker, got lost and had to spend the night in the woods. He won't expect anything more from an Englishman."

"And what will you be doing?"

"I think I remember a back door. I used to come here with my dad, but it was a long time ago. I'll go in the back way, surprise him, then we'll see what he knows."

"You think you remember a door? What if there isn't one?"

"Then you keep him talking a little longer. You're a good talker, aren't you?"

"All right, then."

Colin was beginning to look back on his time up the tree with longing. He approached the front door of the lodge, whistling, a confused but unconcerned hiker. He could just see Redner cutting through some low scrub, then he disappeared from sight behind the looming building.

There was no bell, so Colin rapped on the wooden screen door. "Hallo," he shouted. "Anyone home?"

There was a heavy tromp of boots inside the house, then Edwards appeared on the other side of the screen door, holding a length of cord wood in his hand. "The fuck do you want? This is private property."

The man hadn't shaved in days and he smelled like an ashtray that had been pissed in. With the cordwood in hand, he looked more than capable of running someone off the place. At least he hadn't called for any confederates.

"Sorry to trouble you. I'm with a birding group on an outing in the state park. I spotted a rather rare sort of nuthatch and I'm afraid I took a wrong turn in pursuit of it. Got separated from my group, and had to spend the night in the bush. Can't tell you how relieved I was to find human habitation. I wonder if I could trouble you to use your phone, ring back to the hotel for transport?"

Edwards eyed him with such a look of incomprehension that

he might as well have been speaking Latin. At least he had successfully established himself as an eccentric Englishman, Colin thought.

"I'm lost," he tried again. "Okay if I use the phone?"

Edwards looked suspiciously around, but seeing no one but the harmless Englishman, said, "All right, but make it quick. The senator finds someone trespassing, we'll both be in shit."

Edwards pulled open the screen door, then turned to lead Colin to the phone. When he saw Redner blocking his path, the Winchester levelled at him, he dropped the cordwood in surprise.

"Bobby Edwards. Been a long time."

"Redner? The fuck are you doing here?"

"Looking for my niece Kris. Seen her?"

"Yeah. I had a beer with her in town, couple of days ago. She's working on some kind of story. What's up?"

"Seems she's missing."

"Really?"

Edwards scratched a calloused hand against his unshaven face. "Well, she isn't here. I suggest you boys move out before Bud Naylor and his gang get back. Bud won't be pleased to see you, waving a gun around in the senator's house."

"Bud? There's another fella I haven't seen in a while. Coming by, is he?"

"I expect him any minute."

Edwards rubbed his hands nervously on his pant legs, glancing behind to see what Colin was doing. Colin took a step back, and felt the reassuring shape of the knife under his sweater.

"What's he up to, old Bud?"

"Senator's head of security."

"I meant right now, where's Bud at?"

"Bud? I don't know. He don't check in with me. Just said he'd be here first thing."

"I'm thinking that wherever Bud is, he's got Kris with him. What do you think?"

Edwards shrugged. "I wouldn't know anything about that."

Redner gestured with the gun barrel, pointing to the large room on the other side of the screen porch. "Come on in, Bobby.

Bet I can improve your memory."

"Right, get a move on," Colin said.

Redner lifted his eyebrow, masking a smile.

Edwards reluctantly shuffled into the two-storey room, its log walls rising to an open, planked ceiling. The chimney of the cobblestone fireplace was the full height of the room, and a small fire sputtered in the grate. Colin could smell fresh coffee.

A worn red and blue rug filled the space in front of the fireplace, and Redner prodded the other man on to it. "All right, Bobby. Down on your knees. Hands behind your head."

Edwards sunk stiffly to his knees. "If you want to shoot me, Redner, go ahead. You won't get away with it."

"Really? You imagine anyone knows I'm down here? Or that anyone really gives a shit about you one way or another? You weren't here, senator'd get another guy to fetch his firewood and fix his taps in about five minutes. You don't think guys like Osborne and Naylor care about guys like us, do you Bobby?"

"Us? You think I'm like you? I served my country, Redner. You're a fucking draft dodger."

"Not exactly, but maybe you're right. You're the type does what you're told, asks no questions."

"I call that loyalty."

"OK, maybe you understand why I'm trying to find Kris, then. I wanted to talk to you about Kathy, too."

"What about her?"

"Kris says you were one of the boys that did her, day she died."

"What if I was? Little slut was dying to give it away."

"Colin," Redner said, his tone entirely casual, "can I borrow that fine looking knife you've got?

Colin handed it to him, in the sheath. He wasn't sure he wanted to see what was going to happen next. The words accessory to murder kept flashing in his head.

Redner came up behind Edwards and held the knife so tightly against his throat that a thin trickle of blood began to work down his neck.

"I don't like the way you talk about my family, Bobby," Redner said.

The pressure of the knife distorted Edwards's voice, but he managed to say, "If you cared so much about your family, why'd you run off after two of them was killed?"

"You're right, Bobby. I did run off. Always been sorry about that. Now I'm back to make good. Sure you can't remember where Kris is?"

Edwards said nothing, kept staring straight ahead, impassive.

"You know Bobby, in the old times, they catch a rapist, they'd like as not cut his nuts off. Keep it from happening again."

Redner removed the blade from Edwards's throat, the metal slick with blood. "You know, I like the old times," he said.

Edwards grabbed reflexively at his crotch. "If I tell you, Bud Naylor will just kill me later. How am I any farther ahead?"

"I guess it's just not your day, Bobby."

Redner put the muzzle of the rifle to the back of Edwards's head.

"Tell me, Bobby, and I'll kill you quick. Do you think Bud would?"

37

By the time Bud Naylor walked into the cabin, Kris's captors had her sitting on a hard wooden chair, arms behind the chair back and taped at the wrist, legs bound together just above the knees. Her shoulders were pulled so far back that they hurt like hell, but she was determined not to show Naylor her pain. She struggled for an expression that was impassive, maybe even unconcerned.

Naylor was still wearing the USMC T-shirt and camouflage pants from the day before, but he had added a jacket that went with the pants. He was unshaven and bleary-eyed like he'd been up all night.

"Hey, Bud," Lewis said. "Everything taken care of?"

"I solved the Sloan problem," he said. "The Pat Osborne part is going to be a little trickier. She's not home, and I can't find her."

Solved the Sloan problem? Kris was sure that could only mean one thing. Once all the people who knew about the tape of her sister's rape had been eliminated, it wouldn't really matter whether they found the tape itself, she realized. Now, her life depended on Pat Osborne's ability to elude them. Did she know they were after her, or had she simply gone down to Albany on a shopping trip?

"You need some help with that?" Lewis asked.

"No, we're covered. It's just a matter of time."

Then the senator himself appeared in the doorway of the cabin. Unlike Bud, he was crisp and fresh, as if he were out for a pleasant fall walk. He wore a denim shirt and khaki pants, with an undone denim jacket so new it still looked stiff. Campaign clothes, the kind rich and powerful candidates wore to show the voters they were ordinary folks like them. How did his morning schedule read? Seven a.m. — kill Kris; eight a.m. — coffee with garden club?

"'Morning, Senator," Nick and Lewis said in unison, like grade-school children greeting the teacher. He nodded in acknowledgement.

"Kris," the senator said, offering the same practised smile he would have used if they'd just met at a fundraising barbecue. The guy actually looked like he was pleasantly surprised to see her. Where did he think she was going to be?

"Bud tells me you're not being very co-operative."

"I have this theory that if I tell them where the tape is, your thugs will kill me. Bud thought maybe a beating, followed by a rape, would persuade me."

"Yes, Bud told me that he had to get firm. I'm afraid you've left us no choice. You weren't seriously hurt, were you?"

In truth, it was painful to sit down, and the feeling of being taped down on that table, Bud lovingly running his knife blade across her would stick with her for a long time. She would never give the senator the satisfaction of admitting any of that, though.

"I'm fine," she said. "But now what?"

"The very thing I'm here to determine," the senator said. "Bud, why don't you three get some air, give us a moment?"

Bud grunted, clearly not being pleased at being excluded, but he led the other two out and closed the cabin door.

The senator pulled up a chair like the one Kris was bound to, and turned it around, the back facing her. He straddled the chair, arms draped loosely over its back. He seemed disgustingly relaxed.

"Kris, I have to say I'm very disappointed in you. I tried to make you see that it's time to get past old grievances and move forward, for the sake of the country. I appealed to your higher instincts. I even tried your baser instincts."

He smiled at that, pleased with the line. "That pension, which you really are entitled to, by the way, is a substantial sum of money."

Osborne had a sincere look on his pleasantly bland face, as if, even now, she might still see how reasonable he had been.

"And, I have to say, you've made me very angry, Kris. Why

did you have to drag Pat into this? It was none of her business. Now I'm going to have to do something I don't want to do."

"What, kill your ex-wife? Or as Bud would probably put it, 'take care of the Pat Osborne problem.'"

"It's likely to come to that. How much does she really know about all of this?"

Kris saw that she was being offered a chance to deny Pat's real level of involvement, to save her life at the price of Kris's own. She knew it was a deal that Lowell Osborne would never honour. Pity about Pat, but she had made her decision, just like Kris had.

"Everything," she said. "Why do you think she was helping me? I think Pat is the only person who hates you more than I do."

The senator said nothing. Hard truths weren't to his taste.

"I suppose it was Billy who tipped you off," she said.

"Of course. You say you are doing all this out of family loyalty, Kris. Do you think your family is the only one that has it? Billy called me as soon as you left his place. It was simple to pick up your car on the Northway and tail you until you reached an appropriate location."

Kris shook her head. "My mistake. I thought maybe one person in your family would do the right thing, but I gave Billy too much credit. I suppose the family bank account still subsidizes Billy. Even in Midbury, he couldn't afford a house like that just by cutting grass."

"Very astute, but your observation is a bit late."

"Yes, you've stayed one step ahead of me. Congratulations, Senator, you win the game."

He gave a small nod, as if he had just bested her at chess.

"Now that it's over," she said, "maybe you can tell me a couple of things. Just to satisfy my curiosity."

"Perhaps."

"What actually happened to my father?"

It was a question she had hoped to answer for herself, but with all that had taken place since L.T.'s death, she had never been able to get to the bottom of it.

"Your father? Like I told you, he was a fine man. Very noble. I didn't know him well, of course, but you remind me a lot of him.

He was convinced there was more to your sister's death, and he seemed to be buying into the idea she had been raped. Now, that was a problem, because her wild tales were what forced us to deal with the situation in the first place. Add her death to that, very complicated. Reputations were on the line."

The senator shrugged. "I'm sorry I can't tell you exactly what happened. All I know is that I went to my own father with the problem, and a couple of days later, he told me it was solved."

Kris had assumed as much, but the information still chilled her. She had never really believed her father's electrocution was an accident. The call in the middle of the night had been a set-up. Her father had been murdered in his version of the quest she herself was now on. Did her family have to lose every confrontation with the Osbornes?

"Now your uncle Martin was a much wiser man," Osborne said. "He got the gist after your father's death and headed off for Canada, never to be heard from again. Too bad you didn't have as much common sense."

Martin. She wished he were with them now, to hear that. Did he know the Osbornes had murdered both his brother and his niece? And if he did, how had he lived with that knowledge all these years?

"He was a coward," she said.

"Perhaps. Not everyone wants to seek out a hill to die on. Didn't you understand, when all this started, that you couldn't possibly come out ahead? You've been annoying, I grant you, but my resources and determination so far exceed your own that there was only one way for all this to end."

There was a look on his face that Kris could have mistaken for sadness, if she hadn't already concluded that Osborne lacked any real human emotion.

"I gave you chances to get out gracefully, but you wouldn't take them," he said, shaking his head at her stubbornness.

Kris realized that, in Osborne's mind, she probably constituted nothing more than a moderately difficult problem to solve. One of many he would have to deal with on his way to the White House. He was probably telling himself that leadership was about making these tough calls.

Arrogant bastard, she thought. There must be some way to make him trip over his own ego, but what? Colin knew most of the story, but without her notebooks and the videotape, he could do nothing. If she had only kept L.T. with her, he could have handled any of Osborne's men, but she had sent him on a fool's errand, and it had cost him his life. She had to do something to justify his sacrifice.

"My mother and your father, they were . . ." She was going to use the word "lovers," but surely it wasn't quite that. "They were having an affair. What did that have to do with Kathy's death?"

The senator smiled coldly. "You were right, back at my house," he said. "My mother hadn't been well for some time and my father would occasionally seek relief."

Seek relief, Kris thought. It made it sound like he was using a public toilet.

"Kathy was hired as a favour to your mother. You know what it was like that summer. We were all young, full of hormones. She got caught up in it, but does it matter now what really happened? Your persistent efforts to smear me have made it irrelevant whether I had anything to do with your sister's death or not. You've forced me into a level of damage control that I really wanted to avoid."

Jesus, did he expect her to feel sorry for him because he was going kill her? Was it going to spoil his day? Not that he would kill her himself, she was sure. There were people for that. A leader has to know how to delegate.

"So you're going to kill me. Do it."

"I beg your pardon?"

"You've decided to kill me. Aren't you man enough to do it? How hard can it be, a woman, helpless, taped to a chair."

"Bud handles these kinds of situations."

"Right, because you haven't got the balls. Just like you had L.T. killed by rigging his truck. You'd never have been able to face him man to man. Neither would Bud.

"Gutless bastard," she said, launching a projectile of spit that landed on his perfectly creased khaki trousers.

The senator took a white handkerchief from his pocket and dabbed away the spit.

"Well," he said, the smile returning, "I guess we're done here.

"Bud and I have some business, and then he'll be back. I'm sure you've figured out that once we deal with Pat, it won't matter whether we find that tape or not. The knowledge of its whereabouts will die with you."

He got up from the chair and straightened his jacket.

"One last chance," he said. "Tell me now where the tape is and I'll instruct Bud to kill you quickly. Once we find Pat, you'll just be a problem that Bud and his helpers can deal with at their leisure."

"Fuck you."

The senator shrugged, turned, and walked out of the cabin.

He left the door open, and Kris shivered in the cold, damp morning air. She had used the last of her psychological reserves to tough it out with the senator, but now she knew that all that lay ahead was death. If Bud and his two goons had their way, she would welcome it when it came.

38

The old black pickup bounced jarringly as it descended a hill into a denser area of pines and firs. Colin was thrown about on the springy seat, and had to put a hand on the doorframe to brace himself. In the back, he could hear Bobby Edwards land with a thump every time they went over an obstacle.

"How can we be sure Edwards wasn't steering us wrong?" Colin asked. "This road doesn't look like it leads anywhere."

"Don't worry. I know where I am. This is the back way in. Besides, there's nothing like a knife up against the equipment to get a guy to focus."

When it appeared as if Edwards was quite willing to take a bullet in the skull for his employer, Redner had tried another tack. Before Edwards had even time to realize what was happening, Redner had hauled his trousers down and held the chap's business in his hand like a man holding a chicken by the neck. Once the knife blade was up against his nuts, he was quick enough to tell them where Bud Naylor had taken Kris.

Afterwards, they had tied Edwards up and tossed him in the bed of the pickup. Colin had been relieved that Redner hadn't killed the chap. If he really had raped Kris's sister, then he had it coming, but who was to say what had actually happened? He still hoped they might be able to extricate Kris without any bloodshed. If there were dead bodies to account for, it could get awfully dicey, and from everything Kris told him, this chap Osborne swung a heavy bat.

"That was quite a trick you pulled with the knife," Colin said.

"A man can face death easier than he can face life without his balls," Redner said.

No argument there. Colin was forced to wince and readjust his position on the seat, simply from remembering what Edwards had experienced.

"I thought you were just going to shoot him in the head."

"Thought about it, but it wouldn't have done us any good. The knife thing works real well."

"You've done that before?"

"Couple of times. Once, I had a biker crying like a baby, thinking about his life as a soprano."

"A biker? I thought you were some sort of fishing guide."

"Yeah, but I do a little cash crop on the side. Sometimes a few fellas come up from the city, think they can rip you off for it. You need to persuade them otherwise."

So Redner was a drug dealer who apparently knew how to kick the ass of bikers. Normally, the prospect would have been alarming, but at the moment, Colin took it as rather good news.

"How'd you know I even had the knife?" he asked.

Redner fought with the wheel, taking the truck over a series of logs laid on a swampy spot, then said, "You could see the outline under your sweater. Surprised Bobby didn't see it. Must have been distracted by your crazy birdwatcher act.

"Nice piece of equipment, by the way. Where'd you get it?"

For most audiences, Colin would have embellished an old war story, but he had nothing to match threatening to cut the balls off bikers.

"Wrote a feature on an SAS commando back in the Falklands. He gave it me as a souvenir."

"The Falklands?"

"War between Britain and Argentina."

"Yeah, I'd forgotten that one. Long time ago."

Redner braked, bringing the truck to a halt just short of a sizeable pine that had collapsed right across the rough track they were using as a road.

"All right. This is it," Redner said. "We walk in from here. Any closer and they'd have heard the truck anyway."

The rain had begun to close in again, more a mist than actual drops. Colin couldn't see more than twenty feet in front of him, the forest beyond that fading off into a dark gloom. He hoped that Redner really knew where he was going.

"What about Edwards?" Colin asked.

"He's not going too far."

Redner took the shotgun and two rifles out of the back of the pickup, and handed the sawed-off gun to Colin. After sliding into the shoulder straps of a military-style knapsack, Redner slung one rifle over his shoulder and gripped the other with one hand. He headed left around the base of the uprooted pine and Colin hurried to keep up. It wouldn't be good to get lost in these woods, and Redner was obviously in a hurry.

The dirt from the overturned tree and the smell of freshly fallen leaves combined with the smell of decay that Colin always associated with forests. Tried to avoid them as a rule. Dank places. His stomach roiled, something he preferred to attribute to the lack of a proper breakfast.

On the other side of the tree, the rudimentary road became little more than a path obscured by fallen branches, but Redner moved along it with the ease and confidence Colin only felt when striding across the newsroom. He wished he'd thought to wear something more practical than white Nike trainers, now covered in forest muck, his feet sodden and cold. The sawed-off gun felt heavy and unbalanced in his hands. He kept the barrel pointed up. It wouldn't do to trip and accidentally shoot Redner.

After fifteen minutes' walk, Redner stopped and signalled with his hand for Colin to do the same. They had come to the crest of a little hill, and Redner could obviously see something below that was not yet visible to Colin.

Redner sunk into a crouch, then took binoculars from his knapsack. Colin mimicked his stance, his knees protesting loudly at being asked to bend so much in the cold and damp. Not for the first time, Colin realized that his characteristic bravado had gotten him into a rather sticky spot.

Redner signalled for Colin to move up. When he was in close, Redner said, "This is it."

Colin could see a rundown cabin, little more than the size of a single-car garage. Smoke was coming out the chimney, though, and a shiny black pickup, its fenders splattered with mud, was parked to the left of the building.

"How do we know this is where Kris is?" Colin asked.

"No other reason for anyone to be in that old cabin. Dad sometimes used it for sportsmen who wanted to think they were in the wilderness, but that was years ago. Surprised it hasn't fallen down."

Colin could easily understand why someone would think himself in the wilderness. There were no roads, no power, and nothing in sight but trees.

"What's the plan?" he asked, hoping there was one.

"We sit tight up here for a bit, see what we're up against. Then we take them out, get Kris back."

It all sounded rather simple, expressed that way. Colin assumed the phrase "take them out" would have its usual meaning. He hoped Redner planned on doing the taking out. It certainly wasn't something he fancied having to do himself.

Despite his own reluctance to act, he said, "Do you think we can afford to wait? No saying what they are doing to her down there."

"Chance we have to take. We rush down now, we'll just get her killed."

He raised the binoculars to his eyes again. The rain had stopped, but moisture still hung in the air. Colin himself could see nothing more than the outline of the cabin, no sign of any human activity. He shivered and reached into his hip pocket for his flask. He took a pull and offered it to Redner.

He tossed it back, taking a double jolt. "Not bad," he said.

Half an hour went by. Colin's legs were cramping mercilessly now and he was soaked through. At least the sun had come out, light dappling through the leaves. He thought he could hear the sound of voices coming from the cabin. No screams, thank God, and surely they wouldn't gag her, so far back in the forest.

He found the hanging about frustrating. Redner was obviously a man of action. What was he waiting for?

The answer came almost immediately.

A heavily muscled man in a black T-shirt and camouflage pants came out the front door of the cabin and scanned the sky, checking the weather. Ascertaining that the rain had stopped, he ducked back in the cabin and then came right back out, a rolled magazine in his hands.

Redner clicked the safety off the Ruger.

They could both see where the man was going. A little shack perhaps fifty feet from the cabin itself. The door was open, showing a crude hole cut in the wooden bench.

The man whistled as he headed toward the outhouse, apparently anticipating the pleasures of a good shit.

"Having a splendid day," Colin whispered.

"Not for much longer."

The man reached the outhouse, stepped in, pulled his camouflage pants down and settled onto the seat. He left the door open, to give enough light to read.

Redner raised the Ruger to his shoulder and lined up his shot. After they had spared Edwards's life, Colin had comforted himself with the idea that Redner had a plan to get Kris back without killing anyone. Apparently not.

The flat snap from the rifle was followed almost immediately by a heavy thup, like a baseball bat hitting a watermelon. The man in the outhouse jerked against the back of the building, then slumped forward clutching his stomach. Even from the top of the hill, Colin could see the red flowing over his hands.

"One down," Redner said.

The words had just left his lips when a second man came running from the cabin, carrying a rifle. He was younger, tousle-haired, but dressed the same as the first man.

"Lewis," he shouted, an edge of panic in his voice.

The man called Lewis groaned, and the second one ran toward the outhouse.

Redner dropped him like a stone with a single shot to the head. His body lay, unmoving, on the leafy forest floor.

"That should about do it," Redner said. "Let's go down and get Kris."

Despite having just killed one man and grievously wounded another, the man showed no more emotion than if he'd swatted a fly.

They headed cautiously down the hill. It was unlikely there was a third man, smarter than the first two, but they couldn't rule it out. Redner held the Ruger at the ready, the Winchester on a sling over his left shoulder. Colin held the Remington shotgun.

They were half way down the hill when they heard Kris cry out. "In here," she shouted. "There aren't any others."

Her rescuers broke into a trot.

Redner was first through the door, Colin close behind. He saw Kris taped to a wooden chair, the look on her face a combination of shock and relief.

"Martin?" she said, then "Colin?" the tone of surprise even greater.

"No time to explain," Redner said. "We need to get out of here. Colin, give me that knife."

Colin pulled the commando knife from under his sweater and passed it to Redner, who quickly cut through the tape that bound Kris.

"Can you walk?" he asked.

She got stiffly to her feet and took a couple of shaky steps.

"I'll be all right," she said. "Let's move."

They were only twenty feet from the cabin when the first flurry of shots ripped through the air.

"Down," Redner shouted, pushing Kris under his body and leaving Colin to fend for himself.

Bullets whizzed over them, singing through the air like horizontal hail. Semi-automatic fire. For Colin, the sound brought back instant memories of Lebanon, caught in a crossfire between militias. The shooters were in a heavy clump of underbrush, perhaps a hundred yards back down the rough road that approached the cabin from behind. They were well out of the effective range of Colin's shotgun, which he clutched so hard he thought he might dent the stock.

"Bud Naylor," Kris whispered, although there was no need for stealth. Their opponents were all too aware of precisely where they were.

There was a brief pause in the fire. Reloading, or moving closer, Colin wondered?

"Kris, you know where we are?" Redner asked.

"Grandpa Charlie's old cabin," she said.

"Good. In case something happens to me, the truck's on the old logging road, fifteen minutes back. Keys are in it.

"Let's split up, divide their fire," Redner said. He shoved the cowboy rifle across the wet leaves toward Colin.

"Take this. Run like hell, back the way we came. Kris and I will circle around, meet you at the truck. Everyone ready?"

Still no firing. The shooters were obviously moving closer. Colin reckoned he had to cover fifty feet of open ground before the forest would offer cover. He might have a chance. He wished he were the one looking out for Kris, but realized Redner had a better hope of success.

Redner looked at him expectantly. "Go, go," he said urgently.

Then Colin realized his job was to run first and draw fire. So he would have a hero's role after all. What he had to do went against every instinct for survival, but he couldn't show himself a coward in front of Kris.

Colin leaped to his feet and set off for a heavy stand of firs. Adrenaline propelled him faster than he thought he could go, but he still felt as if he were moving in slow motion. To his left, he saw Kris and Redner make their move. Time seemed to have paused. He was running but the sheltering trees weren't getting any closer. Then the shots started, whizzing by him, smacking into tree trunks. He waited for the sickening thup sound that he had heard when Redner shot the first man.

Behind him, Redner squeezed off a couple of shots.

Then he heard Kris scream.

"Martin!"

39

The general settled comfortably into one of the leather armchairs in Pat Osborne's so-called Great Room. He hated the name, but had to admit the view of Lake Champlain was superior. Framed by two storeys of glass, the lake stretched off for miles in front of him. The morning rain had blown out, and the wind created a heavy chop on the grey water, whitecaps rolling in toward shore.

He would have preferred to sit outdoors, but it would be unwise. No telling who might chance by. He had parked the Lexus behind the house, then let himself in through a set of patio doors that opened on to the terrace. They had a lock a child could have opened, and it took only a few seconds with his pocket knife to release the primitive latch.

Despite all the stickers warning that an alarm system was in place, there was none. He'd checked that in advance. A foolish economy, given the enormous amount of money the woman had siphoned out of Lowell.

The general himself didn't believe in divorce. Too expensive. Not that he had to worry. He and Elizabeth were happily married. Had been for forty-eight years.

He looked at his heavy gold watch, a memento presented by his regiment on retirement. Not that he had ever really retired. He was still serving his country, but in different ways. Pat Osborne should be here within minutes. Their watchers had spotted her Boxster on the highway. Hard to miss it, big show-off car. He'd hurried over immediately.

She would be surprised to see him, he was sure. Just as he'd been surprised when she had showed up at his house with that reporter. What had she been thinking? Pat Osborne had financial security, good looks, and all the freedom in the world. Why did she have to keep haunting Lowell, especially now, when the prize was finally attainable?

It was the fault of the Redner woman, of course. Her reappearance had upset matters greatly. And all because of a problem from so long ago. His work had stood up for nearly thirty years. Now it was all coming undone.

The general had dealt with that situation carefully at the time, one of the first big favours he had done for the Osbornes. He'd had his own motivations, too. It had been Bud who had actually killed the girl. And so sloppily. It was typical. He failed to get into West Point, then had an undistinguished career in the ranks. Bud had always been a disappointment.

The general didn't relish his afternoon's task, but he simply couldn't take the chance of delegating it. Things would be simpler without Pat. She had always been a wild card; the vindictive former wife with a tale to tell. The Redner woman certainly wouldn't have been the last reporter to talk to Pat, digging around for dirt. The media were so bitterly jealous of anyone who was successful that they did their outmost to bring them down into the gutter.

He heard the throaty sound of the Boxster pulling into the driveway, then the screech of the carriage house door going up.

A minute later, Pat appeared, heading across the terrace. She wore a tight-fitting, knee-length red dress, sleeveless, and carried paper shopping bags in each hand. The woman did nothing but spend and meddle.

She put down the bags, fumbling in her purse for a key. Then she realized the door was already unlocked.

The general put a welcoming smile on his face.

Pat Osborne opened the glass door cautiously and called out, "Maria?"

Nope, the general thought. Maid's day off. Another detail he'd checked.

She entered the kitchen, placing the bags on the granite counter top. Then she saw him. "General, what in the world are you doing here?"

She seemed surprised, but not alarmed. Good, he thought. One of the few advantages of becoming old was that people no longer perceived you as a threat.

"We have some things to discuss," he said, keeping his expression friendly.

"Did Lowell send you?"

"Of course."

Pat sighed in exasperation. "What does he want now?"

"Have a seat," the general said. "I'll explain it to you."

Pat came out of the kitchen and into the adjoining great room, her heels clicking on the ceramic tiles of the kitchen, then changing tone as she reached the hardwood of the great room. She had taken her cigarettes and a lighter from her purse.

The general detested smoking, but there was no point in saying anything now.

Pat seated herself across from him in another of the black leather chairs, tapped a cigarette out of her pack and lit it. "What's up, General?" she asked tersely.

"I was wondering if you have seen your friend Kris?"

"No, and if I had, I wouldn't tell you."

"Ah, Pat. After all Lowell has done for you, and still does for you, you seem to have strangely misplaced loyalties."

"All he has done for me? He cheated on me for twenty years of marriage, then dumped me for someone younger. We had a few good months, maybe even a year, then the rest was all a lie. So don't tell me about all the good things Lowell has done for me, General."

She made a gesture that encompassed the room, cigarette clutched in her fingers. "All this was just part of his punishment, and richly deserved.

"If he had anything to do with Kris's sister's death, then he should be punished for that, too. Tell me, General. You'd know. Was Lowell involved in the murder of that girl?"

"It was a complicated situation, Pat. People are reading far too much into whatever it was that did happen to that poor girl up at Cooper Lake. As I understand it, she was just trading sex for the chance to get ahead. You know how it is."

Pat countered that remark with a look of intense disgust. "I think you'd better leave, General. I have nothing further to say to you. Or Lowell."

Pat stood up and started to walk back toward the kitchen.

The general rose, too, slipping on a pair of golf gloves and pulling a heavy plastic bag from the pocket of his windbreaker. He stepped quietly behind Pat, then pulled the bag over her head in one smooth, quick motion.

She twisted and turned, struggling with more strength than he would have credited her with. Her mouth was open, gasping for air. He held the bag firmly closed behind her head with one fist, and twisted her left arm up behind her back. She flailed with her right, ineffectively smacking at his head and clutching at the bag.

He would have much preferred to simply slit her throat or snap her neck, but it would leave too many questions.

Her struggles became less vigorous, and he was able to force her to her knees. It wouldn't be long now. She was already turning a shade of blue, and her breath was rattling. Then she went limp and collapsed onto the floor. He still held the bag tight around her neck, to be sure. When he was certain she was finished, he removed the bag, folded it neatly and put it back in his jacket pocket.

The second phase of his plan had a small element of risk, but not enough to concern him.

He unzipped her red dress and pulled it off her limp body. Then the panty hose, bra and panties. She had been a fine looking woman. Shame he had to waste her this way.

He placed the clothes on the black leather chair. Later, he would take them up to her bedroom and put them on the bed. Not too neatly. That wouldn't have been Pat's style.

He hoisted her body onto his shoulder and headed toward the French doors, pausing briefly to make sure there were no surprise visitors in the yard. Satisfied, he hurried across the terrace toward the pool. When they found her body floating in it, probably some time tomorrow, the police would immediately assume it was a drowning. The chief always had a knack for perceiving the obvious. The only small worry was that Will Hooper would wonder why there was no water in her lungs, if she had drowned. Perhaps he should talk to the doctor, once the body had been found, and explain to him what he was to conclude. He'd always proven reliable in the past.

The general went back inside, to take care of the clothes and make sure he hadn't overlooked anything. Pat Osborne's cigarette still smouldered in the ashtray. He stubbed it out. Filthy habit, smoking.

40

Colin had thought he was off scot-free. His flailing legs had carried him to the cover of the heavy stand of firs, bullets ripping through the air around him. He dived for the soft forest floor and rolled out of sight of the shooters, hardly believing his good fortune. He certainly offered a large enough target. Chaps were damn poor shots.

But where was Kris? He rose cautiously to his feet and was just about to examine the clearing when another volley, fired blind, tore through the firs. He felt his lower left leg go numb, and looked down to see his trousers darkening with blood. Strangely, he could feel no pain, although he knew it would come. He sank back to the ground with a grunt, and used the knife to rip the trousers to the knee. There was a nasty gash through the meat of his calf, bleeding like a stuck pig, but it hadn't hit the bone. He splashed a bit of the whiskey from his flask on the wound, feeling it burn, then took a shot himself. Using the strip of material from the trousers as a tourniquet, he completed the repair job by cutting a piece from the other leg to act as a bandage.

He peered back out into the clearing. Martin Redner's body lay in the open, not moving. Colin found he was having a difficult time taking in the sudden turn of events. Redner had seemed so tough and capable that Colin had felt a modicum of security. Now he was completely on his own.

Two men approached from the road, weapons held at the ready. There was still no sign of Kris. He could only hope that she had gotten away and was heading toward the pickup, as Martin Redner had planned. One of the men he took to be Bud Naylor, from Kris's description. Big fellow with a beer gut, dressed in the same kind of camouflage clothes as the two from the cabin. The other man was turned out the same way. Did this Osborne have his own private army? The second chap was a mean looking bastard, unshaven, with tattoos darkening his arms.

Colin kept low to the ground, clutching the old Winchester. If they came his way, he'd have the advantage now. For a moment, at least.

The heavy one turned Redner over with one foot, then launched a kick to his ribs with a big military boot.

"Fucking Martin Redner," the man said. "Never thought I'd see his face again.'"

"What do you want me to do with him?" the other asked.

"Leave him for now. We'll clean this up later."

Bud knelt and looked at the man Redner had felled with the head shot. His body was relaxed, as if he'd just lain down for a nap, but his head was half gone. The second man had gone down the hill to examine the one in the outhouse.

"Lewis is dead," he shouted back.

Naylor's "Shit!" echoed through the clearing.

Even though he hadn't killed either man, Colin knew he'd pay the price for it if they caught him.

"I'm going after the bitch," Bud Naylor said. "You track down the fat one. Finish him."

"Shouldn't take long," the second man said.

"When he's done, come in behind me, but watch out, for chrissakes. I don't want you blowing my head off by mistake."

The second man gave a derisive snort. "Don't worry. I know what I'm doing."

Colin was certainly convinced. This was no local thug. The chap was almost certainly some sort of former commando.

The second man had obviously marked where Colin went into the bush, because he was heading straight for the clump of firs. Bud Naylor headed off into the maple woods behind the cabin.

Colin hefted the Winchester, working the lever back to make sure there was a shell in the chamber. He had a clear shot, but the sound of the gun would draw Naylor back. He didn't fancy his chances of taking them both.

The man continued to head for the dense stand of trees. His rifle was held at the ready, but he made no effort at stealth. Either he assumed that Colin would be farther away, or that he simply posed no threat.

The little honeymoon period with his leg had quickly come

to an end. The thing was burning like the devil, but at least the tourniquet had slowed the bleeding.

Colin was well concealed where three trees grew densely together. He briefly considered whether he ought to let this man go past him, but then he'd be between Colin and his only chance of a rendezvous with Kris, then escape. He thought he could find his way back if he stuck to the same path they took coming in, but if he tried to get out another way, he would almost certainly end up lost and bleed to death.

The man was twenty feet away. Colin had only seconds to consider his options. He could use the gun as a club, try to knock the fellow down, but it was tight quarters in the bush, and he wasn't sure if he could swing the thing before the other man could turn and fire.

He eased the commando knife from its sheath. It was a nasty little piece of business. About ten inches long, it was black all over and looked rather like a dagger. Thing was sharp enough to shave with. Best English steel.

The man had stopped at the edge of the firs, peering in. Colin froze in position, keeping his breathing shallow. His heart beat like a drum. Could the other fellow hear it?

The man cocked his head and listened. Colin hoped that his hearing had been affected by the semi-automatic fire. He was no weapons expert, but the gun the chap held looked like an M–16. Whatever it was, it would turn him to hamburger with a squeeze of the trigger.

Satisfied that there was nothing in the firs, the fellow began to walk past them. If he stayed on course, he'd pass no more than three feet from where Colin was hiding. This was it, now or never. He seemed to remember his commando friend suggesting it was rather effective to drive the knife first into the kidneys. Quite painful. Then grab the head and slit the throat. He'd have to be awfully fast. If there was any sort of a struggle, this chap could overpower him easily.

Colin figured the odds of his ever having to kill a man with a knife were about the same as being asked to star in the bloody ballet, but there it was. He had one chance to get out of here alive.

He braced himself, hoping that his wounded leg wouldn't fail him.

The man was directly beside him now, looking at the path ahead.

One more step, let him pass.

Colin lunged forward driving the knife at what he hoped was the correct spot. With the weight of his body behind it, the knife met surprisingly little resistance. The man gave a grunt of surprise and half turned. Colin smelled his sweat and some kind of cheap cologne. Now was the critical moment. He withdrew the knife, grabbed the fellow's hair and ripped the blade across his throat with one quick movement. There was a strangled gurgle and bright red arterial blood sprayed on the carpet of yellow leaves. Colin had a quick image of his father killing a chicken on the farm, when he was a lad.

The fellow struggled free of Colin, turned toward him and took a staggering step backward. He dropped the gun. He gave one final look of disbelief and incomprehension, then collapsed to his knees and fell face forward.

Colin was panting, the bloody knife in his hand. He couldn't believe he'd actually succeeded. He had a rush of exhilaration he hadn't felt since he bested George Stannard in a scuffle when they were both twelve. The feeling lasted about five seconds, then he threw up on his shoes. His arms and legs were suddenly weak and trembling.

He'd seen dead bodies in his day, but this was clearly different. The man's warm blood was still on his hands. He picked up a wad of damp leaves and furiously rubbed at the blood until most of it was gone.

The other man's eyes had already started to go glassy and he had released his bowels. Colin knew he had to get moving, to get away from here as quickly as possible.

He wiped the knife on his ruined pants and put it back into its sheath, then stuck it in his belt. He picked up the assault rifle and quickly examined it. No bloody idea how to operate it, but it certainly had the potential to make a bigger impression than the John Wayne special.

Now he had a choice. He could struggle down the path, try to drive out and get help. Or he could go after the man who was chasing Kris.

As attractive as saving his own behind was, it simply wasn't on. By the time he found help, Kris would certainly be dead. He'd come here to rescue her. No time to stop now. The only thing for it was to head off after Bud Naylor. He would be expecting a man to come up behind him. He just wouldn't be expecting Colin.

He hobbled out into the clearing. Two to one now, he told himself. He and Kris against Naylor. Odds were in their favour.

41

For the first few hundred yards, Kris had simply crashed through the forest as fast as she could. Martin's old army knapsack slapped and banged against her back. His rifle had fallen under his body, and she had only had time to grab the knapsack, desperately hoping that it would contain a handgun.

No such luck, but she could feel the blade of a sheathed hunting knife. It was better than nothing.

Once she thought she had established enough of a lead on Naylor, she slowed and moved as quietly as she could. She knew this part of the woods, and she hoped that would be her advantage. Naylor didn't strike her as the type who'd ever spent much time in the bush.

She scrambled up a small rise dense with cedars and slipped into the cover the trees offered. She listened intently for the sound of Naylor moving through the forest. He hadn't the skill to come up stealthily, she was sure, and he was wearing army boots. He was also a guy with an assault rifle tracking an unarmed woman. He wouldn't think caution was necessary.

Finally, she heard him. There was a snapping of branches on the ground, then a muttered "Fuck." Probably a branch whipping him.

She hurried down the far side of the hill. The waterfall was no more than a mile away. If she could stay ahead of him, get behind it for protection, she might be able to slip away once it got dark.

Her legs were stiff from her confinement, but it felt good to be moving again. At least now she had some chance of survival.

She tried to push thoughts of Colin and Martin to the back of her mind. How had they found her? How had they even gotten together? When the two of them came through that cabin door, she couldn't have been any more surprised if they had been Jesus

Christ and Santa Claus.

Now Martin was dead. What had become of Colin? For a second, she had thought he was running off, until she realized that Martin had sent him to draw fire. He had made it as far as the heavier cover, she knew that much. What chance would he have against Naylor's man? He'd be a professional killer, for sure.

There was nothing she could do for him, she knew, so there was no use worrying about it. There would be plenty of time for remorse later — if there was a later.

The forest was fairly open, dominated by a stand of tall maples that shut out the light to everything below. Good for moving, bad for hiding. She slipped behind an old maple that was more than three feet across, and listened.

Nothing. Where was he?

Kris set off again. She thought she could hear the little falls off to her right. Suddenly, she was up to her ankles in cold mud, the dark muck pulling at her borrowed shoes. A flooded area stretched a hundred yards ahead and as far as she could see to the left and right. She doubted it was deep, but she'd leave a lovely set of tracks getting in and out.

She tried to see an alternative, but there was nothing to do but plug ahead. Everything depended on getting behind the waterfall. Naylor would never think to look there.

She slogged through the sloppy mud, every step making a sucking sound she was sure must have been audible far off. Struggling up the other side, she saw the stream and waded in. No footprints, and it would take off the mud. The water was chillingly cold.

Close to the falls, she pulled herself back up on the bank and crouched low. She could hear nothing but the call of a jay. Still no sign of Naylor.

She slipped the knapsack from her shoulders and pulled open its straps. Besides the knife, would it contain anything useful?

She emptied the contents on the ground. The knife was a big, heavy-bladed one in a worn leather sheath, cracked with age. It looked familiar. Was it the same one her grandfather had used to gut deer? This was Martin's survival kit. There was a plastic container of nuts and dried fruit, a compass, a box of 30.06

ammunition, and three large snares with an assortment of pegs. They reminded her of a lesson from her grandfather. Never go into the woods unprepared. You never knew when something might go wrong.

Now she had an idea.

There was a natural path alongside the stream, leading to the small pond below the falls. It was heavy with the tracks of deer that came down to the pond to drink. Midway along the trail, there was a clump of young aspen, about fifteen feet tall and with trunks as thick as Kris's wrist. They might do.

It had been so long since her grandfather had shown her how to set a snare, but she still remembered him crouched to get down to her height, his strong brown hands demonstrating the technique. Her grandfather had relied on a steady stream of game coming to the table, in season or out. Snaring rabbits was a quiet way to achieve that without gunshots that would alert wardens.

Bud Naylor was a hell of a lot bigger than a rabbit, and she'd need to use a spring snare, the type you wanted for a deer. She pegged out the loop of the snare in the centre of the path, then used her weight to pull one of the supple aspens to the ground, attaching the steel cable firmly to the tip of the tree. She was worried the tension would pull the pegs from the ground, but they held. As soon as something got tangled in the snare, say Bud's big army boot, the pegs would release, the slip knot would close, and the tree would whip back into position, leaving the prey dangling upside down. That was the theory, anyway. It was possible that Bud's weight would snap the tree, or prevent it from springing up.

She set the other two snares the same way, creating the effect of a disturbance in the middle of the path, the kind of thing one saw when a larger tree fell, crushing smaller ones under it. She hoped Bud would be drawn to the path. It was the easiest way to get to the pond. Once he got to the tangle of aspens, he'd try to bull his way through. If she was lucky, he'd put a foot in one of the snares.

This trap would need bait, though, to make sure he went down the path. She ripped part of the sleeve off the too-large blue shirt they had put her in, and spiked it on a broken branch.

Now it would look like she also had passed through the tangle, tearing her shirt in the process.

Kris made her way up to the head of the pond and slipped behind the waterfall, the cold water instantly drenching her and causing her to shiver. It was a good hiding place, but if she had to stay long, she'd regret being wet.

The little stone room immediately brought back memories of L.T., and how they'd made love there. If she closed her eyes, she could still imagine him with her. He'd tell her to fight to the end, she was sure of that.

Running through the forest, she had thought of just keeping going. If she could get to the main road, maybe she could flag down a passing car. But surely Naylor's men would be patrolling the roads. She'd be a sitting duck.

She ate half of the nuts and dried fruit, then held the rest in her hand while she filled the container with water and drank deeply.

There was nothing to do now but wait and hope.

42

The general parked his Lexus in front of the Osborne house and let himself in through the front door. He loved the heavy, stone permanence of the place. In a life lived mostly on military bases, the Osborne house had always been the one constant. It had been his second home when he and Lowell's father were growing up together, and it was still.

"Lowell?" he called.

The senator came out of the kitchen and down the centre hallway, lined with portraits of Osbornes past. The smile with which Lowell greeted most any sort of news was missing, but the general felt confident he had just the thing to cheer him up.

"Let's go into my study," Lowell said.

The room was much as it had been in his father's time. Dark walnut panelling, shelves full of books no Osborne had ever read, worn couches covered with a heavy material on which hunting scenes were depicted. Two old muzzle-loading shotguns were crossed above the mantel of the red brick fireplace.

Lowell took an armchair and the general took the one opposite him, no need to be invited.

"Is it done?" Lowell asked.

"Taken care of."

"No problems?"

"None at all."

The senator managed a tight smile, but then ran his right hand through his hair and down the side of his face. "I can't say I feel good about this, General. Was it absolutely essential?"

"Doesn't matter now, does it? But yes. You know that as well as I do. The Redner woman told you Pat knew everything she did. Quite probably has that damned videotape squirreled away somewhere, too. Given all the history, there is no way we could trust her. It would have been like letting her keep a gun pointed at your head. And she couldn't be bribed. Hell, she already had half of your money.

"You didn't still have feelings for her, did you?"

"No, of course not. But we were together a long time. There were a lot of good moments. She understood me better than most."

Lowell looked down at his shoes, then said, "Did she suffer?"

"It was fairly quick. I put her body in the pool, like we discussed. Help will find her tomorrow. It will look like she went for a skinny dip and drowned, probably drunk. Hooper will handle the autopsy. I'm sure we can rely on him to determine the obvious without digging too deep."

"Good, and what about Kris Redner? Is that over, too?"

"Bud's taking care of that. Once she's gone, it won't matter where the tape is. I told Bud to take his time, give the boys a bit of a reward. They've earned it."

The senator winced. "Is that necessary? Why don't we just finish her and get on to other things?"

"After all that she's put us through, we need a little payback. You want to see it?"

"No, of course not. I'll leave all that up to you and Bud. What about the body?"

"We'll bury her up in the woods someplace. No one will ever find it."

It was a good plan, and well executed, but the general could see Lowell still wasn't happy. "Look, son, you're going to have to make some tough calls in the years ahead. This is just the beginning. Remember, always keep your eye on the big picture. Don't let emotion rule you."

Lowell nodded. "No, you're right, General, as always. Still, a difficult one."

The candidate shook his head, as if clearing away the unpleasantness. "While I've got you here, let's talk about some campaign stuff. I've got that fundraiser Friday, and I want to hit the trade issue. Jobs for Americans, jobs in America."

"You should be prepared to cancel. Don't forget that you will have a funeral to attend."

"You think I should go?"

"It will play well. Even though your divorce was bitter, you were still loyal, regarded her as a friend, that kind of thing. A little emotion will help expose your human side to the public. You might want to give a short speech. I'll make sure the media are there. Al will give them the story line in advance."

"All right. I'll have him draft something. Once I learn of her tragic death, of course."

Lowell got to his feet, still looking nervous and unsettled. "Look, can I offer you a drink?" he asked.

"Scotch, single malt."

Lowell pulled two glasses and a bottle from a small walnut hutch near the fireplace. Offering a glass to the general, he said, "I should thank you for everything you've done. That must have been tough today."

The general shrugged. Lowell had no idea how many people he'd killed in his long career. He'd had no particular feelings for Pat Osborne, but even if he had, you did your duty. When Lowell was in the White House, he'd get his reward.

"It's time to focus in on the campaign again," the general said. "This has been a distraction, but we handled it. We've got primaries to think of. It's not too soon to start organizing our people on the ground."

The general's cell phone rang. He pulled it from his jacket pocket with annoyance, saw Bud's number, then took the call.

"We've got a situation."

"Like what?"

"I've got three men down. The girl is on the loose. Martin Redner came in here with another man, killed Lewis and Nick. Stedman and I came up on them, and I took out Redner, then went after the girl. I found some footprints heading toward that little pond, the one with the waterfall, but she could be anywhere in this damned bush. When I doubled back to the cabin, I found Stedman dead. Head damn near cut off. Whoever this second man is, he must be a professional, and he's armed. I need more people out here."

"Where's Edwards?"

"Don't know. He wasn't at the lodge."

"All right. I'll make a call, but it's going to take a couple of hours to get men into position. I'll get them on the roads, seal off every exit."

"Good. I'll go back after the bitch. I want to finish that."

"She can't get far. I want you to stay near the cabin. Keep an eye out for this second man."

Who knew what resources Redner's help had? Transport out, that was for sure. Whoever this guy was, he was the primary target for now.

How had Martin Redner gotten into the game? And three men killed. The day was proving to be even more complex than the general had imagined. He drained his scotch. "Stay where you are. I'm coming in. Let's get this cleaned up."

The general put down the phone and said, "Lowell, have you ever fired a gun?"

43

Colin watched Naylor stand in the clearing, cell phone to his ear, trying to find a position that gave him good reception. The big black SUV was between them, helping shield Colin from Naylor's sight. A crack shot would take the opportunity, but Colin had always had difficulty knocking down the metal ducks at a shooting gallery. He needed Naylor to present himself in the open. Any kind of a clear shot and he'd let loose with everything in the gun. Marquess of Queensbury rules were clearly not in play.

His pursuit certainly hadn't gone well. At first, as Naylor had crashed through the bush, Colin had been able to keep up, or at least able to keep Naylor within earshot. It was difficult to miss the sound of a man cursing at the obstacles nature had placed in his path.

Then Naylor got too far ahead, and Colin had had to admit he was lost. The forest seemed to have closed in behind him. The sun had gone behind heavy clouds, making even that natural compass unavailable. He assumed he had been taking the same general route as Naylor, but it was difficult to determine the direction of sound to a certainty.

Colin estimated he hadn't gone more than 500 yards into the bush before he heard Naylor coming back in his direction. It had been a frightening moment. He had heard a whipping of branches in front of him, alarmingly close. Naylor.

Colin had cautiously swivelled around, staying on the ground. He had seen Naylor no more than fifty feet away, pushing his way through a dense stand of maples. He could have chanced a shot, but he didn't like the odds. Too many trees, and he'd have only one chance to take him out.

He had let Naylor get a couple of hundred yards ahead, then set off cautiously after him, staying parallel and about 100 yards to his right. He had assumed Naylor was heading back to the cabin, having failed to find Kris. With her background, he was sure she'd be adept in the forest. God knew there were enough places to hide. Colin had felt relief, but only for a moment. While he hadn't heard a shot, there was no saying Naylor would have used his gun on her. From what she'd told him, Naylor was the sort who'd want the pleasure of a more personal sort of killing. With a knife, perhaps, or his bare hands.

Once he let Naylor pass by him, Colin had followed close enough to keep the big man in sight. The cabin proved to be nearer than he had imagined. He had made disturbingly little progress, and with the pain, he didn't think he could go much farther. If he was going to take the fellow at all, it had to be at the cabin.

He'd seen an M–16 used often enough, but he'd never thought to ask for a lesson. Hadn't imagined himself having to fire one. He had located a switch on the left-hand side that indicated safe/semi-automatic/automatic. He assumed it would all be as simple as flick the switch, aim and pull the trigger. If it wasn't, he'd be on the receiving end, and it wouldn't matter.

When Colin had finally reached the edge of the clearing that surrounded the decrepit cabin, he had lowered himself to the ground, nearly losing his balance because of his injured leg.

There was shooting pain in the leg now, and it continued to seep blood. He felt light-headed.

It was difficult to make out the words of Naylor's phone conversation, but from the tone, Colin assumed he was reporting to a superior. Senator Osborne, perhaps. From the scowling and shaking of his head, it was apparent Naylor didn't like what he was hearing.

The conversation complete, Naylor flipped the cell phone shut and jammed it in his pocket. He looked at his watch, then said loudly, "Fuck that." Before Colin could react, Naylor took off at a run around the far side of the cabin and disappeared from sight.

44

From her vantage point midway up a densely leafed maple, Kris looked down at the trap she had set, twenty-five feet down the path. It was a hunting trick her grandfather had taught her. Bud Naylor would be looking for her, but he wouldn't be looking up. It worked on deer, at least.

If she'd had a gun, anyone below would have presented an easy shot, but all she had was the heavy knife, tucked into her waistband, and the hope that her plan would work. If it didn't, she'd let him pass by and try to make her way back to the cabin. But what about the other man? Was he waiting behind Bud for her to try exactly such a strategy?

After a brief rest, she had abandoned the hiding place behind the falls. It was fine, as long as hiding was all you intended to do, but the curtain of water left her vision blurred and distorted, like looking through a car windshield in a heavy rain. She couldn't hear much, either, other than the sound of the water sliding over its ten-foot drop into the pool below. If Bud Naylor did come her way, she didn't want it to be a surprise.

She looked at her watch. It would be dark in a couple of hours, and the increasing clouds had already made the forest gloomy. She had reached the waterfall more than an hour ago, but she had neither heard nor seen any sign of Naylor and the second man. Had they pulled back to wait for reinforcements?

She didn't make that as Bud's style. Bull ahead and get it done was more like it. Besides, two men with assault rifles versus one unarmed woman. That wouldn't have caused him any concern. Maybe he wanted to get enough people to advance methodically, like beaters driving game.

She knew she had to just stay calm and wait for Naylor to make his move. "Wait for the game to come to you — don't go chasing it," her grandfather had often said.

She still remembered Charlie Redner, but much of what she actually knew about him was the result of campfire stories related by her uncle. What had they done with Martin's body, she wondered? She had tried not to think about his death.

And Colin, was there any chance that he'd eluded them? If he did, she prayed that he'd have the sense to go for help. Preferably the state police, but even Osborne's tame force would have to respond to a situation like this.

She heard Naylor before she could see him.

He was coming from the direction of the cabin, trying to be stealthy, but every second step seemed to be right on the broken sticks that littered the forest floor. What had he been doing all this time, she wondered, and was he alone?

She began to shiver. Just because she was wet from the falls, she told herself.

What would she do if Naylor actually stepped into her trap? If she left him, the others would find him, and she'd be no further ahead. She'd never killed anyone, or even contemplated it. She still couldn't imagine doing it. Then she remembered what had happened back in the cellar of the lodge. Naylor so close to her she could feel the warmth of his beery breath, saying, "I own you, little girl. Every inch of you." Then the beating and the humiliation. And worse would have happened, too, if he hadn't been interrupted.

No, if she was ever going to kill anyone, Bud Naylor had to be at the top of the list. She put a hand on the knife, feeling its reassuring weight rubbing against her side.

Naylor stepped into the clearing, alone. The black, ugly, M–16 was at the ready as he scanned the open area, head cocked, listening. Then he saw the piece of her shirt snagged on a branch.

The hungry, hard arrogance of his smile told Kris that only one of them could come out of this alive. If she didn't stop him, the man would pursue her like a predator until he made the kill.

He advanced cautiously down the deer trail that led to the pond. Looking down, he saw the tracks her shoes had made. This seemed to reassure him, and he moved forward more quickly.

Kris was almost right above him. She kept completely still,

trying to will herself into a steady calmness. If Naylor saw her, he'd shoot her down like a treed coon.

At the twisted tangle of young trees she had created, he paused, crouched and peered into the leafy mess. Wondering what had caused it, she was sure. No big limb was in sight, no visible reason for what he saw in front of him.

She worried that her trap had been too obvious, that he would simply force his way through the bush and go around it.

She didn't have to worry long.

Naylor held the gun in front of him to deflect the branches and pushed his way into the tangle, seeking the obvious ease of the path on the other side.

Nothing happened. He was past the first snare, she was sure of that.

Then one of the trees released, catapulting Naylor up into the air. She had an excellent view of the shocked look on his face.

"Fuck," he screamed, arms flailing. The assault rifle was long gone, lost in the tangle below. The tree bowed under Naylor's weight, but it didn't snap as she had feared. It suspended him about four feet off the ground, the snare tight around one high-topped leather boot.

Kris hoped it was painful.

"Where are you, you fucking bitch?" he shouted. "Get out here, cut me down."

As if, Kris thought, enjoying the show from her tree. She wished she had a cigarette.

After running the full Marine vocabulary and offering colourful descriptions of what he'd do to her various orifices, Naylor changed tack. "Guys, over here. Help me," he cried.

That's what she had been waiting for. If Naylor had any backup, they'd certainly have responded to all his bellowing by now. It looked as if poor Bud was all alone.

Kris climbed quickly down the tree, then ambled down the path toward the snare, taking her time.

"Hey, Bud, how's it hanging?"

He swung his body around so he could see her. Hanging upside down from the tree, her ferocious opponent looked absurd, beer belly bulging the wrong way, jowls shoving up into his face, which had become a deep red.

"Get me out of this, goddammit."

"Now why would I do that, Bud? You know yourself that an enemy is best dealt with when he's immobilized."

"Enjoy your fun, bitch. It won't last long."

"Why, have you got me surrounded? I don't think so, Bud. I think you're all alone."

Bud tried to spit at her, but only succeeded in landing spittle on his own forehead.

Kris stepped closer, wary of getting within grabbing range. She'd have preferred to whisper right into his ear, but this would do. "Turns out, I'm your worst goddamn nightmare. I own you now, Bud. Every inch of you."

"You're fucking crazy. You know that? Why the hell didn't you back off weeks ago? We gave you enough warnings."

"Like killing L.T., you mean?"

"Yeah, that was easy."

Bud actually laughed. Even hanging upside down like a side of beef, the man hadn't lost his attitude.

"Did I ever tell you how much I enjoyed fucking your sister?" he sneered.

She knew what he was doing, trying to anger her, lure her in close enough to grab her, break her neck. She couldn't let herself fall for it.

"Yeah, you did, you sick shit. Did you enjoy killing her, too?"

"She really struggled. I liked that."

"Who told you to do it?" she asked.

"Who do you think?"

There was no need to say his name. Everything kept coming back to Lowell Osborne.

"And L.T.?"

"I was just the technician. My old man figured that one out. Pretty simple, too. I was never sure, was the guy on your side or ours?"

Kris forced a laugh. "Yeah, he played you pretty good, didn't he? We had some laughs over that."

"Guy couldn't have been too smart. Fucking you got him

killed. No way that was worth it. You do have a sweet little ass, though."

That was enough. The memory of Bud running his hands, and his knife blade, over her reminded her who he really was.

What was she going to do? She hadn't thought beyond the moment of getting him in the trap. Could she actually kill him, and how could she do it without giving him a chance to kill her?

She closed her eyes, and saw Kathy's face, and L.T.'s face, then the faces of her father and mother, from so long ago. And then Martin, gunned down right in front of her. The Osbornes and the Naylors had destroyed her family. Now it was Bud's turn to pay.

Without any more thought, she picked up a heavy stick from the ground. It was smooth to the touch, about four feet long and as thick as a baseball bat. Bud's arms hung distended from his sides. Stepping behind him, she raised the stick and brought it down with all her force in the gap where the upper arm joined the shoulder. There was a satisfying crack, followed by Bud's high-pitched scream of pain. He pulled the other arm protectively against himself, and she smashed the stick into his elbow. No snap this time, but another scream.

As he spun in front of her, screaming and cursing, she timed one more blow. One leg was suspended from the tree, the other hanging to the side. She reached the stick high over her head and drove it down so hard between his legs that she could feel the vibration jar her arms.

Bud uttered a low growling bellow, then tried to curl his body into the fetal position, he got half way up before collapsing back again, his useless arms dangling at his side.

Kris found herself breathing as fast as if she'd just run a mile, every muscle in her body tensed. She crouched, the stick held in front of her, then threw it to the ground, and knelt, one hand on the soft forest dirt. Jesus, she couldn't believe what she had done.

The worst part was, she felt neither sick nor sated. Was she any better than Bud Naylor?

Bud held his broken arm with the one that was still semifunctional, his face distorted in pain as he twirled by one leg.

She withdrew the knife from its sheath.

"I could finish you now, Bud, but I don't think you've suffered enough. How long would you have tortured me, before you finally killed me?"

He tried to answer, but could only manage a groan.

"I could slit your throat and just let you bleed out. Or maybe I could gut you like a deer, leave your entrails hanging out. You'd make a nice meal for scavengers."

Through gritted teeth, Bud said, "Kill me, you crazy bitch."

45

Colin wasn't sure whether he had been dreaming or halluci-nating. He had been crawling on his belly, scuttling to escape as chips of stone and dust flew from the sun-baked wall behind him. Caught in a crossfire, pushing into an area that his inter-preter had told him was unsafe. Damn near shitting his pants. That was the reality of his Lebanese war story, without the embellishments he added for the young ladies. A minute ago, it had seemed like he was back there and now he was in the forest again.

His leg continued to seep blood. Obviously not an artery, thank God, but he'd still bleed to death, given enough time. Would he survive a night in the forest? He knew the temperature was only cool, but he was shivering like it was a January day in Ottawa.

At the sound of a truck engine approaching, he allowed him-self a moment of hope. Maybe it was some kind of help arriving, at last.

He remained tucked in the firs, where he had hidden before killing the tattooed chap. It was still the best cover and offered a good view of the cabin, but the fellow's body was disconcert-ingly close. He was trying to ignore the sound of the flies that had gathered, and forcing himself not to allow the thought of maggots to enter his mind at all.

When he saw another black SUV like the one already parked at the cabin, Colin knew this latest development didn't constitute good luck.

Two men got out of the truck. One was older, trim, silver-haired, the other fortyish and blandly good-looking. Osborne, he assumed. They didn't look terribly threatening, but the older man opened the hatch of the SUV and removed a black assault rifle. Was there anyone in this bloody forest who didn't have one? Colin eased his own into a better position, in case he had to shoot.

"Bud," the older man shouted. "Where are you at?"

His shout echoed through the forest, but there was no response.

"Dumb sumbitch has set out on his own," the older man said.

The man went to the cabin, calling Bud's name again, then advanced across the clearing. He used the toe of his boot to turn over Martin Redner. The sight of his dead body caused the older man to smile.

He advanced toward Colin, checking the bodies of his own two dead men, then retreated to the SUV. In the quiet bowl of the clearing, he was still close enough for Colin to hear everything he said.

"Can you handle an M–16, Lowell?" the older man said.

"I'd be more comfortable with a handgun," the other one said.

The older man reached back into the truck, apparently having brought his own armoury. He produced a large, ugly-looking weapon.

"Colt .45 semi-auto. Ever fired one?"

"Couple of times."

"Good. Remember, aim low. It has a hell of a kick."

The two men were standing directly in front of Colin, no more than 100 feet away. He was no marksman, but he felt reasonably confident he could bring them both down. But if he did, how the devil would he ever locate Kris and Bud Naylor? Presumably, these two knew where they were going. He'd simply have to follow.

The younger one looked at his watch. "Should we give Tom a few more minutes?"

"Did he say he was coming for sure?"

"I'd say he was hesitating."

"Typical," the older one said. "We could never really count on him. We'll deal with him later. Let's just get going. I doubt Tom is any good with a gun anyway, and Bud's ass is hanging out."

"I don't like this," the younger one said.

"You don't need to like it. This is your mess, remember? Now, let's clean it up."

"What about the second man? Bud seemed to think he's a professional."

"He'll be between us and Bud, if he's any good. Long gone if he's smart. Now let's go."

The older chap's analysis was sound, Colin thought. So far, he had proven that he was neither smart nor good.

46

She couldn't do it. That was the cold, hard, fact. Bud Naylor hung from the snare, 250 pounds of evil, and she couldn't finish him.

After the fury that had driven her to beat him with the stick was finally spent, Kris couldn't bring herself to butcher him, because that's what it would be. Naylor was defenceless now, spinning slowly from the bowed tree trunk, moaning quietly.

She could slip in quickly, slit his throat and get the hell out. It would be the smart thing to do. Naylor might have been alone, but there would be more coming. She should be using the last hour of light to head toward the road, then take her chances after dark.

Instead, she crouched ten feet away from Naylor, watching him. The will to fight had finally run out. She felt as if she could just lie down on the ground and fall asleep.

Kris knew she should have felt triumphant. She had beaten Naylor against all the odds. It was only a battle, though, not the war. Osborne had won that. She could never retrieve the videotape and she imagined all the people who could back up the story were dead now. She was the last loose end, but even if she escaped alive, she would never be able to bring Osborne down.

And her casualties were immense. L.T., Martin, probably Colin. All dead because of her crazy, quixotic fight against an enemy any fool would have known was unbeatable.

She felt a single tear trickle down her left cheek. I tried, Kathy, she thought. She consoled herself with the idea that her father would have been proud, at least. He was a man who had never backed down from a fight in his life.

Absorbed in her thoughts, Kris didn't hear Lowell Osborne until he was fifty feet away, at the entrance to the path where she had snared Bud. The large handgun he carried at his side was rather incongruous with his false, political smile.

"Kris," he said brightly, as if he'd just encountered an old friend.

She pulled the knife from its sheath and crouched, ready. No way Lowell Osborne would have the guts to shoot her. What was he doing out here on his own?

Her question was answered by a cold steel muzzle pressed into the base of her neck. She hadn't even heard the other man come up behind her.

"Drop the knife, Kris. It's all over now."

The general's tone was gentle, almost kind.

Kris did as she was told, letting the knife fall to the ground and straightening out of her crouch. The gun barrel remained pressed to her neck.

Bud was moaning more loudly now, even in his haze realizing that help had arrived at last.

Kris wondered why the general hadn't simply shot her, then quickly realized they must have a worse fate in mind. Now she regretted not killing Bud. It would have been her only way to hurt the general, let him feel what it was like to lose someone he cared about.

"You can lower the gun, General," she said. "I'm quite defenceless now."

He kept it in place.

"Perhaps, but you've proven to be surprisingly resourceful. What in the world did you do to Bud?"

"Deer snare. He wasn't watching where he was going."

"Lowell, figure a way to get Bud down from that bloody tree, would you? He needs medical attention."

The senator seemed surprised at being told to do something, but he stepped carefully past Kris and began to examine Bud's situation. Kris finally realized that the general had been the one giving the orders all along. Bud and Lowell were just his front men, one rough, the other smooth. If Lowell made it to the White House, she was sure the general would still be whispering in his ear.

Osborne examined Bud's boot and how it was attached to the tree, then made a tentative attempt to snap the tree using his weight as leverage.

"Going to be tricky to get him down from here without a saw," he said.

"Oh for fuck's sake," the general said.

Kris was nearly deafened as he left off a short burst from the M–16, snapping the tree and causing Bud to fall to the ground with a heavy thud.

If there was a God, Kris thought, the bastard would have broken his neck in the fall, but instead he struggled to his knees.

"Lowell, see if you can get him to his feet," the general said. "We've got to get out of here. We need to clean up that mess back at the cabin, and there isn't much time before dark.'

"What about her?" the senator asked.

"I'll deal with her. If I kill her here, one of us would have to drag the body."

How practical, Kris thought. Maybe the bastards would ask her to dig her own grave.

"How many people do you think you can make disappear, General, before someone in the real world notices?" Kris asked.

"We'll see," he said, with the bright enthusiasm of a man tested by a particularly interesting problem. "The people Martin Redner killed were never here anyway. Him, I doubt anyone will miss.

"Just out of curiosity, how the devil did he know you were here?"

"Good question," she said. She wasn't going to tell them anything about Colin. If he had somehow managed to get away, justice might still be done.

"Well, plenty of time to chat later," the general said. "Let's get moving."

Osborne had helped Bud struggle to his feet. The bigger man was dragging one leg and when Osborne tried to help support his weight by putting Bud's arm around his neck, Bud moaned in pain.

"This is going to be slow," Osborne said.

The general nodded, then poked Kris with the gun barrel.

"You lead the way," he said. "Don't even think about jackrabbiting. You won't get five feet."

Kris had no doubt he was sincere, even if it would mean the inconvenience of having to drag her body. She set off slowly down the path, head down. The other three followed her, no one speaking. The only sounds were Bud's moans and the crunching of sticks underfoot. There was no reason for an attempt at stealth now.

They were halfway back to the cabin, passing through a small clearing dense on both sides with cedars. Their smell was one Kris always associated with these woods. It struck her that she was smelling them for the last time. Her life was measured now in minutes. Surprisingly, she felt no fear. It was as if she were already dead, watching her body go through its last motions.

Then she heard the gunshot. Kris instinctively tensed in preparation for the pain, but there was nothing. She dived to the ground, flattening herself into the wet leaves. Behind her, she heard Osborne shout, "General!"

Kris twisted around to see the general lying face first on the leaves, a large part of the top of his head missing. Tom Larson had stepped from the cedars and stood between her and Bud and Lowell, who looked on with complete incomprehension.

"Tom, what the hell?" Lowell managed.

Tom raised his gun, a Glock by the look of it, casually aimed it at Bud Naylor and shot him twice in the centre of his chest. Bud staggered back like a man who had been punched, then collapsed to his knees dragging Lowell Osborne down with him.

Osborne quickly disentangled himself from Bud's body and scrambled back to his feet. His face had gone ash grey, his lips quivering.

Tom still hadn't spoken a word, but kept his gun pointed at Lowell Osborne. He seemed to have forgotten Kris. She considered running, but stayed where she was, clinging to the ground. If he was here to save her, there was no need to run. If he wanted to kill her, there was no chance she could get away.

"Tom, are you insane?" Lowell Osborne asked. He held his hands out, beseechingly. For once, his look was sincere, and it was one of terror.

"Not at all," Tom said. "Ever since her sister was killed, you three have controlled my life. Didn't you think I would realize that I was your Plan B, in case anyone ever traced her death back to you? The three of you would have set me up without blinking an eye."

"No, Tom, you're wrong," Lowell said, shaking his head now. "We were all in that together. And when it became a problem, we dealt with it. Tom, I paid to put you through medical school. You're like a brother to me," Lowell pleaded.

Tom laughed, but he kept his gun pointed straight at Osborne. "A brother? You mean a guy you pay to stay away and not tell the world what you're really like? You've always acted like you owned me, Lowell. When you offered me all that money to come back here, what would you have done if I'd refused? I know you. You'd have found a way to destroy me."

"No, Tom. I wanted to do something for the town. Bringing you back has been wonderful for the people."

"Don't give me the old Osborne bullshit about the people, Lowell. You wanted me back here so you could keep me under close watch. You've got big dreams, and I'm one of the few who knows the truth about you."

"Look, Tom, we can still work this out. I don't understand why you had to kill the Naylors, but there's no need for it to get out. It can be our secret. Let's just kill the girl and get out of here."

Tom turned to look at Kris. His handsome face was disturbingly blank. She noticed for the first time that he wore black dress pants, a red tie, and a leather jacket. He must have come straight from his office. The clothes were as jarring as his actions. What had brought him here?

"No, Lowell, we've had secrets for too long. My whole life has been about keeping your secrets. I should have turned you in thirty years ago, when you killed her sister."

"But I didn't kill her, Tom. You know that."

Bud gave a low moan. A large patch of blood darkened the centre of his USMC T-shirt, but he wasn't dead yet.

"Tom, you're a doctor. Bud is still alive. How can you stand there and do nothing?"

"You're right, Lowell," Tom said.

He raised his gun and fired one more shot, right into Bud

Naylor's head. The sound was like thunder in the small clearing.

"Tom, I'm begging you. Don't kill me," Lowell said. He was actually on his knees now.

Kris herself had gotten back to her feet. If Tom wanted to kill her, he would. There was no use cowering.

She could see now that she had seriously underestimated Tom. She had taken him for nothing more than a follower, one of Lowell's gang. Another of the many who knew what had happened, but didn't stand up and do anything.

"When the general called me and said you needed help, did you think I wouldn't figure out that I'd never leave these woods alive? He told me he was cleaning up loose ends. I'm a loose end, Lowell."

"No, you're not. We trust you. That's why we asked you to help. Bud's other men were killed. You must have seen the bodies back at the camp."

"Yes. Loose ends."

"Think this through, Tom," Lowell pleaded, still on his knees. "If you kill me, there will be a serious investigation. I'm a U.S. senator. You will spend the rest of your life in jail."

"Oh, don't worry, Lowell. I've already found a solution to that problem. Now get on your feet. You look pathetic."

Tom turned his head briefly in Kris's direction.

"Sorry I didn't help you sooner," he said. "It should never have come to this. Will you help me now?"

To do what, exactly? she wondered. Was Tom insane, or the only one here who wasn't? Either way, there was only one possible answer.

"Of course."

"Good. Let's go, Lowell. We're heading back to your camp."

47

At first, Colin thought he was hearing voices in his dream. He had been slipping in and out of consciousness, the line between the real world and the one in his head now very fine indeed. Then he heard Kris's voice. He was sure it was her.

Two or three people were coming from his left. He couldn't see them yet, but he could hear them making their way through the brush. He could hear two men's voices and a woman's, their actual words still indistinct.

So they had captured her. He would have one more shot at freeing her after all. He rubbed his face and shook his head, trying to focus. The sun wasn't quite down yet, but it was shadowy in the forest. Everything looked indistinct.

He remained in a prone position, but raised the gun so he could shoot. Surely he still had enough strength left to pull the trigger.

Then he saw them enter a gap in the trees, no more than 100 feet away and heading right at him. The man he assumed was the senator was in the lead. The chap with the moustache, the one who had gone in last, was carrying a handgun but he kept it by his side. Kris was between the two of them.

The senator appeared to be unarmed, but he likely had his gun in some kind of holster. Not ready to hand, in any case. The thing was to take out the fellow with the gun first, then play it by ear.

He sighted down the barrel, but it seemed to be swaying. Damned hands were far from steady. He'd have to wait until the chap was in can't-miss range.

They were fifty feet out now, and a bit of a gap had opened up between Kris and the fellow with the gun. This was the moment.

Colin flicked the little lever up to semi-auto. He wasn't sure how many rounds were still in the gun and he didn't want to empty it in one burst. One hit from this black beast ought to be enough, he reasoned.

The man was moving quickly and every time Colin got the barrel on him, it seemed to waver to the left. Damn. If he didn't fire now, they'd be gone and the opportunity lost. Pursuit was out of the question.

He squeezed off three quick rounds and saw all three of them dive for the ground. There was no return fire.

A voice he thought was the senator's called out, "Bobby, is that you?"

Bobby? That was the fellow from the lodge. Still in the back of Redner's pickup somewhere, Colin supposed, if a bear hadn't made a meal of him.

He gathered his energy to put the maximum authority into his voice and said, "Guns down. Everyone get to their feet with their hands above their heads."

"Colin?" Kris said.

"Right. You okay, Kris?"

"Yes, we've captured Osborne. The Naylors are dead."

Who was "we"? he wondered. Did Kris have another ally he wasn't aware of?

"Who's the other fellow?"

"He's all right. He's with us."

"Don't shoot," the man with the moustache said. "I'm on Kris's side."

What if he had a gun to her head, was making her say that, Colin thought. "Get to your feet all three of you," he said.

They rose slowly, Kris and the fellow with the moustache close to each other, the senator about six feet to their right.

"Right then, hand your weapon to Kris."

The man gave his gun to her without hesitation.

"Kris, does the other one have a gun?" he asked.

"No. We're clear. Colin, join us."

He struggled to his feet, then collapsed back to the ground.

48

"How bad is it, Tom?" Kris asked.

He shook his head.

"Not good. Nothing major was hit, but he's lost a lot of blood. We have to get him out of here, fast."

Blood had leaked through the makeshift bandage that Colin had fashioned, soaking his shoe and sock. His normally ruddy complexion was as white as new snow.

"Who is he, anyway?"

"A friend. He came in with my uncle Martin."

Tom nodded as if this made some kind of sense. "Lowell, help him to his feet," he said.

The senator looked reluctant.

"Just do the right thing for once, will you?" Tom said.

Lowell Osborne struggled to get Colin back on his feet. The senator was a large man, but Colin was taller and heavier. Finally, he got him up, but it seemed unlikely that Colin would have the strength to go on.

"I'll take his other side," Kris said.

She looked at the M–16 lying on the forest floor where Colin had dropped it.

"Should we take that?" she asked.

"No," Tom said. "I've seen about enough of those for one day."

Kris was still tempted to sling the thing over her shoulder. She had placed her trust in Tom because she didn't have a better alternative, but she was well aware that he hadn't chosen to act until he himself was imperilled. He was here to cover his own ass, not save hers. What did he have planned?

She half wished that Colin's shot had taken Tom out, but then they would have had to kill the senator, too. She couldn't imagine their doing that. No, she needed Tom's help. For now, at least.

Kris gave Colin her right shoulder to carry some of his weight and they set off toward the cabin, like awkward participants in a three-legged race. Tom followed behind. She had put Tom's gun down when she bent to help Colin and he had picked it up and was carrying it in his hand. Was it just to prevent Lowell from escaping?

Fifteen minutes of stumbling carried them back to the cabin. The first thing she saw was Martin's body, lying stiff and face down. No one had even bothered to move it.

The senator and Kris took Colin into the cabin and lowered him gently on the same thin bed where Kris had spent the night, so many deaths ago. It was almost dark in the dim little cabin.

Tom gave Colin a large glass of water from a bottle left by Lewis and Nick. "See if you can get him rehydrated, Kris," he said. "Give him as much as he'll take."

"We've got to get him to a hospital now, Tom," she said. "Let's take your car."

"Then what do we do with the senator?" Tom asked.

"I don't know. Put him in the trunk?"

"No," Tom said. "We don't have time for detours."

"Look, this is my friend. He risked his life to rescue me. I'm not just going to leave him here to die."

"No, of course not. Lowell, give me your cell phone."

The senator reached into his jacket pocket and produced a BlackBerry. Tom punched in a number and said, "Give me the chief."

After only a few seconds, Kris could make out a familiar voice on the other end.

"Larry, it's Lowell Osborne," Tom said, keeping his gun pointed at the real Lowell Osborne. "We've got a problem up here at the camp."

Kris thought his imitation of the senator was spot on. Tom had caught his bluff heartiness perfectly.

"You know where the old hunting cabin is, the one on the west side? I've got a wounded man here. Long story, but we need an ambulance up here now."

Tom dropped his voice into a more confidential tone. "Larry, I need you to get in ahead of the ambulance. There are three other bodies here. I need them to disappear discreetly. I'll fill you in on all of it as soon as I get the chance."

There was a pause, as Chief Larry Brewster offered his point of view. Kris couldn't make it out.

"Yes, Larry, I know it's risky. Why do you think I've gone to my best man?"

More from the chief, then, "No, Bud isn't available. I'm counting on you, Larry. This will be very worth your while. Come on your own, and you need to get moving now. Just call the ambulance and get on up here.

"No, I won't be here. Still one more thing to attend to, but I'll talk to you before the end of the day.

"Larry, you can do it," Tom said, then hung up.

"All your years of investment in the chief are going to pay off, Lowell," he said.

"Look, Tom. You're right, Larry will clean all this up. We don't need to worry. I'm asking you again. Let this go. What do you want? Name it, it's yours."

"Sorry, Lowell, I'm no longer for sale."

Kris couldn't see Lowell Osborne's face in the dim light, but she could see his arms tense, as if he was going to make some kind of move. She could understand his desperation. What did Tom intend to do? If he was going to kill Lowell, why didn't he do it and get it over with?

"Kris, we have to leave him. The ambulance will be here within thirty minutes. He'll be fine until then," Tom said.

"Why don't I stay with him?" she said. "You do what you need to with Lowell."

"No," he said quickly. "I need you with me. Sorry, Kris, I can't let you go until you and I have agreed on our version of what happened today."

Our version, she thought. So he thinks I will cover up what he did. Tom obviously expected gratitude, and maybe he deserved it. He had saved her life, even if his real motive was saving his own.

Her instinct was to resist him, but he still held a gun in his hand and he had already killed two people. If she went with him now, Colin would be saved.

Then she saw it. Tom wanted her to participate in killing Lowell Osborne. That would make it their secret, not his. Or maybe it wasn't as good as that. Why would Tom trust her, again placing another person in the position of holding a secret that could destroy him? Perhaps he intended to kill them both.

She turned to Colin, who lay limp on the bed.

"Colin, you stay here. There will be an ambulance in a few minutes. You'll be all right. I have to go with Tom. Don't worry, it will be fine."

Kris leaned in close to him, to give him a small kiss. He smelled of sweat and death.

She whispered as quietly as she could. "He killed the Naylors and he's going to kill Osborne. Tom Larson. Tell the state police."

Colin seemed to nod, but perhaps it was just an involuntary movement of the head. She prayed he had heard her, and that he would live to tell the story.

49

Tom opened the trunk of his big, red Lincoln. Even in the faint light, they could see Lowell's eyes, large and pleading. Blood was running down his forehead from a nasty looking bump just below the hairline. They had heard him banging about in the trunk as they went down the rough road away from the cabin, but Tom hadn't slowed down.

"Get out," he said, pointing the gun at Lowell. Kris watched them from a few feet away. She knew she should do something, but what? If she tried to grab the gun, rescue Lowell, it would be like saving a rat from a snake. And why should she? Lowell Osborne wouldn't have hesitated or blinked if it was her facing death. He'd been pleading for Tom to kill her.

"Come on," Tom said. Lowell hadn't made a move, curled into a ball in the big trunk, his hands around his head in a futile gesture of self-protection.

When Lowell still wouldn't move, Tom switched the gun to his left hand, reached in and grabbed him by the collar, roughly yanking him until he fell sprawling to the ground.

Lowell forced himself up on all fours then got shakily to his feet. Holding out his right hand, palm up, he said, "Tom, this is crazy. We've been friends all our lives."

"Not really," Tom said. His voice was exceptionally calm, as if the two were having a chat on the back porch somewhere. "We haven't been friends since her sister died, Lowell. I'd say that's when I really got to know you. Now let's go. Into the house."

Tom gestured with the barrel of his gun, pointing toward Osborne's lodge. It was about 150 feet away, along a path heavily carpeted with brown spruce needles. The big house looked ghostly with no lights on.

Lowell Osborne started reluctantly up the path, his shoulders stooped

"You too, Kris," Tom said, indicating that she should go in front of him.

He would kill them both, she was pretty certain. Did he intend to make it look like they had had some sort of confrontation, then shot each other?

"I hope you've got a good plan, Tom," Kris said. "Lowell's right. It will be the state police investigating this, not Larry Brewster. FBI, Secret Service. Hard to say who will get involved in the end. You really think you can get away with it?"

"Sure," he said. "I'm a well-respected doctor. Besides, I was home with my wife Betsy while all of this was going on. How would I even have known about it? Whereas most everyone around here knows that you've been out to get the senator.

"No, I could certainly make it look like you were the one who killed Lowell, if that was what I wanted to do."

They were at the lodge now.

"Inside," Tom said.

Lowell pushed open the screen door, crossed the porch, and swung open the unlocked door of the house itself. Instinctively, he reached for a light switch and flicked on a series of lamps around the large main room. There were pools of yellow light around two of the plaid couches. The stuffed bear reared harmlessly in one corner. The big cobblestoned fireplace was cold and empty.

Tom pointed to a wooden chair that stood against the wall near the door to the kitchen. "Get that chair and bring it into the middle of the room," he told Lowell.

As the senator crossed the room, Tom still stood near the door. Kris was to his right, too far away to make a move.

Lowell Osborne placed the chair in the centre of one of his worn red Persian rugs.

"Sit down," Tom said. He reached into his jacket pocket and pulled out a roll of grey duct tape. Flipping it to Kris, he said, "Tape him to the chair."

She caught the tape, then wrapped it around Lowell's upper body, finally adding three strips to keep his legs fixed to the chair. He sat rigid. She remembered how she had been taped down, in the basement of this same house. Was it going to happen again?

"Kris, go over to the fireplace. You'll find some newspapers piled there, and kindling. Matches are in a box on the mantel. Bring them over to where Lowell is."

She had an inkling now of what he intended, but it seemed too monstrous to be true.

Loaded with paper, kindling, and matches, she returned to where Lowell sat in the centre of the room, and landed the lot on the rug near him.

"Kris, I'm sure an outdoorsy girl like you knows how to make a fire. Set one up, around that chair."

Did Tom actually intend to light the man on fire, or did he just want to make him squirm? Kris wondered.

"Jesus, Tom. This is madness," Lowell said. "If you're going to kill me, then shoot me. There's no reason for this."

"That's where you are wrong, Lowell. There are thirty years of reasons. I've lived my life carrying your secret, waiting for the day it would come back to get me. Now you can spend a little time sharing the feeling."

"Tom, I know you must have felt guilt. We all did. But if you couldn't live with that, how will you feel after you've done this?"

"Kris, lay the fire," Tom said.

Kris saw no choice but to do as she was told. She still wasn't convinced Tom would actually light the fire, but if he wanted Lowell Osborne to suffer, he was succeeding. Death by fire would be terribly painful, but not nearly as quick as you'd like. What did he have in store for her? she wondered.

She balled up the old copies of Lowell's paper, the *Republican–Patriot*, and piled them under the chair. Then she leaned the long sticks of cedar kindling against the chair legs and the paper, forming a teepee. Lowell made a feeble attempt to kick away the sticks in front of his legs, sending a few clunking to the rug.

"Do you remember the day it happened, Lowell?" Tom asked.

"Of course I do."

Lowell's voice was hoarse, strained. It was cold in the lodge, but Kris saw sweat running freely down the senator's forehead, mixing with the blood seeping from the goose egg on his head.

"I've never seen the videotape, Lowell. Did you rape the girl yourself, or did you delegate it?"

"I never raped her," Lowell said, his chin now hanging against his chest.

"So it was Bud, Billy, and Bobby, then. With you operating the camera."

"No, they used a tripod. I didn't even know about it until it was done."

"Really?" Tom said, unconvinced. "Did you know she was fourteen years old?"

"Who are you to talk? You dated her."

"Yes, and I dropped her when I found out how young she was."

"I thought she was willing. The others were," Lowell said.

"You bastard. You had already done the same thing to my own girlfriend."

Tom was growing angry now, reliving the day. Kris had stood up and moved a couple of feet from the senator. She calculated the odds of dashing across the room, getting out the door and into the protection of darkness. It was about twenty feet.

Lowell looked up, defiant now.

"Liz enjoyed it. Didn't she ever show you the movie?"

"No. She didn't."

"Pity we didn't know little Betsy back then."

Kris saw what he was trying to do, goad Tom into shooting him. Anything was better than being set on fire.

"Tom, what are we doing?" Kris asked.

"I'm giving Lowell a chance to confess, to atone for what he's done."

Lowell said nothing.

"After Kris's sister was raped, she ran away," Tom said. "You sent me and Bud after her, but you didn't say what it was really all about. Just that one of the maids had gotten all upset because Billy had made a pass at her, and she was running off to tell her father. I thought we'd solve the problem with money, like we solved most of your problems. But Bud had another idea. We saw her hitchhiking at the side of the road. Bud pulled over."

Kris could see her sister's final moments now, like an old

black and white movie.

"When she saw Bud, she ran. I didn't understand why then. We chased her down. I was actually the one who caught her. Bud was never much of a runner. When he caught up to us, he threw her on the ground and started to choke her. I was surprised. I didn't know what to do.

"So I just stood there, and watched it happen. It was all over so fast. Then she was dead. My first thought was to turn Bud in, but then I'd be an accessory to murder. My life would have been ruined, along with all of yours.

"So I did nothing, and that's been my lasting shame. Tell me, Lowell, have you ever felt any shame?"

"Of course," he said, too quickly. "It was the darkest moment of my life."

"Really?" Kris said. "You didn't show the slightest remorse when we talked back at the cabin."

"What's done is done," Lowell said. "You move on."

"Yes," Tom said. "I think it's time we all put you behind us, and moved on.

"Here's the deal, Kris. The senator is going to die in a tragic fire. This old lodge will go up like a tinderbox. Poor Lowell will be incinerated. If they do find his body, it will be nothing more than a cinder. Cause of death will be smoke inhalation.

"Now, let's give him a little preview of what he's going to face in hell. Kris, light him up."

She picked up the box of wooden matches and slid it open, her hand shaking. She hadn't been able to kill Bud Naylor, but she thought of her sister, her father, her mother, L.T., her uncle Martin. Maybe Colin. All the people who had died because of Lowell Osborne. And he couldn't care less about any of them. They were just small obstacles to be overcome in his ascent to the top.

"Kris?" Tom said. "You and I were at my place tonight. Betsy will back it up. She knows all about Lowell Osborne. Larry Brewster will take care of the bodies at the camp. And the Naylors? We'll leave them for the dung beetles.

"Go ahead," he said. "Do it."

50

Colin hobbled into the bedroom and threw the Sunday *New York Times* down on the bed with a thump.

"Check out page one," he said, then left the room to put the coffee pot on. It was his morning ritual.

He and Kris had tried to avoid all news for the past week, escaping north of Toronto to the Caledon Hills, where Colin had borrowed a farmhouse that belonged to an old flame. Kris had been touched by how quickly he had hidden away a picture of himself sitting awkwardly atop a horse, a long-haired blonde in a riding helmet smiling beside him. Colin would do anything for love, she thought, but this time he'd really outdone himself.

She snuggled back under the cream-coloured duvet and picked up the front section of the *Times*. "Mysterious Death of Senator Probed," the headline said.

> State police and federal agencies continue to study the death of Senator Lowell Osborne, nine days after he died in a fire that destroyed his family's historic Cooper Lodge at Cooper Lake, in the Adirondacks. Osborne, 48, a two-term senator from New York, was considered a strong candidate for the Republican presidential nomination and was just beginning to gear up his national campaign at the time of his death.
>
> "The lodge, a local landmark, was reduced to little more than ashes by the fire. Authorities say there is no indication that the blaze was deliberately set. Town of Osborne Fire Chief Vic Desmarais said, "The fire was so intense that we had no opportunity to bring it under control. We had to settle for dousing down the surrounding trees, to prevent a forest fire."

Kris smiled at that. What had Vic really thought?

Police are investigating whether Senator Osborne's death was linked to the disappearance of two key aides, Marine General Jack Naylor (ret.), and his son Bud Naylor. Neither man has been accounted for since the day of the fatal fire. Police have officially discounted a theory offered by some local residents, that the Naylors might have played a role in the senator's death.

There was no sign of either man's body at Cooper Lodge, but police have not ruled out their presence there. The heat of the fire was so intense that it is believed to have almost incinerated the senator, who was identified by dental records.

Police are questioning Robert G. Edwards, 54, a handyman at the lodge, who was found wandering in the nearby forest. Edwards has told a story of being kidnapped by an Englishman, and continues to be held for further questioning.

Police are also trying to find the link between the senator's death and that of his ex-wife, Pat Osborne. Mrs. Osborne, a former Miss New York, drowned in the swimming pool of her Osborne, New York, home the same day that her former husband perished in the fire. Police say no foul play is suspected in Mrs. Osborne's death, at this point, but a senior police source confirmed that Edwards is also being questioned in that matter.

In Washington yesterday, senators and members of the House jammed a memorial ceremony for the late Senator Osborne. His fellow New York senator, Democrat Norbert Trice, said, "Lowell Osborne was a great leader and a great American. We'll not see his like again."

In the small town of Osborne, dominated by the senator's family for generations, workers at Osborne Shoes took the senator's death hard. Not only was he a popular boss, but they are worried that without the senator's strong support, the town might lose a major industry.

"Jobs in America, jobs for Americans," was the theme the senator hoped to build his national campaign on.

Dr. Thomas. J. Larson, a lifelong friend of the senator,

said he was shattered by the man's death. Dr. Larson, a
noted orthopaedic surgeon, had only recently returned to
practice in Osborne at a clinic set up by the late senator.

The senator's wife, Terry Osborne, has shunned
publicity since his death, retreating with her two children
to an unidentified island in the Caribbean.

Poor Pat, Kris thought. Another victim of her crusade. And
her uncle Martin. What had become of his body? Chief Brewster
must have been efficient. No mention had been made of the dead
men at the old hunting cabin. Even a half-assed cop like Brewster
must have had a few suspicions about the bizarre trail of bodies,
but having disposed of some of them, he couldn't very well share
those suspicions with the state police.

Or Sharon Sloan. Kris knew nothing of what had happened
to Sharon, other than Bud Naylor's comment that he had taken
care of the problem. The fact that she, too, had disappeared,
didn't seem to interest the media. What had she called herself? A
sad-assed grocery store clerk. Sharon had set all these events in
motion, but she had died without knowing that she had finally
gotten her revenge.

Not that everything the police knew would be in the paper,
she realized. The police told the media only what they wanted the
public to know. Getting the rest was the reporter's job.

Neither she nor Colin had returned to work. He'd phoned in
with the announcement that he'd decided to take a sudden holiday out of the country, and casually mentioned that she'd be
off for another week, too. Kris was sure the newsroom rumour
mill had instantly deduced that they were off for a dirty week in
Provence.

Colin had bribed the ambulance drivers to take him to a private clinic in Plattsburgh, where a further financial inducement
had provided off-the-books treatment. He'd told them it was a
hunting accident. Close enough to the truth, Kris thought.

Every night since she had escaped, Kris had the same dream.
She relived the events leading up to Lowell Osborne's death, and
then she was jolted awake, Osborne's final screams still ringing
in her ears. The most terrifying moment, though, was when she

had put the matches down and walked out of the lodge. She had decided that Tom Larson wasn't going to make her a killer. She had enough to atone for, with all the deaths she had caused indirectly. Setting Osborne on fire was simply too much. She had been prepared to gamble her life that Tom wouldn't shoot her. His real hatred was for Lowell, not her. As she walked towards the door, though, she still expected to feel a bullet in the back.

When she heard the sound of a match being struck, Kris knew she had escaped. She ran like hell and hid in the woods. Tom was gone just a few minutes later, eager to clear out before the fire trucks arrived. Kris had gotten a ride out with Vic Desmarais, who had been kind enough not to ask too many questions. He had also made the company Prius disappear. No use leaving any more clues than she had to. Colin had reported it stolen back in Ottawa.

Kris had heard nothing from Tom and didn't expect to. If he had struggled to live with the guilt he bore over his role in the death of her sister, she couldn't imagine how he would deal with what he had done to Lowell Osborne. That was his problem, though.

The Adirondacks and all she had been through had already begun to seem surreal, and there was only one part of the story Kris wanted to hold on to. The house they were borrowing had a small orchard, heavy with apples. Kris sat there and drank most afternoons, while Colin napped. She used that quiet time to relive the few moments she had had with L.T. Had it been the real thing?

She'd never know now. Just add it to her long list of regrets.

In the days they had spent at the farm, Colin had been supportive and kind, as if she were the invalid, not him. They hadn't discussed the future of their relationship, content to take each day as it was. Kris was seeing a different Colin now, the bluster gone. He had risked his life to save hers. All that war correspondent stuff he loved to talk about wasn't just bravado.

She knew she didn't have the spark with Colin that she had had with L.T., but it hardly seemed the time to raise it. He was a better man than she had realized, and he gave her a feeling of safety that was a welcome relief after all she had been through.

They had also spoken very little of what happened down in New York State, and she didn't know if they ever would.

In particular, Colin had steered well clear of any questions about how the senator had come to die in a fire.

Had she been to some degree responsible for Lowell Osborne's death? She hadn't lit the match, but she had done nothing to stop Tom. She told herself there was nothing she could have done. Tom was armed, after all. Maybe Lowell Osborne had predetermined his own long-delayed execution on the day that he helped cause her sister's death.

When Kris went back to her hometown, she had told herself she was seeking justice, and maybe a form of it had been delivered in the end. It was Old Testament, eye-for-an-eye, justice, but that was the only type to which someone like Lowell Osborne was vulnerable. He was too rich and powerful to be touched by the system, and he knew it.

She had thought she could use the truth, the written word, as a weapon. Judging by their reaction, Lowell Osborne and his entourage had, too. Now, she was burying the truth. It went against every journalistic instinct Kris had, but what choice did she really have? Would people have even believed her story, backed up by a drunken ex-girlfriend and an old videotape? And even if they did think there was something to it, would they have been disturbed, or would they have accepted Osborne's story that he wasn't involved? Voters expected little more from their leaders than feel-good clichés and a nice smile. And they believed what they wanted to believe. It was difficult to forget how voters had re-elected Bill Clinton, despite all that they knew.

Kris remembered her grandfather's telling her that the best way to kill a snake was to cut off its head. Lowell Osborne's death was equally effective. He was definitely done slithering.

Kris threw the newspaper on the floor and pulled the duvet over her. She would try to sleep for a while longer, and hope she would be spared the part of the dream where the senator pleaded as the flames licked up his legs. Then that horrible scream, the one that carried her from the sleeping nightmare to the waking one her life had become.

If that was her burden, though, she could bear it. Unlike the rest of Lowell Osborne's victims, Kris was alive.

ABOUT THE AUTHOR

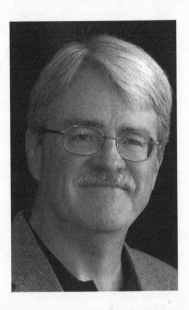

Randall Denley is a veteran *Ottawa Citizen* columnist. Unlike the fictional Kris Redner, his specialty is politics, not crime, but there is sometimes a fine line between the two. He is the author of two previous novels. The mystery *Necessary Victims* was serialized in the *Citizen*. Denley's second book, the *Perfect Candidate*, was a political satire set at Ottawa City Hall.

A native of London, Ontario, Denley began his journalism career at the *Owen Sound Sun–Times* in Grey County. Like the Adirondacks, it's an area noted for strange small towns and trout fishing. Denley has been married for a remarkably long time and is the father of two adult sons.